Camp Club Girls
Sydney

4-in-1 Mystery Collection

Camp Club Girls
Sydney

Jean Fischer

BARBOUR BOOKS
An Imprint of Barbour Publishing, Inc.

Print ISBN 978-1-68322-942-1

eBook Editions:
Adobe Digital Edition (.epub) 978-1-64352-133-6
Kindle and MobiPocket Edition (.prc) 978-1-64352-134-3

Published by Barbour Books, an imprint of Barbour Publishing, Inc., 1810 Barbour Drive, Uhrichsville, Ohio 44683, www.barbourbooks.com

Our mission is to inspire the world with the life-changing message of the Bible.

 Member of the
Evangelical Christian
Publishers Association

Printed in the United Stated of America.
06497   0419   BP

Camp Club Girls:
Sydney's DC Discovery

Go 64

Splaaaashhh! Whoosh!

"Watch out!" someone called near Sydney's ear.

But it was too late. The pent-up explosion of the water landed square against Sydney's back, knocking her to the ground.

Dazed, she rolled onto her back and looked up into the hot summer sky. The water swirled around her whole body. From a distance she heard happy shouting and water gushing onto the street.

A fireman's face appeared above her. "Are you okay, little girl?"

Little girl? Little girl! I'm twelve years old! I'm not a little girl, mister.

The indignation snapped Sydney out of her dazed condition. She looked up and saw that two firemen were now looking at her anxiously. Carefully they helped her to her feet.

"Are you okay, little girl?"

She looked in the fireman's face. He seemed so worried that her irritation melted.

Sydney looked down at her soaked gray tank top and shorts. "Yes, sir, I'm fine," she said. "Thank you," she added, remembering her manners.

Sydney Lincoln had been talking to one of her neighborhood friends. She hadn't even noticed the firemen at the fire hydrant behind her. And she sure hadn't realized she was in the direct line of the nozzle the men were releasing.

Still out of breath from the shock of the water, Sydney dropped onto the curb in front of her house. She tore off her running shoes and socks and stuck her bare feet into the gutter. She watched as the water from the hydrant down the street shot into the air and out the nozzle. The neighborhood kids laughed and splashed in its flow.

As Sydney's clothes began to dry in the torrid sun, the water rushed along the curb like a river. It streamed between Sydney's toes and sent goose bumps creeping up to her knees.

Sydney lived in the middle of a row of brick houses. The two-story houses were connected so they looked like one long building. The only windows were in the front and the back. The houses were close to the street, and each had a narrow front porch with three steps leading to a tiny front yard and the sidewalk.

The screen door on Sydney's house swung open, and her mom stepped outside. "Sydney, have you seen your Aunt Dee yet?" Her curly black hair was pulled back with a blue band to keep it off of her face.

"No, Mom," Sydney answered. "I ran past the Metro station looking for her, but she wasn't there."

"Well, when she gets here, you two come inside. Dinner's ready."

Sydney dipped her fingers into the water and splashed some onto her long, thin arms.

"Don't you want to come in by the air-conditioning?" Her mother fanned herself with a magazine. "Aren't you hot in the sunshine?"

"No, Mom," Sydney answered. She didn't think it was necessary to tell her mom about her little brush with the explosion of water.

The cell phone in the pocket of her pink shorts buzzed. Sydney took it out and found a text message from one of her best friends, Elizabeth Anderson. It said: ALMOST PACKED.

Sydney tapped a reply on her keypad: CAN'T W8 TIL U GET HERE.

Sydney and Elizabeth had met at Discovery Lake Camp, and although Elizabeth lived in Texas, they talked every day. Four other girls had been with Sydney and Elizabeth in Cabin 12B. They were Bailey Chang, Alexis Howell, McKenzie Phillips, and Kate Oliver. When camp ended, Kate set up a website so the girls could stay in touch. It was password protected, so it was like their own secret cabin in cyberspace. They'd all bought webcams with babysitting money, chore payments, and allowances so they could see each other and talk online. The Camp Club Girls—as they liked to be called—made webcam calls, sent IMs, and frequently met in their own private chat rooms.

Sydney continued typing her message: WILL PIC U UP @ D APORT @ 4 2MORO.

"Sydney, I really wish you'd come inside." Sydney's mother crossed her arms.

"Okay, in a few minutes, Mother!" Sydney said without looking up.

The screen door slammed shut.

This was the worst heat wave Washington, DC, had seen in twenty-five years. Everyone had air conditioners blasting. The energy load was way too much, and the night before, the power had gone out. Sydney hated being in total darkness. She was relieved that today seemed normal.

PACK SHORTS, she typed. REALLY HOT HERE!

While she sat texting, Sydney heard the *thump, thump, thump* of music getting closer and closer. A green jeep raced around the corner, and the booming bass from its stereo echoed inside Sydney's chest. In the passenger seat, Aunt Dee held on to her tan park ranger hat to keep it from flying off of her head. The jeep screeched to a halt in front of Sydney's house, and her aunt hopped out.

"Thanks for the ride, Ben!" she yelled over the music. "See you tomorrow."

The young driver waved and drove off.

GOTTA GO, BETH, Sydney wrote. ANT D'S HOME.

Sydney stood and wiped her feet on the grass. "You're late again," she said. "Mom's mad."

"I know," Aunt Dee apologized. "There was trouble at the Wall." She took off her ranger hat and perched it on Sydney's head. Aunt Dee always blamed her lateness on her job at the Vietnam Veterans Memorial. Sydney didn't understand how she could be so enthusiastic about a long black wall with a bunch of names carved onto it.

"So what was the trouble?" Sydney asked.

"I'll tell you at dinner," said Aunt Dee. She linked her arm through Sydney's. "It's hot out here, girlfriend. Let's go inside."

By the time Sydney washed and sat at her place at the table, Mom and Aunt Dee were already eating. Sydney had learned at camp to pray before every meal. So she bowed her head and said out loud, "Dear Lord, make us truly grateful for this meal and for all the blessings of this day." She noticed that her mom and Aunt Dee stopped eating and bowed their heads too. "And please keep Dad safe," she said. Sydney always added a blessing for her dad, who was serving in the military overseas.

"Amen!" Mom and Aunt Dee chimed.

Sydney poured iced tea into her tall glass and scooped pasta salad onto her plate. "So what happened at the Wall?" she asked, reaching for a piece of French bread.

"Someone spray-painted the sidewalk last night," Aunt Dee replied. "Graffiti."

Sydney's mom got that look on her face—the one where her forehead turned into wrinkled plastic wrap. "You mean *vandalism*," she said. "I think it's just terrible what kids do these days—"

"How do you know it was kids?" Sydney interrupted. Her mouth was full of creamy macaroni. "Kids aren't the only ones who do bad stuff."

"Don't talk with your mouth full," said Aunt Dee.

"Most times it is," her mom argued. "Just look around our neighborhood." She waved her hand toward the kitchen window. "Vandalism everywhere! Who do you think did all that? Not the adults. The kids don't care about our community. Do they care that this neighborhood used to be a military camp to help slaves that escaped from the South? No! They just want to mess up the nice things that good folks worked so hard to build." Sydney's mother sighed and took a long drink of her iced tea.

Mrs. Lincoln worked at the local historical society, and she was very protective of the neighborhood and its landmarks. She liked to talk about how, in the old days, kids had manners and didn't do anything wrong. Sydney hated it that her mom blamed everything on the kids in the neighborhood.

"There are good kids too," Sydney argued. "You don't see my friends and me running around spray-painting everything. Give us some credit!" She looked at her plate and pushed the rest of her pasta salad into a neat little pile. "We care what happens."

"We don't know who did it," said Aunt Dee, trying to stop the argument. "Someone painted 'GO 64' in front of panel 30W—in orange paint. Ben and some other volunteers scrubbed it this morning. They'll work on it again tonight when the air cools off some. They're having a hard time cleaning it. Pass the bread, please."

"What does 'GO 64' mean?" Sydney asked, handing her the basket of bread.

"That's what we're trying to figure out," Aunt Dee answered. "We're wondering if the number 64 is a clue to who did it. Ben said that in some rap music, 64 means a 1964 Chevrolet Impala. Another volunteer plays chess and said 64 is the number of squares on a chessboard. We don't know what it means."

"Maybe it's Interstate 64," Sydney's mom suggested. "There's construction on that freeway and plenty of orange construction cones. Maybe the orange paint is to protest all that."

"But if it's about the freeway, or a car, or a chessboard, why would they complain by painting graffiti at the Vietnam Wall? Besides,

Interstate 64 is in Virginia," Aunt Dee said.

"Yes, but there's some military bases out that way," Mother said. Then she added, "It's probably just kids."

The air-conditioning kicked in again, and a cool draft shot from the air vent, making the kitchen curtains flutter.

"The Wall's lighted at night," Sydney said. "And the park police keep an eye on all the monuments. So why didn't anyone see who did it?"

"The lights were out," Aunt Dee reminded her. "The whole city went dark for a while, and the park police were busy with that. That's when it happened, I'm sure. Anyway, it's a mess, and we have to clean it up fast. The TV stations are already making a big deal out of it." She dipped her knife into the butter container and slathered butter onto her French bread. "I had such an awful day at work. Everybody blamed everyone else for letting it happen. Like we would *let* it happen! People don't know how hard the Park Service works—"

"May I be excused?" Sydney asked, swallowing her last bite of pasta.

"You may," her mother answered.

Sydney put her dishes into the dishwasher. Then she went upstairs to her room.

The computer on Sydney's desk was on, and her screensaver cast an eerie blue glow on her yellow bedroom walls. Syd's bedroom had no windows, so it was always dark. That was the trouble with living in a row house. If your room was in the middle of the house, you had no windows. She flipped the switch on her desk light and tapped the spacebar on the computer. The monitor lit up, and Sydney noticed that McKenzie Phillips was online. She sent her an IM: *Talk to me?*

The phone icon on the computer screen jiggled back and forth. Sydney clicked on it, and McKenzie's freckled face appeared. She was sitting at the work island in her family's kitchen. "What's up?" she asked.

Sydney turned on her webcam. "Not much," she said. "I just finished dinner."

"Me too," McKenzie replied. "Well, almost." She held a slice of cheese pizza in front of her face so Sydney could see it. "We ate early because Dad and Evan have to drive some cattle to pasture. Then they want to practice for the rodeo this weekend." She pointed to the blue baseball cap on her head. Its yellow letters said SULFUR SPRINGS RODEO.

"I didn't want to hang out downstairs," Sydney told her. "Someone spray-painted graffiti by the Vietnam Wall last night, and Mom blamed it on kids again."

McKenzie took a bite out of her pizza. "I saw it on the news. Why did she blame it on kids? I mean, anyone could have done it."

"She blames *everything* on kids," Sydney answered. "I think it's because a lot of the kids around here get into trouble. I try to tell her that we're not all like that, but she doesn't listen. Lately she doesn't listen to anything I say."

"My mom's like that too," McKenzie said. "Nothing I do is ever right." Her face lit up. "Hey, the news said it was *orange* paint, right?"

"Yeah," Sydney said, fidgeting with her cornrows. "Orange graffiti that said 'GO 64.' So what?"

"So maybe it's some crazy nutcase with Agent Orange."

"Agent who?" Sydney asked.

"Agent Orange!" said McKenzie. "Agent Orange was a chemical they used in Vietnam. I read about it in school. It made some Vietnam soldiers really sick, and some even died. So maybe it wasn't a kid who wrote it. Maybe it's a guy who got Agent Orange, who's mad at the government and wants to get even. By the way, I can't see you well."

"You think too much," Sydney answered. She pulled her desk light closer to her computer and bent it toward her face. "They're trying to figure out what 'GO 64' means. My aunt and mom think it could be about some sort of car, or highway, or maybe even a chessboard—"

"A chessboard!" McKenzie screeched. "A person who plays chess won't spray-paint a national monument."

"I know," Sydney said. "Some gang member probably wrote it. Anyhow, I don't care. I don't want to talk about it anymore."

"I can see you fine now," McKenzie said, changing the subject. "So when is Elizabeth coming?"

"She and her Uncle Dan are flying in from Texas tomorrow," Sydney answered. "Aunt Dee and I are going to pick them up at the airport at four. We'll take her uncle to his hotel, and then Elizabeth will come here to stay with us."

"Can Elizabeth's Uncle Dan get around all by himself?" McKenzie asked. She twisted a strand of her shoulder-length hair around her fingers. "I mean, he's in a wheelchair and everything."

"As far as I know, he can," Sydney answered. "Elizabeth said he plays wheelchair basketball and competes in wheelchair races, so I suppose he gets around just fine by himself. I'm sure once he gets to the hotel, his Vietnam buddies will help him out if he needs help."

McKenzie reached for a gallon milk container on the kitchen

counter. She poured herself a glass. "Well, at least you and Elizabeth don't have to hang around with him the whole time. He'll be busy with his reunion stuff, right?"

"Right," Sydney agreed. "We'll see him Monday at the Vietnam Wall. Aunt Dee wants to give him the tour, and she thinks that Elizabeth and I should be there. Otherwise, we're on our own." Sydney heard strange sounds coming from her computer speakers. "Is that mooing?" she asked.

"Can you hear it?" said McKenzie. "That's Olivia, our old milk cow. About this time every day, she wanders up to the kitchen window and talks to us. I'll move the camera, and you can see her."

McKenzie's face disappeared from the screen. Sydney watched her friend's bare feet move across the kitchen floor as she carried the webcam to the window. Then a big, black-and-white cow head appeared. Olivia stood chewing her cud and looking at Sydney with huge brown eyes.

"Earth to Mac! Earth to Mac!" Sydney called into her computer's microphone. "Come back, Mac!"

Sydney watched McKenzie's bare feet walk back to the computer. Then her face showed up on the screen.

"Isn't Olivia awesome?" she said. "You really should come to Montana, Syd. We have tons of animals. I know you'd love it, and we could ride horses and hike, just like we did at camp."

"Maybe I will someday," Sydney replied. "But right now, I'm signing off. I want to clean up my room before Elizabeth gets here from Texas. All of my junk is piled on the other bed. If I don't move it, she won't have a place to sleep."

"Okay then," McKenzie said. "I'll sign off too—and eat more pizza." She picked up the gooey slice from her plate and took another bite. "I'll talk to you tomorrow."

"See ya," Sydney answered, switching off her webcam.

Everything in her room looked neat except for the other twin bed. It was hardly ever used, so that was where Sydney stored most of her stuff. It held boxes filled with colorful papers and art materials, magazines, piles of clothes, and posters she planned to put up in her room. Sydney had so much stuff stored there that she didn't know what to do with it all. *Under my bed, I guess,* she thought.

Before long, the bed was cleaned. Sydney changed the sheets. Then she went to her closet and pulled out a new black-and-tan bedspread that matched her own. She threw it on top of the bed and tucked it neatly around the pillow.

"Sydney?" Aunt Dee stood in the doorway. She held a long white envelope. "This came for you."

The letter was from Elizabeth. Sydney tore open the flap and found a note taped to an information sheet.

Uncle Dan wanted me to send you this so your mom can keep track of him. Just in case of an emergency. It's his reunion schedule.

Sydney Lincoln read the heading on the sheet of paper. It said, *"Annual Reunion—64th Transportation Company, Vietnam."*

The Wall

Thunderstorms in Texas delayed Elizabeth's flight. By the time Aunt Dee, Sydney, and Elizabeth dropped Uncle Dan off at his hotel and got back to Sydney's house, it was almost midnight.

After the girls got ready for bed, Elizabeth handed Sydney a small package wrapped in polka-dot-covered paper. "I got this for you," she said.

Sydney grinned. She loved getting presents. Carefully she peeled the tape off the paper. Then she reached in and pulled out a square gray box. On the top of it, gold script letters spelled out HIS WORLD, AMARILLO, TEXAS. Sydney opened the lid and found a thick, coppery bangle bracelet. Etched all around it was a scripture verse: *Be strong and courageous. Do not be terrified; do not be discouraged, for the LORD your God will be with you wherever you go. Joshua 1:9.* "This is so cool!" Sydney exclaimed. "Thank you, Beth." She slipped the bracelet over her left wrist.

"My uncle gave me a pendant with that scripture," Elizabeth said. She reached for the pendant on a long silver chain around her neck. Then she held it up so Sydney could see. "It has a special meaning."

Sydney settled into her bed and covered herself with the cool white sheet. "What's the meaning?"

"Well, when Uncle Dan was in Vietnam, he always carried a small Bible in his hip pocket. When he got shot, the bullet went through his pocket and right through the Bible. The doctors said that the Bible slowed down the bullet. If it hadn't, he might have died instead of being paralyzed." Elizabeth stretched out on her own bed and got under the covers. She switched off the light next to her bed. "And do you know what else? In the hospital, Uncle Dan opened his little Bible with the bullet hole, and it fell open to the words, 'Be strong and courageous. Do not be terrified; do not be discouraged, for the LORD your God will be with you wherever you go.' It was Joshua 1:9!"

"Wow," said Sydney. "What a coincidence, huh? Good thing he had the Bible in that pocket."

"Coincidences don't exist," Elizabeth answered. "That was God."

Sydney shut off the light on her nightstand. "Your uncle is lucky to be alive. Maybe he can't walk, but he sure does seem to get around fine. He just zipped around the baggage carousel and grabbed that suitcase. It was—"

"Not that great." Elizabeth finished Sydney's sentence. "Because he still can't walk. I pray every night for God to make him well again. But so far, nothing has happened. If it weren't for you, I wouldn't even have come here with him. Aren't there a lot of statues of soldiers and reminders of wars here? I don't like statues like that. They make me think of Uncle Dan."

Sydney heard tears in her friend's voice. "Washington's not so bad," she said. "We'll go to the Wall first thing tomorrow when Aunt Dee shows your uncle around. Then, the rest of the time, we can do fun stuff."

Elizabeth said nothing.

"Good night, Elizabeth," Sydney said. "Thanks for the bracelet."

"Good night, Sydney," Elizabeth whispered.

●—●—●

The girls got up early the next morning and were glad to find the weather had cooled and left a beautiful, sunny day. They ate breakfast, and then they walked from Sydney's house to the Metro station. From there, they took the Metro, the name everyone called the subway system, to L'Enfant Plaza. They transferred to another train and ended up in a neighborhood west of downtown called Foggy Bottom.

Elizabeth was impressed by how easily Sydney got around. "I'm glad I'm not doing this alone," she said. "You know how directionally disabled I am!"

"Do I!" Sydney replied. "Remember at camp when we were in the woods, and we scared off that cougar? You didn't have a clue where we were. And *you* were the one who'd been to Discovery Lake Camp before!"

They ran up the stairs from the train platform to the street.

"And who got us out of that one?" Sydney added.

"You did!" Elizabeth laughed. "Like I said, I'm directionally disabled."

Quickly they walked a few blocks to the Vietnam Wall.

Elizabeth was surprised to see that the Wall was in a big, grassy park with lots of trees. The girls had agreed to meet Sydney's aunt at the Three Servicemen statue near the west entrance. By the time they got there, Aunt Dee was already telling Uncle Dan and two of his buddies about the memorial.

"The total length of the Wall is 493 feet and 6 inches," Aunt Dee said in her park ranger voice. "Its two arms meet at the central point to make a wide angle of 125 degrees, creating a V shape. One end points toward the Washington Monument and the other end toward the Lincoln Memorial. The wall is ten feet three inches high at the center and is made of black granite—Oh, hello, girls!"

Uncle Dan and his friends turned to look at Sydney and Elizabeth standing behind them. "Hi, Elizabeth," Uncle Dan said. "Boys, this is my niece, Elizabeth Anderson, and her friend Sydney Lincoln."

The men shook hands with Sydney and Elizabeth. "Are you any relation to Abraham Lincoln?" one of them asked jokingly.

"Not that I know of," said Sydney.

They moved toward the wall as Aunt Dee continued her tour. "The Wall was designed by a young American sculpture artist named Maya Lin."

"Violin," Sydney whispered into Elizabeth's ear. The girls giggled, and Aunt Dee frowned.

"The names of 58,220 men and women are etched into these panels," she said. "You already know these were the men and women killed in the Vietnam War, or listed as missing in action. If you'd like to find specific names, I can help you with that, and our volunteers have tracing paper if you'd like to make tracings of any names. Also, feel free to leave a note or other mementos at the Wall. People leave things here every day, like these—" She hesitated. "Oranges?"

A row of oranges lined the base of the Wall. Actually, they were tangerines, but Sydney kept that fact to herself. Aunt Dee got annoyed when Sydney corrected her about such facts. The tangerines were neatly placed about three feet apart, stopping halfway down the west part of the Wall.

"We've had some strange things left here lately," Aunt Dee said. "Last week, it was lemons."

"Lemons?" Uncle Dan chuckled. "That does seem strange."

"I know," Aunt Dee answered. "They were arranged in a neat little pyramid in front of panel 4E. The week before that, a box of blueberries was left by 48W; and the week before that, a row of limes led to panel 14W. They were set there just like these oranges."

"Tangerines!" Sydney corrected her. She couldn't help herself.

"Whatever," Aunt Dee replied. "And then, of course, the other day some vandals struck."

"I heard about that on the news," said one of the buddies. "It made me mad that someone disrespected the Wall like that. Did they catch them yet?"

"No," Aunt Dee answered. "Since it was graffiti, we think it was kids, probably some gang members. Most cities seem to have that problem."

Sydney and Elizabeth walked away, leaving the adults to discuss gang activities and whatever else people their age talked about.

"This place is so quiet and depressing," Elizabeth observed.

Sydney agreed. "A lot of people treat it like it's a cemetery. I don't come here unless Aunt Dee needs me to. . . . Too many sad people. But we have to hang around until your uncle and his friends leave."

"I guess," said Elizabeth.

"Then we can walk to the Tidal Basin and ride the paddle boats," Sydney continued. "That'll be fun."

The girls wandered along the Wall with groups of tourists. They noticed all the different things left by people who wanted to remember the dead soldiers: a teddy bear here, a pair of combat boots there, letters addressed to loved ones, identification tags soldiers had worn in Vietnam, and plenty of tiny American flags. Nearby, a man was busy making a rubbing of one of the names on the Wall. Not far from him, an old woman laid a red rose on the brick walkway in front of one of the panels.

When they were about halfway down the west side of the Wall, Elizabeth noticed her uncle and his friends behind them. Uncle Dan had his head in his hands. He seemed to be crying, and each buddy had an arm around him. Elizabeth looked away. She couldn't stand to see her uncle being sad. Bitter anger crept up inside of her. *Refrain from anger and turn from wrath; do not fret—it leads only to evil,* she reminded herself. *Psalm 37:8.* The shiny granite wall reflected images like a mirror, so Elizabeth stopped to put a clip in her long blond hair.

Sydney was next to her by panel 30W, setting up a little American flag that had toppled over. She saw a tall man approaching them. He looked about the same age as Tyler, Sydney's brother, who was away at college. The man's fair cheeks and chin were almost hidden by his bushy red beard, and Sydney noticed that he smelled like cigarette smoke. His blue T-shirt was stained and his black cargo shorts were too big for him. He wore shabby brown sandals at the ends of his long, sunburned legs. Each was decorated with a silver peace sign about the size of a quarter.

The man read the names on the wall. Then he picked up the last tangerine in the long row of them. He tossed it into the air and caught it in his right hand. "This is the place, Moose," he said.

A big, burly guy had sauntered next to him. His head was shaved and his walnut-colored eyes darted about as he scanned the names on panel 30W. His gray T-shirt showed the picture of a fierce bulldog with the words Nice Doggy.

"You're right, Rusty," he said. "Looks like they got the sidewalk cleaned up already. Good thing there was a picture in the paper." He took a handkerchief out of his pocket and blew his nose.

"Yeah, these guys work fast," Rusty muttered. "Bet it took a lot of scrubbing." He reached down and picked up a note someone had attached to a flag by the wall. He read it aloud. "Patience is bitter, but it bears sweet fruit." He laughed. "The Professor has a sense of humor. I think I'll eat my orange now."

Sydney wanted to say that they were tangerines, not oranges. Instead, she and Elizabeth listened while trying not to be obvious.

Moose retied the laces on his dirty tennis shoes. "This one was a little different from green, blue, and yellow," he said. "But I didn't have to look long before I found it, Rusty. You saw it too, right?"

Rusty peeled the tangerine and stuffed the peelings into his pocket. Then he gave the fruit to his friend. "Yeah, I saw it Moose. Right away."

"Saw what?" Elizabeth whispered to Sydney.

Sydney shrugged.

Moose bit into the tangerine. Juice ran down his chin, trickled onto his hairy arms, and dripped onto his shirt. When he finished eating, he wiped his sticky hands on his jeans. "We should probably leave something for The Professor, so he knows when—"

"Shut up," Rusty grunted.

"But we have to—"

"Shut. . .up!" Rusty whispered, spitting out each word. He tipped his head slightly toward Sydney and Beth. Then he nodded toward the other tourists.

"I get it," Moose said. He sounded like he'd just discovered the answer to a riddle. He faced the Wall. Then, after about thirty seconds and a quick jab in the ribs from Rusty, he saluted. "We should leave something nice for our dearly departed fellow soldier," he said loudly.

Rusty picked up another tangerine and tossed it to Moose. "Let's go sit down and have a snack," he directed.

The two men walked away.

"What do you think that was about?" Elizabeth asked.

"Beats me," Sydney answered. "But we should walk; otherwise they might think it's weird that we're standing here for so long."

The girls strolled toward the center of the Wall, the place where the west wall met the east. Uncle Dan and his buddies were halfway down the east wall, and one of the buddies was kneeling on the ground making a tissue paper rubbing of a name.

"I think those guys were creepy," Elizabeth said. "They were obviously looking for something and found it. Who do you think The Professor is?" Elizabeth was so busy thinking and talking that she almost bumped into a lady in front of her.

"And that stuff about this one being different from green, blue, and yellow," Sydney added. "You're right. They were kind of creepy."

"Maybe we should tell your aunt," said Elizabeth. "I think they're up to something. Maybe they're the guys who painted the graffiti on the sidewalk."

Sydney stopped in front of panel 10E and pretended to search for a name. "No, I don't think so, Beth. I hate to admit it, but kids probably did the graffiti. And I don't think we should tell my aunt. I mean, they weren't doing anything wrong."

"But they were acting suspicious," Elizabeth argued as she joined Sydney and pretended to look for a name on the shiny black panel.

"Think about it. *We* might look suspicious," Sydney suggested. "We've been standing here for five minutes acting like we're looking for a name. Not exactly what a couple of kids would do."

The girls walked to Elizabeth's uncle and his friends.

"There you are!" Uncle Dan said. "Listen, we're almost done. Would you girls like to have lunch with the boys and me?"

Sydney looked at Elizabeth.

"I'm buying," Uncle Dan said, smiling.

"Well, okay," Elizabeth replied. "How about if we meet you by the statue of the ladies when you're done?"

"You mean the statue of the *nurses*," one of the buddies corrected her. "We can tell you some stories about them over lunch." He grinned and winked at Uncle Dan.

"Okay, we'll meet you over there," Sydney said. "Let's go, Elizabeth!" She linked her arm with her friend's and tugged on it, pulling Elizabeth back toward the center of the Wall.

"What?" Elizabeth balked.

"Look." Sydney pointed toward the middle of the West Wall. Moose and Rusty were back, putting something near the bottom of panel 30W.

"Slow down," Elizabeth said. "Let them leave it, and then we'll see what it is."

The girls stopped walking and pretended again to look for a name on the Wall.

"Okay, they're leaving," Elizabeth reported. "Let's *slowly* walk down there so we don't draw attention to ourselves."

The girls strolled toward panel 30W. When they got there, they found a note written on lined notebook paper. It was stuck onto the thin plastic stick of a small American flag. Elizabeth knelt down and read it aloud. "Meade me in St. Louis, July 1."

"Huh?" Sydney bent down to see.

"That's what it says," Elizabeth told her. "All in capital letters. 'MEADE ME IN ST. LOUIS, JULY 1.'" She hesitated for a few seconds. "Sydney? Do you know how it is when God puts a thought in your head and you know that it's true? Well, I just got one of those thoughts, and it's not good!"

Elizabeth felt a heavy hand rest on her shoulder.

"It's time to go, little girl," a man's voice ordered.

The Lincoln Memorial

Elizabeth's heart jumped to her throat. She whirled around. Uncle Dan stood behind her.

"Did I scare you, honey?" he said. "I'm sorry. Are you ready to go to lunch?"

Elizabeth brushed some dirt from the knees of her new blue jeans. "You know what, Uncle Dan? I think Sydney and I will skip lunch today. I really want to see stuff in Washington, DC, and we're only here for a week."

What? Sydney thought. She was looking forward to a free lunch in the city. Most of the time when her family went out to eat, it was to a place in her neighborhood called Ben's Chili Bowl. Anywhere else was a treat.

Uncle Dan looked disappointed but didn't try to persuade the girls any further.

The girls walked with Uncle Dan and his friends to the west end of the Vietnam Wall to say their good-byes.

"Check in with me this week," Uncle Dan told his niece. "Your mom will be furious if I don't take good care of you."

One of his buddies, Al, chuckled. "And we'll take good care of your uncle," he said. Al was the one who had corrected Elizabeth about the nurses' statue. Elizabeth didn't like something about him.

She kissed her uncle on the forehead. "Don't worry, Uncle Dan. I'll be fine."

The men had barely walked away when Sydney said, "You know, a free lunch sounded pretty good to me."

Elizabeth took Sydney's arm and pulled her. "We have to find Rusty and Moose," she said. "I think they went that way." She pointed toward the Lincoln Memorial.

The girls started walking along Henry Bacon Drive toward the big white building with the famous statue of Abraham Lincoln.

"When I read the words 'Meade me in St. Louis,' well, I got a thought," Elizabeth said. "If I'm right, those guys are terrorists."

"What!" Sydney shrieked. "They're weird and creepy, but they don't look like terrorists."

A police car rushed past them, weaving through traffic on the drive. Its siren briefly interrupted their conversation.

"Remember that Bible verse: 'Outside you look good, but inside you are evil and only pretend to be good'?" Elizabeth asked.

"No," Sydney answered. "Why do you know so much scripture?"

"Because just about everybody in my family is a minister or a missionary. That's from Matthew chapter twenty-three." Elizabeth said.

The girls split up and walked around two ladies pushing baby strollers.

Elizabeth had to run a few steps to catch up with Sydney. "As soon as I read those words, 'Meade me in St. Louis,' I thought about a few years ago when terrorists tried to assassinate President Meade. Do you remember? It was at the Smithsonian, at the National Air and Space Museum. Slow down a little, please."

Sydney never did anything slowly. Her friends often had a hard time keeping up with her fast, long legs. "Oh yeah," she answered. "The president was there to celebrate some sort of anniversary."

"The anniversary of Charles Lindberg's flight across the Atlantic in his plane, the Spirit of St. Louis," Elizabeth added.

"I almost forgot about that," Sydney continued. She walked a little slower. "That was the first year that Meade was president. Someone tried to shoot him but got away, and the government said it was terrorists. The Spirit of St. Louis. . .President Meade. . . Elizabeth! You don't think the note was about that?"

"They never caught who did it," Elizabeth reminded her. "I think Rusty and Moose might at least know something about that."

The girls passed a crowd of people at a food cart near the Lincoln Memorial. Sydney suddenly realized how hungry she was.

"You and the rest of the Camp Club Girls always accuse me of jumping to conclusions," she said. "But this time, I think *you're* jumping to conclusions. Even if you *are* right, Moose and Rusty are gone by now. We'll never find them in this crowd. And since you cost me a free lunch today, let's get in line and buy some sandwiches."

"Okay," Elizabeth replied. "But I wish I knew where they went."

When the girls finally got their food and drinks, they sat on a bench facing the street. The Lincoln Memorial towered to their left, almost one hundred feet tall. Its huge white columns made it look like an ancient Greek temple.

Sydney peeled the paper off her BLT wrap and took a bite. "As long as we're here, do you want to tour the memorial?" she asked.

"Not really," Elizabeth said as she opened her chocolate milk. "Did you know that a long time ago, Vietnam War protests went on at the Lincoln Memorial? Being here reminds me of what happened to my Uncle Dan."

"Elizabeth," Sydney groaned. "You can't visit Washington, DC, and not see the monuments. Sure, there have been protests here, but that's not what it's all about."

Elizabeth said nothing. It was just like the night before when they'd been talking about Uncle Dan before going to bed.

"This place is a memorial to the president who freed the slaves. Martin Luther King Jr. made his famous 'I Have a Dream' speech here, and Marian Anderson sang here when they wouldn't let her sing in Constitution Hall because she was black. I like the Lincoln Memorial, Elizabeth. Some really good things happened here!"

Sydney didn't like being annoyed with her friend, but she couldn't understand Elizabeth's attitude. She was always easygoing and understanding, but since she'd arrived, she just didn't seem to be herself.

"I'm sorry," Elizabeth apologized. She picked at her burrito with a black plastic fork. "I just don't understand why people have to fight in wars where good folks get hurt—like my uncle."

Sydney thought hard for something to say. "Wars have happened since way back in Old Testament times, Beth. Remember when David fought Goliath? Can you try not to think about bad stuff and just have a good time?" She offered her friend a dill pickle.

Elizabeth screwed up her face. "No, thank you," she said.

A shiny black limousine pulled up in front of them. It stopped on the wrong side of the street and held up traffic. The driver got out and walked briskly toward the back door.

"Wow," said Elizabeth. "Who do you think is in there?"

Sydney took the last bite of her wrap and tossed the container into a trash can by the bench. "Probably a senator or a congressman. You see tons of limos in the District."

The driver opened the back door, and a short, dark man in a black suit got out. His crisp white shirt gleamed against his tan skin, and a thin black necktie hung neatly inside the front of his suit jacket. His mirrored sunglasses reflected the image of Sydney and Elizabeth sitting on the bench nearby. "Twenty minutes," he said to the driver. He walked toward the memorial, and the limo drove off.

Sydney turned around to look at him. "Elizabeth!" she gasped.

"What?"

"There are Rusty and Moose."

Sure enough, Moose and Rusty stood on the sidewalk, not far from where Sydney and Elizabeth sat. The girls watched the man in the suit approach them. Moose stuck out his hand for the man to shake it, but the man ignored him. Then all three walked briskly toward the Lincoln Memorial.

"Let's see what they're up to," Sydney said.

"But you think they're good, upstanding citizens," Elizabeth reminded her.

"I didn't say that," Sydney argued. "I said that they don't look like terrorists. It won't hurt to check them out. Maybe you're right. Maybe they did have something to do with the graffiti."

The men were a good distance ahead of them now. The girls wove through the crowd trying to keep them in sight. Sydney, being taller than Elizabeth, focused on Rusty's shaggy red hair. The short man was impossible to see. He was dwarfed by Moose's big, hulking body.

"Do you see them?" Elizabeth asked. She walked a few steps on her tiptoes.

"I see the top of Rusty's head bobbing up and down," Sydney answered. "Looks like they're heading for the stairs."

The Lincoln Memorial had fifty-six wide marble stairs leading to the statue of the sixteenth president of the United States. People sat on the staircase talking and reading. Tourists climbed to the top to gaze at the Reflecting Pool on the Mall and, beyond it, the Washington Monument and the United States Capitol Building.

The men started to climb the stairs.

"Now what?" Elizabeth asked.

"We should try to get close enough to listen and find out, once and for all, if they're up to something," Sydney told her. "But we'll have to be careful that they don't see us. They might remember us."

"How about if we split up?" Elizabeth suggested. "They're less likely to recognize us if we're not together."

The men were halfway up the stairs now.

"Good idea," Sydney agreed. "But let's keep an eye on each other. Just in case."

The girls split up. Elizabeth ran up the left side of the staircase, and Sydney ran up the right.

At the top of the stairs, a sign read QUIET, RESPECT PLEASE. Just beyond it was the nineteen-foot-tall statue of President Lincoln. He towered over the tourists, looking relaxed but alert, sitting in his chair, watching over the nation's capital. Moose, Rusty, and the short man didn't seem to notice the president. They whisked past him as if he wasn't even there.

The memorial was surrounded by thirty-six huge columns. They were thirty-seven feet tall and fat enough to hide behind. Sydney saw the men hurry to the column farthest to the right of the president. They disappeared around it.

Sydney searched for Elizabeth and saw her standing at the foot of the Lincoln statue. She was watching Sydney like a hawk. Sydney pointed to herself and then toward the column where the men went, showing Elizabeth that she would follow them. Elizabeth put her right index finger to her lips.

Silently, like a shadow, Sydney slipped from one marble column to the next. Finally she was just one column away. It would be tricky to shift to the last column where the men were standing. If the men changed their position, she would be caught. Sydney peeked around the column to be sure the coast was clear. She said a short prayer and took a deep breath. Then she slithered to the column hiding the men. With her back plastered against the pillar just a few feet from where they stood, Sydney listened.

"We left a note for you," Moose was saying, "because we didn't expect you to show up."

The short man snickered. "You never know when I'll show up." His deep voice didn't fit his small, slim body. "That's why you'd better do exactly what you're told."

"We are, boss!" Rusty spoke this time. His voice was almost a whisper, nervous and hushed. "We're doing it just like you told us to."

"That's good," said the man. "Otherwise, we might have to send you on the trip with Meade."

What does that *mean?* Sydney wondered. She pressed tighter against the marble pillar and shifted, ever so slightly, to her left. She tried to listen even harder.

"Waaaaaaaaaa!" A high-pitched shriek filled the air. Sydney's heart stopped as she looked toward the Lincoln statue. A woman near Elizabeth was trying to calm her unhappy little boy. As Elizabeth and Sydney watched, the mother led her screaming child down the steps and away from the president's statue. Sydney sighed.

"Who came up with the tattoo idea?" The short man was talking now. Sydney had missed part of the conversation.

"I did, boss," Moose said uncertainly.

There was a short pause.

"Good work," he said. "I didn't think you had it in you, Percival."

Percival! Sydney thought to herself. *Moose's real name is Percival?* She stifled a laugh. What a funny, old-fashioned name!

"Thanks, boss!" Moose's voice relaxed.

"Don't you want us to go check out the place?" asked Rusty. "We could go right now."

"I warned you about being impatient," the short man snapped. "I'll talk it over with him first. If it's a go, then we'll move up to the next level. When that happens, *then* you can go and check it out."

"Tomorrow?" Rusty asked.

"Tomorrow," the man said.

Sydney saw Elizabeth with her right arm in the air. Beth was frantically making counter-clockwise circles with her right hand. Sydney heard footsteps on the opposite side of the pillar. The men were leaving. She inched her way counter-clockwise around the gigantic column, making sure she was opposite of where they were. If they saw her, she couldn't imagine what would happen.

Sydney held her breath and didn't let it out until she was sure they were gone. She peeked around the back of the column and looked toward Elizabeth. The men were almost to her, but she had her back to them. She was talking with a group of old ladies, trying to edge her way in front of them as she pointed up at the Lincoln statue.

She's acting like a tour guide so they won't recognize her, Sydney thought. The men walked by, not seeing Elizabeth, and continued down the stairs.

Sydney came out from her hiding place and hurried toward her friend.

"And if you'd like to learn more about the Lincoln Memorial, you can ask one of the park rangers down there." Elizabeth pointed down the steps toward the Reflecting Pool where a ranger, wearing a uniform like Aunt Dee's, was talking with tourists. The women started down the stairs.

"So what did they say?" Elizabeth asked.

"I don't have a good feeling about them," Sydney confided. "Moose and Rusty called the suit guy 'Boss,' and they seemed afraid of him. They were extra polite. The suit guy said Meade is taking a trip, and if Moose and Rusty don't do what they're told, they might go with him. They talked about a tattoo and taking things to the next level, and they asked the boss if they should go check someplace out. But I don't know where that is. Something's happening tomorrow too, but I don't know that either. And would you believe that Moose's real name is Percival?"

"*Percival!* Do you think the suit guy is The Professor?" Elizabeth asked.

"I don't know," Sydney said. "But I think it's too late for us to go to the Smithsonian now. And I think we should tell the other Camp Club Girls what's going on and see what they think. Let's text McKenzie and ask her to schedule a group chat for tonight."

"Great idea," Elizabeth responded. "Especially since all the time I watched you, I felt like someone was watching *me!*"

CHAPTER 4

Colors of Danger!

Promptly at 6:55 that night, Sydney was waiting at her computer with Elizabeth seated next to her. She entered the Camp Club Girls' chat room, and right away, the messages began to arrive.

Alexis: *Are you guys ok? I got an uncomfortable feeling about you today and prayed for you.*

Sydney: *When everyone logs on, we'll explain all.*

McKenzie: *I'm here. I bet something to do with Agent Orange is involved.*

Alexis: *Let's hope it's just kids playing a prank and not something worse. However, I did see a mystery movie last week that had terrorists masquerading as kids.*

Kate: *Biscuit started barking like crazy as soon as I pulled up this screen. I think he knows it's you guys, and is trying to tell you he misses you.*

Sydney: *How is Biscuit? I wish he could text with us.*

Kate: *He's wanted to play ball with me all day.*

Bailey: *I'm here! Just got home from a day with Mom in Chicago. Good thing we came home early. We're an hour behind you here in Peoria.*

McKenzie: *I was beginning to wonder if you were home when I sent an email and didn't hear from you.*

Sydney: *Okay, since we're all here, let's get started. . . .*

●—●—●

Sydney spent the next few minutes telling the girls about all that had happened that day. She told them about Moose and Rusty and everything that had gone on at the Wall that morning. Then she explained how she had listened to their conversation at the Lincoln Memorial.

Elizabeth took the keyboard and slid it over to where she sat next to Sydney at her desk.

Elizabeth: *When I read the note, "Meade me in St. Louis, July 1," the Lord gave me the memory of President Meade and when he was almost shot a few years back. It was at the National Air and Space Museum at the Smithsonian Museum, here in Washington. The president was there to honor Lindberg's flight in his plane, the Spirit of St. Louis. So I've been wondering, do you think they could be planning something evil at the same place on July 1st?*

Alexis: *Are you sure that the thought was from God, Elizabeth? Sometimes Satan gives us thoughts to throw us off track. You probably know where the Bible says that.*

Elizabeth: *It's in 2 Corinthians: "Even Satan tries to make himself look like an angel of light. So why does it seem strange for Satan's servants to pretend to do what is right?" But, Alex, I know that this thought was from God. Oh, and I forgot to tell you about the fruit.*

Bailey: *Fruit? This is beginning to sound really crazy, Lizzybet.*

Elizabeth: *I know. Someone has been leaving fruit at the Vietnam Wall: a small pyramid of lemons, a box of blueberries, and rows of limes and oranges.*

Sydney took the keyboard back.

Sydney: *Tangerines!*

McKenzie: *I think the fruit is important. That one guy found the note about patience being bitter and bearing sweet fruit.*

Kate: *I looked that up online. It's a Turkish proverb. Whoever wrote it might want those guys to be patient about whatever they're up to.*

Bailey: *That one guy's name is Red. Why? What do they look like?*

Elizabeth: *Moose and Rusty, that's his name, look messy, like they haven't combed their hair or washed their clothes in a while. The short guy. . .well. . .think of an FBI agent. He looks like that.*

McKenzie: *Rusty said, "This one is different from green, blue, and yellow." Think about it. Limes are green, blueberries are blue, lemons are yellow.*

Sydney: *And tangerines are orange! But what do those colors mean. . .if anything?*

Kate: *Was the fruit always left in the same spot?*

Sydney turned to Elizabeth. "Do you know?"

Elizabeth twisted the pendant on her necklace. "It wasn't in the same spot," she said. "I remember your aunt told Uncle Dan where they left it, but I wasn't really listening. Why don't you ask her? But don't be too obvious about it."

"Okay," Sydney replied. "I'll get a banana from the kitchen. Then I'll use that to start a conversation. I'll say that it reminded me of the fruit at the Wall. Aunt Dee will love it if I ask her. She likes talking about her work."

Sydney pushed the keyboard back to Elizabeth and hurried downstairs to find Aunt Dee.

The other girls chatted for a while as they waited for Sydney to return. Elizabeth told them a little about her uncle and that he had been wounded in Vietnam. She asked them all to pray that the Lord would heal Uncle Dan's legs so he could walk again.

Suddenly Sydney burst back into the room repeating, "4E, 48W, 14W." She took the keyboard from Elizabeth.

Sydney: *Write this down. 4E lemons, 48W blueberries, 14W limes.*

Kate: *And the oranges were where?*

Elizabeth: *They were in a long row from the beginning of the Wall to the same place where the graffiti was painted on the sidewalk—panel 30W.*

Kate: *Everyone go to www.viewthewall.com/demo_wallbrowse. htm. Let me know when you're there.*

Sydney: *We're there.*

McKenzie: *Me too.*

Bailey: *And me.*

Alexis: *Hang on. My browser is acting up. I have to try it again. Okay, I'm in. Now what?*

Kate: *Click on any panel number and it will take you to a*

photograph of that panel on the Wall. Then you can zoom in and read the names on the panel. I think that's what we need to do. We need to read each panel where the fruits were left, and look for clues.

McKenzie: *That will take forever! I think we should research Agent Orange. That's the obvious answer.*

Alexis: *Maybe the obvious answer isn't the one we need. I think we should check out Kate's idea. Then, if that doesn't work, we can check out Agent Orange.*

Sydney clicked on panel 4E. A photo popped up of that panel on the Vietnam Wall. She and Elizabeth began reading the hundreds of names on the panel.

Sydney: *There are 136 rows. Why don't we divide them up? It'll go faster that way.*

She assigned each girl a group of rows.

Bailey: *What am I supposed to be looking for?*

Sydney: *Any name that might connect with lemons. Think about what they look like, how they taste, that sort of stuff.*

"I don't like doing this," Elizabeth told Sydney. "All of these names represent someone who was killed in Vietnam. This is more than just a list of names; it's real people."

"I know," Sydney agreed as she searched the rows. "I don't like doing it either."

Bailey: *I think I might have found something. I see someone with the last name Gold in row 34. Lemons are sort of gold.*

Alexis: *That's great work, Bailey! I wrote that down. Lemons, gold, row 34, panel 4E.*

Kate: *Did anyone else find anything? If not, let's move to the next panel, 48W. Look for anything that connects to blue or blueberries.*

Again Sydney assigned rows, and she and Elizabeth searched their lists of names. Before long, McKenzie's name popped on the screen.

> McKenzie: *I think Bailey might be on to something. A soldier is on my list with the last name Blue!*
>
> Kate: *I'm looking on panel 14W, where the limes were. There's a Green on my list.*

Sydney shrugged her shoulders and looked at Elizabeth. "If there's a soldier named Tangerine on panel 30W, I'll make your bed the rest of the time you're here," she promised. Sydney figured that it was a safe promise to make, because no one, especially not a soldier, would be named Tangerine.

> Bailey: *I'm on 30W. And guess what? I found a guy named Orange.*
>
> Sydney: *Oh, come on, Bailey. No one is named Orange. I mean, have you ever met any Oranges?*
>
> Alexis: *Bailey is right. And this one is different from Green, Blue, and Yellow. . .I mean Gold. Orange is his first name.*

Sydney clicked to the photograph of panel 30W. Sure enough, there was a man named Orange.

> McKenzie: *And do you see where it is? Row 64. That's what 64 means in "GO 64." It was a clue for Rusty and Moose to look at that row. The leader must have thought that they needed some extra help, since this name is a little different from the others.*

Elizabeth took the keyboard from Sydney.

> Elizabeth: *So we know the boss, or professor, or whoever he is, was telling Rusty and Moose to look for colors. But why?*
>
> Kate: *You'll never believe this. I was doing a search for colors, and Biscuit put his red ball in my lap.*
>
> Bailey: *Pet Biscuit for me!*
>
> Sydney: *What's hard to believe about Biscuit putting his ball in your lap?*
>
> Kate: *The ball is red. I pushed it out of my lap as I was typing a search for the colors we talked about. When I saw the red ball bouncing, I accidentally typed in red too. Guess what!*

These colors are the colors of the Homeland Security Terror Alert System. Green is a low risk of terrorist attacks. Blue is a general risk of attacks. Yellow means a significant risk of attacks. And orange is a high risk. There's only one more level above that, and it's red—a severe risk of terrorist attacks!

Elizabeth looked at Sydney, and Sydney knew what she was thinking.

Elizabeth: *That's what the short man meant when he told Moose and Rusty that they'd be taking things to the next level.*

Sydney grabbed the keyboard back.

Sydney: *Oh my goodness! They really are terrorists!*

CHAPTER 5

A Plan to Track Trouble

The next morning, Sydney and Elizabeth were at Union Station in Washington, DC, waiting for Kate Oliver to arrive. She was on the ten o'clock train from Philadelphia. During their group chat the night before, Kate had come up with a brilliant idea that involved a piece of electronic equipment. Since Philadelphia was only a few hours away and trains ran frequently up and down the coast, the girls had decided she would join Sydney and Elizabeth. If all went well, they would put her idea into action before the terrorists stepped up their plan to Level Red.

The old, cavernous train building was alive with activity. Its white marble floors echoed with the footsteps of tourists, people on business, and government workers as they rushed to and from their trains. Music drifted from stores on the upper level, adding to the chaos.

Sydney stood by the doors nearest the train tracks to the Philadelphia–Washington, DC, line. Kate's train would arrive at that platform.

Sydney and Elizabeth opened the big glass doors that led out to the tracks. A blast of air, heavy with the smell of diesel fuel, swept past the girls' faces. They waited and watched while some trains sat idle on the tracks and others chugged in and out of the station.

Sydney soon spotted a single headlight on the Philadelphia track. Slowly an enormous, shiny, bullet-shaped engine chugged into the station pulling six cars behind it. It stopped at the platform where the girls waited. The doors slid open, and passengers spilled out and scurried into the building like ants toward a crumb.

"Do you see Kate?" Sydney asked.

"Not yet," Elizabeth replied.

The crowd was thinning out. Only a dozen or so people remained.

The girls worried that Kate had missed her train, but then they saw her. She waved to them as she exited the third car and stepped onto the concrete platform. She ran toward them, her sandy-colored hair bouncing. With her yellow T-shirt, fuchsia backpack, and bright green shorts, she looked as if she'd stepped off a tropical island.

"Hi, Syd. Hi, Elizabeth," Kate said. She briefly hugged each friend.

"We were afraid you missed the train," Sydney said as they walked into the crowded station.

"I was listening to Casting Crowns on my iPod," Kate answered. "I decided to hang out on the train until most people got off. It was a zoo in there."

Sydney led the girls down the escalators to the street level of the station. Then they walked toward the Plaza exit. "We'll go to West Potomac Park," Sydney announced. "Then we can talk."

Kate and Elizabeth scurried, trying to keep up with Sydney's long stride.

"I have the equipment ready," Kate announced. "I just have to show you how to use it. Do you have the rest of the stuff?"

"Yes. In my backpack," Elizabeth answered.

They were outside Union Station now and walking across the Plaza. They passed the Columbus Memorial Fountain where the statue of Christopher Columbus stared steely-eyed into the distance. To the right of him was a carving of a bearded man, sitting. To the left of him was a carving of an American Indian from long ago, crouching behind his shield and reaching for an arrow.

The friends caught a bus on Constitution Avenue. Cars, taxis, and delivery vans whizzed by them as they traveled west to 15th Street. They got off on 15th and walked toward the Washington Monument. Then they covered the short distance to the Tidal Basin in the park.

The girls found a quiet bench under the cherry trees. Nearby, children and grown-ups rode paddleboats through the cool, clear water in the Tidal Basin. In the peaceful setting, no one could have known that Kate, Elizabeth, and Sydney were worried about a terrorist attack on President Meade.

Kate unzipped her backpack and pulled out a small black cell phone. "Here it is," she said. "I've programmed it so any of us can access the data from our computers. It works like this: We have to make sure that this phone is with Moose all the time. From what you said, he's the dumber of the two, so it'll be easier to get him to take it. As long as he has this phone, we can track him wherever he goes."

Kate handed Sydney and Elizabeth each a slip of paper with some writing on it. "When you get home, just go to this URL and type in your password. Elizabeth, yours is 'Indiana.' Sydney, yours is 'Jones.' Once you do that, you'll see a screen with a map on it. It will show you exactly where Moose is. He'll appear as a little, green blip on the screen."

Sydney laughed when she thought of the big, hulking Moose as nothing more than a small, green blip.

Elizabeth opened her yellow backpack and took out the box that Sydney's bracelet had come in. Then she pulled out a brown paper lunch bag, a pair of scissors, and a roll of tape. "I have everything we need," she said.

Kate handed Elizabeth the phone, and carefully Elizabeth placed it into the box. She cut the paper bag and made it into a piece of wrapping paper. Then she folded it around the box and sealed it with tape.

"Now we have to create the note," Sydney began. "I know what we should say."

"You dictate and I'll write," Kate offered, taking a black permanent marker out of her backpack.

"Okay, here goes." Sydney dictated the words and Kate wrote them on a leftover scrap of the paper bag:

> *Moose, it is very important that you keep this package with*
> *you at all times. DO NOT OPEN IT or talk to anyone about it,*
> *including people you trust—not even the person giving you this!*
> *You will be asked for this package at the end of your mission.*
> *Keep it safe, keep quiet, or else!*

"That sounds good!" Kate said, smiling.

"I think so too," Elizabeth agreed. "From what Sydney overheard at the Lincoln Memorial, Moose seems to want to please the guy in the suit. So he'll probably take very good care of this package."

She folded the note in half, hiding the message inside. Then she wrote *Moose* on the blank side and taped it to the top of the wrapped box.

"We should go now," she said. "Idle hands are the devil's playground."

"Is that in the Bible?" Sydney asked.

"No, but it's a good proverb," Elizabeth replied.

Within moments, the girls arrived at the Vietnam Wall. When the friends got there, they found the place crowded with visitors.

The girls hid near the trees at the south yard of the Wall.

"Kate, I think you should do this alone," Sydney suggested. "Moose and Rusty have never seen you. So if you run into them, it'll be no big deal. Plus, if my aunt is around and she sees us, she'll wonder why we're here."

"I think you're right," Kate said. She dropped her backpack on the ground. "Watch my stuff."

Elizabeth handed her the small package wrapped in brown paper. Then Kate went toward the Wall.

Sydney and Elizabeth stayed hidden in trees. Sydney had brought a pair of binoculars she liked to use for bird watching. She was peering through them, watching Kate.

Kate purposefully looked indifferent as she casually strolled past the panels etched with names. On the west end, the panels began with the number 70. Only five names were etched onto that first panel. It was the shortest one on the west part of the Wall. Each panel beyond it stood a little bit taller until the east and west walls met in the middle at their highest points. Kate walked on past panels 61. . .60. . .59. . .58. . .57. Then something caught her eye. She hurried to a spot five panels down.

"Hey, she's stopping!" said Sydney, squinting through the binoculars.

"She must be there," Elizabeth added.

"No. She's a long way away from it still," Sydney disagreed.

Sydney watched as Kate stopped in front of a quart-sized box of huge red strawberries on the ground at the center of panel 52W.

"She's at the wrong panel!" Sydney exclaimed. "Didn't we agree that she'd leave the box by panel 30W?"

"Yes," Elizabeth confirmed.

"Well, she's a long way from there," Sydney said, focusing her binoculars.

"What's she doing now?" Elizabeth wondered. She could see Kate crouching down in front of the Wall.

"I don't know. I can't tell, because she has her back to me. I think she might be leaving the package there," said Sydney.

"But it's the wrong place!" Elizabeth said with exasperation.

"Oh Elizabeth! What are we going to do? Come on, girl!" Sydney said under her breath. "You're at the wrong spot!"

The girls watched as Kate set the package down.

"I'm going in," Sydney exclaimed, handing the binoculars to Elizabeth.

"Do you think that's a good idea?" Elizabeth asked nervously.

"Probably not, but I'll be careful. If that phone gets into the wrong hands, we're sunk. Keep an eye on us." Sydney sprinted across the grass toward the Wall.

Just as Kate stood up, she felt someone grab her arm. She jumped.

"What are you doing?" Sydney whispered. "This is the wrong place."

"No, it's not!" Kate whispered back. "Let's not talk about it here."

"But this isn't 30W!" Sydney reminded her. "It's down that way." She pointed to her left.

"Don't point!" Kate scolded. "Someone might be watching us. Let's get out of here."

Sydney was about to cut across the grass again.

"Uh-uh," Kate said. She took Sydney by the arm. "You'll show them where we're hiding!" Kate was right. Obediently, Sydney followed her to the entrance to the memorial. They doubled back toward the trees where Elizabeth was.

"I knew what I was doing!" Kate said when they were away from the crowd. "As I walked to panel 30W, I saw a box of strawberries by panel 52W. I had to check it out."

The girls were approaching Elizabeth now. She was still watching the Wall through Sydney's binoculars.

"Hey, Beth, Kate found some strawberries!" Sydney didn't mean to startle her friend, who swung around, dropping the binoculars on the ground.

"Don't do that to me!" Elizabeth said.

"I'm sorry," Sydney apologized. "But Kate found some strawberries by panel 52W."

Elizabeth picked up the binoculars and handed them to Sydney.

"That's not all I found," Kate said. "A soldier on that panel had the last name Redd. You know what that means, don't you? They've accelerated their plot to Level Red. Anytime now, they could put their plan into action—and we have to find out what it is before someone gets hurt!"

Kate picked her backpack up off the ground and took out her notepad and marker. She printed the words *Hail to the chief at the twilight's last gleaming.* "There's a note with the strawberries, attached to a small American flag. This is what it says," Kate told them.

Elizabeth read the words. "Were the letters all capitalized like you've written them here?" she asked.

"I didn't really pay attention," Kate answered. "But no, I don't think so. I'm almost sure that they weren't all caps."

"Then this note must be from The Professor, or the guy in the suit," Elizabeth decided. "The note that Moose and Rusty left for him was written all in capital letters, the one that said 'Meade me in St. Louis.'"

Kate reached into her backpack and took out a plastic bottle of water. She plopped down on the ground and drank some. "Who do you think The Professor is?" she wondered. "Do you think it's the suit guy?"

"I doubt it," Sydney said, watching the Wall with her binoculars. "At the Lincoln Memorial, Rusty wanted to go and check out *the place*, whatever that meant, and the suit guy said no, that he'd have to talk it over with *him* first. I think *him* might mean The Professor."

"So, we think they might be plotting to do something to President Meade," Kate sighed, "but we don't know who the *him* is or where the place is."

"You've got it," Sydney replied, still watching through her binoculars. "But if your plan works, we'll know soon. Hey, Elizabeth, isn't that your Uncle Dan's friend?"

"Huh?" Elizabeth answered.

"I think I see that Al guy," Sydney went on. "The one who asked me if I was related to President Lincoln. He's over by the center of the Wall."

"Let me see." Elizabeth took the binoculars from Sydney. She focused them until she could see clearly. "Yeah, that's him," she said. "He's just standing there leaning against the Wall." She moved the binoculars away from her uncle's friend and scanned the east part of the Wall and then the west. She saw no sign of Uncle Dan or of the other man who had been with them yesterday morning.

"He's looking all around now," Elizabeth reported, "like he thinks someone might be watching him. There he goes. He's walking along the west part of the wall. Still looking around. Acting sort of nervous."

"I see him," Sydney said. "He's too far away to see what he's up to, though, so keep telling us."

"Who are we looking at?" Kate wondered as she put the water bottle inside her backpack.

Sydney explained, "Yesterday morning Elizabeth's Uncle Dan and two of his friends met us here at the Wall. My Aunt Dee showed them around, and we hung out too, just to be polite. That man was with us. His name is Al."

Kate was still confused. "Which man? Where?"

"He's walking past 30W now," Elizabeth informed them.

"The guy in the white shirt and khaki cargo shorts," Sydney told Kate. "See, he's almost to where the strawberries are."

"And he's stopping there," Elizabeth reported. "He's looking at the berries. . . . Now he's looking around again. I wonder what he's doing. . . . He's kneeling. Is he praying? No. . . . He's reading the note that's on the flagpole. Hey! He's picking up our package!"

"Oh no!" Sydney cried. "What's he going to do with it?"

"Is he one of the bad guys?" Kate asked in disbelief.

"Now he's lifting the tape on our note. I think he's reading it," Elizabeth continued. "Yeah, he *is* reading it. I knew yesterday that I didn't like something about him."

"He's leaving," Kate observed. "And he seems to be in a hurry. Did he take our box?"

"No, it's still there," replied Elizabeth.

"Let me have the binoculars," Sydney said. She took them from Elizabeth and scanned the Wall from right to left. "Look over there, where the two walls meet. It's Rusty and Moose!"

CHAPTER 6

"We've Got Legs. . ."

"I'll follow your uncle's friend," Kate announced. She stood and grabbed her backpack. "I'll meet you guys at Union Station before my train leaves at two, at that little café on the upper level. If Moose takes our package, send a text message to the Camp Club Girls so they can track him online."

Kate ran off to follow the guy named Al.

Sydney watched Moose and Rusty through her binoculars. The two men walked slowly, looking at all the items that visitors had left to honor the fallen soldiers. They worked their way, panel by panel, along the west part of the Wall, obviously looking for a clue.

"They're getting closer," Sydney reported to Elizabeth. "I don't think they've seen the berries yet. . . . They're almost there. Oh, Rusty sees them! There they go. They're nearly to panel 52W now. Okay, they've stopped."

Elizabeth could see the men in the distance, but she relied on Sydney to tell her what was happening. "What's going on with our package?" she mused.

"Nothing yet," Sydney answered. "It looks like they're reading the names on the panel. At least Rusty is. Moose is bending over. Oh, wouldn't you know it? He's eating one of the strawberries."

Moose had picked out the biggest and best strawberry of the bunch and popped the whole thing into his mouth.

As Moose reached for another berry, Sydney watched his focus land on the brown-paper-wrapped package.

"He's reading our note, Elizabeth!" Sydney watched through the binoculars. "He's turning sideways now so Rusty can't see what he's doing. Yeah, he's reading it!"

"Can I have a turn, please?" Elizabeth asked.

Reluctantly, Sydney shared her binoculars.

Elizabeth peered at the men through the strong, thick lenses. "Oh, now he's putting the package into the back pocket of his shorts. Yuck! He has the hairiest legs that I've ever seen."

"Elizabeth!" Sydney said.

"Well, he does," Elizabeth confirmed. "Rusty looks upset, and Moose is grinning. He's probably thrilled that the boss gave him such an important job. Moose is picking up another strawberry now. He's giving it to Rusty. Hey! Rusty just hit Moose on the arm. I wish we could hear what they're saying," she added.

"He just hit Moose again," Elizabeth observed. "Just before that, Rusty wrote something on a piece of paper and stuck it on the little flag. Now they're leaving."

"Just like yesterday," Sydney said. "They've left a note for The Professor. We have to go see what it says."

Elizabeth gave the binoculars back to Sydney. "But shouldn't we wait and watch for The Professor to come? I mean, at some point he or the suit guy is going to read it, right?"

"Probably," Sydney answered. "But if The Professor is smart, he won't take that note in broad daylight. If anything, he'll just stroll by, looking like a tourist. He'll take a quick look at it, like anyone else being curious. I think he does his dirty work at night, Elizabeth. That's when the graffiti happened, and no one saw him do it."

"I guess you're right," Elizabeth answered. "I'm going to send a text message to the girls." She took her cell phone out of her pocket and typed: MOOSE HAS PHONE. TRACK HIM! BETH.

Then Elizabeth turned to Sydney and said, "So how do we go over there and look at the note without being seen?"

"Girl! You don't see the forest for the trees," Sydney exclaimed. "Look at that crowd. There are so many tourists that it'll be easy for us to blend in. We'll just get in line and go with the flow. Come on!"

The girls walked to the Vietnam Wall and joined the crowd. Surprisingly, though many people gathered there, the noise level was low. The Wall, that morning, reminded Sydney of being in church just before the service began. People talked, but in hushed voices.

As they neared panel 52W, Sydney and Elizabeth heard children laughing. When they got closer, they saw the reason. Two squirrels were busy eating the strawberries. Each squirrel sat with a berry in its tiny front paws and nibbled at it until it was gone. Soon, just one berry was left. Both squirrels lunged for it, but only one got it. The lucky squirrel raced away with the berry in its mouth. It ran across the grassy area toward the trees where the girls had been hiding. Then the second squirrel tore Rusty's note off the little flag. Off it went, in pursuit of the first squirrel, with the precious note in its mouth.

"Oh my goodness!" Elizabeth gasped. Sydney sprinted across the grass, chasing the squirrel. She ran at lightning speed, almost catching up as the squirrel scampered for the trees.

By now, a crowd of people stood watching. Hurriedly, Elizabeth followed Sydney.

"Sydney! Where are you?" Elizabeth was annoyed by the time she got to the trees.

"Up here," came a voice from overhead. Elizabeth looked up and saw Sydney sitting on a thick lower limb of the tree. Sydney grinned as she waved the note at Elizabeth. "The squirrel dropped it, and I caught it."

Far up in the tree branches, the angry squirrel sat on a branch, shaking its tail and scolding.

"What does the note say?" Elizabeth asked.

Sydney unfolded the paper and read: " 'LIEUTENANT DAN, WE'VE GOT LEGS.' In all capital letters—"

"Girls! What are you up to?" Aunt Dee stood behind Elizabeth, looking very official in her park ranger's uniform.

"Hi, Aunt Dee," Sydney said brightly. "We were just goofing off." She slid down the tree trunk and brushed herself off. "We were in the neighborhood and decided that we'd visit the Wall again. How are things going?"

Aunt Dee stood with her hands on her hips. "Sydney Lincoln, did I just see you chasing a squirrel across the lawn by the Wall? With a whole bunch of people watching you?"

The smile disappeared from Sydney's face. She had no idea that she'd made such a scene. "Yes, ma'am," she answered.

"Girlfriend!" Aunt Dee said. "This is a national monument where people come to pay their respects. I'm glad that you and Elizabeth want to come here, but it's not a place to play."

As Elizabeth looked beyond Aunt Dee toward the Wall, she saw Moose and Rusty by panel 52W. They were too far away to tell what was going on, but Rusty was holding the little flag and pointing toward the trees. Had they seen Sydney run off after the squirrel?

"We're sorry, Miss Powers," Elizabeth said. "We were just about to leave. Sydney wants to take me to Union Station." She shot Sydney a desperate look. Sydney had no idea why.

"That's a good idea," Aunt Dee said. Her voice was less stern when she spoke to Elizabeth. "I have some tour buses coming soon, so I'll see you girls at supper. Have fun!"

As soon as Aunt Dee left, Elizabeth grabbed Sydney's arm. "Look!" she said, pointing toward the Wall. Rusty and Moose were walking across the grass toward the trees. "I don't think they see us yet. Drop the note on the ground, and let's get out of here."

"Why should I drop the note?" Sydney questioned.

"I'll tell you later!" Elizabeth exclaimed as she tore the paper from Sydney's hand and threw it to the ground. "Run!" she said.

They ran as fast as they could, through the trees and away from the Wall. They ran until they were almost to the Tidal Basin.

"Why did you leave the note behind?" Sydney asked.

"So they'd think the squirrel got it!" Elizabeth dropped to the ground and stretched out on her back, trying to catch her breath. "What if they saw you chasing the squirrel, Syd? At least if they find the note, they might think you never saw it. What if Moose and Rusty were watching the whole time? We could be in big trouble."

Sydney plopped on the grass and sat cross-legged with her head in her hands. "I didn't stop to think," she said. "When that squirrel took off with the note, I just started running. Did other people see me?"

Elizabeth sighed. "I can't believe you just said that. Do you know how fast you can run? Everyone was watching you. You were amazing!"

Sydney looked at Elizabeth. "What if they did see? We're not talking about some common thugs here, Elizabeth. These guys are out to get President Meade."

Elizabeth sat up. "We'll have to be extra careful now," she said. "We'd better get going. Kate's train leaves in an hour."

The girls walked to the bus stop on 15th Street. They watched for Rusty and Moose. Before they paid the fare on the bus and walked to their seats, they looked around to be sure that the men weren't on board. By the time they got to Union Station, they were reasonably sure that they hadn't been followed.

Kate was waiting for them at a café on the upper level of the station. She sat at a small white table with three chairs, sipping a cold soda. Elizabeth and Sydney both noticed that Kate looked serious.

"Hi, you two," she said. "You'd better sit down. I have a lot to tell you."

"We have a lot to tell you too," Elizabeth replied.

"I'll buy some sodas," Sydney told them. "They don't like it if you sit without buying something."

By the time Sydney returned, Elizabeth had told Kate about the new note that Rusty and Moose left on the little flag and what had happened with Sydney and the squirrel. Sydney placed two Cokes on the table and sat down. "We might be in big trouble," she said.

"Maybe more trouble than you know," Kate responded. "I followed that guy, Al, to a hotel on East Street Northwest."

"That's where the Vietnam Veterans' Reunion is," Elizabeth said. "My uncle is staying there."

"I know," Kate said. "I think I saw him. What does he look like, Elizabeth?"

"Well, he's in a wheelchair. . . ," said Elizabeth.

"A flashy one with lots of chrome," Sydney added.

"He has blond hair, a little on the longish side," Elizabeth continued, "and big muscles on his arms, because he wheels himself around in the chair. He won't use one of those motorized ones. And he usually wears khakis or camouflage, especially when he's with his Vietnam friends. Oh, and I forgot, he has a bushy mustache."

"That was him," Kate said. She took a long drink of her soda. "You're not going to like what I have to tell you."

"What?" Elizabeth said cautiously.

"Well, I followed Al to the hotel. He got on an elevator, and I watched to see what floor he got off on. It was the third. So I ran up the stairs, and by the time I got there, he and your uncle were going into one of the rooms. When they shut the door, I went to the door and listened."

"Kate! Are you out of your mind?" Sydney asked. "What if someone had seen you?"

"I was okay, because the room was next to a broom closet. If I had to, I could have hidden in there," Kate said. "Beth, they were talking about the stuff at the Wall. Al told your uncle about every place that you've been. He knew about the 'Meade me in St. Louis' note and about your going to the Lincoln Memorial and that Sydney listened to those guys behind the pillar. He even knew that you met me at the station this morning, but he doesn't know who I am. And, of course, he knew about the latest note. The one the squirrel got."

Elizabeth said nothing.

Sydney remembered, "At the Lincoln Memorial you thought you were being followed, Elizabeth. I guess it wasn't your imagination. It was your uncle's friend. He's been watching us!"

"I can't believe that," Elizabeth said. "Why would he do that? And why would Uncle Dan let him?"

"There's more," Kate said. "Your uncle said something about talking to a man named Phillips. He said Phillips was watching the situation closely. Then your uncle said, 'If the girls get too involved in this, we might have to—.' I didn't hear the rest because someone around the corner turned on a vacuum cleaner."

Elizabeth spilled her soda, and Sydney hurried to get napkins to wipe it up.

"Beth," Kate said softly, "I think your Uncle Dan might be one of the terrorists."

Suspicions

"My uncle is *not* a terrorist!" Elizabeth exploded.

Kate looked at her solemnly and handed her a sheet of folded-up notebook paper. "Stick this in your pocket," she whispered. "Don't lose it, and don't open it until you get back to Sydney's house."

— ● — ● —

By three o'clock, Sydney and Elizabeth were back in Sydney's bedroom. Elizabeth read Kate's note aloud:

> *"Elizabeth,*
> *I think a tracking device might be hidden in your backpack. That might be how Al knows where you are all the time. From now on, leave your backpack at Sydney's house, but not in your room where a mic could pick up your discussions. Be careful what you say in public too. Someone might be listening.*
> *Kate"*

Elizabeth flopped down on her bed as Sydney booted up the computer. "I don't care what anyone says. My uncle is *not* plotting to do something terrible to the president."

Sydney watched the monitor screen turn from black to blue. "You're probably right, Beth, but we have to be careful until we find out what's going on."

"And do you know what else?" Elizabeth continued. "We need to pray. In 1 Timothy the Bible says to pray for those in authority. So we should be praying for President Meade. In Matthew scripture says we should pray for our enemies. We should be praying for Rusty and Moose, the suit guy, and The Professor. And most of all, we should be praying for ourselves that we're doing the right thing."

Sydney clicked on the icon to bring up her email program. "You're right, Beth. We'll form a Camp Club Girls prayer group. If we all join together to trust God, I know He'll help us save the president."

"*If* the president needs saving," Elizabeth reminded her. "We don't know what this is all about yet."

Sydney clicked her mouse a couple of times to bring up a list of new mail messages. Only two waited: one from Bailey and the other from McKenzie. "Elizabeth, even before I agreed with you, you'd decided those guys were terrorists."

"I know," Elizabeth answered, "but now it's getting personal."

Sydney opened Bailey's email.

I've been tracking Mr. Green since I got your text message. He went from the Wall a little bit south. Then he turned around and went north. He's been a little northwest of the White House all afternoon. He hasn't moved at all. I hope you guys are okay! Let me know what's happening.

"I'm going to log on to Kate's tracking site," said Sydney. "My password's Jones, and you're Indiana, right?"

"Right," Elizabeth said. She got up from the bed and walked across the room to sit with Sydney at the desk. Sydney typed the password into the log-in box. Soon a map appeared. A little off from the center of it was a small, glowing green dot. Sydney clicked the zoom icon. The map morphed into a bird's-eye view of Washington, DC. You could see the tops of trees and buildings as if you were looking down at them from an airplane. All the important streets, highways, buildings, and monuments were labeled.

"This is so neat!" Elizabeth exclaimed. "Kate's outdone herself this time."

"And Bailey's right with her directions," said Sydney. "Moose is northwest of the White House, in Foggy Bottom. From this view, it looks like they're in an apartment house."

Elizabeth remembered that she and Sydney had gotten off the train in Foggy Bottom, but she had no idea that it was northwest of the White House.

"Well, now we know that Moose and Rusty didn't follow us," Sydney said. "According to Bailey's email, they walked from the Wall a little bit south. That must have been when they were coming after us, just before we ran."

Sydney minimized the map screen and brought up her email program. "Then if they turned and went north, they must not have seen that we ran to the Tidal Basin."

Sydney typed her reply to Bailey:

Great work, Bailey! That area northwest of the White House is called Foggy Bottom. Keep watching, OK? In a little while, we'll set up a schedule so we all can take turns watching Moose. We're fine. More later. Syd.

"Did you notice that the blip didn't go anywhere near where my uncle is staying?" Elizabeth asked. "I just know that he's not a part of this."

"You're right, it didn't," Sydney replied. Then she opened McKenzie's email.

Call me online as soon as you get this. Kate has texted me the whole time she's been on the train. She told me everything that's going on. Call me!

Before Sydney could respond, the videophone rang. It was McKenzie. Sydney turned on the webcam and picked up the call.

McKenzie sat at the computer desk in her bedroom. She wore a pink baseball cap with a picture of a racehorse embroidered on the front. Her orange tomcat, Andrew, lounged on the back of her desk chair.

"We were just going to call you," Sydney said.

"I couldn't wait," McKenzie replied. She twisted a lock of her hair between her thumb and her index finger. "Do you realize what a big deal this is if you've uncovered a plot to assassinate the president? I couldn't believe half the stuff that Kate told me."

"Believe it," Sydney said. "It's all true."

Elizabeth slid her chair closer to Sydney's. "Hi, McKenzie," she offered.

"Hi, Elizabeth," McKenzie answered. "Listen, I've been thinking. That first note you found said 'Meade me in St. Louis, July first,' right?"

"Right," Elizabeth confirmed.

"Get off!" Andrew had jumped from the chair onto McKenzie's keyboard. He loved to act up when she was online. "I just googled the president to find out where he'll be on July first. He's not anywhere near St. Louis. He's going to be in Baltimore. So could you be on the wrong track with all of this?" She picked up Andrew and put him on her lap.

"Your guess is as good as ours," Elizabeth said. "The first of July is Friday. That gives us two days to find out if we're right. If nothing happens by the end of the weekend, I'll have to help out from Amarillo. We're going home on Sunday night. Uncle Dan has a class starting on the fifth."

Sydney picked up a red, fine-point marker and scribbled the word *Baltimore* on a scrap of paper. She doodled all around it. Drawing flowers and animals somehow helped her concentrate.

"What kind of class is your uncle taking?" McKenzie asked.

"He's not taking it; he's teaching it," Elizabeth replied.

Sydney penned the words: *Teaching. . .Teacher.*

"My uncle teaches American history at Amarillo Community College," Elizabeth continued.

Sydney scribbled the words: *Teacher. . .College. . .Professor!*

Oh my goodness, she thought. She decided not to say what she was thinking. As Elizabeth and McKenzie talked, Sydney tore the paper into little pieces and tossed it into the trash can under the desk.

"So what's the president doing in Baltimore on Friday?" she asked. She tried hard not to let her feelings show. Inside her brain, a voice shouted, *"Oh no! Kate's right! Elizabeth's uncle is The Professor, the top guy in the plot to kill the president!"*

McKenzie was feeding Andrew now. She held his bowl of food while he sat on the desk and scarfed it down. "He's going to be at Fort McHenry for some Fourth of July weekend concert thing. I can't remember exactly what it's called. Just a minute, I wrote it down." McKenzie set the cat's dish on the desk. The girls heard paper rustling as she looked for the note she'd jotted about the president. "Here it is. It's called a Twilight Tattoo."

Elizabeth gasped.

"What?" McKenzie asked.

"That was Moose's big idea," Elizabeth said. "He made a plan that involved a tattoo, and the suit guy couldn't believe that Moose was bright enough to think of it—"

Sydney interrupted, "Only we thought he meant tattoo, as in a picture branded on your skin."

"Tattoos aren't *branded* on people," McKenzie corrected her. "You brand cattle."

"Obviously that's not what it means," Elizabeth said. She found a dictionary in Sydney's bookcase. She opened it to the *T* section and searched. "Tattle. . .tattler. . .tattletail. . .*tattoo*! Here it is. Oh girls, listen to this: 'an outdoor military exercise given by troops as evening entertainment' and 'a call sounded shortly before taps as notice to go to quarters.' It all fits! Taps is a bugle call that's sounded at the end of a day and at military funerals. They plan to assassinate the president at the tattoo!"

McKenzie leaned back in her chair and put her hands on top of her baseball cap. "I can't believe this is happening," she said. "What are you guys going to do? I mean, if you say something and we're wrong, can you imagine all the trouble it will cause?" She took off her hat and set it on the desk. "Just a second, I'm getting an IM from Alexis. She wants to know what's going on—"

"Listen, McKenzie," Sydney said. "We have to go. Will you tell Alexis and the rest of the girls what we just talked about?"

Elizabeth got up and started unpacking her backpack. "Tell her to get a prayer group going too," she said as she looked through her backpack for anything odd, like a tracking device.

"I heard," McKenzie said. "Will do, and I'll tell the girls to try to figure out more of this. We'll be in touch with you later." McKenzie waved at the camera and signed off.

Elizabeth had everything out of her backpack now. Her camera, a tube of sunscreen, her hot-pink iPod, a pair of socks, lip gloss. . .all of it lay in a pile on her bed. She turned the yellow backpack upside down and gave it a few hard shakes. Nothing fell out. "See," she said. "No tracking device. If anyone is tracking me, it's not with this backpack."

Sydney sat quietly at her desk pretending to straighten papers and organize her bookcase. There was one important clue that she and Elizabeth hadn't discussed, and they couldn't avoid it any longer. "That note we left behind," Sydney said. "The one that said 'Lieutenant Dan, we've got legs.' What do you think it meant, Beth?"

Once again, Elizabeth said nothing.

Sydney felt anger inside of her. She didn't want to be mad at her friend, but something was very different about Elizabeth. She wasn't acting like the same girl Sydney knew from Discovery Lake Camp.

"What's going on with you?" Sydney asked. "Every time I try to talk about your uncle, you clam up. Don't you know you can talk to me if something's bothering you?"

Elizabeth sighed and sat down on the edge of the bed. "My uncle saved his whole company of men in Vietnam by putting himself in the line of fire," she said. "He got shot, and he might never walk again, and, Sydney, that's not right! I get mad at God sometimes because bad things happen to good people. I get mad at my uncle's Vietnam buddies because they can walk and he can't. Then I get mad at myself for feeling that way. I know what kind of a man my uncle is, and now you want me to believe he's a bad guy and is trying to kill the president. Well, he's *not*! I don't know what the note means, but it isn't what you think."

Sydney walked across the room and sat on the bed next to Elizabeth. "I don't want your uncle to be a bad guy, Beth, and he probably isn't. Help me prove that he isn't, okay? I'm on your side. I really mean that."

Elizabeth held the pendant that hung around her neck. It was a habit that helped her to remember the scripture verse engraved on it: *Do not be terrified; do not be discouraged, for the Lord your God will be with you wherever you go.*

"I want your uncle to walk again," Sydney continued, "but sometimes bad things do happen to good people, and you just have to accept that."

As Elizabeth held the pendant, it came off the chain. The pendant remained in her hand, and the chain slipped to the floor. "Oh," she said. "I can't believe that happened. Uncle Dan just took this to the jewelry store the day before we came out here. He had it matched to this nice silver chain." She picked up the chain and checked out the clasp. "That's strange. It doesn't look broken. I guess I must not have fastened it right. Will you do it, please?" Elizabeth held up her long blond hair while Sydney fastened the clasp.

"There," Sydney said. "It's as good as new. And how about us? Are we good as new?"

Elizabeth smiled. "We are," she said softly. "Let's make a pact to prove that my Uncle Dan isn't a terrorist. Agreed?"

"Agreed!" Sydney said.

Just then, Sydney's cell phone began to buzz. She took it from her pocket and found a message from Bailey: MR. GREEN IS ON THE MOVE! LOG ON NOW AND WATCH WHERE HE GOES.

Quickly Sydney and Elizabeth logged on to Kate's tracking site. The green blip was moving steadily away from Foggy Bottom. Its rate of speed told the girls that Moose was not traveling on foot. The blip was on New York Avenue heading northeast out of town. Elizabeth and Sydney sat at the desk and watched for more than an hour as it slowly traveled to the Baltimore-Washington Parkway, on to Maryland 295 North, and along I-95 North. Then it stopped.

"Why is he stopping?" Elizabeth wondered. "Isn't he in the middle of a freeway?"

"Maybe a toll booth or traffic," Sydney answered.

"So now we know he's in a car," Elizabeth added.

"Or a taxi or a bus," Sydney said.

Soon the green blip left I-95 and began weaving through the streets of Baltimore.

"Either he's lost, or he's looking for something," Sydney observed. "It doesn't look like he knows where he's going."

Eventually the green blip traveled east of Baltimore's Inner Harbor and stopped again. The girls waited for about twenty minutes, wondering if the blip would move. It didn't.

"I know that neighborhood," Sydney said. "It's just across the harbor from Fort McHenry. I've been there with my Aunt Dee; sometimes she fills in at the fort when a ranger is on vacation. Anyway, that neighborhood where Moose is now was once upon a time a place where pirates hung out."

"Interesting," Elizabeth said. "So now what do we do?"

Sydney was busy typing an email to the Camp Club Girls.

Subject: *Camp Club Girls Unite*
> *Moose has moved from Washington, DC, to Baltimore's Inner Harbor. (Rusty is probably with him.) Let's group chat tonight at 8:30. We need to make a plan to save President Meade, and we have to pray for guidance and safety. Tomorrow Elizabeth and I will go to Baltimore to check out Fort McHenry and to find out more about the Twilight Tattoo. We'll meet you in the chat room.*

"We're going to Baltimore?" Elizabeth exclaimed. "How will we get there?"

"That's easy," Sydney answered. "Aunt Dee! The National Park Service has a van that travels from the Wall to Fort McHenry every day. I'll tell Aunt Dee that I want to take you to see the fort, and we can hitch a ride with a ranger. We can spend the whole day in Baltimore sleuthing things out. Plus, we can get into the fort for free."

"What if we run into Moose and Rusty?" Elizabeth asked.

"We won't as long as the girls are tracking them," Sydney replied. "They can let us know if Moose and Rusty are near, and then we can ditch them. Right now, we have other things to think about. The Camp Club Girls need to get organized. We're on a mission to save the president."

On the Move. . .

The girls wasted no time getting to the chat room at 8:30. None of them had much of an appetite at supper that night. Their minds were on how to solve the mystery of Moose, Rusty, and President Meade.

Alexis Howell was the first to "talk." She had been working on the latest clue left by the Wall.

> Alexis: *Have any of you seen the movie Forrest Gump?*
> *That note, "Lieutenant Dan, we got legs," is like a line from the movie. The line goes: "Lieutenant Dan, you got new legs." In one part of the movie, Forrest Gump is a soldier in Vietnam. His platoon gets ambushed and Forrest saves his wounded officer, Lieutenant Dan. Afterwards, the lieutenant is real mad at Forrest.*
> Bailey: *Why is he mad at him?*
> Alexis: *Because Dan wanted to die in battle as a hero. Instead he lost his legs and was disabled for the rest of his life. He figured he'd be better off dead.*

Elizabeth and Sydney sat at the computer watching the words flash across the screen.

"Some of it is like what happened with my uncle," Elizabeth said to Sydney. "But Uncle Dan never complains that he lost the use of his legs, and I'm sure that he doesn't think he'd have been better off dead. The clue has to have another meaning."

Sydney typed on her keyboard.

> Sydney: *Then what happened?*

Alexis: *Forrest and Dan went into shrimping together and got rich. Years later, when Forrest got married, Lt. Dan showed up at the wedding walking. Forrest said, "Lieutenant Dan, you got new legs." The Lt. showed Forrest his new metal legs and said, "Custom-made titanium alloy. It's what they use on the space shuttle."*

McKenzie: *I'm sorry, Elizabeth, but this seems to point right to your Uncle Dan. He was wounded in Vietnam and can't use his legs. So Moose and Rusty are using their legs to help him. I bet that's what it means: Lieutenant Dan, we got legs!*

Alexis: *McKenzie, we can't jump to conclusions. Elizabeth's uncle is innocent until he's proven guilty.*

An uncomfortable pause filled the chat room and Sydney's bedroom. Neither Sydney nor Elizabeth said a word. The only sounds were the soft hum of the computer and the gentle patter of rain on the roof.

Bailey: *What's titanium alloy?*

Kate: *It's a metal made of titanium and other chemical elements. It's super-strong, lightweight, and it can withstand high temperatures. The military uses it to make stuff, like planes and weapons.*

The storm was getting stronger. The girls heard the rain falling harder on the roof.

Sydney: *Let's make a plan for tomorrow when Elizabeth and I go to the fort. A storm's coming, and we'll have to shut down the computer soon.*

Kate: *It's been here already. Would you believe Biscuit was outside digging in the pouring rain? He tracked mud all through the house. He's never done that before.*

As the storm raced toward Sydney's neighborhood, the girls made a plan for the next day. Kate told Sydney and Elizabeth how to set up their cell phones to view the tracking site. That way, Sydney and Elizabeth could see where Moose was at any given time.

Bailey and Alexis would be their backup. They'd watch Moose too and would report to Kate and McKenzie what was going on. Meanwhile,

Kate and McKenzie would dig deeper into the clues to look for any new leads.

Before they signed off, Sydney and Elizabeth promised to stay in touch with the girls by texting them from the fort, and all the girls promised to pray.

Rain poured down on the brick row house. A huge clap of thunder exploded over the house, making the girls jump.

Just then, Elizabeth's cell phone rang. She looked at the caller ID and pressed the answer button.

"Hi, Uncle Dan," she said.

"Hi, honey," her uncle replied. "I'm just checking on you. There's quite a storm outside. Are you girls all right?"

"We're fine," Elizabeth answered. "We were just getting ready for bed. I'm glad Sydney's room doesn't have any windows. I'd rather not see all the lightning."

"So what's on your agenda for tomorrow?" Uncle Dan asked. "Do you and Sydney have something fun planned?"

"We're going to Baltimore to see Fort McHenry," Elizabeth said.

Sydney sat on her bed waving her arms to get Elizabeth's attention. "No!" she whispered. "Don't tell him!"

But the damage was already done.

"I have to go now," Elizabeth said abruptly. "It's probably not a good idea to talk on the phone in a storm. Good night, Uncle Dan."

She ended the call before her uncle could ask anything else about their plans. "I'm sorry. I forgot," Elizabeth said. "Besides, I won't treat my uncle like he's a criminal. Like Alex said, he's innocent until he's proven guilty."

As the wind howled outside, the two girls shared a time of prayer. They asked God to guide them and protect them. They prayed for their friends and family, and especially for President Meade. Elizabeth asked the Lord to do something soon to prove that her Uncle Dan was innocent, and she prayed that her uncle might walk again.

Then Sydney and Elizabeth climbed into their beds and said good night.

●—●—●

Sydney awoke the next morning to someone gently shaking her. It was Aunt Dee. The room was dark and quiet, and Elizabeth was still asleep.

"What time is it?" Sydney groaned.

"It's 7:00 a.m.," Aunt Dee answered. "If you girls are going to catch a ride to the fort, you have to get up soon. The power went out for a while overnight, so your alarm clocks are behind."

Elizabeth stirred in her bed across the room. "What's going on?" she asked, sitting up and rubbing her eyes.

"It's time to get up," Sydney told her. "We have to leave in an hour to go with Aunt Dee to the Wall."

The girls got dressed and logged on to Kate's tracking site. The green blip was still in the same spot as the night before, just east of Baltimore's Inner Harbor.

"I'm going to email the girls," Sydney said.

> *We're leaving in a few minutes to go to the Wall with Aunt Dee. Catching a ride to the fort at 10:00 a.m. Make sure you let us know if Moose moves, in case we're not looking at our phones.*

●—●—●

At ten o'clock, Sydney and Elizabeth met Ranger Hank Ellsworth at the Visitor Center at the Vietnam Memorial. As they rode along in the backseat of his white park service van, Ranger Hank told them about the fort.

"My great-great-great-grandpa fought at Fort McHenry," the ranger said, scratching the short, gray beard on his tan, weathered face. "But you girls probably aren't interested in hearing about that."

He turned the van onto the highway into heavy traffic.

"No, we want to hear," Sydney said. "We want to learn as much as we can about the fort."

The ranger checked his rearview mirror and changed lanes. "Well, when you get there, you'll have to use your imagination," he said. "The story goes like this: Way back in the 1700s, Baltimore was afraid of being attacked by the British. We were at war with Britain. So the people decided to build a fort to protect themselves. They picked a site called Whetstone Point. It was a good place to build a fort, because it was near the city and was surrounded on three sides by water."

"A peninsula," Elizabeth said.

"Right," the ranger agreed. "And it was smart to build the fort on a peninsula, because any ships sailing in to attack Baltimore had to pass it. When they first built the fort, it was just big mounds of dirt. But later a politician named James McHenry raised money for a new and better fort."

A car cut in front of the van, and Ranger Hank maneuvered to another lane. "The people named Fort McHenry after him because he was so generous and also because he was President George Washington's secretary of war."

Sydney took her cell phone out of her pocket.

"The fort is built in the shape of a five-pointed star," Ranger Hank explained. "They did that so each point of the star could be seen from the point on either side. It only took five men to guard the whole thing. One man could watch from each point of the star."

"That was smart," said Sydney. "Then they could see if the enemy was coming by land or by boat."

"Right," said the ranger. "And the new fort was strong. It was made of brick to protect the soldiers who lived inside. When you get there, you'll see how they lived in houses called barracks. There's the Commanding Officer's Quarters, the Junior Officers' Quarters, and two buildings for the enlisted men. That's where my great-something grandpa lived.

"And don't forget to check out the magazine—that's the strong room where the soldiers stored their gunpowder. They added it to the fort during the Civil War to keep ammunition safe from any sparks or explosions. There's a guardhouse on the grounds too with some jail cells. That's where they locked up prisoners."

Sydney checked her cell phone, and Elizabeth leaned in toward her to take a look. The green blip hadn't moved.

"Do you know why the fort is so famous?" asked Ranger Hank.

Sydney slipped her phone back into her pocket.

"It's because of 'The Star-Spangled Banner,' " Elizabeth said. "That's where the song was written."

"And the Battle of Baltimore," Ranger Hank added. "That was the one my great-grandpa fought in."

They came to a stretch of highway that was lined with orange barrels and construction cones, slowing traffic even more.

"Sydney, it's a good thing that you didn't live here back then," said Ranger Hank. "If you had, you'd have seen most of Washington, DC, burned by the British. Thunderstorms, like the ones we had last night, dumped rain and helped to put the fires out. But the White House and the Capitol Building were destroyed.

"After that, the British sailed toward Baltimore. They planned to take Fort McHenry and then sail into the Baltimore Basin and attack the city. They made it to where Key Bridge is today. From there, they fired on the fort, and that was the start of the battle. My grandpa and the other soldiers were ready for them and put up a brave fight."

Elizabeth was looking out the window, watching the traffic inch along. "That's where Francis Scott Key comes in," she said. "I studied about him. When the Brits attacked Washington, they took an old doctor prisoner. He was being held on a British ship, and his friends worried that he would be hanged. So they asked Francis Scott Key for help because he was a lawyer. He and another guy were allowed to get on the enemy ship and make a deal with them to release the doctor."

"A dangerous proposition," inserted Ranger Hank. The traffic was thinning, and he increased the van's speed. "The British agreed to release the doctor, but not until the battle was over. They figured that Key and his friends knew about their battle plans, so they were stuck on a ship that was shooting bombs at Fort McHenry."

He turned the van onto I-95 North and headed into Baltimore.

"So how does 'The Star-Spangled Banner' fit in?" Sydney asked.

"Well, there was a huge battle," said Hank. "For twenty-five hours the British attacked Fort McHenry. They used bombs that weighed two hundred pounds and had lighted fuses that made them explode when they reached their targets. The Brits used cannons on their ships and fired fifteen hundred bombs at the fort. All the while, Francis Scott Key was on the enemy's ship watching Fort McHenry under attack."

"Key was a religious man," Elizabeth said, "so he was probably praying as the bombs flew through the air. He was a writer too, so while he watched, he wrote a poem about what he saw. He didn't know what was going on at Fort McHenry, because it was all smoky from the bombs. But when the smoke cleared over the fort, the big American flag was still there. Baltimore had won the battle."

"If they hadn't won," said Ranger Hank, "Key would have seen the British flag flying over the fort instead."

They turned off of I-95 onto Exit 55. The fort was only a couple of miles away now.

"And that poem that he wrote," said Hank, "was 'The Star-Spangled Banner.' "

The Ranger picked up the yellow ranger hat on the seat next to him and put it on his head. Then he entertained the girls by singing:

"Oh, say, can you see, by the dawn's early light,
What so proudly we hail'd at the twilight's last gleaming?
Whose broad stripes and bright stars, thro' the perilous
    fight,

O'er the ramparts we watch'd, were so gallantly streaming?
And the rocket's red glare, the bombs bursting in air
Gave proof thro' the night that our flag was still there.
Oh, say, does that Star-Spangled Banner yet wave
O'er the land of the free and the home of the brave?"

Just as he finished the song, they turned left onto Fort Avenue. As they drove down the road, soon the girls saw Fort McHenry and the huge American flag towering over it, blowing in the wind. Ranger Hank drove the van to the Visitor Center.

"Here we are, girls," he said. "Come inside and I'll set you up with free passes. They'll get you in here today and for the next seven days, if you want to come back."

"What about the tattoo tomorrow?" Sydney asked. "Will the pass get us into that too?"

"It will," the ranger answered. "Are you coming to the tattoo then? Probably with your aunt, since she has to work here tomorrow. Lots of us got called in because the president is coming. It'll be special for you girls to see President Meade. Most people never get to see a real, live president."

"And we hope to keep him that way," said Sydney.

Elizabeth elbowed her. "Thanks for the ride," she said. "What time should we meet you back here?"

"Closing time is 4:45," said the ranger. "I'll be here to pick you up."

As the girls walked out of the Visitor Center, they checked their cell phones. The green blip was moving on water!

"Sydney, he's headed this way," Elizabeth said. "What will we do when they get here?"

Sydney grinned at Elizabeth. "We're going to follow them," she said. "I was hoping that this would happen. Following them is the only way we're really going to find out what's going on."

"But it's too dangerous," Elizabeth protested.

"We'll be careful," Sydney replied. "We can hide in any of the points of the star, and we'll always know where Moose is. We'll be fine."

As the girls walked toward the entrance to Fort McHenry, their cell phones began to vibrate. It was a text message from Bailey: MR. GREEN IS ON THE MOVE. HEADED RIGHT AT YOU. ON THE WATER. IN A BOAT? B CAREFUL.

Fort McHenry Fiasco

Sydney and Elizabeth walked on the weathered brick pathway into the arched entranceway of Fort McHenry. The short, dark hallway was flanked by vaulted doors.

"This is awesome," Elizabeth said. "These doors are ginormous!"

The hallway opened into the bright sunshine and the fort's grassy parade grounds. Just beyond this grassy area were redbrick buildings, the barracks that Ranger Hank had told them about. The barracks were two stories high with red roofs, white balconies, and green shutters on the windows. Red-white-and-blue banners hung from the balconies in honor of the Fourth of July, and actors dressed in costumes wandered the grounds making the fort seem more like 1814 than the twenty-first century.

"I just got an idea," Sydney said. "Follow me."

Elizabeth followed Sydney toward a short, stout lady who was one of the actors. She sat on a wooden bench outside the barracks wearing a floor-length, blood-red dress with a tan bonnet. It seemed like way too much clothing for the hot summer day.

"Good day," the lady said as the girls approached her.

"Good day," Sydney and Elizabeth said in unison.

The woman gave each girl a tour map of the fort. "Is this your first visit to Fort McHenry?" she asked.

"It is," Elizabeth answered.

"Nice dress!" said Sydney enthusiastically. "Do you have to get dressed like that at home, or do you change into your costumes here?"

The woman smiled and said, "Oh my! We don't dress like this at home. All our volunteers change here at the fort."

"Neat!" Sydney said. "Elizabeth and I took drama classes at summer camp."

Elizabeth smiled and nodded.

"We had a big room where we stored all the costumes," Sydney continued. "I suppose you do too?"

"We do," the woman answered. "In that enlisted men's barrack." She pointed to a building across the courtyard. "All kinds of costumes are stored there. You can take a look, if you'd like."

"Oh, that would be great," Sydney said. "Do you think we could try some on too? My aunt is Deandre Powers, the park ranger. I promise we'll be careful."

The woman thought for a minute. "I know Dee," she replied. "You must be Sydney. She talks about you all the time. Well, I suppose it wouldn't hurt, but make sure you put everything back the way you found it."

"We will," Sydney answered. "Thank you!"

Sydney grabbed Elizabeth's arm and hurried toward the barracks.

"Sydney, what are you up to?" Elizabeth asked.

"We can dress like the volunteers," Sydney answered. "Moose and Rusty will never recognize us, and we can get right up to them and find out what's going on. Then we'll put the costumes back before we go."

The girls opened the door to the enlisted men's barracks and went inside. It was like walking through a time warp into the 1800s. The air smelled musty and cobwebs hung from the rafters. The cobwebs glowed in rays of sunshine that streamed through the only window in the room. It was made up of twenty-five little glass squares, and in front of it sat a small wooden table and chair. An old military jacket hung over the back of the chair, and an inkwell was on the table with some yellowed writing paper and an old oil lamp.

The stuffy room held three rows of simple wooden bunk beds. Each uncomfortable-looking bed had a thin straw mattress and a single flat pillow. Soldiers' shoes hung from several of the bedposts, and muskets stood in their holders, ready for troops to grab them as they hurried out the door. The wooden plank floor creaked as the girls walked on it.

At the back of the barracks was a door marked WARDROBE. Sydney opened it, and the girls found a room filled with racks of costumes: soldiers' uniforms as well as costumes that citizens wore in the early 1800s. The girls went inside and bolted the door behind them.

"So do you want to be a soldier or a lady?" Sydney asked.

"A lady, definitely," said Elizabeth. She picked out an apple green dress and a white bonnet. Sydney helped her pull the dress on over her sleeveless top and shorts. It fit perfectly. Its hem was even long enough to cover the tops of her sandals.

"I'll roast in this!" Elizabeth complained as she pinned her long blond hair on top of her head and tied the bonnet over it. "What will you be?"

"A soldier," Sydney replied. She wiggled into the soldier's uniform—white pants and a dark blue coat with long sleeves and brass buttons. A white sash crisscrossed the front of the jacket, and the jacket's blue-and-gold collar fit snugly against Sydney's neck. She pulled on a pair of tall black boots. Then she set a blue soldier's hat on top of her cornrows, pulling the visor down just below her eyebrows. "There," she said. "How do I look?"

"Like you're ready for a winter storm," Elizabeth said. "Sydney, you'll be too hot."

"I'll be fine," Sydney argued. "Don't forget to take your cell phone with you. I'll take my binoculars too. And we should hide my street clothes and our backpacks in here somewhere."

Sydney searched for a place to hide their things.

"Why don't we just hang them up neatly with the costumes?" Elizabeth said. "There are so many clothes in here that no one will notice ours."

"Good idea," Sydney agreed.

The girls made sure that no one was coming. Then they left the barracks through a back door. As soon as they got outside, they checked their phones. The bright green blip was just offshore now, and they saw a string of messages from Bailey and an urgent message from McKenzie: I THINK HE'S ON A WATER TAXI. LOOKS LIKE IT'S LANDING NEAR THE FORT. BE CAREFUL!

"What's a water taxi?" Elizabeth asked, looking prim and proper in her old-time dress.

"It's a tour boat that shuttles visitors around the Baltimore Harbor," Sydney said. "Listen. It says here on the Fort McHenry tour map that each point of the star-shaped fort is called a bastion. We can walk out on the bastions to look all around the fort. It says the big park we saw around the fort is often used for recreational purposes, like hiking, picnicking, and looking out at the harbor. Let's go to the bastion that faces the water taxi dock. Maybe we can see Moose from there."

Elizabeth and Sydney, wearing their costumes, walked onto the long, raised, grassy area that made up one point of the star-shaped fort. The sides of the bastion had strong brick walls, and several old cannons faced outward, reminders of days when soldiers defended the harbor. Sydney took out her binoculars and looked in the direction of the boat landing.

"Perfect timing!" she said. "There they are." She handed the binoculars to Elizabeth.

Moose and Rusty walked toward the fort. Elizabeth noticed that Moose carried a long slender case strapped over his shoulder. "What do you think he's carrying?" she said. "A gun?"

"I don't think they'd be that obvious," Sydney answered. "Watch where they go."

"They're not coming into the fort," Elizabeth reported. "It looks like they're going to hang out in the park instead. They're walking by the water now. . . . They're sitting down on a bench near some trees."

Sydney's cell phone vibrated like crazy. It was another message from Bailey: PERCY ALERT! HE'S WALKING AROUND OUTSIDE OF THE FORT! WATCH OUT!

Sydney sent a reply: WE SEE THEM. NO MORE TEXT MESSAGES UNTIL YOU HEAR FROM US. WE'RE GOING TO FOLLOW THEM.

"Let's go," said Sydney. "I want to get close so we can hear what's going on."

"I still don't like the idea of this," Elizabeth said, following Sydney, careful not to trip on the hem of her dress.

The girls walked back to the fort entrance. They went through the brick hallway and then followed a brick path toward the waterfront. They saw Moose and Rusty sitting on the bench. Moose had opened the long slender case and was putting together some sort of contraption. It resembled a weed trimmer.

"What's that?" Sydney asked.

"I don't know," Elizabeth replied. "Let's see what he does with it."

Moose had the thing put together now, and it looked like he was plugging headphones into its handle.

"What in the world is he doing?" Sydney wondered.

Moose got up and put the headphones over his ears. He started walking with the contraption in one hand. He waved it back and forth over the grass while he listened through the headphones.

"I'm calling Kate," Elizabeth said. "She'll know what it is." Elizabeth took out her cell phone, took a picture of the contraption, and transmitted it to Kate. Then she dialed Kate's number. Kate answered on the first ring.

"Are you okay?" she asked. "Bailey said you're following them!"

"We're fine—don't worry," Elizabeth replied. "We need your help."

Since the picture hadn't come out well, Elizabeth described to Kate what Moose was doing with the tool.

"It's a metal detector," Kate told her. "He's waving it over the ground looking for something that's buried there. If the thing detects something metal underground, it gives a signal through the earphones."

When Elizabeth hung up, she told Sydney what Kate said.

"Let's split up," Sydney suggested. "You walk over there, like you're playacting. Say good day to them, and see if you can discover anything."

"I can't do that!" Elizabeth said. "You want me to talk to them?"

"Yes!" said Sydney. "Do it for President Meade."

"You'd better protect me," Elizabeth warned as she walked toward Rusty and Moose.

As she approached the bench, Elizabeth heard Rusty giving Moose instructions. "Try ten paces east. . . . Now go ten paces north. . . ."

Moose walked along, counting to himself.

Elizabeth walked right up to Rusty. She saw that he was holding some sort of map. "Good day!" she said brightly. She startled Rusty, and he gave a little jump.

"Yeah," he said gruffly.

"Are you enjoying your visit?" Elizabeth asked. She leaned in to get a better look at the map.

"Humph." Rusty grunted, almost ignoring her.

Elizabeth saw a big red X on the map.

"Is there anything you'd like to know about the fort? Anything that I can help you with?" Elizabeth bravely sat on the bench near Rusty to get a closer look at the map. Under the red X was the word *BUM* in all capital letters.

"You can help by leaving me alone, lady," said Rusty.

His steely gray eyes gave Elizabeth the creeps. She got up quickly. "Well, good day then," she said. But instead of walking back toward Sydney, she circled around the park and met her friend near a grove of trees.

"He's creepier than you could imagine," Elizabeth said.

"So what did you find out?" asked Sydney.

Elizabeth told her all about the map, the red X, and the word *BUM*. Then she texted the other Camp Club Girls to let them know what was going on.

All afternoon, Sydney and Elizabeth watched as Rusty and Moose wandered around the park with the metal detector. Whatever they looked for didn't seem to be there, or maybe they were even more directionally disabled than Elizabeth. Then, just as the park was about to close, something happened.

Sydney watched through the binoculars. The men were searching back where they'd started, near the bench. Moose stopped by a tree about twenty feet from the shoreline. Rusty hurried to Moose. Then he went back to the bench and picked up his backpack. He took it to where Moose was standing and pulled out a small folding shovel. He knelt down and dug in the dirt beneath the gnarly old tree. After a few minutes, Rusty pulled out a metal box about the size of a box of animal crackers.

"I'm heading over there to see what's going on," Sydney said. "Watch me." She gave the binoculars to Elizabeth.

Sydney walked like a soldier, steadfast and straight, toward Rusty and Moose. She slowed her pace as she neared them. Then she stopped, turned her back to them, and pretended to look across the harbor. Rusty and Moose were so excited about the box that they didn't seem to notice her.

"Handle it real careful, Rusty," Moose was saying. "We don't need accidents."

Rusty opened the lid of the box and peeked inside. Just then, an enormous explosion rocked the ground and rumbled across the water. Sydney nearly jumped out of her boots.

"What time is it?" Rusty asked Moose.

What time is it? Sydney thought. *Something just exploded inside the fort, and you're wondering what time it is?*

She turned around just long enough to see Rusty close the box and carefully place it in the backpack.

"It's 4:30," Moose said. "When that cannon goes off, it means the fort's closing, doesn't it, Rusty?"

Sydney sighed with relief.

"Yeah," Rusty said, sounding annoyed. "And because you took so long to find this, now we'll have to take it with us."

"But the boss said we should get it done today," Moose protested. "I don't think he wants us hauling that thing all over Baltimore."

"We don't have time," Rusty snarled. "The last boat leaves at five o'clock, and we have to be on it. We'll come back tomorrow. What the boss doesn't know won't hurt him."

Sydney followed behind the men as they walked toward the Visitor

Center. They passed Elizabeth on the pathway near the fort's entrance. Sydney saw Elizabeth curtsy. When Sydney caught up to Beth, she told her what was going on.

"The fort closes in fifteen minutes, and we have to return these costumes," Sydney said. "The girls will track Moose. They can tell us where he goes."

The girls scurried back to the wardrobe room and bolted the door. Elizabeth was grateful to get out of the long, heavy dress. Even the stuffy, humid air in the back room felt good against her skin. She hung the dress on a rack and offered to hang up Sydney's uniform while Sydney slipped on her street clothes. Elizabeth was about to return Sydney's cap to a cabinet near the door when she heard a familiar voice.

"Well, here we are, the last stop. A bed for two and nobody sleeps waiting for the alarm," the voice said. "We've been to every room inside the fort."

"Yeah," said an unfamiliar voice. "And the minutes are ticking down."

There was shuffling outside the door. The visitors seemed to be searching for something.

"I can't imagine where they went," said the first voice. "Maybe they've given up spying on our friends."

"Hey, what do you think is in here?" the second voice asked. The doorknob rattled.

"Hide!" Elizabeth whispered. She pulled Sydney toward the racks of clothes.

"No! Out the window!" Sydney exclaimed.

The girls rushed to the only window in the room. Just as they were about to climb out, Elizabeth felt the silver pendant fall from the chain on her neck.

"My pendant!" she gasped.

"Leave it!" said Sydney. "Let's get out of here."

Caught!

The girls barely said a word on the ride home with Ranger Hank. Elizabeth's heart was so heavy that her chest hurt. She was horrified at losing her favorite necklace. But even worse, with a dull ache, Elizabeth had to admit to herself that she knew that first voice they'd heard in the barracks. It was Uncle Dan. And she suspected that Sydney had recognized his voice too.

When the girls finally returned to Sydney's room, Elizabeth dropped down on the bed and cried.

Sydney booted up the computer and emailed the Camp Club Girls. Soon they were all talking in the chat room about the voices near the wardrobe room. The girls agreed that in some way Uncle Dan was involved.

> McKenzie: *You know that note you found: "Hail to the chief at the twilight's last gleaming"? "Hail to the Chief" is the song they play when the president shows up. "Twilight's last gleaming" could mean the end of the Twilight Tattoo. Those words are in "The Star-Spangled Banner" too. They plan to kill the president at the end of the tattoo.*

Sydney doodled on a sheet of paper as she remembered something Aunt Dee had said.

> Sydney: *The president isn't scheduled to appear until just before the fireworks start. There's a concert and marching presentation at twilight. When that's over, the president will show up and make his speech. When he's done, it'll be dark, and then the fireworks start.*

"In more ways than one," Elizabeth said. She had come to sit next to Sydney at the desk and was reading the words on the screen.

Kate: *I'm almost certain a weapon is in that little metal box they dug up. Maybe a bomb.*

Sydney scribbled words from "The Star-Spangled Banner" on her paper: *the rocket's red glare. . .the bombs bursting in air. bombs. bomb. BUM!* "Bum!" she said out loud. She grabbed the keyboard.

Sydney: *Elizabeth saw the word BUM on the map near the red X. Maybe it meant bomb. Maybe whoever wrote it couldn't spell.*
Bailey: *So Percy has a bomb in his backpack?*
Sydney: *I think so. And it's your job to keep an eye on him. Let us know the minute he moves.*
Alexis: *I've been thinking about The Professor. I remember a story about Sherlock Holmes, the English detective. His worst enemy was this guy named Professor Moriarty. In the story, the professor was a mastermind criminal. He knew about a secret hiding place for storing bombs during war. So maybe our Professor has a secret hiding place inside the fort.*
Sydney: *Maybe you're right. We're going to Fort McHenry with Aunt Dee tomorrow afternoon. She has to work there from five o'clock until the tattoo is done. We won't have much time to find the bomb.*

"Find the bomb?" said Elizabeth. "Oh Sydney."

"We have to," Sydney said. "Remember, we're not sure any of this is true. We might be way off track, but if we're not—"

The Camp Club Girls agreed to follow the green blip while Sydney and Elizabeth were at the fort. Only very important text messages would be sent, and those would come through Kate.

•—•—•

The next afternoon, Sydney, Elizabeth, and Aunt Dee arrived at Fort McHenry when it closed, at about a quarter to five. Guests for the tattoo wouldn't be allowed in until six. Aunt Dee gave the girls permission to wander around, but she told them to be back at the Visitor Center by nine o'clock, when President Meade was scheduled to speak.

As they walked through the arched hallway into the fort, the girls took out their cell phones and logged on to Kate's tracking site.

"Moose hasn't moved since they took the water taxi back to the Inner Harbor," Elizabeth observed. "So they probably still have the bomb."

"Not necessarily," Sydney replied. "Maybe Rusty brought it back here overnight; we wouldn't have known if he did."

"I hadn't thought of that," said Elizabeth.

When the girls entered the parade grounds, they saw uniformed troops practicing drills. In the distance they heard drummers and buglers rehearsing for the tattoo.

"Elizabeth," Sydney said. "I think you should call your uncle."

"Why?" Elizabeth asked.

"Because we need to know where he is," Sydney responded. "But don't let on where *we* are."

Reluctantly Elizabeth took out her cell phone and called her uncle's number. It rang several times before Uncle Dan answered.

"Hey, Beth!" he said. "How are you doing?"

"I'm fine, Uncle Dan," Elizabeth said. "Just checking in to see what you're up to. Do you have plans with your friends for tonight?"

Her uncle paused before answering. "We're going fishing," he said. "And where are you going?"

Elizabeth thought quickly. "Oh, we're hanging out with Sydney's Aunt Dee."

Sydney put her index finger up to her lips.

"Well, I'm glad to hear that," said Uncle Dan. "Stay close to Aunt Dee tonight, all right?"

What a strange thing to say, Elizabeth thought. "I will," she promised. "I have to go now. I'll talk to you tomorrow." She ended the call.

"So what did he say?" Sydney asked.

"They're going fishing tonight," Elizabeth answered.

Sydney spoke without thinking. "Fishing for President Meade."

As a line of soldiers marched past them wearing 1800s uniforms, Elizabeth said, "I have faith in my uncle, Sydney, almost as much as I have in God."

Sydney didn't say a word.

For the next hour, the girls searched Fort McHenry for the mysterious metal box. First, they checked each of the bastions. As they walked on the ramparts, they looked into the gun barrels of the cannons along the way. They checked the magazines on the bastions—storage areas built into mounds of earth used for stockpiling gunpowder and weapons. Then they moved inside the fort near the barracks and looked underneath the wooden platform that surrounded the enormous flag-pole. Above them, they could hear the huge American flag, a replica of the one from the Battle of Baltimore, flapping in the breeze.

Next, the girls went to the barracks, searching each one. Starting on the upper level, they looked under each bed, through every drawer, and inside all the wooden barrels that held supplies. They left no door unopened, and explored every nook and cranny. Nothing!

The last place they checked was the enlisted men's barracks. While Sydney searched, Elizabeth decided to go back to the wardrobe room and look for her pendant. She found the door bolted shut. Inside, she heard men's voices.

"Look alive, boys!" a man shouted.

"Ready arms. By twos!" shouted another.

As Elizabeth listened, she heard the sound of heavy boots moving toward the door. Quickly she crouched behind some barrels in a corner of the barracks. The door to the room opened and several actors dressed as 1800s soldiers came out. They walked across the wooden floor, past where Elizabeth was hiding, and out the front door.

Elizabeth slipped inside the wardrobe room. Methodically she scanned every square inch of the floor, but found nothing. She also kept her eyes open for the important metal box.

"It's not here."

Elizabeth sucked in her breath and her heart skipped a beat. "Don't scare me like that," she told Sydney.

"The metal box isn't here," Sydney repeated. "I looked everywhere."

"Neither is my pendant," said Elizabeth. "Maybe we should just give up."

"We're not giving up," Sydney protested. "Not until we can prove that nothing evil is going on."

Just then, both girls' cell phones began to vibrate. It was a message from Kate: MOOSE IS ON THE MOVE. ON THE WATER AGAIN. HEADING FOR THE FORT.

"So what do we do now?" Elizabeth asked.

"We hide outside of the fort and wait," said Sydney. "When they get here, we follow them. Only this time, we have to be careful not to be seen."

Elizabeth and Sydney hid near some trees between the Visitor

Center and the fort entrance. Before long, crowds of people arrived. They lined up four or five deep to walk into the fort.

"We'll be lucky to see Moose and Rusty in this crowd," Sydney said. "What if we miss them, Beth? Then what?"

Elizabeth had her cell phone out and was busy watching the tiny screen. "We won't. Not as long as we rely on Kate's website. We just have to watch where the green blip goes and keep following it. Even if we can't see them with our own eyes, we'll know where they are."

"And we have to be careful that they don't see us," Sydney added.

The girls watched the blip come onshore. It traveled slowly past the Visitor Center and along the pathway toward the entrance.

"There they are!" said Elizabeth.

Moose and Rusty shuffled along in the middle of the mob. Sydney almost missed them. They looked oddly respectable. Each wore a pair of neat blue jeans and a polo shirt, and Rusty sported a neatly trimmed beard. They blended well with the patriotic crowd.

"Let's go," Sydney said.

Both girls apologized as they cut into the line a few steps behind Rusty and Moose.

"Keep them in sight," Sydney whispered. She fixed her eyes on Rusty's red hair.

The crowd squeezed into the narrow hallway and then swarmed toward the bleachers set up around the parade grounds. Sydney and Elizabeth were pushed along, forced to go with the crowd. When they exited into the fading sunlight, they saw that someone was missing.

"Where's Moose?" Sydney asked.

Elizabeth checked the green blip on her cell phone. "He's still in the hallway," she said.

They found a bench near the barracks and watched Rusty as he sat on a lower tier of the bleachers. They waited for Moose to come out. But he didn't!

"Something's wrong with Kate's website," Elizabeth complained. "We've lost Moose."

"I'm going to check out the hallway," Sydney told her. "I'll be right back."

Cautiously Sydney walked to the entrance hall. The crowd had begun to thin out, and Moose was nowhere in sight. She hurried back to Elizabeth. "He's not there," she said. "Tell Kate. Maybe she can fix the website."

Elizabeth sent a text message to Kate telling her what was going on.

Everything seems to be working fine, Kate answered. But I'll double check.

"Now what?" Elizabeth asked.

"We wait," Sydney told her. "Keep your eyes on Rusty. Sooner or later, Moose will show up."

"I hope so," said Elizabeth.

The girls watched as the troops marched onto the field. Some soldiers played fifes and others played drums. All marched as if they were going to the battlefield. Swords hung from their belts and some carried muskets.

The troops surrounded the parade grounds and then stood at parade rest. Soon the United States Army Band marched to a stage on the far end of the field. They sat on metal chairs and opened folders of sheet music on their music stands. An announcement boomed over the loudspeaker: "Ladies and gentlemen, please stand for 'The Star-Spangled Banner.'"

Then the concert began. Sydney and Elizabeth had no choice but to sit, listen to the music, and watch Rusty. Kate sent several text messages insisting that the website was not broken. Still, no sign of Moose.

After about an hour, the sunset faded to dusk, and the dim crescent moon hung almost overhead.

"Sydney," Elizabeth gasped. "Look!"

Moose came sneaking out of the hallway. He carried the metal box as he prowled close to the fort's brick wall. Just then, Rusty got up and left the bleachers.

The girls' cell phones were vibrating with Kate's message: He's on the move. Exiting the hallway NOW.

Elizabeth sent a quick reply: We see him.

"You follow Rusty, and I'll take Moose," said Sydney. "I have a feeling we'll end up at the same place."

With their hearts pounding, Sydney and Elizabeth took off.

Quietly and carefully, Sydney stayed close to the fort's wall. She watched Moose slinking from barracks to barracks in the shadow. Finally he paused at an old guardhouse not far from the podium where President Meade was supposed to speak. Sydney saw Elizabeth hiding behind whatever she could find as she followed Rusty. Both girls watched as the men entered the guardhouse, leaving the door open behind them.

The girls met at the open door. Sydney stood on the left and Elizabeth on the right. They could hear the men talking.

"I didn't think you were ever coming out from that secret room," said Rusty. "It's about time!"

"Sorry," Moose answered. "It was dark in there, and I couldn't see my watch. I didn't know what time it was."

"Come on!" Rusty ordered. "That old jail cell is just around the corner. There's a bucket inside where the boss wants us to put it."

Carefully Sydney peeked into the room. The men had disappeared around a corner behind an old jailer's desk. She motioned for Elizabeth to follow her inside. Elizabeth took a deep breath. Then the girls slipped into the guardhouse.

Silently Sydney walked across the room. She peeked around the corner. Straight ahead was a short hallway. At its end was an old jail cell with a heavy iron door. The cell was made of thick brick walls, with no windows. Moose and Rusty were both inside, and Sydney noticed that the cell door had a lock. She watched Rusty take an old tin pail from one corner of the cell, and then Moose gingerly placed the metal box inside.

"We'd better get out of here fast," Moose said.

"I don't think so!" Sydney shouted.

Elizabeth watched with horror as her friend leaped into the hallway and rushed the jail cell. She slammed the door, locking Moose and Rusty inside. Rusty's steely eyes glared at her.

"Who are *you*?" asked Moose.

"I'm your worst enemy," Sydney snapped.

Elizabeth dashed beside her.

"It's those girls from the Wall," Rusty said. "I told you I didn't like something about them." Rusty's voice echoed inside the dark, musty cell. The only other sound came from the tin pail. It was ticking!

"You'd better tell us what you're up to," said Elizabeth. "Or else."

"Or else, what?" Rusty laughed.

In the dim light from the hallway, the girls saw sweat pouring down Moose's face. He stuttered, "There's a b—bomb in here. It's going to g—go off when the f—fireworks start. P—please, let us go. We all g—gotta get out of here." He looked nervously at the pail, inches from his feet.

Through the doorway, the girls heard the loudspeaker announce that President Meade would soon be at the podium.

"You'd better let us go, or we'll all die!" said Rusty. "This is a high-tech military bomb made from titanium alloy. It'll blow this place to smithereens." He took the metal box out of the pail and held it menacingly in front of the girls.

"Run and get help," Sydney told Elizabeth. "Hurry! Go!"

"You come too!" Elizabeth said.

"*Just go!*" Sydney commanded.

Elizabeth raced out of the short hallway, around the corner, and past the jailer's desk. She bolted out the door and into the darkness. She was almost to the parade grounds when she felt one strong arm wrap around her waist. Then a hand covered her mouth, and someone was dragging her away from the fort and toward the water. The kidnapper pulled her onto a pier and into a small boat. Only then did she get a look at him. It was her uncle's friend Al.

The Rockets' Red Glare

Elizabeth struggled with her kidnapper until she saw Uncle Dan sitting in the boat. Al let her go, and she ran into her uncle's arms.

"I can't believe you're involved in this!" she sobbed. "I always thought you were a good man who loves the Lord."

Uncle Dan hugged her. "I am, and I do," he said. "Now listen to me."

A stranger appeared from the darkness in the back of the boat. He was dressed in black and carried a gun!

"We think there's a plot to assassinate President Meade right here, tonight—and very soon. This is Agent Phillips from the FBI. If you know anything, Elizabeth, tell him right now! It's a matter of life and death. Why were you running, and where is Sydney?"

Elizabeth's heart pounded.

"Sydney has Moose and Rusty locked in a jail cell in the guardhouse." She pointed in the direction from which she'd run. "They have a bomb and it's set to go off when the fireworks start. Sydney told me to run for help. She insisted on staying there to guard them."

Al stood behind Elizabeth and put his hands gently on her shoulders. "See, I knew there was a bomb," he said. "I could sense it from our combat days in Vietnam."

"Tell me exactly what the bomb looks like," Agent Phillips said. "And who are Rusty and Moose?"

"Rusty and Moose work for the boss and The Professor," said Elizabeth. "They're the bad guys. The bomb is in a small metal box that they dug up yesterday afternoon over there." She pointed to the area. "I don't know what's inside the box, but it's ticking, and Moose is nervous. He said if they don't get out of that jail cell, everyone is going to die."

Agent Phillips jumped from the boat onto the dock. He ran as fast as he could toward the guardhouse.

"I'm going too," Elizabeth demanded. "I have to save Sydney!"

She started to move, but Al and Uncle Dan held her back.

"Let Agent Phillips handle this, Elizabeth," Uncle Dan said. "He knows what he's doing. Sydney will be all right."

Al had one big, strong arm around her shoulder now. This time, instead of it making her feel terrified, she felt safe.

"I'm sorry, Elizabeth," he said. "I didn't mean to scare you back there. We knew that something was going on, but we weren't sure what it was. If you had screamed, who knows what might have happened. I had to get you to the boat so you'd be safe. I don't know what your uncle would do if he lost you."

Uncle Dan took something from the pocket of his Levi's and held it in his closed fist. "And speaking of losing things," he said, "did you lose this?" He opened his hand and revealed Elizabeth's pendant.

"Oh," Elizabeth gasped. "You found it."

"After you and your friend climbed out the window yesterday," he said. Uncle Dan read the inscription out loud: " 'Be strong and courageous. Do not be terrified; do not be discouraged, for the Lord your God will be with you wherever you go.' Joshua 1:9. I gave you this pendant for times like this, Beth. The Lord is with us. He'll save President Meade and your friend. Just you wait and see."

Uncle Dan fastened the chain around Elizabeth's neck. "And by the way," he said. "What were you and Sydney doing in the wardrobe room?"

Elizabeth explained how they had dressed in costume and followed Rusty and Moose. She also told her uncle about the package Moose was carrying, and she showed them Kate's website and the green blip that was inside the jail cell.

●—●—●

Meanwhile, Agent Phillips rushed into the guardhouse. He passed the old jailer's desk and turned the corner into the shallow hallway. Sydney was standing guard over the prisoners, and Rusty was pleading, "Kid, just go and get the key!"

The FBI agent flashed his badge. "Phillips, FBI!" he said. "Sydney, get out of here. I'll handle this."

Sydney stood straight and tall. "No," she said. "Where's Elizabeth?"

"She's safe," said Agent Phillips. "Get out!"

Sydney didn't move.

"Unlock this door!" Rusty thundered. "We have less than a half hour before this thing blows."

Moose stood next to Rusty, hanging on to the bars. His eyes were glazed, and his face was an odd gray color. "I think I'm going to throw up," he said.

"Sydney, where's the key?" the agent asked calmly.

Sydney felt like she was in an old spy movie, the kind that Alexis was always talking about. "I don't know," she answered.

Agent Phillips stayed calm when he spoke. "We have to find the key. The only thing that might stop that bomb from going off is to drown it in water. We need to get it out of this jail cell and into the harbor. *Now!*"

Agent Phillips began searching the guardhouse. Sydney helped. They dumped the contents of all the jailer's desk drawers and found nothing. They looked in cabinets, under a pile of books, and beneath the mattress of the jailer's cot in the corner. Then Phillips got on his radio and called for help. Within seconds five men wearing black suits burst through the door.

"Oh!" Sydney gasped.

One was the short, dark man she and Elizabeth had seen at the Lincoln Memorial—the boss.

"Arrest that guy!" Sydney cried. "He's the boss!"

The man looked at her as if she were crazy. "Peter Daniels, Secret Service," he said to Agent Phillips.

"Daniels, get President Meade out of here right now!" The FBI agent commanded. "He's in danger."

The Secret Service agent bolted out of the room.

"But you can't let him get away!" Sydney said. "He's the boss!"

Everything was so mixed up. Sydney had no time to tell Agent Phillips the whole story, and he had no idea what she meant. Meanwhile, she watched the boss get away.

"Elizabeth and I were spying on Moose and Rusty," she blurted out. "At the Lincoln Memorial. That guy is the one who was giving them the orders. He's part of the plan to get President Meade!"

Agent Phillips looked at her with disbelief.

"Oh, please, just trust me," said Sydney.

Phillips nodded toward the other men, and two of them ran into the darkness.

"Sydney, I need your help," said Agent Phillips. "Run as fast as you can to the Visitor Center, and see if you can find where they keep the key. Radio the information back to me." He handed her a small walkie-talkie.

"Whatever you do, don't come back here. Get as far away from Fort McHenry as you can."

Sydney Lincoln took the walkie-talkie in one hand and started to run. She ran faster than she ever had. Everything was at stake now: the president's life and the lives of everyone in the fort, including her own.

●—●—●

In the Visitor Center, Aunt Dee sat at a desk watching the fort entrance on a security monitor. The entrance was deserted. All of the visitors were in the bleachers waiting for President Meade. Dee looked at a wall clock. It was a few minutes past nine o'clock, and the president was late getting to the podium. The loudspeaker played patriotic music as the visitors waited for him to appear.

Aunt Dee glanced back at the monitor just in time to see Sydney dash through the entrance from the fort. It didn't seem at all odd that she was running. After all, Dee had told her and Elizabeth to be back at the Visitor Center by nine. And they were late.

Sydney ran through the front door.

"Aunt Dee! Aunt Dee! Help!"

Dee jumped up from her desk and hurried to Sydney. "What's the matter?" she demanded. "Did something happen to Elizabeth?"

"Aunt Dee, an FBI agent sent me. There's a bomb in the guardhouse, and we need the key to the jail cell!"

"What?" Aunt Dee asked doubtfully.

Sydney held the walkie-talkie up to her mouth and pushed a button. "Agent Phillips? Please tell my aunt what's going on. I don't think she believes me."

The walkie-talkie crackled. "This is Agent Phillips from the FBI," the voice said. "We have a code red situation in the guardhouse, and we need the key to the jail cell right away!"

"There's a plot to kill the president," Sydney added.

Sydney's aunt rushed into a back room and returned with a big, black skeleton key hanging on a bigger metal ring. "Tell him I've got it," she said.

Sydney tore the key from her aunt's hand and took off.

"Sydney, no!" Aunt Dee shouted. But it was too late. Sydney charged through the darkness grasping the key. As she ran, she remembered the scripture verse on the bracelet Elizabeth had given her: *Be strong and courageous. Do not be terrified; do not be discouraged, for the Lord your God will be with you wherever you go.*

By now, fifteen minutes had passed. A quarter of an hour was all that was left to drown the bomb and get to safety. As the loudspeaker played "Stars and Stripes Forever," Sydney cut across the parade grounds, past the barracks, and into the night. Several Secret Service agents, not knowing who she was or what she was up to, chased her. Sydney was faster than they were. She didn't dare slow down by looking over her shoulder to see if any of them was the boss. Instead, she ran with all her might to the guardhouse.

Sydney slammed through the door. "Here!" she gasped, pushing the key to Agent Phillips.

"Leave her alone!" Phillips ordered the agents who were about to tackle Sydney. Phillips ran to the jail cell with Sydney behind him. "Get out of here!" he told her.

"No!" Sydney exclaimed. "I can help."

Moose was lying on the floor. He had passed out from fear. Rusty clung to the cell bars, his face ashen. He was no longer the gruff character who talked down to Moose and made demands. Instead, he looked like a frightened boy.

"You'd better say your prayers," Sydney told him as Phillips put the key into the lock.

"I don't know any prayers," Rusty answered.

As Agent Phillips tried to unlock the door, Sydney prayed out loud: "Our Father who art in heaven, hallowed be Thy name. Thy kingdom come. Thy will be done on earth as it is in heaven. Give us this day our daily bread. And forgive us our trespasses as we forgive those who trespass against us. And lead us not into temptation, but deliver us from evil: For thine is the kingdom, and the power, and the glory, forever. Amen."

"Amen," Rusty echoed.

The cell door creaked open, and a team of FBI agents tackled Rusty. Another agent snapped handcuffs onto Moose as he lay unconscious on the cold brick floor. A third agent reached for the metal box with the bomb, but Sydney was faster. She grabbed the box and ran.

"Sydney!" Agent Phillips shouted.

"Let her go," another agent said. "She's faster than any of us. We can't do anything about it now."

●━━●━━●

On the boat, Elizabeth waited with her uncle and his friend. In the distance, they could hear "Stars and Stripes Forever" playing on the parade grounds' loudspeakers.

"It's almost time for the fireworks to start," Elizabeth said. "I suppose that by now Agent Phillips has canceled them and they've dismantled the bomb. Where in the world is Sydney?"

Uncle Dan smiled weakly. "They'll probably have the fireworks anyway," he said. "It's all done by computer these days."

The two-way radio on the boat started to crackle. Agent Phillips's anxious voice came through: "Dan, Sydney has the bomb, and she's running toward the harbor. As soon as she drops it in the water, get her into the boat and get as far out in the harbor as you can—as fast as you can. Good luck!"

Elizabeth had a sick, sinking feeling in the pit of her stomach.

Al started the engine and untied the boat from the dock. Then a shadowy figure appeared on the crest of the hill near the harbor. It almost flew toward the boat docks.

"There she is!" Elizabeth cried. "She's running to that dock!" She pointed to a boat dock south from where they were. Immediately Al backed the boat out and sped in that direction.

"Run, Sydney! Run!" Elizabeth cried. "We're coming to get you!"

As Sydney ran, clutching the metal box, she prayed that the bomb wouldn't go off. Her heart was pounding when her feet hit the wooden dock. Although it was at most thirty feet long, to Sydney it seemed like a mile. Finally she reached the end of the dock. She dropped the box into the water.

"Swim to us!" Uncle Dan shouted.

Sydney dove in and swam to the boat. Elizabeth helped pull her inside. Then, with Al at the controls, the powerboat sped out into the Baltimore Harbor.

Sydney lay on her back on the boat's floor, wet and gasping for air. "W—we. . .d—did it," she said. "We s—saved P—President Meade."

Elizabeth held her friend's hand. "No, Sydney," she said. "*You* did it."

As the boat sailed a safe distance into the harbor, Elizabeth sent Kate a text message: WE'RE ALL RIGHT. TELL THE OTHER CAMP CLUB GIRLS THAT WE'LL HAVE A LONG STORY TO TELL AROUND OUR CYBER CAMPFIRE.

Kate texted: MOOSE IS ON THE MOVE AGAIN. HE'S HEADING TOWARD THE FORT'S ENTRANCE NOW, REALLY SLOW.

Elizabeth typed back, I KNOW. HE'S IN HANDCUFFS AND SHACKLES.

Kaboom! Pow! Bang! Several explosions thundered across the water making the boat rock.

"Oh no," Sydney said, still lying on the floor. "Did it go off?"

In the following seconds, Elizabeth only saw the stars and the crescent moon in the black sky. Then several bright dots shot into the air over the fort, leaving smoke trails behind them. One exploded into a silver fountain, another into long golden spider legs, and a third showered the fort with sparks of red, white, and blue. "It's only the fireworks starting," she said.

The radio crackled again. "All suspects are in custody," said Agent Phillips. "Percival Malone, Rusty Gates, and also the Secret Service guy Peter Daniels. A fourth suspect is in Washington, DC, and our agents have him surrounded. Good work, Sydney and Elizabeth. But if you ever do anything this dangerous again, I might have to arrest you!"

Uncle Dan looked at the girls and nodded in agreement. Then they all laughed, happy that the whole thing was behind them.

"Do you think that Agent Phillips will tell us the whole story?" Sydney wondered as she accepted a blanket Uncle Dan found in a seat. "I mean, we still don't know why those guys wanted to kill the president or who The Professor is."

Al settled back in his captain's chair and watched as fireworks spilled over the fort. "I'm sure he'll tell us what he can," he said. "Your uncle and I would like to know the whole story too."

Sydney sat looking toward the fort. The exploding fireworks cast a strange flickering light on the huge American flag flying near the barracks. Sydney couldn't help but imagine what it was like for Francis Scott Key as he stood on the deck of an enemy ship in the Baltimore Harbor, watching bombs explode over Fort McHenry. She thanked God that tonight's rockets' red glare came from the fireworks.

CHAPTER 12

According to His Plan

The next morning, Elizabeth and Sydney went to the police station to provide information on Moose, Rusty, and the plot to kill the President. Uncle Dan and Al went too, and Agent Phillips was there to help.

●—●—●

Meanwhile, Alexis, Bailey, McKenzie, and Kate were all in the chat room waiting for them to return. The only information they had came from an email that Sydney sent after she and Elizabeth got back from the tattoo. It told everything that had happened at the fort, but there were still lots of missing pieces.

Finally Sydney and Elizabeth logged in.

> Bailey: *So tell us what you found out at the police station. And don't leave anything out.*
> Alexis: *Yeah. I'm dying to know what happened. I've had "The Star Spangled Banner" playing in my head ever since I read your email. Sometimes I hate it that my brain is so musical.*
> McKenzie: *I didn't see anything about it on the news this morning. Why not?*

Sydney and Elizabeth sat at Sydney's desk. In front of them was an open box of chocolates, a gift from Agent Phillips. Two pieces of candy were missing from the box, and Sydney reached for another. On the shelf near Elizabeth sat a big glass vase filled with two dozen red roses. A white card with gold lettering hung from it, reading: *WITH SINCERE GRATITUDE—PRESIDENT WILSON MEADE.*

> Sydney: *They're keeping the assassination plot quiet. The*

visitors to the tattoo had no idea that anything was going on, because the FBI didn't want them to panic. It was quicker to get the bomb away from the crowd than to get the crowd away from the bomb. When it was all over, President Meade made his speech as if nothing had happened, and then the tattoo ended with the fireworks.

Alexis: *So you're not going to be on the news?*

Sydney: *Not unless someone leaks it to the media. The FBI hopes it won't happen. They don't want other bad guys to get ideas.*

Elizabeth borrowed the keyboard from Sydney.

Elizabeth: *You can't say a word to anyone about what we're going to tell you. This is a Camp Club Girls' secret. Let's do a cyber pinkie-promise that we'll take it to our graves.*

Bailey: *I promise.*

Alexis: *And me.*

McKenzie: *I'm in.*

Kate: *Me too. Biscuit promises too.*

Sydney and Elizabeth linked their pinkie fingers and promised to keep the secret forever.

McKenzie: *So who was The Professor?*

Kate: *And what was up with the Secret Service guy, the boss?*

Elizabeth: *One thing at a time. We have to start at the beginning, way back in 1967 in Vietnam. The boss—his real name is Peter Daniels—was a soldier then in the United States Army. He was the Dan in the note, "Lieutenant Dan, we've got legs," not my uncle.*

Alexis: *I'm glad, Elizabeth. None of us wanted your uncle to be one of the bad guys.*

Elizabeth chose a square piece of chocolate from the box before she continued.

Elizabeth: *Peter Daniels had a twin brother named Adam, and they fought together in the Vietnam War. They were both in a platoon called White Skull, and they were in the worst of the fighting.*

Sydney took over the keyboard while Elizabeth ate the chewy caramel.

Sydney: *One day, there was a terrible battle. The White Skull troopers were under attack, and they were outnumbered. So their leader, Sergeant Kuester, told them to retreat. He figured if he didn't get his men out of there, they'd all get killed.*

McKenzie: *How do you know all this?*

Sydney: *Because Sergeant Kuester is here in DC at the Vietnam Veterans' Reunion, the same one Beth's uncle is at. The FBI found out that Sergeant Kuester had been Daniel's platoon leader, and they figured he might have an idea why Daniels wanted to kill the president. It was his information that got Peter Daniels to confess.*

Bailey: *So why did he want to kill the president?*

Sydney: *President Meade was in the White Skull platoon too when he was a young soldier. When Sgt. Kuester told his men to retreat, Meade froze. Adam Daniels, the boss's twin brother, tried to get Meade out of there, but Meade went crazy. He started fighting with Adam, like he was the enemy or something—*

McKenzie: *It was Agent Orange, wasn't it? I've thought from the beginning that whoever we were looking for was sick from that.*

Sydney: *Sorry, McKenzie, but you were wrong about that. It had nothing to do with Agent Orange. Meade just froze in fear.*

Sydney helped herself to another piece of candy before going on with the story.

Sydney: *Sgt. Kuester realized that two guys were missing, so he went back to get them. When Peter Daniels found out that one of the missing guys was his brother, he went to help. Of course, when they got to them, they found Meade fighting with Adam Daniels. Adam was trying to drag Meade out of there while they were under attack. Kuester managed to get between them and wrestle Meade to the ground. But the enemy fired at them. The sergeant got shot in the leg and Adam Daniels fell to the ground—dead. Kuester managed to get out and Peter Daniels rescued Meade, but secretly he blamed Meade for the death of his twin brother.*

Sydney pushed the keyboard toward Elizabeth. "You tell the next part," she said.

Elizabeth: *After he got out of the army, Peter Daniels became a police officer in Washington, DC. He worked his way up to the rank of lieutenant.*

Kate: *And that's why they called him Lieutenant Dan in the note.*

Elizabeth: *Right. Wilson Meade became a politician and was elected to the United States Senate. He and Peter Daniels were friendly, but Daniels was just like Jesus' disciple Judas. He pretended to be Meade's friend, but in the end, he betrayed him.*

When Meade got elected president, he wanted Peter Daniels as one of his Secret Service guys, because he trusted Daniels with his life. In fact, we found out today that it was Daniels who saved President Meade when he was almost shot at the National Air and Space Museum.

Kate: *So the boss saved Meade's life twice. Once in Vietnam and again at the Spirit of St. Louis thing.*

Elizabeth: *Meanwhile, Daniels was getting angrier that his brother was dead. He hated it that Meade was not only alive, but had also become the president of the United States. He just couldn't get it out of his head that Meade was responsible for Adam's death.*

McKenzie: *So he decided to get even.*

Elizabeth wiped her chocolaty fingers on a piece of scrap paper.

Bailey: *What about The Professor?*

Alexis: *And how do Moose and Rusty fit into all this?*

Sydney asked Elizabeth to go down to the kitchen to get some bottles of water. They needed something to wash down the chocolates. In the meantime, she went on with the story.

Sydney: *Daniels knew a scientist who had helped create the space shuttle. He was a troublemaker and hated the government, so he got kicked out of NASA. Daniels figured he'd be more than willing to help get rid of Meade, so he got Professor Hopkins to create a miniature smart bomb made of titanium. It was tiny enough to fit into that little metal box Moose and Rusty had, but powerful enough to destroy all of Fort McHenry and most of the peninsula it's built on.*

Alexis: *So Hopkins was the mastermind professor, like Professor Moriarty in the Sherlock Holmes stories.*

Elizabeth returned with two bottles of water. Sydney opened hers and took a drink.

Sydney: *The Professor was the brains behind it all. Plus, he knew his way around the fort, so he decided where the best place was to plant the bomb. When they arrested him last night, he confessed to his part in the plot, but he blamed it all on Daniels.*

Bailey: *And what about Moose and Rusty?*

Sydney gave the keyboard to Elizabeth.

Elizabeth: *Daniels and The Professor turned out to be cowards. They didn't want to get killed if the bomb went off too soon, and they didn't want to be connected with the assassination, so they got Moose and Rusty to do their dirty work.*

Moose and Rusty were both in trouble for not paying their taxes, and Daniels promised they wouldn't go to prison if they helped him plant the bomb. As much as possible, Daniels tried to stay out of it. That's why he left those messages at the Wall. He didn't want to be seen with Rusty and Moose.

Kate: *So did Moose and Rusty confess?*

Elizabeth: *They sure did. They told the FBI a lot of stuff. They* said since Daniels was a Secret Service agent, he was allowed at Fort McHenry to bury the box with the bomb. He told the park ranger he was checking the place ahead of the president's visit.

McKenzie: *Then he's the one who made the treasure map.*

Elizabeth: *He made the map. But Rusty and Moose messed up. They were supposed to plant the bomb that afternoon. The Professor wanted them to put it in a secret room in the fort's hallway, the one that Moose hid in last night. But Daniels wanted it closer to where President Meade was supposed to give his speech. He told Moose and Rusty to hide it in the jail cell. It was all supposed to be done the day before the tattoo. But it got too late and Moose and Rusty took the bomb with them. They weren't supposed to be anywhere near the fort on the night of the tattoo. Kate, if not for your tracking device, last night would have been a disaster.*

McKenzie: *What did your uncle say, Elizabeth?*

Kate: *And what about his friend Al? Was he following you?*

Elizabeth took a drink from her bottle of water.

Elizabeth: *That first day at the Wall, when I found the "Meade me in St. Louis" note, my uncle was suspicious. When I didn't want to go to lunch, he figured something was going on. He was worried because I'd told him about our sleuthing at camp. So he asked his friend Al to keep an eye on me for a while. He was afraid I wouldn't be safe in the city.*

Kate: *Was I right that they put a GPS in your backpack?*

Elizabeth: *No. There was no tracking device. But Al soon figured out that we were on to something. He was reading those notes at the Wall too. None of them made sense to him and Uncle Dan, but they figured out, like we did, that something was going on with President Meade.*

Elizabeth helped herself to one more piece of candy.

Elizabeth: *Uncle Dan called Agent Phillips from the FBI. Phillips was Uncle Dan's old army buddy. My uncle told Phillips about the notes at the Wall and also the two suspicious-looking guys who left them there.*

Kate: *So that's what I heard when I was listening outside their hotel room that day.*

Elizabeth: *Right. Phillips wasn't sure what was going on, but decided that by following us they would keep us safe, and maybe find out what, if anything, we knew. I'd accidentally told my uncle we planned to go to Fort McHenry, so he, Al, and Agent Phillips followed us. But they lost us when we changed into costumes. They saw us go into the enlisted men's barracks but didn't see us come out. When I heard them outside the door to the wardrobe room, it sounded like they were looking for something. Turns out that they were looking for us!*

She pushed the keyboard over to Sydney's side of the desk and asked her to finish the story.

Sydney: *By the time Uncle Dan found Elizabeth's pendant, we had already left the fort. Agent Phillips figured we'd gone out the window. So Al went looking for us, and guess what he found instead—Rusty's map. He must have dropped it on his way to the water taxi. And guess what it was written on—the back of a flyer announcing the Twilight Tattoo. So that's how Uncle Dan and his friends found out that maybe something was going to happen at the tattoo. Then when they found out that we were there last night, they were doubly suspicious.*

Alexis: *It's a good thing they followed you last night. You both might have been killed.*

Sydney: *I don't think so. I think we'd have found a way to save the president. I don't know how, but the Lord would have helped us.*

Alexis: *He did help you! It all worked out according to His plan. By the way, what does your mom think about all of this?*

Sydney put the lid on the box of candy. She and Elizabeth had decided to save some for later.

Sydney: *Mom didn't know anything about it until we got home last night. Aunt Dee brought us here in one of the ranger's vans. Uncle Dan and Al came along and explained the whole thing to my mom. At first she was mad. But then she understood that we saved President Meade's life. She cried and hugged us because we were safe. Then I couldn't believe my ears. She said kids like us made the world a better place!*

McKenzie: *All right! Let's hear it for the Camp Club Girls!*

A soft knock sounded on Sydney's bedroom door and her mom peeked inside. "I'm sorry to interrupt," she said, "but I just invited Elizabeth's uncle and his friend over for some barbeque. Dee's starting the grill. Would you girls come help us get ready, please?"

"Sure, Mom," Sydney answered. "We'll be down as soon as we've said goodbye to our friends."

Sydney's mom smiled and closed the door.

Elizabeth: *We have to go. Uncle Dan and Al are coming over for a cookout.*

Bailey: *Have a safe trip home.*

McKenzie: *We'll keep praying that your Uncle Dan will walk again real soon.*

Elizabeth: *Do you know what? I'm not angry about that anymore. This whole adventure taught me that Psalm 37:8 is true: "Refrain from anger and turn from wrath; do not fret—it leads only to evil."*

Camp Club Girls:
Sydney's Outer Banks Blast

Sydney's Ghost Story

"It wasn't a UFO," said Sydney Lincoln as she and Bailey walked along the beach. "There's a logical explanation for it."

Bailey Chang disagreed. "I looked out at the ocean at two o'clock this morning, and there it was. It had red, flashing lights, and it was hovering over the water. It spun around and around, and then *poof*, it was gone. It was a UFO!"

Sydney bent and picked up some small stones from the sand. "What were you doing up at two o'clock?" she asked as she walked to the water's edge.

"I couldn't sleep in a strange bed," Bailey told her.

Sydney waited a few seconds before skipping a stone across the waves. "I think what you saw was just a coastguard training exercise, or something."

"It was a UFO," Bailey insisted. "I'm sure of it."

"I don't believe in UFOs," said Sydney skipping another stone. "Anyway, I'm glad your parents let you come. Ever since camp, I've wanted to show you the ocean."

Sydney had invited her friend Bailey to spend a week at her grandparents' beach house on the Outer Banks of North Carolina. Sydney loved to escape the activity of her home in Washington DC for the peace and quiet of the long, narrow string of barrier islands that separated the Atlantic Ocean from several sounds off the edge of North Carolina.

Bailey was always willing to accept an invitation to anywhere. She couldn't wait to leave her hometown of Peoria, Illinois, and see the world. Now, in the early morning sunshine, Bailey was getting her first taste of the salty ocean air as she and Sydney walked together through the sand.

"It's not exactly what I expected," Bailey said.

She had imagined that the Atlantic Ocean would look vastly different from the huge Great Lake that bordered her home state. In fact, the ocean *was* very different—much larger and far grander—but just not as different as Bailey had hoped for. She was often disappointed when real life didn't match up to her imagination.

"The ocean sort of looks like Lake Michigan," she said. "Lake Michigan also has waves, and it's so big that you can't see to the other side."

She picked up a handful of sand and let it sift through her fingers. "This beach looks like it's not taken care of. In Chicago, a tractor pulls a machine that combs the sand and keeps it nice and clean. There aren't weeds and stuff sticking up, like here. And they test the water to make sure it's not polluted."

Sydney kicked at the sugar-fine sand with her bare feet.

"Nobody tests the water here," she said. "It's clean. I swim in it all the time." She waded into the ocean a few yards offshore.

"Come on!" she told Bailey. "Check it out."

Bailey hesitated. "What about jellyfish and sharks?" she asked.

"If I see some, I'll introduce you," Sydney said, joking.

Bailey rolled the legs of her khaki pants over her knees. Then she tiptoed into the breakers. All at once, she felt the world between her toes as she imagined thousands of miles between herself and the nearest shore.

Sydney and Bailey had met at Discovery Lake Camp where they bunked in Cabin 12 with four other girls: Alexis Howell from Sacramento, California; Elizabeth Anderson, from Amarillo, Texas; McKenzie Phillips, from White Sulphur Springs, Montana; and Kate Oliver, from Philadelphia, Pennsylvania. The Camp Club Girls, as they called themselves, were the best of friends. They loved to explore, and they'd become quite good at solving mysteries together. When they weren't at summer camp, the girls kept in touch by chatting on their Camp Club Girls' website, sending instant messages and emails, and even by phone and cell phones.

"I still think it was a UFO," said Bailey splashing in the water. "I'm sure that it wasn't an airplane, so what else could it be?"

"Oh, I don't know," Sydney answered. She added with a fond grin, "Maybe your imagination?"

As the girls waded and splashed in the water, only one other person was in sight, and he kept a very safe distance away from them.

"Who's that?" Bailey asked, pointing a shell she'd picked up towards the boy.

"I think his name is Drake or something," Sydney said. "He's kind of different. I see him alone on the beach sometimes. But it seems whenever people show up, he just kind of disappears."

"He's about your age, it looks like," Bailey said, squinting to see him better. "Looks like he's kind of cute too."

"I don't know how anyone can tell if he's cute or not," Sydney said. "He always keeps his head down, digging around in the sand."

"What's he looking for? Shells?" Bailey asked.

"I dunno," Sydney said, shrugging. "It seems whenever he picks up something, it's bigger than shells, though. Some friends of mine who live here all the time, the Kessler twins, say he's a relative of the Wright brothers. Remember where we drove across the causeway? The Wright brothers did their famous flying around there."

"Well, that's neat! To be related to the Wright brothers!" Bailey exclaimed.

Sydney waded out of the ocean and stood on the shore. She watched Bailey scoop water into her hands, smell it, and then carefully stick her tongue in the water.

"It tastes sort of like potatoes boiled in salt water," Bailey observed.

"Whatever you say," Sydney answered. Her wet legs were caked up to her knees with sand, and against her chocolate-colored skin, the sand looked like knee socks. She bent over and brushed it off. "Let's take a walk up the shore," she said.

Bailey hurried out of the water and fell into step alongside her friend. The boy saw them coming, and he walked quickly on ahead of them. After they had gone around a hundred feet along the beach, Bailey's right foot landed on something hard. "Ouch!" she said.

Sydney, who was a few steps ahead, stopped and turned around to see what was the matter. "What's wrong?" she asked, "Crab got your toe?"

Bailey jumped. "Where?"

"Where what?"

"Where's a crab?"

"I didn't see a crab," Sydney answered. "I just wondered if you got pinched by one."

"No," Bailey told her. "I stepped on something."

Sydney explored the sand where Bailey stood. "Do you have crabs in Lake Michigan?"

"We have crayfish," Bailey answered. "I don't know if they live on the beach, or if they're just bait that fishermen leave behind, but I've seen them there a couple of times. They're brown and ugly, and they have big claws. They kind of look like lobsters."

Sydney saw a white bump protruding from the sand. She reached down and pulled it up. It was a long, slender bone, a rib bone, maybe, from a wild animal, or possibly left from a beachfront barbeque. Tiny bits of dried flesh clung to its underside. Sydney held it up and showed it to Bailey. "This is what you stepped on," she said. "It's a bone."

"Eeeewwww!" said Bailey. "Where do you think it came from?"

"Oh, I don't know," Sydney teased. "Maybe from the body of an old sailor who died at sea. They call part of the Outer Banks the Graveyard of the Atlantic, you know."

"Eeeewwww!" Bailey said again. "Are there really dead sailors floating around out there?"

"Oh sure," Sydney said matter-of-factly. "Not to mention the ones from the ghost ship."

Bailey shuddered. "Ghost ship! What ghost ship?"

"The *Carroll A. Deering*," Sydney replied. She tossed the bone into the water and walked on with Bailey at her side.

"The story of the *Carroll A. Deering* is really spooky," Sydney went on. "I don't know if I should tell it to you. You might be too afraid." She looked at Bailey and grinned.

"I will not!" Bailey protested. "I'm not scared of anything."

"Well, okay then," Sydney answered. "But if you can't sleep tonight, don't blame me."

She stopped and picked up a stick at the ocean's edge. Frothy, white fingers of water washed across the beach, scrabbling at the firm, wet sand. Sydney used the stick to write BEWARE OF UFOs on the gritty, light tan canvas. Then she tossed the stick back to the ocean. The girls walked on leaving two sets of footprints behind them.

"The *Carroll A. Deering* was a tall ship, a schooner," Sydney began. "Pirates used several types of sailing ships. The ships they used had to be fast and strong. The *Carroll A. Deering* was bigger than most schooners. It had five tall masts with billowy sails—"

"I know exactly what you're talking about," Bailey interrupted. "Those kind of tall ships came to Navy Pier in Chicago last summer. Of course, they weren't old ones. They were only made to look like the old ones. Mom, Dad, my sister, Trina, and I went to check them out.

They looked really old, and we even got to sail on one of them out on the lake."

"Cool," said Sydney. "So, since you've been *on* a tall ship, you can imagine what it was like to be a sailor on the *Carroll A. Deering* back in 1921. Imagine that it's the middle of winter. Some coastguardsmen are looking out at the ocean, sort of like we are now. They're about a hundred miles south of here near the Cape Hatteras Lighthouse, down by Diamond Shoals."

"What's that?" asked Bailey. She carefully stepped through the sand watching for bones and other hidden objects.

"What's what?"

"Diamond Shoals."

"It's a bunch of sandbars just off the coast of the Outer Banks, down at the southern end," Sydney replied. "Anyhow, that's where they saw it."

"The ghost ship?" Bailey asked. Just saying the words sent a little shiver up her spine.

"The ghost ship—the *Carroll A. Deering*," Sydney answered. "There she was, half washed up on one of the shoals, with her sails still opened wide and flapping in the wind. The ocean was pushing at her from behind. Her prow, that's the front end of the ship, was scraping against some rocks in the sand. *Scrape. . .scrape. . .*" As Sydney said the words, she brushed the tips of her fingers along the side of Bailey's arm.

"Stop it!" Bailey said. "You're spooking me out."

"I thought nothing scared you," Sydney answered. "Maybe I shouldn't tell you the rest."

A seagull swept over Bailey's head. It dove and snatched a small fish out of the ocean. "Go on," she said tentatively. "I want to hear."

"It was a foggy, cold, misty morning," Sydney continued, "and the sea was rough. The men of the coast guard knew it would be really hard getting to the wreck, but they had to, because they knew that the crew was in danger. So they got into their heavy wooden rowboat, and they rowed through the boiling waves toward the shoals."

"But it was the middle of winter," said Bailey.

"So?" Sydney asked.

"You said that the waves were boiling, and if that's true, it was summertime. You're making this up, aren't you?"

"Bailey!" Sydney protested. "It was a figure of speech. The sea was rough. The waves were rolling *like* boiling water. That's all. The ocean never gets hot enough to boil, and this is a true story. You can ask anyone on the Outer Banks, and they'll tell you—it's true."

Bailey stopped in the sand and let the edge of the ocean tickle her toes. "Okay," she conceded.

"So anyway," said Sydney. "They got into their big rowboat, and they rowed out to the *Carroll A. Deering*. When they reached her, they climbed up onto her deck."

"How'd they climb onto it?" Bailey wondered. "Did they have a ladder? Weren't the waves too rough?"

"I don't know. They were the coastguardsmen, and they know how to climb up on decks and stuff." Sydney swatted at a deerfly that landed on her elbow. "And when they got up on the deck, it was eerily quiet except for the waves lapping at the sides of the ship and that awful *scrape. . . scrape. . . .*"

Bailey pulled away as Sydney's long fingers reached for her arm.

"Ahoy!" Sydney yelled.

Bailey jumped.

"Did I scare you?"

"I just didn't expect you to yell, that's all," said Bailey. "And why did you?"

"That's what the coast guard yelled," Sydney said. "They stood on the deck, and they yelled, 'Ahoy there! Is anyone here?' But nobody answered. So they searched the deserted deck, and the only sounds they heard were the echo of their own footsteps."

"Don't forget the waves and the scraping," Bailey interjected.

"And the waves and the scraping," said Sydney. "And after looking around the top deck, they went down into the center of the ship, and then they opened the door to the crew's quarters. And do you know what they found?" Sydney stopped. She looked at Bailey and grinned.

"Stop playing with me," Bailey said. "What did they find?"

"Nobody," said Sydney. "There was no one there. The beds had all been slept in, and everything was shipshape, except that eleven crewmen and their stuff were gone."

"Gone?" Bailey wondered.

"Just like that. Disappeared. Then the coastguardsmen went to check out the galley. There was food standing out like someone had been preparing a meal, only nobody had eaten anything. The table was all set with plates, cups, and silverware, but nothing had been touched. So the men checked out the officers' quarters next. The beds had been slept in, and the officers' boots were on the floor next to their beds, but nobody was there. Their personal stuff was gone and so was the ship's log, the navigating instruments, all of it—gone."

"So where did everybody go?" Bailey asked.

"Nobody knows," Sydney answered. "It's a big mystery around here. It was like they vanished into thin air. The sailors were never found. The shoals are near enough to shore that something should have washed up, if not their bodies, then some of their belongings, but nothing ever did—"

Sydney's story was interrupted by a powerful, rhythmic noise. All at once, a swirling cloud of sand covered Sydney and Bailey as something huge and brown rushed past them.

Bailey screamed. She gripped Sydney's arm. "A horse!" she cried.

In the swirling dust, she saw a muscular, brown stallion galloping on ahead of them. Its black mane stood on end as it raced against the wind.

Sydney caught her breath. The horse had frightened her as much as it had Bailey. She wondered if God was having a good laugh, getting even with her for trying to scare Bailey with the ghost story of the *Carroll A. Deering*.

"It's a wild horse," she said. "Probably one of the mustangs."

"What mustangs?" Bailey asked.

"Usually, they're not this far south," Sydney told her, "and they don't typically come near people. They're wild horses—they don't belong to anyone. They wander as free as any other wild animal around here. I'm pretty used to seeing them. They've lived on the Outer Banks for at least four hundred years, so people who live here don't pay much attention to them. They're another mystery of the Outer Banks. No one knows for sure how they got here."

"Oh great," said Bailey. "The sailors disappeared and nobody knows where they went. The wild horses showed up, but nobody knows how they got here. And this morning I saw a UFO.

"What kind of a place is this, Sydney? First you tell me a story about a ghost ship, and then a wild horse comes galloping by almost close enough to touch. You know, this sort of reminds me of *The Legend of Sleepy Hollow* where the headless horseman comes dashing out of nowhere."

"You never know," said Sydney. "We might have a headless horseman roaming around here too. The Outer Banks is loaded with folklore about all kinds of stuff. It's even known for pirates like Captain Kidd, Calico Jack, and Blackbeard. They all walked along this beach once upon a time. Who knows, maybe they still do."

"Do you believe in ghosts?" Bailey asked.

Before Sydney could answer, a small ghost crab popped out of the sand and skittered toward the girls. It stopped briefly and looked at them through two black eyes set atop its head like periscopes sticking up from a submarine.

"Maybe," said Sydney, "and maybe not."

The Disappearing Captain

The girls left the beach and walked to Corolla Village and the Curri-tuck Beach Lighthouse. It was one of Sydney's favorite places, and she wanted to show it to Bailey. Something was wonderfully mysterious about the way the lighthouse rose from the trees and almost touched the sky. Its weathered red bricks sat tightly atop each other, forming rows around and around. They stopped at an iron-framed lookout. The lookout encircled the lantern house, the highest part of the tower. There, inside a giant glass dome, was the powerful beacon of light that swept across ocean and sound.

Not far from the tower, nestled in a grove of trees, was a small lightkeeper's house. It had a steep red roof and white paint. The place was a gift shop where tourists could buy everything from tee shirts to figurines. Its wide front porch was empty but for a pair of old, wooden rocking chairs that often rocked alone in the wind.

Bailey and Sydney sat in the chairs looking up at the tower. Bailey nervously sipped the root beer that she'd bought at a little post office and convenience store nearby.

"You have to at least try," Sydney said.

"But I'm afraid of heights," Bailey answered. "You know that, Syd. In fact, if I could have, I would have walked here from Peoria instead of taking a plane." She swirled the root beer around in its plastic bottle.

"But you got on the airplane, and you got here in one piece," Sydney pointed out. "The next step is to climb to the top of the lighthouse."

Bailey glanced toward a short line of tourists waiting at the entrance. "How tall is it, anyway?"

"Not that tall," Sydney answered. She wrapped a napkin around the bottom of her ice-cream cone and licked the melting vanilla custard as it dribbled down the sides.

"How tall?" Bailey asked again.

"What difference does it make?" said Sydney.

"How tall!" Bailey demanded.

"I think two hundred fourteen steps to the top!"

"That's a lot."

"The Statue of Liberty has three hundred fifty-four steps," Sydney added. "You're always saying you want to go to New York and climb the Statue of Liberty. Think of this as your training. Once you've climbed the lighthouse, Lady Liberty will be a piece of cake."

"I dunno." Bailey sighed.

"And what about the Eiffel Tower?" Sydney went on. "You want to go to Paris and climb the Eiffel Tower. You told me that. And the Eiffel Tower is a whole lot scarier than the Currituck Beach Lighthouse."

"I guess so," Bailey agreed.

By now, Sydney had finished eating her custard and chomped on the cone. "Come on, Bailey," she said. "If you don't face your fears, you'll never climb the Statue of Liberty, or the Eiffel Tower either."

"I suppose you're right," Bailey said. She gulped down the rest of her root beer, got up, and tossed the empty bottle into a trash can. "Let's go."

"Go where?" Sydney answered.

"Let's climb to the top of the lighthouse before I chicken out."

The girls followed a curving brick path to the lighthouse entrance. A small, blue sign sat in front of the six concrete steps that led to the front door. It said: PLEASE WAIT HERE TO CLIMB. A family with three boys, all of them younger than Bailey and Sydney, stood waiting in line. The oldest one shoved his little brother and knocked him to the ground.

"Trevor!" his mother shouted. "Why did you push your brother?"

"He called me a name," Trevor said.

"I did not!" said the little brother getting up and standing next to his mom. "I want to go home."

"Behave!" said the dad.

Just then a gray-haired gentleman came from behind the lighthouse. He walked toward the family, looking as if he'd stepped off a page in a history book. He wore a blue captain's cap, and his face was framed with a neat, gray beard. Although the weather was hot, he wore an old-fashioned blue wool officer's coat with shiny brass buttons and a name-tag that read CAPTAIN SWAIN.

As Sydney and Bailey watched, the captain stopped in front of the boys. He opened his left fist and showed them four silver coins. "Spanish doubloons," he announced.

The boys gathered to see the treasure in the captain's hand. "Is this your first trip to the Outer Banks?" the captain asked.

"Yeah." The boys answered in unison.

"Then you don't know about the pirates," said the captain.

"What pirates?" Trevor asked. He grabbed Captain Swain's hand and pulled it closer to get a better look at the coins.

The old man smiled and looked Trevor straight in the eyes. "Blackbeard," he whispered.

Trevor stepped back.

"Blackbeard the pirate used to hide out on this very land," the captain said mysteriously. "He and his crew attacked ships at sea, robbed them, and brought their treasures back here to the Outer Banks. And these coins, my little friends, are some of the treasure that Blackbeard stole."

The boys' eyes grew big. They were so busy studying the doubloons that they didn't even notice when a group of visitors left the lighthouse.

"You're up next," Captain Swain told the family. "And when you get to the top, look out in the ocean as far as you can see. Maybe you'll spy Blackbeard's ship."

"Blackbeard doesn't exist," the older boy said. "He died a long time ago, and your coins are probably fakes."

"Trevor!" his mother scolded.

"Now, would I tell a tale?" said the captain. "Sure Blackbeard's dead, but some say his ghost haunts the sea while he and his crew sail on their ghost ship. You know about the ghost ships, don't you?"

The boys shook their heads.

"Then visit the museum down in Hatteras," the captain replied. "Graveyard of the Atlantic, it's called. They'll tell you all about Blackbeard and the ghost ships. You'll find a brochure inside." He pointed to the front door. Then, as the family disappeared into the entrance, Captain Swain turned to the girls. "Aren't you going with your family?" he asked.

"Oh, we're not with them," Sydney replied. "We're next in line."

The captain looked surprised. "How old are you young ladies?"

"Thirteen," said Sydney. She noticed the captain's sparkling, blue eyes.

"I'm nine," Bailey announced.

"Oh dear," said the captain. "Young people thirteen and under have to be accompanied by an adult. I'm afraid you won't be able to climb the lighthouse."

Bailey breathed a sigh of relief.

"But I'm *from* here!" Sydney protested. "Well, I'm not actually from here, but my grandparents have a beach house in Corolla Light. I visit them every year."

"Ah, the resort community," said the captain. He shook his head sadly. "I rarely get there. It's too crowded, and there's far too much traffic on the highway. This is the *real* Corolla, you know. This tiny village was here long before Corolla Light or any of the other subdivisions."

"I know," said Sydney, "but can't we please climb the lighthouse? My friend Bailey is trying to overcome her fear of heights."

The captain winked at Bailey. "So, you're afraid of heights, are you? Well, we need to do something about that. The view from the top is outstanding. On one side there's the Atlantic Ocean, on the other side Currituck Sound."

Bailey's heart sank. She didn't really want to climb to the top of the lighthouse no matter how beautiful the view.

Captain Swain scratched his beard.

"I'll tell you what," he said. "I'll take you to the top. And, Bailey, you'll be fine. There's nothing to be afraid of. Nothing at all." He looked up at the tower, and Sydney noticed his mouth curl into a wistful smile.

Suddenly, the front door burst open. Trevor's little brother scuttled out with his father close behind. "I am *not* being difficult," the boy shouted. "I don't want to climb those curvy steps. They're scary!"

His mother and brothers came out too.

"Chicken!" Trevor taunted. He stood with his hands on his hips. "I wanted to go to the top, and now you've wrecked everything!"

"Let's go," said Trevor's dad. "I've had enough of this."

The mother grabbed the smallest boy's hand, and the family rushed to the parking lot.

" 'When justice is done, it brings joy to the righteous but terror to evildoers,' " said Captain Swain.

"What?" Sydney asked.

"Nothing," replied the captain. "Just God and me talking out loud. Looks like it's our turn to climb."

When they went inside, Bailey noticed how cool and stuffy the lighthouse felt. An ancient, brick wall circled them, and the narrow space smelled old. Sunlight streamed through several tall, narrow windows up high. In the center was a green, spiral staircase that reminded Bailey of a loosely coiled snake. Its metal stairs went up and up. When Bailey looked to where they led, she felt dizzy. She hesitated, afraid to take the first step.

Captain Swain seemed to know how she felt. "'I can do all things through Him who strengthens me,'" he said.

Sydney gave him a quizzical look.

"Just God and me talking again," the captain announced.

Sydney knew that Bible verse from camp. It had given her courage when she was afraid.

"I want you to go first, Bailey," said the captain. "Your friend here— what's your name?" he asked, turning to Sydney.

"Sydney Lincoln," Sydney replied.

"Sydney Lincoln and I will be right behind you. We'll take very good care of you all the way. There's nothing to worry about. Absolutely nothing. I climbed these stairs a lot—back in the day."

The captain's voice echoed inside the tower. It seemed to drift all the way to the top and then disappear.

"I'll watch every step you take," Sydney told her. "You'll be fine. I promise."

Tentatively, Bailey put her right foot on the bottom step. She looked down to make sure that her shoes were tied. She didn't need to trip over any loose laces. Then she breathed deeply and whispered, "'I can do all things through Him who strengthens me.'"

She put her left foot on the first step, and then Bailey Chang was on her way. She was ready to conquer her fear of heights and tackle all 214 steps. "One. Two. Three. Four." She counted each step unwaveringly, bravely marching upward. But then, she made the mistake of looking down. The stairs weren't solid. They had holes, like Swiss cheese, and when Bailey looked down at the fifty or so stairs she'd already climbed, she felt sick to her stomach. She stopped and Sydney almost tripped over her.

"Bailey! What?" Sydney wondered.

"I can't," Bailey whispered. "I'm afraid."

"Just move!" said Sydney. "This staircase is only wide enough for one person, and right now you've got us stuck here."

Bailey gripped the railings with both hands. Her feet wouldn't move. She was afraid to look up and afraid to look down. Her mind drifted to a strange place where she imagined she was the main character in a ghost story. She was stuck forever on that one step, an eerie mist that visitors sensed as they climbed to the top. Bailey Chang, Ghost of the Currituck Beach Lighthouse.

"Bailey." The captain's calm voice startled her. She grasped the railings even tighter. "I'm right here with you," he said. "I won't let anything happen to you. We're on our way now. You can do it. Just keep telling yourself that."

Bailey's heart slammed in her chest. Her mouth felt like sandpaper. She couldn't speak.

"Just one step, Bailey," said the captain. "Take one more step."

Bailey's feet moved up to the next step, whether she wanted them to or not.

"That's good," said the captain. "Now, one more."

Bailey felt Sydney close behind her. She decided if she fell backward onto her friend, and Sydney fell too, the captain was strong enough to catch them both. So Bailey took the next step, and the next, and she kept going. Whenever she got to a landing and one of the tall, narrow windows, Bailey avoided looking out. She wouldn't look down or up either. She just concentrated on one step at a time.

"'I can do all things through Him who strengthens me,'" she murmured.

As she climbed the last steps, Bailey noticed a small landing and an old wooden door that stood wide open. She couldn't see where it led, but from where she stood Bailey caught a glimpse of blue sky and puffy, white clouds on the other side of it. She took the last step to the top and then turned away refusing to look beyond the door.

"You did it!" Sydney exclaimed. She stepped onto the landing and hugged her friend, but Bailey stood frozen.

"I'm not going out there," Bailey said. "I don't even want to see."

The captain stood between Bailey and the door. "It's your decision," he said. "But someday you might regret that you didn't. You might be sorry that fear got in your way."

Bailey swallowed hard.

"Come on, Bailey," Sydney coaxed. "Do you want to be an old lady telling your grandkids how scared you were? What kind of an example will that set?"

Bailey turned around. Beyond the captain's broad shoulders, she saw nothing but sky and clouds. Then, slowly, Captain Swain stepped aside. Bailey suddenly saw the tops of trees and in the distance, the Atlantic Ocean. She felt like she was back in the airplane flying over

North Carolina. But this time, if she chose to, she could step outside onto a narrow, open platform that was rimmed by a thick, iron railing.

The captain stepped outside. "I won't let anything happen to you," he said. "Sydney Lincoln, would you like to join me out here?"

Sydney's heart did a little flutter. She would never admit that she was scared too. She had never climbed to the top of the lighthouse, and it was higher than she had imagined. Still, she wouldn't make Bailey more afraid than she already was.

Bravely, Sydney stepped through the door. She leaned against the captain and felt his strong arm holding her steady.

"It's not so bad, Bailey," she said, holding onto the railing. "Come on, we'll help you."

The captain held out his hand.

The image of herself as an old woman flashed through Bailey's mind. She heard herself say, *"When I was little, I almost went out that door."*

Bailey took the captain's hand, and then nothing stood between her and the world but the black, iron railing. Her stomach churned, but she inched along the lookout with her friends. They rounded the bend. Now, instead of seeing the ocean, they could see the sound—the strip of water between the Outer Banks' island and the shore of North Carolina.

"I knew you could do it, Bailey," said Sydney. "I watched you all the way, and you were really brave. I'm glad I convinced you to do it."

Bailey grabbed Sydney's arm. "Syd," she said. "Where'd the captain go? He was right behind me."

Captain Swain was gone! Just as if he had vanished into thin air!

CHAPTER 3

A Mysterious Mug

"That's odd," said Sydney. "Where is he?"

A strong wind swept across the lighthouse. Sydney noticed Bailey's fingers gripping the railing. She grabbed Bailey's hand, and they carefully walked back to the door. When they got there, a lady whose name tag read MEGHAN was waiting.

"I was wondering if anyone was up here," she said. "I'm closing the lighthouse now. Storms are coming, and it's not safe up here when there's lightning."

The woman led the girls down the curving staircase. It was scarier going down than up because Sydney and Bailey had no choice but to look at their feet and imagine how far they'd fall if they tripped.

To keep her mind off it, Bailey began to talk—she tended to talk a lot whenever she got nervous. "So, do you like working in a lighthouse?" she asked.

"It's fascinating!" Meghan answered. "It's fascinating to go up to the top and see how the ocean changes every day."

"I live like two-and-a-half hours from Lake Michigan," Bailey told her. "And we go there in the summer to the beach and I think the lake looks a lot like the ocean, only it's not as big, and we have perch and trout instead of sharks and jellyfish."

She gulped a breath and went on. "Lake Michigan has fresh water and, of course, the ocean has salt water. This is the first time I've climbed a lighthouse. I'm afraid of heights, you know, but I climbed to the top—"

Sydney interrupted her. "Did you see Captain Swain come down the stairs?"

"Captain Swain? No," said Meghan. "Why?"

"He took us up to the lookout but disappeared. We didn't see him leave. We were wondering where he went." They were almost to the bottom of the stairs now, and Sydney sighed with relief.

"When was this?" the woman asked.

"Just a few minutes ago," said Sydney.

"I didn't see him come downstairs," Meghan replied as they reached the main floor. "As far as that goes, I didn't see him go up either. I must not have been paying attention."

"You weren't here," said Sydney. "When we came in, no one was around."

"That's odd," said Meghan. "I've been here for the past hour or so. I don't know how you got by without me seeing you, unless I was in my office. Did you say this was your first lighthouse visit?"

"It is," Bailey answered. "I'm visiting from Peoria. That's in Illinois."

"You know what?" said the lady. "I have something for you." She went to a desk in a little room nearby and picked up two small cardboard folders. "These are lighthouse passports," she said. She gave one to each of the girls. "You can visit lighthouses all over America and get stickers to put in your passport book. There's already a sticker from this lighthouse inside."

"Wow!" said Bailey. "I'm going to visit every lighthouse and collect all the stickers."

"If you do that, come back here and show me your passport. I'll buy you a cheeseburger," said Meghan.

"It might take me awhile to get them all," Bailey responded.

"Like, years!" Sydney added.

The woman smiled. "I imagine I'll be here."

After the girls left the lighthouse, Sydney pointed at two girls on the other side of Schoolhouse Lane. They were eating ice cream by the Corolla Village Bar-B-Q. "Come on," she told Bailey. "I want you to meet my friends." She led Bailey to a picnic table where the girls were sitting outside the restaurant. "Hi, Carolyn. Hi, Marilyn," said Sydney.

"Hi, Sydney!" the twins answered in unison. The Kessler twins often spoke in unison, Sydney had noticed. They were so much alike that Sydney still had trouble telling them apart, and she had known them for six years. The Kessler family owned a house near Sydney's grandparents' place. She knew they lived there year-round since Mr. Kessler ran a company that made recreational water vehicles and racing boats.

"What are you guys doing here?" Sydney asked.

"Hanging out," they answered together.

"This is my friend, Bailey Chang," said Sydney.

"I thought so!" said Marilyn.

"I thought so too," Carolyn echoed. "You're one of the Camp Club Girls. Sydney talks about you guys all the time."

Bailey slid onto the bench at the picnic table. "Nice to meet you," she said. "We just finished climbing the lighthouse."

"You did!" the girls exclaimed.

"I've lived here since I was five, and I've never climbed it," said Marilyn.

"I haven't either," said Carolyn.

They both looked at Sydney as she slid into the bench next to Bailey. "Okay, I confess. I hadn't either," she said.

Bailey couldn't believe her ears. "What do you mean, you hadn't either? You acted like you'd climbed it a million times."

"I've always wanted to climb it," Sydney told her. "Would you have gone if I'd acted scared?"

Bailey thought for a second. "Well, no," she conceded. "But I wish I had known."

Two odd-looking bikes were propped against the picnic table. Each had two seats, two sets of handlebars, and two sets of pedals. "Are those your bikes?" Bailey asked the twins.

"They're tandems," said Carolyn.

Marilyn nodded in agreement. "Bicycles built for two." She took a lick of the chocolate ice cream that was melting in her cone.

"How come you *each* have one?" Bailey wondered. "Can't you both just ride on *one*?"

"One of them belongs to our brothers," said Carolyn. "The other one is ours."

"We just dropped them off at a friend's house on the Sound," said Marilyn. "They're spending the night there."

"And we're taking their bike home," Carolyn added. She popped the last bit of ice-cream cone into her mouth and Marilyn did the same with hers. "You can ride back with us if you want to," she said. "We have our brothers' helmets you can wear."

Bailey looked at Sydney hoping she would agree.

"Okay," Sydney answered. "We probably should get home soon anyway. Gramps said Nate Wright might try to take a cluster balloon flight off the beach this afternoon. That'll be cool to watch."

"Who's going to do what?" Bailey asked. She looked at her reflection in the side-view mirror of one of the tandem bikes and smoothed her jet-black hair.

"Nate Wright is going to do a cluster balloon flight," said Sydney. "He ties a bunch of extra large helium party balloons to a chair contraption and sails up into the sky. Then he releases the balloons gradually to come back down."

"Why would he want to do that?" Bailey asked.

Carolyn climbed onto the front seat of one of the tandems and put on her helmet. "Mr. Wright's an inventor," she said, pointing for Bailey to get on the back seat.

"Well, sort of," said Marilyn, picking up the other bike and climbing onto the front seat. "He's kind of strange. He's always trying to invent weird ways to get around. Lately he's been experimenting with cluster ballooning."

"Mr. Wright's a distant relative of the Wright brothers," Carolyn explained. "Usually, people cluster balloon in the early morning when there's no breeze, but today, he's doing it in the afternoon."

"We saw his son on the beach this morning," Sydney said. "What's his name? Drake?"

"Yes, that's Drake Wright, Nate Wright's son," Marilyn said. "He's a beachcomber."

"They call him Digger," said Carolyn.

"He picks up junk along the beach and digs stuff out of the sand. Then he sells it to people who sell it in their shops or use it for crafts. Driftwood and glass floats and old fishing nets and stuff," Marilyn added. "And he hardly ever talks."

Carolyn gave her bike a shove with one foot and then started to pedal. Bailey held tight to the handlebars. She didn't know what to do when the pedals under her feet began to spin.

"Don't try to steer!" Sydney told her. "Just keep your feet on the pedals and help Carolyn push."

Soon the girls were riding down Schoolhouse Lane heading for Corolla Light. They were almost to Highway 12—the two-lane road that was the main road for the Outer Banks—when Sydney's cell phone rang.

"Can we stop for a second?" she asked Marilyn. The twins steered their bikes to the side of the road. Sydney pulled her cell phone out of the pocket of her shorts. "Hello?"

"Sydney," said a concerned voice that Sydney recognized as her grandfather. "Where are you?"

"We're biking home with the Kessler twins," Sydney answered. "We should be there in about ten minutes."

"Come straight home, and don't stop anywhere," said her grandfather. "A bad storm is coming, and I don't want you girls out in it."

"Okay, Gramps," said Sydney. "We're on our way." She folded the phone and slipped it back into her pocket. "There's a storm coming," she said. "Gramps wants us home."

"The sky does look kind of greenish and black over there," said Bailey, pointing to the right. "Do you guys have tornado warning sirens here?"

"I don't know," Sydney answered. "If they do, I've never heard one."

"Me neither," said Marilyn, steering her bike back onto the road.

"I haven't either. We don't usually have tornadoes here," said Carolyn, following her.

"They go off a lot in Peoria," Bailey said. "Sometimes, the sky looks ugly like this, and then we get a tornado warning."

Suddenly a bolt of lightning sliced through the black clouds.

Whoosh! The wind picked up. The girls pedaled as fast as they could. By the time they got to their street, big droplets of rain started to fall. Then the rain turned into a rushing waterfall that spilled onto the girls' helmets and soaked their clothing. The twins made a perfect turn into Sydney's driveway, and Sydney and Bailey hopped off the bikes. Then the Kesslers sped off toward home.

Sydney's grandparents stood on the upper deck of the beach house. "Hurry!" Gramps called to the girls. "Come on up here."

Sydney ran up the two flights of stairs with Bailey close behind.

Crash! At the sound of thunder, Bailey nearly tripped on the last step. She caught the railing and climbed up onto the covered deck.

Bailey, Sydney, and her grandparents stepped inside the sliding screen doors and watched the storm from the safety of the family room. The fierce purple cloud was right over their heads now. To the south, near the ocean's horizon, the sky was clear and the sun was shining. But north of the beach house, the scene was very different. A long, thin, white tail dropped from the cloud until it met the ocean. It turned brown as it sucked up water.

Bailey screamed. "Oh my goodness! Oh my goodness! It's a tornado!"

"If they're over the water, they're called waterspouts," Sydney's grandmother explained. "Then when they come to land, they're called tornadoes."

Bailey squeezed Sydney's arm.

"It's heading away from us," Sydney said as the cone swept out to sea. "Pretty soon it'll dwindle to nothing."

Gramps added, "We're safe here, but can you imagine being in a sailboat out in the ocean? A decent-sized waterspout could easily drop on one of those and smash a small boat to smithereens. In fact, that *did* happen. There are so many shipwrecks near the Outer Banks that folks have lost count."

"Maybe that's what happened to the sailors on the ghost ship," Sydney suggested. "They got sucked into a water spout."

Bailey watched the long, coiling twister disappear. Beyond it, in the distance, two more waterspouts formed as the ocean carried the storm away. The back edge of the dark cloud passed over the beach house now, and the rain turned to drizzle. Bailey wasn't afraid anymore. She thought the tumbling waves and the waterspouts were awesome.

"Lake Michigan has waterspouts too," she said as the sun broke through the clouds. "I remember reading about them in current events, but I've never seen one. Very cool, although a bit scary."

"Look over there," said Sydney. The end of a rainbow was barely visible near the beach opposite of where the waterspout had been. Its colors gradually became bright, clear ribbons of red, orange, and yellow, blue, green, indigo, and violet.

"See?" said Sydney's grandmother. "God is sending us a message, just like He did to Noah on the ark. He's telling us we don't have to worry about the waterspout. It won't hurt us. A rainbow is God's way of saying, 'I promise.' "

"Let's go stand in the end of it!" Bailey was already out the door and running down the stairs toward the beach. Sydney followed, but by the time they got to where it looked like the rainbow ended, they realized it was out over the ocean.

"You can't touch it," Sydney explained when she caught up with Bailey. "Rainbows are sunlight bouncing off raindrops. I've chased them before, but you can't catch them. They move with the rain."

Bailey looked at her sand-caked feet. "Hey, look!" she said. "I'm wearing sand shoes."

She dropped to her knees and began scooping wet sand into a big pile. "Come on, Syd, let's make a sandcastle or something."

Sydney sat near her friend and helped form sand into a mound. "You know, don't you, that the tide will come in and wash it away."

Bailey patted the sand with both hands, sculpting it into a tower. "I don't care," she said. "Building it is the fun part."

"I see something we can use," said Sydney. A cylinder-shaped container was half-buried in the sand nearby. Sydney went to get it. "This'll work," she said. "We can put wet sand in here and mold it into turrets."

The container that Sydney found was a tall, insulated coffee mug. The top was screwed on so tight that she couldn't get it off. She tipped the mug, and water dribbled out of the tiny hole on top. She shook it, and the inside rattled.

"Something's in here," she said. Sydney shook the mug again, but nothing fell out. She shook it harder. Still nothing. Then she peeked into the hole.

"I can't see anything," she said. "This is kind of gross. We should wash it or something." She walked to the water's edge and swished the mug in the ocean. Then, once more, she looked inside. Nothing. She turned the mug upside down and shook it hard and fast.

A beam of light jiggled across the sand!

"Bailey? I think it's glowing!"

"Huh?" said Bailey, who hadn't been paying attention.

"It's glowing. The mug is glowing!" Sydney repeated.

She turned the mug upright. A bright beam of light streamed out of the tiny opening. She put her eye to the opening, but the light was too bright to see what was inside.

Bailey put her hand a few inches above the tiny hole. A small circle of light reflected on the palm of her hand.

"Weird," she said. "What do you think this is?"

"Beats me," Sydney answered. "I've never seen a coffee mug that lights up."

"Me neither," Bailey replied. "Maybe it's not a coffee mug at all. Maybe we've stumbled onto something else."

"Like what?" Sydney asked, handing her the mug.

Bailey sat down and chewed her lip, a nervous habit that she vowed to break. "Like, maybe, some sort of secret weapon," she said. "Something the UFO left behind."

"If it were a secret weapon, we'd probably be dead by now," Sydney told her. "Your imagination is getting away from you again."

The girls sat for a few minutes pondering the odd gadget and then—

"Hey, the light went out!" Bailey exclaimed.

UFO!

The object was indeed strange. It seemed to light up only after Bailey or Sydney shook it for a while. Then, it cast an eerie glow for about five minutes and went dark. They brought it back to the beach house, and Sydney put it on a metal bookshelf in the guest room. She had the idea that they might try to dissect it later.

When the Camp Club Girls met in their chat room after supper, Sydney told them about the mug.

Kate: *A coffee mug that glows from the inside? Why would you need it to light up inside?*

Alexis: *Maybe it's so you can see how much coffee's left.*

McKenzie: *But you have to shake it to make it light. That doesn't make sense, because if there's hot coffee, you'll get burned when it leaks out of the hole on top.*

Elizabeth: *I think you can close the hole. My mom's coffee mug has a flippy thing you turn to open and close the hole. Oh, and by the way, the kind of mug you have is a travel mug. Some of them aren't supposed to be submerged in water. At least my mom's can't.*

Sydney: *Maybe it got dropped in the ocean and the salt water wrecked it or something, and then it washed up on the beach.*

Bailey took the laptop from Sydney.

Bailey: *Hi, Bettyboo. Hi, everyone else.*

Elizabeth: *You know I don't like being called Bettyboo.*

Bailey: *Just kidding, Beth. I have a theory about the mug. It was half buried in the sand. I don't think it washed up on the shore. Someone put it there. I think it's some kind of secret weapon.*

She bit her lip hard and waited for someone to reply.

Alexis: *Something like that happened in one old alien movie I saw.*
McKenzie: *Why would you think it's a weapon?*
Bailey: *I don't know. It's too creepy to be anything ordinary.*

She pushed the laptop back to Sydney and went to get the mug from the bookshelf. She grabbed the handle, but the mug wouldn't budge.

"Hey," she said. "It's stuck."

"What do you mean?" Sydney asked.

"It's glued to the bookshelf, Bozo," said Bailey. "I can't pick it up!"

"Oh for goodness' sake," said Sydney. She set the computer on the twin bed, where they had been cyber-chatting, and she went to help Bailey.

Sydney grasped the mug's handle. Bailey was right. It was stuck. She pulled hard. The mug let loose, almost catapulting her backward.

"See?" said Bailey. She examined the spot where the mug had been. "I don't see any glue or other sticky stuff."

Sydney moved closer to inspect the bare spot. All at once, the mug shot out of her hand and stuck itself to the shelf. "It's a magnet!" Sydney gasped. "Look at this." She yanked the mug away from the metal shelf and then let it fly back. "I didn't notice it when I put the mug here before."

"Way cool!" Bailey squealed.

Sydney hurried back to the laptop to tell the girls. When she looked at the screen, she found a string of messages.

Alexis: *Syd? Bailey? Where are you?*
McKenzie: *Hey, did you log off without saying goodbye?*
Kate: *Where did everybody go?*
Sydney: *Sorry. Bailey went to get the mug, and we found out it's a magnet! It was stuck to my metal bookshelf.*
Kate: *DANGER! DANGER! Do not—I repeat—DO NOT put that mug anywhere near the computer.*

Bailey was just about to plop down on the bed next to Sydney with the mug in her hand. "No!" Sydney yelled. She shoved Bailey off the bed and onto the floor.

"Hey!" Bailey protested. She sat there looking startled. "What did you do that for?"

"I'm sorry," said Sydney. "Kate just wrote that the mug is very dangerous—"

Bailey shuddered and flung the coffee mug over her shoulder. It landed somewhere across the room. "What's the matter with it?" she asked nervously.

"You didn't let me finish," said Sydney. "It's dangerous to put it near the computer."

Sydney told the girls what had just happened.

Alexis: *Well, at least now you know that it's not a bomb. The way you two are messing with it, it would have gone off by now.*

Bailey joined Sydney on the bed. She read what Alex had just written.

Bailey: *Not funny. Why is it dangerous to put a coffee mug next to a laptop?*

Kate: *I read a magnet will kill the pixels on your computer screen, so it's best to keep the mug away from it. Can you take a video with your cell phone?*

Sydney: *No, but I can with my digital camera.*

Kate: *Good. Stand away from the computer and shoot a video to show us what you do to make it light up.*

Sydney retrieved the mug from a corner of the room.

"You hold it," said Bailey. "I don't want to touch it."

"It won't bite you," Sydney answered. She got her digital camera out of her dresser drawer.

Bailey took the pink camera out of Sydney's hand and turned it on. She switched the button to VIDEO MODE. "All set," she said. "Ready?" Bailey pushed another button and started recording. "The case of the mysterious cup. Take one!"

Sydney held the mug and shook it hard, but nothing happened.

"It stopped recording," said Bailey. "The LCD says, 'Out of Memory.' "

"My camera only takes a forty-five-second video," Sydney answered. "Don't start recording as soon as I shake it."

Bailey deleted the first video, and the girls tried again. Sydney shook the mug hard and fast, but again, the time ran out before anything happened.

Sydney sighed. "Hang on a minute. I'll shake the mug to see how long it takes to light up." Sydney shook the mug hard, but it wouldn't light. "Bailey, I think you broke it."

"I did not!" Bailey defended herself.

Sydney tried again, but the mug stayed dark.

By the time they returned to the computer, Kate had an idea.

Kate: *You know, that thing reminded me of my shake flashlight, so while you were away I went on the internet and looked up how it works.*

McKenzie: *What's a shake flashlight?*

Kate: *Don't you have them in Montana? It looks like a regular flashlight, but it doesn't work on batteries. It has a strong magnet inside. When you shake it, the magnet passes up and down through a coil. That causes the capacitor to charge and the flashlight lights!*

Alexis: *Now you have a perfectly reasonable explanation.*

Bailey: *But there's nothing reasonable about a glowing coffee cup.*

"Mug," Sydney corrected her. It bugged her when people misused words.

Bailey: *In fact, a lot of unreasonable stuff has gone on since I got here last night.*

McKenzie: *Like what?*

Bailey: *I saw strange lights over the water that looked like a UFO. Today I stepped on a bone on the beach and Syd said it might have come from a dead sailor. A lot of them have disappeared around here. Like when a ghost ship washed up on the beach down the coast. The sailors vanished into thin air. Then, today we climbed a lighthouse with an old sea captain but he disappeared. Maybe he was a ghost too.*

Elizabeth: *Bailey, calm down. There are no ghosts!*

Bailey chewed on her lip as her fingers flew across the keyboard.

Bailey: *There are too! There's the Holy Ghost. We learned about Him at camp, and I heard my pastor talk about Him.*
Elizabeth: *The Holy Ghost is a part of the Trinity of God. Sure, He's a spirit, and you can't see Him, but He's not out to get you. There are no such things as ghosts.*

Bailey said no more. Elizabeth was the oldest of the Camp Club Girls, and she seemed to know everything about God. Sometimes, Bailey felt like such a kid when she was around her.

Kate: *So what are you going to do with it?*
Sydney: *I don't know. Throw it in the trash, I guess.*
Kate: *Gotta go. Biscuit just made a mess, and I have to clean it.*

It was getting late, and the rest of the girls decided to sign off too.

Bailey and Sydney's guest room in the beach house was on the second floor. It had two twin beds with matching striped bedspreads and big, fluffy pillows. A white wicker nightstand separated the beds, and it held an alarm clock and a table lamp made out of seashells. The room was painted a soft blue, and instead of one wall, two big sliding glass doors led to a private covered deck that overlooked the ocean. Gramps had said that Bailey and Sydney could sleep out there if they wanted to. It would be like camping, only instead of sleeping in a cabin near Discovery Lake, they would sleep under the stars near the beach. The girls got their sleeping bags and went outside.

"Hey, what's going on down there?" asked Bailey. She leaned over the deck railing to get a better look. Below, children ran around on the beach with plastic buckets and flashlights.

"Ghost crab hunting," said Sydney as she settled into a hammock on one end of the deck.

"Ghost crabs? You mean that ugly thing that we saw on the beach this morning?"

"They're not ugly," Sydney said. "I think they're kind of cute."

"They look like monster white spiders," said Bailey. "Why is everyone trying to catch them?"

Sydney rolled on her side and gazed at the ocean. "Because they're fun to chase," she said. "They pop in and out of their holes so fast you never know when you'll find one. Little kids especially like looking for them."

She paused and watched the moonlight dance across the waves.

"They're hard to catch, because they blend in with the sand. Some-times, if you stay real still and wait, it's like the sand comes alive around your feet. The ghost crabs come up out of their holes all around you, and then they start scurrying sideways and if you move—even one tiny little bit—*they bite your toes!*" Sydney made a quick grab at Bailey's foot.

Bailey jumped. "Ooo! Don't scare me like that," she said. "I've heard enough ghost stories for one day."

Sydney rolled onto her back and gazed up at the stars. "Like Eliza-beth said, Bailey, there's no such things as ghosts."

"Then how do you explain the captain disappearing?" asked Bailey.

"I don't know where the captain went," Sydney said, "but I don't think he was a ghost that just floated off the top of the lighthouse."

Down below, on the beach, children giggled and screamed with delight as they tried to put crabs into plastic buckets.

"Be careful!" a man's called in the darkness. "They pinch!"

"Hey, look up there. It's the big dipper," Sydney said, changing the subject. She pointed out the constellation to Bailey, and the girls settled down to watch the stars, Sydney in the hammock and Bailey on a mat-tress on the deck. Soon they were sound asleep.

Bailey had a nightmare. She dreamed that she was climbing the stairs in the lighthouse, and they disappeared beneath her. There was no way down and no way out.

She awoke with a start. The full moon was high in the sky, casting a glow on the water. The beach was deserted, and Bailey had no idea what time it was. She stood and looked out at the sea.

The waves washing up on the beach glowed an eerie blue green, and she saw what looked like glowing ghost crabs skittering across the sand.

"Sydney!" she whispered. "Wake up!"

Sydney groaned and rubbed her eyes. "What's the matter?"

"Get up!" Bailey demanded. "The ocean is glowing and so are the crabs."

"Huh?" asked Sydney. She sat up wearily and looked at the beach. "It's just bioluminescence."

"Buy a luma what sense?"

"Bioluminescence," Sydney repeated. "It's a phenomenon caused by phosphorous in the water. On moonlit nights, it makes the waves glow."

"And crabs too?" Bailey wondered.

"I suppose," said Sydney. "It's nothing to worry about. Go back to sleep." Sydney rolled over, and in no time at all, Bailey heard her breathing heavily.

She felt lonely on the deck with Sydney sleeping. At night, the ocean didn't seem at all like Lake Michigan. The Atlantic was huge, and it held sharks and stingrays, and who knows what else. And scorpions and snakes might be nearby. If they were on the beach, they could find their way up to the deck where the girls slept.

Although it was muggy outside, Bailey climbed into her sleeping bag and zipped it up tight. She sat on the deck with her back against the wall, fighting sleep. She worried that if she slept she might have another nightmare.

Dawn was peeking over the ocean when Bailey lifted her head. She had dozed off sitting up and now her back ached. The moonlight had faded, and the ocean was like a black, gaping hole. She thought she heard something on the beach. It was a soft whirring sound, kind of like the blade of a helicopter spinning. It stopped. Then she heard nothing but the waves lapping up on the sand.

Bailey climbed out of her sleeping bag and stood by the railing. Something caught her eye. There, not far offshore, was some sort of flying thing. Bailey could barely make out its shape, but it was the size of a car and covered with blinking, multicolored lights. It moved slowly, hovering above the water.

"Sydney! Wake up!" Bailey commanded. She ran to the hammock and shook her friend awake.

"What!" Sydney exclaimed.

"Get up!" said Bailey. "The UFO is out there!"

Sydney sat up and looked toward the ocean. "Bailey, nothing is there. That story I told you about people seeing things at night? It's just a story. I don't believe there's anything to it."

When Bailey looked toward where the lights had been, she saw they were gone. "Oh Syd," she gasped. "You have to believe me. Something dreadful is out there."

"I believe you," Sydney said halfheartedly. "Now forget it, and go back to sleep."

"I won't!" said Bailey. "Look!"

Mysteries on the Beach

"Whoa! What on earth is that?" Sydney exclaimed.

The object was making small, tight circles above the water and darting to and fro. It's blinking lights alternated from red to multicolored, and it didn't make a sound that the girls could hear from their balcony.

"It's not on earth," Bailey answered, "And it's not *from* earth either. It's a UFO! I told you so. I'll go get your grandparents." Bailey started for the sliding glass doors.

"Not yet," said Sydney. "It's probably nothing. Let's go check it out." She climbed out of the hammock and put on her sandals.

"Are you crazy?" Bailey shrieked.

"Sshhhh!" Sydney told her. "You'll wake everybody."

"We are *not* going to check it out," Bailey whispered. "What if the aliens on it abduct us and take us to their planet? No way, Syd!"

But Sydney was already hurrying down the stairs to the beach.

"Don't leave me alone," Bailey begged.

"Then come on," her friend said.

The UFO was just offshore now. The blinking lights faded to black, and the object disappeared into the darkness. Soon a strange whirring came from the water's edge. It turned into a soft *flop flop flop*, sounding like a flat tire on asphalt. Whatever it was had landed on the beach. And it was moving!

Sydney walked toward the noise, but she couldn't see a thing.

The noise stopped.

Bailey had Sydney by the arm now and held her back from going even closer.

Whoof!

A strong puff of hot air hit the girls in the face. Something whizzed past them only a few yards away.

"A wild horse!" Bailey gasped.

"That was no horse," Sydney said.

"Are you sure?" asked Bailey. She loosened her grip.

"I'm sure," said Sydney. "It was going so fast that it's probably to the sound by now."

Sydney decided to run home to get a flashlight. Bailey insisted on coming along. In only moments, the girls returned to the place where whatever it was had rushed past them. Sydney focused the light onto the sand at the water's edge.

"Oh my," she said, "look at that!"

Along the water was a line of strange footprints in the wet sand.

Or were they footprints?

The prints were like big, oval waffles. Their pattern of lines and squares looked like someone had gone along slapping the sand with a tennis racket. The prints came out of the sea and stretched only across the wet sand at the ocean's edge. When they reached the dry part of the sand, they disappeared.

"Bigfoot!" said Bailey. "You know, that gigandamundo monster that leaves his footprints but is hardly ever seen!"

"There's no such thing as Bigfoot," Sydney said. She crouched down to get a better look.

"And until a few minutes ago, you didn't believe UFOs existed," said Bailey.

She had a point. Sydney had no idea what they had just witnessed. She had no explanation for the strange thing that hovered over the water or for the way that it had rushed past them on the beach without a sound.

As she looked over the ocean, Sydney saw the sun beginning to rise. It painted the sky a beautiful salmon orange and sent diamonds of light dancing across the lavender-colored sea.

"Bailey, go get the camera," Sydney said. "We have to get a picture of these prints before they wash away."

Bailey ran to the beach house. She quickly returned to where Sydney waited. By the time she got there, the water was already lapping at the prints.

Sydney snapped a half dozen shots until the prints had almost disappeared.

"Looking for ghost crabs, Sydney Lincoln?"

A man's deep voice came from behind them.

"Captain Swain!" Bailey exclaimed. "What are you doing here?"

The captain stood in front of them dressed in a crisp, blue jogging suit. Sydney noticed it had a coastguard emblem on one sleeve. He had a dog with long black fur, about the size of Kate's dog, Biscuit, by his side.

"McTavish and I are taking our morning walk," the captain replied. "And what brings you girls out so early on this fine, summer morning."

"We saw a UFO," Bailey answered. "And then we went to check it out, but it disappeared. Now there are Bigfoot prints in the sand."

Bailey didn't notice that Sydney was shooting her a look that said, *"Be quiet!"* By now, the footprints had been completely washed away.

"'So we fix our eyes not on what is seen, but on what is unseen. For what is seen is temporary, but what is unseen is eternal,'" the captain said.

In the back of her mind, Sydney remembered reading those words in her Bible study class at camp, but she wasn't quite sure what they meant.

"Just God and me talking out loud," said the captain. He bent and patted McTavish on the head. The dog wagged its tail, sending sand flying in all directions. "Go play, my boy," the captain said, and McTavish scampered along the water's edge leaving footprints trailing behind him.

"I thought you said you never come to Corolla Light," Sydney reminded him.

"I said I *rarely* come here," the captain corrected her. "I *never* come here in the daytime when things are busy unless I absolutely have to. Too many tourists! But often in the morning hours, I hear the ocean calling me."

Bailey still wasn't sure about Captain Swain. Something about him was different. He seemed not to fit in with the residents and tourists on the Outer Banks. She imagined him instead in the days of the ghost ships, hoisting the billowing sails, and standing at the ship's wheel. He seemed mysterious. From a different time in history.

She decided to come right out and ask, "Are you a—"

"Girls! Breakfast!" Sydney's grandmother stood on the upper deck of the beach house calling to them. "Come on now."

"We have to go," Sydney said. She and Bailey ran back to the house.

"Who was that man?" Sydney's grandma asked. "And why were you girls on the beach so early?"

"We saw a UFO," Bailey announced. "And we went to check it out, but we didn't find anything but Bigfoot's footprints. And then Captain Swain showed up. I think he's a ghost because yesterday he disappeared into thin air." She looked down at the beach, but the captain was gone.

"See," she said. "He disappeared *again*!"

Sydney looked toward the beach and tried to come up with a logical explanation.

"Did you see where he went, Grandma?" she asked.

Sydney's grandmother looked north and south.

"No," she replied. "But I had my eyes on you and not on the beach. Bailey, UFOs and Bigfoot and ghosts don't exist. Those are all just stories." Her brown eyes twinkled as she smiled at Sydney's friend. "We're so happy to have you here, but we don't want you to be afraid of things that don't exist. We just want you to have fun."

Bailey still wasn't convinced. She had seen the UFO with her own eyes, and she had seen the footprints too. And those footprints weren't from any animal or human.

"But those things do exist," she whispered to herself. "At least, I think so."

The girls hurried to their room to dress. Sydney quickly emailed the photos to the Camp Club Girls, telling them what had happened at the beach that morning. Then she and Bailey dashed to the kitchen table. Grandpa said the mealtime prayer:

"Loving Father, we thank You for this food,
And for all Your blessings to us.
Lord Jesus, come and be our guest,
And take Your place at this table.
Holy Spirit, as this food feeds our bodies,
So we pray You would nourish our souls. Amen."

"Is the Holy Spirit the same as the Holy Ghost?" Bailey asked as she chose a piece of cinnamon bread.

"He is," Gramps answered, scooping some scrambled eggs onto Bailey's plate.

"And He's truly a ghost?" Bailey wondered.

"He's a spirit, Bailey," Gramps answered. "Many things about God are a mystery and beyond what we humans can understand. The Holy Spirit is one of them. He's a part of God, but He isn't a ghost who haunts or hurts people. He's the Helper, the One who guides us through every day. Grandma says you've been seeing things since you got here."

Bailey shook some pepper onto her eggs. She didn't know what to say except that she had seen strange things, and they were real.

"You girls are good at solving mysteries," Sydney's grandfather went on. "I think you've discovered, by now, that when it comes to mysteries there's usually a logical explanation."

Sydney went to the refrigerator and got a slice of American cheese. She put it on top of her scrambled eggs and zapped her meal in the microwave.

"I think it's my fault," she said. "Yesterday, I told Bailey about the ghost ship. Since then, she's been thinking about ghosts." Sydney carried her eggs back to the table and stuck her fork into the gooey cheese.

"Ah, the ghost ship," Gramps said. "That's an unsolved mystery on the Outer Banks. Folks like to make up stories about it. Somewhere, though, there's the truth about what happened to those poor missing sailors. You can be sure there's a good explanation."

Gramps stirred cream into his coffee. "You know, I think tomorrow I'll take you girls to the Graveyard of the Atlantic Museum. Then you can learn all about the ghost ship and the other shipwrecks off the coast."

While the girls continued eating and talking about shipwrecks, someone knocked on the door and Sydney's grandmother went to answer it.

In a moment, the Kessler twins walked into the room, greeting the girls. Grandpa offered them some cinnamon bread, but they declined.

"Hey, Nate Wright is down at the beach near Tuna Street, and he's setting up his chair," Marilyn said.

"Digger is starting to blow up the helium balloons," Carolyn added. "And I thought Bailey might want to see."

"Can we?" Sydney asked her grandparents as she picked up her plate and Bailey's to carry to the dishwasher.

"Go ahead," Grandma said. "But when he takes off, you girls stay a safe distance away. I don't want you getting hurt." Grandma sipped her coffee. "Cluster ballooning is dangerous, even when it's done the ordinary way, but when Nate does it, it's even more dangerous. He takes too many risks if you ask me and is even a bit crazy. And that son of his is an odd duck too."

Grandma poured a little more creamer into her coffee. "Why, you wouldn't believe the junk that boy picks up on the beach. One day, I was near their house in the village, and you should have seen the junk piled up by their equipment shed!"

"One night, our dad had to go to the village, and he saw Mr. Wright and Digger welding stuff in their yard," Marilyn said. "The sparks lit up their place like fireworks on the Fourth of July. He said he heard that they get real busy at night moving stuff around in the dark—"

"And using hammers and power saws too," Carolyn added.

Grandpa buttered a piece of bread for himself. "Nate says he's an inventor, but the only invention I've seen so far is that silly balloon chair. He thinks he can use that idea to someday create travel that's fast, clean, and inexpensive. Can you imagine all of us flying around in chairs tethered to party balloons?"

The girls laughed.

"Let's go," said Sydney. "Are we walking or taking our bikes?"

"Walking," said the twins.

The girls joined a small crowd that had gathered on the beach just off the sandy beach access lane. Nate Wright was checking the chair, adjusting the straps and making sure they were secured. The seat looked like it came from an airplane cockpit. It had lots of instruments and a big joystick.

"It'll never get off the ground," Bailey said. "It'll be too heavy with all that stuff on it."

"No, it won't," said Sydney. "You won't believe your eyes."

An old beat-up school bus was parked at the edge of the beach on the end of the access road. On its side was a hodgepodge of words:

LASERS
LEVITATING
ELEVATING
WRIGHT &
SON
ORIENTEERING
RACING

"What does it all mean?" Bailey asked.

"I guess it advertises things they're working on. I don't really know," said Sydney.

"Why don't we ask them?" said Bailey.

"Because they don't talk to anybody," Sydney replied. "The only time the Wrights say anything is if they think you're getting close enough to get hurt."

Drake Wright, Digger, was on the roof of the bus with a helium tank.

One by one, he filled balloons with helium and fastened them to big hooks on top of the bus roof. Each hook held several dozen colorful balloons.

"What's he doing?" asked Bailey.

"He has to have a place to store the balloons until they get attached to the chair," said Marilyn. "So he ties them to the bus, because anything lighter than a bus would lift right off the ground."

"No way!" said Bailey. She took her cell phone out of her pocket and snapped a few pictures. "I'm going to send these to Kate right now," she said. "She'll love this!"

Once Digger had filled all of the balloons, he helped his dad slide the chair to the front of the school bus. Then they chained and locked it to the bumper. Mr. Wright sat down, strapped himself in, and put on a helmet, the kind the astronauts wear.

"Now what?" asked Bailey.

"Watch," said Carolyn.

"Watch," Marilyn echoed.

Methodically, Digger carried the balloons from the rooftop to his dad's chair, one bunch at a time. He attached them to special fasteners on the chair frame and the chair soon began to rise.

"Awesome!" Bailey gasped, snapping more pictures.

"You haven't seen anything yet," said Sydney.

When all of the balloons were in place, the chair hovered near the hood of the school bus. It strained to break loose.

"Get back!" Digger yelled at the crowd.

Everyone took several steps backward.

Drake shook his dad's hand and released the chains. The chair shot up into the air like a rocket. It kept soaring up and over the water.

"Oh wow!" said Bailey.

Digger disappeared from sight.

"Where'd he go?" Bailey asked, snapping a few more pictures.

"He's probably gone to get the boat," said Carolyn.

"Mr. Wright can only go so high before the oxygen gets too thin," said Marilyn, "so he has to start popping balloons to slowly come down. When he splashes down in the ocean, Digger will be there to pick him up."

"But Digger has to go down the shore a bit to get the boat in the water," Carolyn explained to the girls. "There's no dock or boat ramp here, and you have to have a boat with some power to withstand the waves."

"He usually flies over the sound side of the Outer Banks," Marilyn said. "That's where most of the smaller boats and jet skis are because the water is calmer."

Bailey's cell phone rang. It was a text message from Kate: READ THE FIRST LETTERS OF EACH WORD ON THE BUS FROM BOTTOM TO TOP. THEY SPELL ROSWELL! K8.

"Check it out," Bailey said handing the phone to Sydney. "What's Roswell?" Sydney read the message. "Roswell is a town in New Mexico famous for UFOs," she explained. "People think one crashed there years ago."

Pop! Pop-pop! Pop!

As a series of a loud bangs rang over the ocean the girls wondered about UFOs as they watched Nate Wright's chair fall slowly toward the sea.

CHAPTER 6

Aliens

Dear Syd and Bailey,

Kate emailed me about the Wrights and the Roswell connection. How creepy! Do you think that the Wrights are connected with the UFO you saw this morning? I don't know if you've seen the movie Close Encounters of the Third Kind, *but in the movie people tried to make contact with a spaceship by using a code—five musical notes, re-mi-do-do-sol. I wonder if that flashlight thing you found on the beach is some sort of signaling device. Do you think the Wrights are trying to communicate with aliens?*

Be careful,
Alex

Alexis's email, marked "Highest Priority," was waiting for Sydney and Bailey when they got back from the beach.

"Now do you believe me?" Bailey asked flopping on her bed in the guest room. "Even Alex thinks we're being invaded by spaceships."

Sydney sat on her bed fidgeting with her cornrows. She was trying to find a practical explanation.

"I don't know what to believe," she answered. "I mean, Roswell is another unsolved mystery like the ghost ship. According to the story, a UFO crashed in Roswell, in the desert. A rancher found pieces of metal scattered all over his property. He called the authorities and even the army got involved. It was a very big deal back then. They roped off his land and didn't let anyone inside. At first the government said they found pieces of a flying saucer. Later they said that the pieces were from a weather balloon. No one knows for sure, but just like the ghost ship story, rumors have kept going around."

Bailey lay on her bed thinking. She was sure the UFO she saw was not a helicopter, boat, or other ordinary thing. If the Wrights were involved, it would make sense, because they were so different and secretive.

"Hey," said Bailey. "Maybe they're aliens!"

"Huh?" said Sydney.

"Mr. Wright and Digger," Bailey answered. "Maybe their spaceship crashed in the ocean, but they survived. That would explain Drake Digger picking up stuff along the shore. He's picking up pieces of the spaceship!"

Sydney sighed. "Oh Bailey, your imagination is getting away from you again."

"No, it's not," said Bailey sitting up on the bed. "At night, when most people are asleep, the Wrights are trying to reconstruct their spaceship from the pieces Drake finds. That's why they're welding and stuff. And meanwhile they're trying to create an alternate vehicle that could go high enough to meet a rescue ship, or something. That's why they're experimenting with the cluster balloons. And that thing we found on the beach? Alex is right. It's a signaling device."

"Bailey!" said Sydney.

"And you know what else?" Bailey went on. "I think Captain Swain is one of them. He was on the beach this morning when the UFO was there. He saw the whole thing! *He* knows what that thing was hovering over the ocean, and he knows what scooted past us in the dark. He knows about those footprints too!"

"Oh Bailey, stop," said Sydney. "Yesterday, you thought the captain was a ghost." She got up from her bed and got the coffee mug from the bookshelf.

"I don't think he's a ghost anymore," said Bailey. "Now I think he's a space alien."

Sydney shook the coffee mug, but nothing happened. She shook it again. Still nothing. Then she tossed it into the wastebasket. It landed with a thud. "Enough of the alien stuff already!" she said. She slid open the glass doors to the deck and went outside.

Bailey screamed at the top of her lungs.

"What's the matter?" Sydney exclaimed, hurrying back inside.

Bailey was sitting on the bed, her knees pulled tight to her chest with her arms wrapped around them. She looked terrified.

"Bailey, what's wrong?" Sydney asked again.

Bailey pointed to the wastebasket. The inside of it was lit with an eerie, flashing light. Sydney looked more closely and saw that it was coming from the hole in the lid of the mug.

This was too weird. For the first time, Sydney believed no logical explanation existed for the mug, the UFO, or any of the other strange things that had been going on. She bent to take the mug out of the trash, but then she stopped.

Better to leave it alone, she thought.

"Count 'em, Syd. Count 'em," said Bailey.

"Count what?" Sydney asked.

"Count the flashes of light," Bailey answered. "One, two, three, four, five. . . One, two, three, four, five. . ."

The mug sent out five quick flashes of light. Then it stopped briefly and sent out five more.

"So?" said Sydney.

"So, remember what Alex said in her email?" Bailey answered. "In the *Close Encounters* movie, the signal was five musical notes. One, two, three, four, five notes. One, two, three, four, five flashes of light. It's a code, Sydney."

Bailey's phone dinged. It was a text from Kate. Bailey read aloud. "BAILEY, DO YOU KNOW ABOUT THE LAKE MICHIGAN TRIANGLE AND THE FOOTPRINTS? IF NOT, LOOK IT UP ONLINE. K8." There was a URL address.

"What's the Lake Michigan Triangle?" Sydney asked.

"Never heard of it," said Bailey. "Let's check it out."

Sydney typed the URL address into the browser window on her computer. An article from a Michigan newspaper appeared on the screen. She read, then explained.

"This says the Lake Michigan Triangle has a history similar to the Bermuda Triangle. The lines of an imaginary triangle run from Ludington, Michigan, down to Benton Harbor, Michigan, then across the lake to Manitowoc, Wisconsin, and back across the lake to Ludington."

"I know where Manitowoc is," Bailey said. "Our family rented a cottage near there one summer."

Sydney continued. "Ships have disappeared inside the triangle. This even says one of them is seen sailing on the lake from time to time, but then disappears."

"Another ghost ship!" said Bailey. "And that's not too far from where I live. Do you know what, Syd? I just remembered something."

"What?" Sydney asked.

"A couple of years ago, there was a report of a UFO over O'Hare International Airport, in Chicago. Pilots saw it, and some other people did too. They said it was shaped like a saucer and spun around slowly, but didn't make any noise. The air traffic controllers couldn't see it on the radar. Then, *zoom!* It shot straight up into the sky."

"For real?" asked Sydney.

"Really," Bailey answered. "It was in the *Chicago Tribune* and on the TV news too. Nobody ever found out what it was."

"Check this out," said Sydney, reading the article. "There have also been reports of strange footprints on the beach near the points of the triangle."

Bailey gasped. "Footprints! Syd, maybe those footprints were like the ones we saw this morning. Alien footprints!"

Sydney logged off her browser. "You know, Bailey," she said, "maybe UFOs do exist."

Bailey got up the courage to walk to the wastebasket and peer inside. The flashing light had stopped. Once again, the thing looked like an ordinary travel mug. "So what do we do now?" she asked.

"We put the mug back where we found it," said Sydney. "Then we stay up tonight to see what happens."

At sunset, the girls took the mug to the beach. They tried to find the exact spot in the sand where it had been buried. They put it there and hoped children hunting for ghost crabs would leave it alone. After that, they set up the deck for spying. Sydney hung a pair of binoculars around her neck. Bailey had a mini audio recorder in her pocket, a gift Kate had given her for her birthday. The girls had their digital cameras, flashlights, and a notebook and pencils. Now they only had to wait.

Two hours later, Sydney wrote in the notebook:

> *UFO Log*
> *9 p.m. Kids on beach with flashlights looking for*
>   *ghost crabs.*

"Can you see if our mug is still there?" Bailey asked.

"I think so," Sydney answered from a folding chair set up near the hammock. "I can only see when one of the kids shines a flashlight in that direction, but so far, it's there."

Bailey settled into a chair next to Sydney's. She opened a bottle of water and sipped. "So did you talk to Beth while I was in the shower?"

"I did," Sydney answered.

"What did Bettyboo say when you told her what was going on?"

"She already knew about it," said Sydney as she took the cap off her water bottle. "McKenzie heard about it from Kate, and she emailed Beth. And don't call her Bettyboo. She hates that."

"What did she think about the UFO?" Bailey asked as she put her feet on the deck railing.

"She doesn't believe in UFOs, and she sure doesn't think the Wrights are aliens. She said we should be careful, and she suggested that we look for a logical explanation instead of thinking about UFOs and spirits." Sydney gulped her water.

"What do you think, Syd?" asked Bailey. "Do you think that God created UFOs?"

Sydney put her feet up on the railing and settled back in her chair. "In my heart of hearts, I don't," she said. "I mean, the Bible says that He created the heavens and the earth and humans and animals, but it doesn't say anything about UFOs."

Bailey looked up at the stars. "I don't want to believe in UFOs and ghosts and stuff, Syd. I don't think that God would create anything bad. But, I know what I saw, and I don't see any other explanation for it." She sighed.

"Tomorrow, Gramps is taking us to the Graveyard of the Atlantic Museum," said Sydney. "Maybe we'll find some answers there. And do you know what, Bailey? We both need to get some sleep. Otherwise we'll be really tired tomorrow. We should watch the beach in shifts. One of us sleeps while the other one watches."

Sydney wrote in the notebook:

> *Sydney—10 p.m. to midnight*
> *Bailey—midnight to 2 a.m.*
> *Sydney—2 a.m. to 4 a.m.*
> *Bailey—4 a.m. to dawn*

At ten o'clock, Bailey stretched out in the hammock and was soon asleep. Sydney had a hard time staying awake. The beach was deserted except for a couple of four-wheelers heading back up north. She watched the moon dodge in and out of clouds. Besides it, the stars, and an occasional airplane flying above the ocean, nothing was in the sky.

When the little travel alarm clock she'd brought on the deck said 12:00, Sydney wrote in the notebook. *"Midnight and all is well".* Then she woke Bailey.

"What time is it?" Bailey groaned.

"It's midnight," Sydney said. "I didn't see anything, and it's your turn. Try hard to stay awake. It's easy to get bored." Sydney and Bailey traded places, and Sydney fell asleep.

At first, Bailey scouted every inch of the beach with the binoculars, but she couldn't see anything in the darkness. There was no sound except the waves rolling up on shore. She tried to occupy her mind by singing songs in her head and reciting scripture verses Elizabeth had taught her. Finally, it was 2 a.m. She wrote in the notebook *"2 a.m. Nothing to report".*

"Syd?" she said, shaking her friend awake. "It's your turn."

Sydney rolled over in the hammock. "Anything?" she sighed, rubbing the sleep from her eyes.

"Nothing," said Bailey. Then the girls again traded places.

By 3:30 a.m., Sydney was ready to give up. She was bored out of her mind sitting on the deck looking at nothing. She felt her chin hit her chest as she fought off sleep. Then, out of the corner of her eye, she saw something. At least, she thought she did. She thought she saw a flash of bright, white light in the ocean. It flashed briefly and then it disappeared. She waited a few minutes, but there was nothing. Then it flashed again. Five quick bursts of light!

"Bailey! Bailey! Get up. I see something," she urgently whispered.

Bailey rolled so fast in the hammock that she almost sent it flying upside down. "What?" she asked, trying to sit up.

"Sshhh," Sydney whispered. "Look out there." She pointed at the ocean in front of where they sat. After a few seconds, the light flashed again. Sydney noticed that the bursts of light were sometimes long and sometimes short. "It's a code!" she said. "See? Sometimes it flashes longer than others. Write it down, Bailey."

Bailey shone her flashlight onto the notebook paper. "Hide under something," Sydney commanded. "They might see your flashlight."

Bailey dodged under the sleeping bag. As Sydney dictated, Bailey wrote:

> *Short short long*
> *Short short short*

SS
LS
LSL. . .

She wrote for what seemed like forever. Then Sydney stopped dictating. "What's going on?" Bailey asked from under the sleeping bag.

Sydney didn't answer.

"Syd?" Bailey asked. Her muscles tightened and her heart began to race.

"It stopped," Sydney said. "I think you can come out now."

Bailey turned off the flashlight and crawled out from under the sleeping bag. "How weird was that?" she asked.

"Pretty weird," Sydney answered. "Did you get it all written down?"

"Every flash of it," said Bailey proudly. "What do you think it means?"

"I don't know," Sydney answered. "I think we should email it to McKenzie. She's good at analyzing things."

It was just past 4:30 a.m. now, and the beach was pitch-black. It was about the same time that Bailey had seen the UFO the morning before. As the girls looked out at the water, nothing was above it but fading stars. In a little while, the sun would come up over the Atlantic, and another day would begin.

"Hey," Sydney whispered. "Listen."

The girls heard footsteps along the wet sand at the edge of the beach. They came from the south and plodded along rhythmically, passing Sydney's grandparents' beach house, and then stopping just to the north.

"Did you see?" said an older male voice in the darkness.

"It's Captain Swain!" Bailey gasped.

"I saw," a younger male voice answered. "I didn't put the vehicle in the water. Probably best not to until that girl leaves. At least I got my light back." Suddenly, Sydney and Bailey saw their coffee mug flash on and off.

"I think they broke it," said the younger voice.

"That's too bad," said Captain Swain. "We should get out of here before the sun comes up."

Bailey and Sydney sat quietly until they thought the men were gone.

"See?" said Bailey. "The captain is one of them, and they do have a vehicle. I think that they're trying to get back to the Mother Ship, Syd."

"Let's email McKenzie right away," said Sydney. "She won't be up for a few hours, but I know she checks her email first thing in the morning. Maybe she can tell us what the code says before we leave for the museum."

The girls went inside, and Bailey copied the code from her notebook pages to the email document. "There," she said, typing the last *Long short long*. "Let's hope she can figure this out." She hit SEND, and the message flew off through cyberspace.

In less than a minute, they got a reply.

I'm up. Our horse, Princess, foaled about an hour ago. She had a darling colt that we named Benny. I just came in from the barn. I'll check out your code and email you back.

As the sun rose, Bailey and Sydney got dressed and packed their backpacks for the drive to Hatteras. After breakfast, just before Gramps went to get his pickup truck, they checked the email. A message was waiting from McKenzie.

It's morse code. It says: "I think we're being watched from the Lincoln house. Someone is on the deck with a flashlight."

CHAPTER 7

Double Trouble

After a long drive down Highway 12 from the top of the Outer Banks to the bottom, the girls and Gramps stopped at the museum, ready to stretch their legs.

"It kind of looks like a shipwreck," said Sydney as she climbed out of her grandfather's truck. She had never been to the Graveyard of the Atlantic Museum, and she had no idea what to expect. The front of the building was outlined in weathered timbers shaped like the hull of a wooden sailing vessel. The building resembled a long, gray ship. Four porthole windows protruded from its roof, reminding Sydney of giant bug eyes.

"I think you'll find some pieces of the ghost ship in here," Gramps said as they walked to the front door.

"Pieces?" said Bailey holding the door for them. "What happened to the rest of it?"

"It stayed aground on the shoals," said Gramps. "After weeks and months of the wind and waves pounding against it, it started to break apart. Then the coast guard dynamited what was left of it."

"Why did they do that?" Bailey asked.

"Because it was a hazard to ships sailing out there. Most of the pieces ended up on the beach. Some of them floated down here to Hatteras Island and got put in the museum. Look over there. There's the capstan. It was used to haul in the ropes on the ship."

The heavy, rusty metal device of the *Carroll A. Deering* rested in front of them. The top was shaped like a lampshade, and a pole came out of the bottom like a rusty old water pipe.

"Was that really a part of the ship?" Sydney asked.

"Yes," said Gramps. "It's the part that raised and lowered the anchors."

Bailey was busy looking at other pieces in the exhibit. She saw timbers from the hull and also pieces of the ship's boom—the long wooden pole that had held up the sails.

"Can you imagine," she said. "This thing was on the ship when all of those sailors disappeared." She felt a shiver run down her spine. "It was there when it happened. The wind probably tore the sails off it when it rocked back and forth on the shoals."

Something ran up the side of her arm and made her jump.

"*Scrape. . .scrape. . . ,*" Sydney whispered as her fingers tickled Bailey's shoulder.

"That's not funny!" Bailey protested. "If this thing could talk, it would tell us exactly what happened."

"Interested in the *Carroll A. Deering*, are you?" The museum curator walked toward them. He was a short, older man with a bald head and a happy smile.

Gramps shook his hand. "Travis Lincoln," he introduced himself.

"David Jones," said the curator.

"We'd like to know what really happened to the sailors on the ghost ship," said Sydney. "They couldn't have just disappeared. There has to be a logical explanation."

Mr. Jones stood with his elbow resting against a glass cabinet that held more artifacts from the ship. "Well," he said, "that depends on who you talk to. What do you girls think?"

"I'm not sure," said Sydney. "A lot of ships have wrecked off the coast around here. But this one seems so mysterious." She looked inside the glass case at a model of the *Carroll A. Deering*.

"I think they were abducted by aliens!" said Bailey. "I'm almost sure of it."

"Aliens," said Mr. Jones. "Why, that's a theory I haven't heard before. What makes you think it was aliens?"

Bailey waited for a few visitors to pass out of earshot before she answered. "Because we've seen them," she said softly. "With our own eyes."

Sydney frowned at Bailey. "We're not sure what we saw," Sydney said. "We saw some strange lights over the ocean the other night and unusual footprints on the beach."

"Big footprints that looked like waffles!" Bailey added. "And then an alien spacecraft whooshed past us on the beach in the dark. It didn't make a sound, but it hit us with a big puff of air."

Gramps looked confused.

"Young lady, you have quite the imagination," said Mr. Jones. "Let's sit down and talk about this. Maybe I can shed some light on what really happened to the crew of the *Carroll A. Deering.*"

He led them to a small, round table and some chairs. The table held a book about the ghost ship and some brochures about the museum. "Now, tell me. What are your names?"

"Sydney Lincoln."

"Bailey Chang."

"Well, Sydney and Bailey, folks have come up with three *logical* explanations. The first one is that the crew abandoned ship. When the coast guard got to the *Carroll A. Deering*, the rope ladder was hanging over the side, and both lifeboats were gone. Someone had run red flares up the rigging to indicate trouble on board."

"Red flares?" said Sydney. "The lights we saw over the ocean the other night were red."

"And sometimes multicolored and flashing," said Bailey. "Maybe it wasn't a spaceship we saw. Maybe it was the ghost ship!"

"I doubt that, Bailey," said Mr. Jones. "Because what's left of the ghost ship is right here."

"You have a point," Bailey said. "But how about a ghost of the ghost ship?"

Mr. Jones smiled and continued. "Now, if the crew did jump ship, they did it in a big hurry, because the galley was set up for a meal, and everything was left behind. However, the theory of abandonment doesn't add up."

"Why?" Sydney asked.

"Because the men were professional sailors who knew what they were doing. In stormy seas, they would be able to steer the ship away from the shoals, but the evidence shows that they sailed right into them!

"Two days before that they'd sailed past the Cape Lookout Lightship, and a crew member reported to the lightkeeper that they had lost both of their anchors, but they'd gotten through the worst of the storm.

"And something was strange about that. Usually a ship's officer makes the report. But on that day the lightkeeper didn't see an officer on deck with the men. Not the captain or a mate or even an engineer. So the officers might have already been missing by then. And the ship ran aground so near the Hatteras Lighthouse that the crew would have been better off to wait for a rescue than to jump ship. The ship didn't seem to be taking on water or anything."

Bailey nervously folded the pages of a brochure. "So maybe the crew member was a ghost?"

"No," said Mr. Jones. "But the crew member might have been up to no good. The officers might have been tied up on board or thrown overboard or even killed."

Gramps had been listening and looking through the book about the *Carroll A. Deering.* "What's your second theory?" he asked.

"Mutiny," said Mr. Jones.

"What does that mean?" Sydney wondered.

"Mutiny means the sailors take over the ship," said Gramps. "If the sailors didn't like the captain, they sometimes found a way to get rid of him."

"That's right," said Mr. Jones. "Captain Willis Wormell was the captain of the *Carroll A. Deering,* and he and his first mate, a man named McLellan, probably didn't get along. Some folks think there was a mutiny at sea. Something strange must have happened because it should have taken the ship about twelve hours to get from Cape Fear to Cape Lookout, but it took six days!"

"Why so long?" Bailey asked.

"No one knows," Mr. Jones answered. "It's part of the mystery. But some of the ship's charts were found in the wreck. After the ship got past Cape Fear, none of the entries in the charts were in Captain Wormell's handwriting. Three sets of boots were found in the captain's cabin, but none of them were the captain's. Some folks think he was killed and thrown overboard."

"Was he?" Sydney asked.

"No one knows," said Mr. Jones.

"Boy," Bailey said. "There sure is a lot of stuff that no one knows. So it still could be aliens, right?"

"I doubt it," said the curator. "Plenty of things point to a mutiny, but there's no evidence, and if you know anything about solving a mystery, you know you need evidence."

"Oh, we know that!" said Sydney. "Our group of friends, the Camp Club Girls, have solved several mysteries now."

Gramps smiled. "The girls and their friends from summer camp have quite the reputation for solving mysteries. You wouldn't believe some of the adventures they've had."

"I can only imagine," said Mr. Jones.

"I suppose it could have been mutiny," said Sydney. "But without evidence, we can't make that conclusion. If McLellan killed the officers and the crew, he had to do something with the bodies, and they were never found. Were there any signs of a fight on board?"

"No," said Mr. Jones. "Wormell was a big man and could have put up quite a fight. And *both* lifeboats were missing, and that doesn't make sense if McLellan was the only one left on board."

"That is weird," said Bailey. "But there's not enough evidence in either of those theories to convince me the crew members weren't abducted by aliens."

"Is there evidence to convince you that they *were*?" Sydney asked.

Bailey bit her lower lip. "No," she confessed. "What's the third theory?"

"Pirates," said Mr. Jones.

"Like Blackbeard?" Sydney asked.

"No," Mr. Jones replied. "He died long before then. But pirates still sailed in the sea. One theory is that pirates took over another ship named the *Hewitt*, killed everyone, and then threw a tarp over the ship's name-plate. So, if anyone saw the ship, they wouldn't know which one it was."

"And shortly after the *Carroll A. Deering* passed the Cape Lookout Lightship, another ship sailed by—"

"What's a lightship, anyhow?" Bailey interrupted.

"A lightship is a special ship equipped with a really bright light," said Mr. Jones. "Lightships are used in places where a lighthouse can't be built. They're moored off the coast in places that are dangerous for ships to navigate." He found a picture of a lightship in the book on the table and showed it to the girls.

"Maybe the signals we saw were from a lightship?" Bailey said.

"Signals?" said Gramps.

"We think we saw someone flashing a white light in Morse code early this morning," said Sydney. "It was in the ocean straight out from our house at around four o'clock."

"What were you girls doing up at four o'clock?" asked Gramps.

"Watching for UFOs," said Bailey.

"Oh girls," said Gramps, shaking his head. "There are no such things as UFOs. . . Mr. Jones, please tell us more about the *Hewitt*."

"Well, that second ship, the one that was following the *Deering*, was hailed by the lightship at Cape Lookout. Usually, someone on board would shout a report, like the crew member from the *Deering* did. Only, this time, the ship sailed right on by without reporting. The lightship keeper said he couldn't find a nameplate on the ship, so no one knows, but it could have been the *Hewitt*."

"Another unknown," said Bailey.

"The theory is that pirates killed everyone on the *Hewitt* and then stole the vessel. After that, they attacked the *Deering*, killed its crew, and stole anything valuable. Then they transferred their treasure to the *Hewitt*, steered the *Carroll A. Deering* in the direction of the shoals, and jumped ship."

Sydney was fidgeting with her cornrows again, like she often did when she was thinking. "But what about the bodies of all those sailors? They were never found."

"They never were," Mr. Jones agreed. "And some of their remains would have probably appeared sooner or later."

"Except that we found one of their bones on the beach," said Bailey.

"What?" Gramps exclaimed.

"I stepped on a bone in the sand, and Sydney said it was part of a dead sailor."

"I did not!" said Sydney. "I was telling you a ghost story. The bone was probably left from someone's barbeque lunch."

Mr. Jones chuckled. "It sounds like you girls are having quite the time up there in Corolla."

Sydney remembered what she had been thinking about before Bailey had mentioned the bone. "What happened to the *Hewitt*?" she asked.

"Well," said Mr. Jones. "That's another great mystery. It disappeared around the same time the *Carroll A. Deering* was found stuck in the shoals. It was never heard from again."

"Another ghost ship!" said Bailey. "It sounds like there's no more evidence to support those theories than mine: I still think they were abducted by aliens."

Mr. Jones sighed. "I guess I can't argue with you, Bailey. But I don't believe in UFOs."

"Me neither," said Gramps.

Bailey looked to Sydney for support.

"I don't know," Sydney said. "We've seen and heard some strange things lately and haven't found any logical explanations."

"You're the Camp Club Girls!" Mr. Jones said. "Be good detectives, and see if you can find an explanation for your UFOs. If nothing else, you'll come up with some good theories. Who knows, maybe fifty years from now, people will discuss your UFO theories the way we just discussed the theories about the *Deering*."

The girls thanked Mr. Jones for his time. Then they went to explore the rest of the museum.

Bailey was excited to see a lighthouse exhibit, including a model of the Cape Hatteras black-and-white striped lighthouse. She enjoyed looking at the exhibits for each of the lighthouses on the Outer Banks, including the Currituck Beach Lighthouse, in Corolla.

"Hey, Kate would be interested in this," said Sydney. "When the lighthouse we climbed was first built, it didn't have electricity. The lighthouse keeper had to rotate the lens at the top of the tower by hand so the light appeared to flash."

Bailey looked at a diagram of the lighthouse showing all of its parts. "If Kate had lived back then, she'd have found some sort of high-tech gadget to make it easier. Hey, if there was no electricity, where did the light come from?"

Sydney read the caption under a picture. "It came from a giant oil lamp," she said. "The lens was rotated with a system of weights, sort of the way a grandfather clock works. The lighthouse keeper or his assistant had to crank the weights by hand every two and a half hours. Look, here's a picture."

Bailey studied the old, yellowed photo of the lighthouse keeper cranking the weights. "Captain Swain!"

"What?" said Sydney.

"It says here, 'Captain Nathan Swain Rotates the Lens on the Currituck Beach Lighthouse, 1910'. Sydney, that's a picture of him. It's Captain Swain!"

Sydney looked carefully at the photo. "It does sort of look like him," she said, "but it can't be, because this picture was taken one hundred years ago."

"It's him," Bailey insisted. "He's a ghost."

"What are you girls so interested in?" asked Gramps. He had been looking at another exhibit across the room.

"Just this picture of the Currituck Beach lighthouse keeper," said Sydney. "He looks like someone we saw there the other day."

"There's a whole book about the lighthouse keepers over there," said Gramps, pointing across the room. "Maybe you can find him in there."

Bailey and Sydney found the book *Lightkeepers of the Outer Banks* on a table near the exhibits. Sydney looked in the table of contents and found "Currituck Beach Lighthouse." She turned to page 87 and found a list of lightkeepers beginning in 1875. Sydney read them aloud, "Burris, Simmons, Shinnault, Scott, Simpson, Hinnant, another Simmons. . . Here he is—Nathan H. Swain! He was the lighthouse keeper from 1905 until 1920."

"Is there a picture of him?" Bailey asked, looking over Sydney's shoulder.

"No," she answered. "But there's a footnote." She turned to the back of the book, and there she found a photograph of an old newspaper article, " 'Captain Nathan H. Swain Retires as Keeper of the Currituck Beach Lighthouse.' "

There was a picture, a close-up of the captain wearing his uniform. Sydney caught her breath. "It's him!"

"Oh my," Bailey said. "He really is a ghost!"

Theories

After their day in Hatteras, the girls were relaxing in their room. Sydney was on the bed studying a photocopy of the Captain Swain article. She even used a magnifying glass to look at his picture better.

"This photo is a little blurry. It sure does look like our captain," she said. "But it can't be the same man."

Bailey sat at the desk painting her fingernails with a light blue nail polish called Gonna' Getchu Blue.

"He's a ghost!" she insisted. "That explains why he disappeared at the lighthouse and on the beach the other morning."

"Yeah, but what about *this* morning?" said Sydney. "We heard him talking with that other guy on the beach—"

"The alien," Bailey added, blowing on her nails.

Sydney got up and slid open the glass doors letting the warm ocean breeze rush into the room. "Think about this, Bailey. You're telling me that a ghost was on the beach this morning, and he was talking to a space alien. Do you know how crazy that sounds?"

Bailey tightened the cap on the nail polish bottle. "Okay, so do you have another explanation? If he's not a ghost, how do you explain that the Captain Swain in the newspaper article isn't the same guy?"

"I don't know yet," said Sydney. "But I'm going to find out." She sat down on the bed and opened her laptop. "I'm going to email the girls everything we know so far, and if we work together we'll get to the bottom of this."

Sydney wrote an email to the Camp Club Girls. She included her list of facts:

1. *Before Bailey arrived, there were reports of strange*

lights over the Atlantic Ocean near the Outer Banks.

2.   On Bailey's first night, she saw flashing red lights over the water.

3.   The next day, after we climbed the lighthouse, Captain Swain seemed to disappear.

4.   That afternoon, we found the mysterious mug on the beach.

5.   Early yesterday morning, we saw a UFO. We heard a whirring noise, but then the sound quit. Something rushed past us on the beach with a puff of air. It left waffle-like footprints. Then we ran into Captain Swain on the beach. He seemed to disappear in a hurry again.

6.   Later, we went to watch Nate Wright cluster balloon. The words on the Wrights' bus spelled "Roswell" backward.

7.   In the afternoon, the mug started flashing, so we put it back on the beach where we found it.

8.   Early this morning, someone out in the ocean was using a flashing light to send Morse code. The message said: "I think we're being watched from the Lincoln house. Someone is on the deck with a flashlight."

9.   We heard Captain Swain on the beach talking to another guy. The guy said he wasn't going to put the "vehicle" in the water until Bailey left. He also said the mug was his and that we broke it. He took it with him.

10. Today, we went to the Graveyard of the Atlantic Museum. We found an old newspaper article with a picture of a guy named Captain Nathan Swain. He looks just like our Captain Swain. But the picture was taken 100 years ago!

So, Camp Club Girls, who is this man, and what are the mysterious lights over the ocean?

Sydney and Bailey

Sydney attached a copy of the article with the picture of Captain Swain. "There," she said. "Now we'll see what the girls come up with."

Bailey was looking at her nails, "Do you like this color," she asked, "or should I try Sparkle Me Purple?"

"I like the blue," said Sydney. "You know, I just remembered something. Didn't the captain say he'd climbed the lighthouse before?"

"Yeah," Bailey answered. "He said, 'I climbed these stairs a lot back in the day,' or something like that—which would make sense if he was the lighthouse keeper. I mean, they had to rotate that thingy by hand to make the light work, right? Didn't they have to do that every couple of hours? So he would've climbed those stairs lots of times. He's a ghost, Syd. Admit it."

Sydney sat fidgeting with her cornrows. "Remember what Mr. Jones said? We should rule out all the other theories before we decide that he's a ghost or an alien or a mystery that we can't explain." She picked up Bailey's bottle of blue nail polish and shook it.

"So what's your theory?" asked Bailey.

"Well, I thought that maybe our captain was the son of the man in the article." Sydney opened the bottle and brushed some Gonna' Getchu Blue onto her thumbnail. "But then I read the article again, and Captain Nathan Swain only had one child, a daughter named Nellie." She held her right hand out to look at the color.

"Any other theories?" Bailey asked.

"Not yet," said Sydney. "How about you?"

"Maybe he just happens to look exactly like the guy in the photograph and just *happens* to be a captain too and just *happens* to have the same last name."

"Are you being sarcastic?" Sydney asked, wiping off the polish.

"Of course I am," said Bailey. "There's maybe room for one coincidence, but not three."

Sydney next chose a bottle of pale Tickle Me Pink nail polish and began brushing it onto her nails. She was almost done when her cell phone rang. "Bailey, will you get that, please?" she asked. "My nails are wet."

Bailey got Sydney's phone out of her backpack. "It's a text message from Mac. It says: I'M SETTING UP A GROUP CHAT FOR TONIGHT. WE NEED TO DISCUSS THIS!"

"Great," Sydney said. "We need all the help we can get."

●—●—●

When Bailey and Sydney logged into the chatroom after supper, the other Camp Club Girls were waiting.

McKenzie: *We were talking before you got here. Do you
know much about your Captain Swain, the one from the
lighthouse?*

Sydney and Bailey sat next to each other on Syd's bed.

Sydney: *No, we didn't really get to know him at all. He walked
up the stairs with us and helped Bailey get over her fear of
heights. Then, once we were up there, he left, or something,
and we didn't see him go.*
McKenzie: *What does he look like?*
Sydney: *He's about as tall as I am and sort of round. He had a
gray beard and was dressed like a sea captain. He had on
a blue captain's cap and a blue, heavy jacket with shiny
buttons.*

"Don't forget about the dog," said Bailey.

Sydney: *And he has a shaggy black dog about the size of Biscuit.
Named McTavish. When we saw the captain on the beach,
he wore a dark blue jogging suit with a coast guard emblem
on the sleeve.*

"And he talks about God," Bailey reminded her.

Sydney: *And he talks about God.*
Elizabeth: *What does he say about God?*
Sydney: *He quotes the Bible and says that he and God are
talking out loud.*
Elizabeth: *Then he must be a Christian. And I think that's your
best reason to believe that he's not a ghost.*

Bailey borrowed the laptop from Sydney.

Bailey: *Why?*
Elizabeth: *Because when Christians die, their souls go to
heaven. The Bible says in 2 Corinthians 5:8 that when*

*we're absent from our bodies, we're present with the
Lord.*

McKenzie: *So we know your captain is somehow involved with
the lights, right?*

Bailey: *He had something to do with whoever was flashing the
Morse code this morning. But we don't know for sure that
he had anything to do with the strange lights flashing over
the water.*

Alexis: *What do you know about the cluster ballooning guys,
the ones with the Roswell bus?*

Bailey looked at Sydney and shrugged her shoulders. She didn't
really know much about the Wrights except what she'd heard from Sydney, her grandparents, and the Kessler twins. She gave the laptop back
to Sydney.

Sydney carried it over to the desk and turned on a lamp in the room.
It was nearly dark outside, and it had begun to rain. Bailey pulled up a
chair and joined her.

Sydney: *They're related to the Wright brothers. You remember
them, don't you? They invented the airplane, and they
made their first flight down the coast from here near Kitty
Hawk. Nate is a distant cousin or something. He has a son
named Drake, but everyone around here calls him Digger. I
think he's around fifteen.*

Kate: *How cool is that? You actually know relatives of the
Wright brothers!*

Sydney: *I don't know them. They keep to themselves. The only
time anyone sees Mr. Wright is when he's testing an invention, and Digger only comes out when no one else is around
or when he's helping his dad.*

Elizabeth: *Why do they call him Digger?*

Sydney got up and slid the glass doors closed. It was raining hard
now, and the beach was empty. It was too rainy for ghost crab hunting,
or anything else for that matter. She sat back at the desk.

Sydney: *Because he picks up junk on the beach. I'm not sure
what exactly, but it's usually stuff that washes up on the*

shore. The other morning, Bailey and I saw him stuffing things into his backpack. Sometimes he walks along the water with a strange cart. He fills it with driftwood and stuff, but if he sees anyone coming, he leaves.

Bailey took the computer from Sydney.

Bailey: *I've seen him a couple of times. He's kind of cute. He's tall, thin, and tan, and he has shaggy blond hair. He looks like a surfer.*

McKenzie: *Mmm. What's Mr. Wright like?*

Sydney: *Imagine Santa Claus on a bad day. He's older with a sunburned face, a scruffy white beard, and white hair that hangs over his collar. He always wears a red baseball cap and bib overalls.*

"And cowboy boots," Bailey added.

Sydney: *And cowboy boots. Mr. Wright is an inventor. At least that's what people say. He doesn't talk much. This summer, he's experimenting with cluster ballooning as a green way of transportation.*

Elizabeth: *So in the future, we'll all travel in chairs powered by balloons?*

Sydney: *If Mr. Wright has his way.*

Alexis: *I think your captain fits in with the Wrights, but I can't figure out the missing piece. So far, we have a 100-year-old Captain Swain, a younger Captain Swain who looks like him, a kid who picks up junk on the beach, and an inventor who flies in a chair powered by balloons.*

Bailey was busy thinking. She licked her lips and borrowed the laptop from Sydney.

Bailey: *Maybe they're all modern pirates. Mr. Jones, at the museum, said pirates were still around when the ghost ship disappeared. Maybe Nate Wright has invented a flying machine that scopes out ships at sea. Maybe it has a big hook that snatches the cargo. Then, he drops it on the beach, and Digger picks it up. I'm still not sure what the ghost captain does, though.*

McKenzie: *Maybe they're divers and scavengers. Divers find old shipwrecks and rummage through them looking for stuff to sell. Aren't there tons of old wrecks off the shores of the Outer Banks?*

The rain was falling harder now. It drummed on the roof over Sydney and Bailey's room.

"That's the best theory yet," Sydney said to Bailey. "Don't you think so?"

Bailey was chewing her lower lip. "It makes sense," she answered. "But what about the captain? We still don't know who he is, or how he's involved."

Sydney: *We like your theory, Mac, but how does Captain Swain fit in?*

Kate: *And what about that other guy on the beach, the one the captain was talking to this morning. Do you have any theories about him?*

Elizabeth: *A kid's young voice, or a man's young voice?*

Sydney: *A young man's voice. Lots of boys are around here. It could have been anyone.*

Kate: *Could it have been Digger?*

McKenzie: *I was just going to suggest that.*

Alexis: *I was thinking it too.*

The rain was pelting the windows in the guest room, and Bailey sat watching the water stream down the panes. "What do you think?" Sydney asked her. "Could the voice we heard on the beach this morning have been Drake Wright?"

"I suppose it could," said Bailey. "The only time I've heard him is when he yelled 'Get back' yesterday morning, and I don't really remember what he sounded like."

Sydney sighed. "Well, that would connect the Wrights with the captain. It's an idea worth exploring."

Sydney: *We're not sure, but it might have been. We need to investigate.*

Alexis: *The scavenger theory is beginning to make sense. But we*

*still need to figure out Captain Swain. Do you know anyone
else who knows him?*

Sydney leaned back in her chair and thought.

Sydney: *I don't know many people in the village. I only go there
when I ride my bike. I like to get ice cream at a little restaurant there and hang out by the lighthouse sometimes. I've
never seen the captain before, but I could ask around and
see if anyone knows him.*

Bailey's face lit up. "Hey," she said. "What about the lighthouse lady?"
"Huh?" Sydney asked.
"You know. The lady who gave us the sticker books. You asked her
if she'd seen the captain coming down the stairs, and she said, 'Captain
Swain.' I remember. She used his name."
Sydney remembered too. "You're right! She did use his name, didn't
she? Then she definitely knows who he is. She's new at the lighthouse
this summer, so I didn't even think about her. Good work, Bailey."

Sydney: *Bailey just remembered the lady who takes care of the
lighthouse talked about the captain, so we'll go there tomor-
row and ask her.*
McKenzie: *That's great! If you can find out about him, you'll be
closer to solving the mystery of the lights over the ocean.*
Elizabeth: *I know he's definitely not the ghost of Captain Swain.
I'll pray tonight that you find out your beach isn't haunted
by ghosts or being invaded by aliens.*
Alexis: *Keep us posted. Goodbye for now from Sacramento.*
McKenzie: *And from big sky country.*
Kate: *And from Philly.*

"Well," said Sydney, shutting down her laptop. "It's a good theory
that they might be scavenging old shipwrecks." She turned off the desk
lamp.
"I guess so," said Bailey. "Maybe the lighthouse lady will have some
answers about Captain Swain when we go there tomorrow."

Camp Club Spies

"It's locked," Sydney said. She stood on the lighthouse porch and pulled the door handle. "Maybe storms are coming."

Bailey laid her bike in the grass next to Sydney's and took off her backpack. "I don't think so. I watched the weather this morning. We're in for a bright, sunny day." She threw her backpack on the ground next to Sydney's.

"Everything's still wet from the rain last night," Sydney observed. "There are puddles all over the place."

"And mud," Bailey added. "Look at the mess you're leaving." She pointed to the footprints going up the front steps to the door.

Sydney lifted each foot and checked the bottoms of her tennis shoes. They were wet, but clean. "It's not my mess," she said. "Someone else has been here." She knocked on the lighthouse door, but no one answered.

"The footprints are too big to be the lighthouse lady's," Bailey said. "They're more like boot prints."

Sydney knocked again.

"So now what?" Bailey asked.

"Maybe there's a back door," Sydney replied. She walked down the steps and disappeared around the side of the lighthouse with Bailey close behind.

The lighthouse was attached to a small, brick house. The girls discovered that it had no back door. Instead, where a back door would be, the house was connected to the tower. The sides of the house had several tall windows flanked by green shutters. Each narrow window was made up of ten little panes of glass.

"I wish I could look inside," said Sydney. "But the windows are too high." She jumped up trying to peek in, but still wasn't tall enough.

"Boost me up," said Bailey.

"Huh?"

"Boost me up." Bailey stepped behind Sydney. She grabbed her shoulders and swung her legs around Sydney's hips. Then she stretched her neck to see through the window. "I'm not high enough," she said. Bailey put her feet back on the ground. "Can you boost me up on your shoulders?"

"I can try," said Sydney. She bent over. Bailey climbed onto her shoulders and wrapped her arms around Sydney's neck. Then Sydney stood up and teetered against Bailey's weight. "Can you see anything?" she asked.

"The sun's reflecting off the glass," Bailey answered. "Move me closer."

Sydney took a giant step forward while trying to balance Bailey and keep herself from falling.

Bailey let go of Sydney's neck and rested her hands on each side of the window. She pressed her nose against the glass. The room she was looking at was the office.

"Nobody's in there," she said. "The blue WAIT HERE TO CLIMB sign is in the middle of the room, so the lighthouse must be closed. Hey wait. Someone is moving in there. I see a shadow." For a few seconds, Bailey said nothing. Then she pushed herself off Sydney's shoulders and fell to the ground. "Run!" she said. She got up from the ground and scrambled with Sydney toward a grove of trees.

"What did you see?" Sydney asked as they slipped behind a big evergreen tree.

"It was Nate Wright," Bailey answered. "He had a really long chain and was heading for the curvy staircase. I think he might have seen me."

"*Shhhh,*" said Sydney. "Look."

Nate Wright came around the side of the lighthouse. He was dressed in his bib overalls and red cap, and he looked as scruffy as ever. He stopped and looked left and right. Then as the girls watched through the thick, needled branches, he took off his cap, scratched his head, and walked back toward the front of the lighthouse.

"I think he saw you," Sydney whispered. "I think he was looking around for you."

"Yeah, but he has no idea who I am," said Bailey. "Unless he recognized me from when we watched him cluster ballooning on the beach."

"I doubt it. He was too busy to pay any attention to the crowd."

"So now what?" Bailey asked.

"We find a safe place to watch, far enough away, where we can keep our eyes on the front door. There's no other exit from the building."

Bailey stepped out of the grove of trees and began walking toward the lighthouse. Sydney grabbed her arm and pulled her back. "Where are you going?"

"We have to get our bikes and backpacks," said Bailey.

"Not now," Sydney told her. "We should leave them there. Otherwise, he might see us."

Bailey sighed. "But if we leave them, it's a dead giveaway that we're here."

"We have to take that chance," Sydney answered. "Let's double back through these trees. We'll end up on Schoolhouse Road by the Village Bar-B-Q. Then we can cross the street and watch the lighthouse from there."

Bailey followed Sydney through the trees, along a winding footpath, and over to Schoolhouse Road. They made a wide circle to avoid walking close to the lighthouse. Then they found a park bench not far from the lighthouse museum shop. From there, they could see the lighthouse and its front door.

"Look," said Bailey, pointing upward. "He's up on the lookout."

From where the girls sat, Mr. Wright appeared to be a tiny figure. His red baseball cap made him easy to see. His back was to the heavy, iron railing, and he seemed to be busy doing something, but they couldn't tell what.

"I wish I had my binoculars," Sydney said. "They're in my backpack."

"No problem," said Bailey. "I'll get them."

Before Sydney could stop her, Bailey was running up the brick path toward the lighthouse door. With lightning speed, she snatched Sydney's bike and backpack. Then she hurried back to Sydney.

"There," she said, handing her the backpack. "Mission accomplished." She laid Sydney's bike on the ground.

Sydney unzipped a deep pocket on the outside of the backpack and pulled out her binoculars. Then she put the eyepiece to her eyes, pointed the lens at the lookout, and focused.

"He's pulling on something," she said. "Wait. It's that chain you saw. He's pulling it through the little doorway that leads out to the lookout. Boy, is it ever long! He's already got a bunch of it lying on the floor up there."

"Why do you think he's doing that?" Bailey asked. She squinted, trying to see.

"Beats me," said Sydney. She handed the binoculars to Bailey.

Just then, a rumble came from Schoolhouse Road. Sydney looked in that direction and saw a man driving a small, green tractor. The tractor pulled an open trailer that held a tall, wooden crate. The tractor left the road and turned onto the lighthouse grounds. Sydney watched it weave around the trees and onto the path near where they sat. Then she recognized the driver.

"Bailey, turn away!" she hissed.

"What?" asked Bailey.

"Turn and face me, right now!"

The urgency in Sydney's voice made Bailey do as she was told. She put the binoculars on her lap, turned her body sideways on the bench, and looked at Sydney's back.

"Syd, why are we sitting like this?" she asked.

By now the tractor had passed them and was moving toward the front of the lighthouse. Sydney turned and looked at Bailey. "I didn't want him to recognize us," she said.

"Who to recognize us?" Bailey wondered.

"The man driving the tractor was Captain Swain!" said Sydney.

The captain was barely recognizable without his navy blue clothing. He was dressed in a pair of jeans and a black tee shirt. The only thing that made Sydney sure that it was him was his neat, gray beard and the captain's cap on his head. He drove the tractor to the lighthouse steps and stopped. As the girls watched, Captain Swain walked to the front door, took out a key, and entered.

"Look, he has a key to the lighthouse," said Sydney.

"That's strange," Bailey replied. She handed the binoculars to Sydney. "Why would he have a key? Maybe it's a skeleton key, the kind that opens any old door."

"Hi, Sydney!"

"Hi, Bailey!"

The Kessler twins came from behind them. Each was walking with a tandem bike.

"I didn't know you guys were going to the Village this morning," said Carolyn.

"Me neither," said Marilyn. "What are you doing with those binoculars?"

Sydney wasn't about to tell the Kesslers what was going on. They had a reputation for not being able to keep a secret.

"Sometimes I like bird watching," she said, which was totally true.

"Bird watching!" Marilyn exclaimed.

"Sydney's a nature nut," said Bailey. "At Discovery Lake Camp she was the only camper who knew about every animal in the woods and every bird in the sky. What are you guys doing here?"

"We're going to pick up our brothers," said Carolyn.

"We stopped at the Bar-B-Q first to get root beer," said Marilyn. "Are you guys going to the crab fest tonight?" She rested her bike against the bench where Sydney and Bailey sat.

"What's a crab fest?" Sydney asked. Captain Swain came out of the lighthouse now, and Sydney nudged Bailey with her elbow.

Sydney watched the captain as he unhitched the gate on the trailer. Mr. Wright was still on the lookout, but without using her binoculars Sydney couldn't tell what he was up to.

"So are you going?" said Marilyn.

"Where?" Sydney asked. She was busy watching the captain as he climbed into the trailer and took the straps off the crate.

"To the crab fest!" Marilyn replied.

"Sydney asked you what it is," Carolyn reminded her.

"Oh, yeah," Marilyn said. "The Village is having a crab boil tonight."

"The restaurant is sponsoring it," Carolyn added. "They'll have a big crab dinner—"

"With corn, potatoes, deep-fried onion petals, and homemade cherry pie," said Marilyn.

"And ice cream!" Carolyn said. "And they're having bands and some carnival games. It's to raise money for the lighthouse renovation. That's a good cause, don't you think?" She picked up her tandem and held onto the front handlebars.

"Uh-huh," said Sydney. She noticed that Mr. Wright looked even busier up on the lookout. She nudged Bailey again, and Bailey nudged her back.

"So are you going?" asked Marilyn picking up her bike.

"I'm not sure yet," said Sydney. "We'll let you know." Her fingers were wrapped around the binoculars in her lap. She couldn't wait to look through them to see what Nate Wright was up to.

"It sounds like fun," Bailey said halfheartedly. "So maybe we'll see you later then."

"Okay," said Marilyn, hopping onto her bike and shoving off. "See you later!"

Carolyn got onto her bike and followed, "See you later," she echoed.

Sydney sighed with relief. "I'm glad they're gone."

She already had the binoculars to her eyes. "He's lowering the chain down to the captain." Mr. Wright had the big chain wrapped around a heavy wheel-like machine up on the lookout. He was lowering one end of it to Captain Swain who was standing inside the trailer. Sydney noticed a big hook on the end of the chain.

"What do you think's in the box?" she asked.

"I don't know," Bailey replied. "It's about as tall as I am, so it must be big."

"Too big to carry up that spiral staircase," said Sydney.

Bailey watched. "You know, Syd, I'm wondering where the lighthouse lady is. Do you think she knows what's going on in there?"

"I don't know," Sydney answered. "Captain Swain just hooked the chain onto the crate."

From somewhere above them came the whirring of an engine. Bailey looked up expecting to see a small plane flying overhead, but nothing was in the sky.

"What's that noise?" she asked.

"It's coming from the lookout," said Sydney as the crate lifted off the trailer and up into the air. "Mr. Wright has a gasoline-powered pulley up there. That's what's making the noise. It's lifting the crate to the top of the lighthouse."

Sydney and Bailey took turns with the binoculars watching the crate rise. Mr. Wright guided it over the top of the railing and set it on the narrow floor. Once it was safely secured, Captain Swain went inside.

"He's going up by Mr. Wright," said Sydney. "Now's a good time to get your bike. You watch, and I'll go this time." She handed the binoculars to Bailey before heading up the narrow, brick path. When Sydney got near the door, she heard two men talking inside. She hid next to the porch and listened. One of the voices she recognized as the captain's. The other was the younger voice they'd heard on the beach.

"She's locked up in our equipment shed," said the young man.

"Good," said Captain Swain. "A job well-done, Drake, a job well-done."

Digger! Sydney thought. *He was on the beach with the captain.*

"I've taken care of all the paperwork," Captain Swain continued. "You won't have to keep it a secret anymore. Tonight, I'll help you fix the problem with the rudder. Then you're on your way."

"I'm nervous about people seeing it," Drake answered.

"My boy, an anxious heart weighs a man down," said the captain. "Just me and God talking to you."

Sydney grabbed Bailey's bike and rushed back to the bench. "Drake's in there too!" she told Bailey. "They have someone locked in their equipment shed!"

"Who?" Bailey asked.

"I don't know," Sydney answered. "Drake said, 'She's locked up safe in our equipment shed.' "

"The lighthouse lady!" Bailey gasped. "They've kidnapped her."

"I didn't think of that," Sydney answered as she laid Bailey's bike on the grass. "Do you really think they've kidnapped her? And why would they do that?"

"What else did they say?" Bailey asked as she handed the binoculars to Sydney.

"Tonight, the captain is helping them fix some sort of problem, and then they're leaving. The captain said that after that they'll be on their way." Sydney sat down next to Bailey.

"See," said Bailey. "I *am* right. They're aliens, and Captain Swain is helping them. They're taking the lighthouse lady with them. She's being abducted by aliens!"

Sydney watched while the Wrights and Captain Swain pried open the wooden crate. "Bailey, I still believe that there's a logical explanation for all this. I just don't know what it is yet."

Bailey sighed. "So now what?"

"I think we need to go to the crab fest tonight. We can go to the Wright's place when it's dark out, and then we can see what's going on."

Up on the lookout, the men were lifting something out of the crate.

"It's a big telescope!" Sydney said as she handed the binoculars to Bailey.

"They're setting it up," Bailey observed. "They're attaching it to the railing up there. Now the captain is looking through it. He's looking out at the ocean." Bailey handed the binoculars back to Sydney. "I think they put it there so they can watch for the Mother Ship tonight."

Sydney didn't even bother to argue with Bailey about the alien idea. Mr. Wright was lowering the chain, and the empty crate dropped to the ground.

"I think they're leaving," said Sydney.

The girls waited to see what would happen next. Mr. Wright and Digger were the first to come out the front door. They walked across the grass to Schoolhouse Road. Then they turned west toward home. The captain came out next. He locked the door behind him and started down the front porch stairs. When he got to the bottom, he stopped.

"Oh no, my backpack!" said Bailey.

Captain Swain picked up the backpack and read the name on its ID tag: BAILEY CHANG. He looked around. Then he set the backpack on the lighthouse steps and drove away on his tractor.

Questions

Sydney's grandparents agreed that the crab fest would be a fun activity for the girls. As they got ready to leave, Bailey flung her backpack over her shoulders.

"At least he didn't take it with him," she said. She was talking about what had happened that morning when Captain Swain saw her backpack by the lighthouse porch.

"I'd feel better if your name wasn't on it," said Sydney. "If Mr. Wright saw you looking through the window and described you to the captain, he might have put two and two together."

"I didn't think of that," Bailey answered.

"Let me check in and see if any of the girls have sent anything," Sydney said.

Sure enough, when she logged on the computer, she found a couple of notes on the private wall of the Camp Club Girls' website.

> Alexis: *I watched an old TV show today and it made me think about your problem with the identity of Captain Swain. On the show, two grown-up cousins looked so much alike that they were mistaken for twins. Sometimes that happens—a family resemblance may be strong in several people, even if they're not brothers and sisters, or children of the person they look like.*
>
> *We know the original Captain Swain didn't have any sons, so your Captain Swain couldn't be his son. But maybe he's a cousin of the original Captain Swain or something.*
>
> Kate: *I've been thinking about Captain Swain too. Bailey, I'm like Beth—I don't believe in ghosts. And ghosts don't own*

property—according to the law, no dead people can own property. But I looked on the internet and found that there's a Captain Swain with the address of Duck, North Carolina. When I googled Duck, I found out it's just south of Corolla. So it sounds like your Captain Swain is a legitimate resident of the area!

"Sounds like one mystery is solved, anyway," Sydney said.

"I don't know," Bailey said. "It sounds convincing, but I think I'm going to confront Captain Swain and ask him for myself."

Sydney grinned. Sometimes Bailey was so dramatic!

"Well, come on," Sydney said. "Maybe you'll see him at the crab fest and you can ask him there!"

By the time the girls arrived in Corolla Village, the sun had just set. A crowd had gathered at the Corolla Village Bar-B-Q where glowing paper lanterns were strung from tree to tree. On the front lawn, steam rose from a huge, black pot over a fire. Two cooks from the restaurant dumped buckets full of crabs into the boiling water. Then they added Old Bay seasoning, ears of corn, onions, and small new potatoes.

"Yum, that smells good," said Bailey. On a small stage, at the edge of the parking lot, the Wild Horse Band was playing a tune. Bailey grabbed Sydney's hands and swung her around in time with the music.

"Woo-hoo! Let's hear it for the crab fest!" Bailey squealed.

As the girls spun, Sydney glimpsed the Kessler twins arriving with their brothers and mom and dad.

"The twins are here," she told Bailey when the music stopped. "We probably have to hang out with them, but we need to get away to investigate the Wrights' place. Listen, don't say anything about what we're up to, okay? They can't keep a secret."

"Have they seen us?" Bailey asked.

"I don't think so," said Sydney.

"Then why don't we go over to the Wrights' now? We can see what's going on and then come back here and hang out with the twins."

Sydney agreed, and soon she and Bailey were walking up School-house Road in the direction of the sound. When they got to Persimmon Street, they saw a narrow, sandy road marked PRIVATE DRIVE.

"This must be it," said Sydney. She remembered her grandmother saying the Wrights lived on a wooded, private road off Persimmon. "Gram knows a potter who lives on this road, and the Wrights' place is just beyond hers. It's at the end of the drive, I think."

The girls turned onto the sandy lane and walked along the edge of the woods.

"I wish we had a flashlight," said Bailey. The only light came from porch lights along the way. The road was barely wide enough for two cars to pass, and it was deserted. Either all the residents were at the crab fest or they were inside their houses.

Bailey noticed that these houses weren't like most others on the Outer Banks. These were old-fashioned, two-story cottages with narrow front porches and gabled roofs. They looked like they had been there forever.

Who-who-whooooo-who-who. A great-horned owl called from a distant tree.

"I feel like I'm back at Discovery Lake Camp," said Bailey. "This place is spooky. It's so dark and deserted. Syd, are you sure you want to do this?"

"Look. Here's the potter's house," said Sydney. At the edge of the road, an old, tin mailbox sat atop a lovely statue of a mermaid. The name on the box said WILMA HEISER, POTTERY PLUS.

"The Wrights' place has to be over there." She pointed ahead to a sharp bend in the road.

"Listen!"

A loud rumble came from behind them. Some sort of vehicle had just turned off Persimmon Street and onto the private drive.

"Someone's coming. We have to hide!"

Sydney grabbed Bailey and pulled her behind some tall bushes in the potter's front yard. They could see the road.

Thud-thud. . .thud-thud. . .rumble. . .thud-thud. . .thud-thud. . . rumble. . . Whatever it was grew closer. It chugged along slowly, its headlights illuminating the sand. Soon, the girls saw a big, yellow wall. They could almost touch the school bus as it lumbered by, and in the darkness, they could barely make out the words:

LASERS
LEVITATING
ELEVATING
WRIGHT &
SON
ORIENTEERING
RACING

"It's the Roswell bus," Bailey whispered. She and Sydney watched it disappear around the bend at the end of the road. "What do we do now?"

"Let's wait a few minutes," Sydney answered. "Until we're sure they're inside."

Soon the girls heard the sounds of hammering and sawing coming from the Wrights' place. Cautiously, they walked to the bend in the road and, keeping in the cover of the trees, they got close enough to see the Wrights' equipment shed. It was set about fifteen yards away from the grungy old house that Mr. Wright and Digger lived in.

The equipment shed was almost as big as the house, and its heavy front doors were wide open. A shower of sparks rained inside.

"Welding," said Sydney. "They must be working on the whatever-it-is."

An eerie, blue glow came from fluorescent lights hanging from the rafters, and a strong smell of hot steel wafted through the air.

The noise stopped for a few seconds. After a ghostly silence, the inside of the shed went dark.

"Look!" Bailey exclaimed. The shed lit up with flashing lights, first red, and then multicolored. "It's the spaceship. Remember? I said that they were reconstructing their ship from parts Digger found on the beach. Now do you believe me?"

Sydney had to admit that they were looking at something very strange. "Let's get closer so we can see what's going on," she said.

"I wish we had that listening thing Kate has," said Bailey. "You know, that little gadget that lets you hear a conversation from a block away? Then we could know what's happening without having to go right up to the building. Syd, do you think they have the lighthouse lady locked up in there?"

"I don't know," her friend replied. "But we're going to find out."

She took Bailey by the hand and they crept along the side of the road, careful to stay in the shadows. A soft whirring sound came from the shed now, and Sydney and Bailey made a wide circle, staying clear of the open doors. Then they tiptoed to the side of the shed, just below the window.

"I don't think it's safe to look inside just yet," Sydney said. "We should listen for a while."

She'd barely gotten the words out when the colored lights stopped and a bright, white light started to flash. One, two, three, four, five flashes. Then nothing. One, two, three, four, five more.

"It's that code from *Close Encounters of the Third Kind!*" Bailey whispered. "That's the light we saw in the ocean yesterday morning."

The flashing stopped. For a few seconds, the shed went dark again. Then it was suddenly lit up by the overhead lights and the bluish fluorescent glow.

"Well, the signal lights work fine," the girls heard Digger say. "I wish I could program the other lights to change color so opponents can disguise themselves. It would add more strategy to the battle. Imagine that you're approaching a friendly craft, but when you get there, you find it's an enemy craft disguised as a friend."

The girls sat on the ground beneath the window with their backs pressed against the side of the building. Sydney could hear Bailey breathing fast and heavy. She felt her own muscles growing more tense.

Relax, Syd, she told herself. *Think! There has to be a logical explanation.*

Bailey whispered so softly that Sydney could barely hear her.

"Maybe they're not trying to get home to their planet," she said. "It sounds like they're going to wage war on an enemy spaceship, or something. Syd, they're planning a space war!"

"I doubt it, Bailey," Sydney whispered back. "You know at the lighthouse they said something about Captain Swain helping with the rudder. A rudder is part of a boat. Could that be some sort of funky boat?"

"That's a great idea," Mr. Wright boomed out. The girls jumped. Then as he continued, they realized he wasn't talking to them but to Digger. "But if I were you, son, I'd leave the lights alone for now. Save changing the colors for Phase Two. Hit 'em with what you've got. Then, after it takes off, surprise 'em with something even better."

"I guess you're right, Dad," said Digger.

"See? They're planning to strike with some sort of weapon," Bailey whispered. "It probably has to do with that coffee mug thing that we found on the beach."

Sydney was feeling very vulnerable sitting under the window. If anyone came along, they would surely see the girls. She noticed a brown tarp in the grass nearby. Staying close to the ground, she shimmied over and pulled it back to where Bailey sat.

"Here, let's cover up with this," she said, draping it over herself and Bailey.

"The noise problem is fixed now," Mr. Wright was saying. "When these crafts are on the ocean at night, the folks near the beach won't hear them. So there won't be any trouble."

"And I've got the hover fan working fine now," said Digger. "As soon as the craft hits the beach, a blast of air lifts it off the ground, and you can go anywhere without it being heard."

Bailey linked her arm with Sydney's.

"That was the puff of air that we felt on the beach!" she said. "Drake Wright went past us in the dark with that thing just a few yards away from us. Do you think he saw us?"

"I'm almost sure of it," Sydney answered. "Now we know the Wrights are responsible for those strange lights over the water."

"I'm telling you, it's a spacecraft!" Bailey insisted.

The word *hover* brought a picture in Sydney's mind.

"Listen, Bailey!" she exclaimed. "The word *hover*. . .one day at home, I thought I saw something just floating around outside my window. When I looked out, it was a remote-controlled helicopter one of my friends was flying. Do you think this is some sort of remote-controlled device? Like a spaceship-shaped, remote-controlled thing?"

"No. How could they fly it in the dark?" Bailey said.

"I'm going to text Kate," Sydney said, wiggling around to pull the phone out of her pocket. "She'll be able to tell us if it's at least possible."

Sydney had started texting when the sound of a hammer pounding against metal startled the girls. Digger said, "We need to get this rudder fixed. When that's done we can load her up."

The pounding started again.

"See, they do have the lighthouse lady," Bailey said. "I hope she's all right. They're planning to load her onto the spacecraft."

Sydney didn't answer. Her mind was racing trying to come up with answers for her questions. "*Test the spirits to see whether they are from God.*" She remembered hearing her pastor preach about that in church. As Sydney sat there thinking, she believed more than ever that Mr. Wright and Drake Wright were not space aliens.

"You know if it's some sort of boat—since rudders are part of boats—they always call boats 'she,' " Sydney explained.

"Cap has the paperwork done and everything is in order," Mr. Wright said. "It's up to you now, son. You have to get it out there for the right person to see. Plenty of investors are vacationing in Corolla and the other subdivisions around here. If you show it around, surely you'll find a backer or two."

"Huh?" Bailey whispered to Sydney under the tarp. "What are they talking about now?"

"Beats me," Sydney answered.

Listen, said a little voice in her head.

"We should just listen," she told Bailey.

"You have to get the word out," Mr. Wright continued. "I'm not going to help you this time, son. If you're going to be successful, you need to get out there with people and show them what you're up to. Why, think about our cousins. Some people thought they were crazy to keep jumping off cliffs with their flying machine, but they didn't let that get to them. They kept at it, and today—"

"But, Dad," Digger said, "I don't think I can do it. Besides, I don't mind keeping to myself. I like having time alone to wander and pick up stuff on the beach that we can sell to scrap yards. Last night, I found another doubloon for the Cap. He likes giving them to the kids at the lighthouse, you know."

The girls heard a few more strikes of the hammer against metal.

"Are you going to spend the rest of your life selling junk you find on the beach?" Mr. Wright asked his son. "Or are you going to face your fear and live the life God gave you. Remember what the Cap always says."

"'I can do all things through Him who strengthens me,'" Digger replied.

"That's what Captain Swain said to me when I was afraid to climb the lighthouse," Bailey whispered.

"I know," Sydney answered. "I want to look inside and see what's going on."

"Me too," Bailey said. "But I'm scared."

The girls stood, still wrapped in the tarp. They dropped it around their shoulders and peeked through the dirty window.

"Oh my." Bailey gasped.

"Awesome," Sydney exclaimed in a whisper.

In the center of the shed sat a vehicle beyond her imagination. It was about the size of a small car, but round. It was painted a soft gray-blue, the color of the ocean on an overcast day. The paint sparkled the way sunlight dances on waves.

In the center of the craft a cockpit was covered with a clear glass bubble. It reminded Sydney of pictures she'd seen in school textbooks of fighter jets. As she watched, Digger climbed into the cockpit and flipped a switch. The flashing colored lights encircled the craft and spun around its middle. Drake Wright sat in the driver's seat and grinned.

"What do you think it is?" Bailey asked.

"I don't know," Sydney replied. "It's not like anything I've seen in my whole life. It's kind of beautiful."

"But scary too," Bailey added.

"Maybe it wouldn't be if we knew what it was," said Sydney.

A muted *whoosh* came from the craft. It sounded like a choir softly singing *"Shhhhhh..."*

As Bailey and Sydney watched, the machine rose off the ground. It hovered several feet above the floor. Then it slowly began to rotate. It spun around faster and faster, and the girls heard Digger laughing gleefully. Slowly, it stopped and dropped gently back to the floor. Drake opened the cover on the cockpit and said, "Well, if it doesn't make it as a water sport, maybe I can market it as a carnival ride."

Mr. Wright chuckled. "You're a Wright, my boy," he said. "You always have a backup plan."

Sydney motioned to Bailey to sit. The girls sank back to the ground and covered themselves with the tarp.

"Now I'm really confused," said Bailey. "I'm not so sure it's a space-ship anymore, are you?"

"I was never sure it was a spaceship," said Sydney. "I just don't know what it is yet."

She started to crawl out from under the tarp again.

"What are you doing now?" Bailey asked.

"Stay put," Sydney answered. She crawled to the window. When she was sure the Wrights had their backs to her, she took several photos of the contraption. Then she climbed back under the tarp.

"I didn't use the flash," she said. "I think it's bright enough in there for the pictures to turn out." She looked at the display on her phone and saw she was right. The photos were clear enough to show the craft in the middle of the equipment shed floor.

"Now what?" Bailey asked.

"I'm texting Kate," Sydney replied. "And sending her these pictures. You know how smart she is about technological stuff. She might know what this is."

SYDNEY: K8, WE'RE HIDING OUT NEXT TO THE WRIGHTS' EQUIP-MENT SHED. LOOK AT THESE PICTURES. THEY'VE BUILT THIS THING. IT HAS FLASHING LIGHTS THAT SPIN AROUND IT. IT CAN HOVER A FEW FEET OFF THE FLOOR AND IT ROTATES REALLY FAST. WHAT IS IT?

Sydney sent the message and stuck her phone back in her pocket.

"I don't think the Wrights are aliens," she told Bailey. "It looks like that thing is just another one of their crazy inventions. But what is it?"

"Digger said something about a water sport," said Bailey.

"I don't think a water sport would be remote-controlled," Sydney said reluctantly. "And we'll wait to hear back from Kate, but I think anything that is as big as that would be too heavy to be remote-controlled. . ."

"Unless the battery was as big as a bus!" Bailey said.

"Hmm. Could they have a giant battery in that bus of theirs?" Sydney asked. "Nah. I don't think that's the answer."

"But they talked about battles and enemies. That doesn't fit with any water sport I know of. And what about the lighthouse lady? Where has she disappeared to? And then there's Captain Swain. Who do you think he *really* is? And where is he? Wasn't he supposed to be here helping the Wrights tonight?"

"I'm right here, Bailey Chang," said a voice in the darkness. "And I can answer all of your questions."

Answers

Bailey and Sydney crawled out from under the tarp.

Captain Swain stood in the shadows looking at them. He was still wearing jeans, as he had been that morning, and now he had on a sweatshirt that said NAVY on its front. His captain's cap sat squarely on his head.

"What are you girls doing here?" he asked gently.

"You answer our question first," said Bailey. "Who are you, really?"

"You know who I am, Bailey Chang," said the captain. "I'm Captain Nathan Swain."

"No you're not!" Sydney answered. "Captain Nathan Swain is dead. We saw his picture in an old paper. He was the lighthouse keeper here about a hundred years ago, so you can't be him unless you're an imposter."

"Or a ghost!" Bailey added.

"Well, I don't think you're a ghost," Sydney said with a smile. "But Captain Nathan Swain, the lighthouse keeper, didn't have any sons, so you can't be his son. But I suspect you're another relative."

The captain smiled. "Kudos. Congratulations to you for figuring it out, Miss Sydney Lincoln. Captain Nathan Swain, the lighthouse keeper, was my uncle," he said. "I resemble him, but I can assure you, Miss Bailey Chang, that I'm *not* his ghost. Now, as far as being an imposter, Sydney Lincoln, I'll admit to that. I sometimes masquerade as my uncle."

"Why?" Sydney asked.

Before the captain could answer, Bailey interrupted.

"If you're for real, why did you disappear when we were at the top of the lighthouse?" She climbed out from the tarp and stood up. "One minute you were there, and then you were gone. And the same thing happened on the beach. You were there walking your dog, we talked to you, and then you disappeared. What's up with that?"

The captain leaned against the side of the equipment shed.

"Bailey, my girl, you have quite the imagination. I'm sorry if you thought I had abandoned you. Once you girls were safe on the lookout, I hurried to an appointment I was already late for. I should have said farewell, at least. I sincerely apologize for being rude." He tipped the brim of his cap. "As for the incident on the beach, McTavish saw a cat and ran off. I ran after him. McTavish is a good boy, you know, but he hates cats and would do harm to one if he caught it. I'm sure by the time you looked for me, I was chasing my dog across the dunes."

The clues were beginning to add up for Sydney. There was no ghost of Captain Nathan Swain, and she was certain the captain wasn't helping the Wrights build a spaceship.

"But you were wearing a captain's uniform at the lighthouse," she said, getting off the ground. "The kind captains wore years and years ago."

"I was acting," said the captain. "I volunteer at the lighthouse where I play the role of Captain Nathan Swain, the lighthouse keeper. When schoolchildren tour, I tell them the story of the lighthouse and about the pirates and shipwrecks of the Outer Banks. In fact, years ago, I *did* work in the lighthouse, helping maintain the beacon up top."

Bailey was beginning to feel a bit foolish for thinking that the captain was a ghost, but she still had some unanswered questions.

"So why were you on the beach yesterday morning with Digger?" she asked. "We heard you talking with him about not putting *the vehicle* in the water until after I went home. What exactly is he up to, and what's that thing in the shed?"

The captain shook his head. " 'Let the words of my mouth be acceptable in Your sight, O Lord. . .' Just me and God talking out loud," he said. "I know that folks around here call him Digger, but Drake Wright is the young man's name. And Bailey, before I tell you what young Mr. Wright and I were discussing yesterday morning, why don't you tell me why you girls are hiding here in the dark."

Bailey sighed. She was almost certain her theory about space aliens and space wars was wrong. "We thought. . .well, actually *I* thought the Wrights were space aliens and you were helping them get back to the Mother Ship after their spacecraft crashed into the ocean. I thought Digger, I mean Drake, was picking up pieces of the spacecraft along the beach and that the Wrights were rebuilding it in their equipment shed.

And I think they've kidnapped the lighthouse lady. I thought they were going to take her to wherever with them. We're spying on them to find out what's going on."

The captain chuckled. "And you, Miss Lincoln, do you believe in aliens from outer space?"

"I guess I always thought there was a logical explanation," Sydney said. "But I agree with Bailey that a lot of things are happening that just don't add up. Why did you and the Wrights put a telescope on the lighthouse lookout this morning?"

The captain chuckled again. "That telescope is part of the lighthouse renovation. It's there so visitors can view the ocean from the tower. And, Bailey Chang, the lighthouse lady—I assume you mean the young woman who works at the lighthouse and is named Meghan Kent, by the way. She's—"

"Wait, don't tell me," Sydney said. "She's just taking a day off and when the Wrights were referring to 'she' they meant their invention."

"Again, cheers to you, Sydney Lincoln," said Captain Swain. "Miss Meghan Kent is on vacation for a few days while some remodeling takes place. People who are vacationing here don't stop to think that sometimes we natives need vacations ourselves!"

The captain paused and smiled at the girls.

"Come on inside," said the captain. "There are a couple of fellows I'd like you to meet."

The girls walked with Captain Swain around the side of the equipment shed and through the open front doors. Drake turned and greeted the captain with a smile, but when he saw the girls, his smile faded. "Oh," he said, softly.

Mr. Wright walked toward them wiping his hands on a rose-colored rag.

"Hi, Cap." He greeted his friend with a handshake. "I see you've brought some visitors." His voice held a hint of disapproval, and his blue eyes flashed at Sydney and then at Bailey.

"It's all right, Nate," said the captain. "These are my friends and they can be trusted. This is Sydney Lincoln and Bailey Chang." His right hand swept toward the girls.

"You're the kid who looked at me through the lighthouse window this morning," Mr. Wright said gruffly.

"I'm sorry, Mr. Wright," Bailey apologized.

"The girls have been watching us test Drake's invention, and they're curious to know more about it," the captain said.

Sydney noticed that Drake's face had turned a bright shade of red. He looked shyly down at his feet as he stood next to the mysterious craft. Sydney walked up to him with a smile, "Hi, Drake," she said, extending her hand. "It's very nice to meet you."

Drake Wright looked up, but not directly into Sydney's eyes. He grasped the tips of her fingers, gave them a little shake, and then dropped his hand to his side. "I've seen you around," he mumbled.

"Drake, why don't you tell the girls about the Wright D-94 Wave Smasher?" said the captain. "It's okay to talk about it now. You own the patent. I have the paperwork to prove it."

Drake swallowed hard. He looked more embarrassed than ever.

"Go on, son," Mr. Wright encouraged him. "Tell them what this is."

"Yeah," Bailey said, stroking the shiny blue paint. "We can't wait to know."

When Drake saw Bailey's hand touch the paint on the D-94, he stopped looking embarrassed. "Please don't touch it," he said firmly.

Bailey quickly pulled her hand away and stepped backward. "Why? What's it going to do?"

"It's not going to do anything," Drake answered. He pulled a rag out of the back pocket of his blue jeans and polished the spot Bailey had touched. "I just finished waxing it."

"Oh," said Bailey.

"So tell us about this," Sydney said. She walked around the craft so she could see it from all sides. "You were talking about a rudder. Let me guess. This is a new form of transportation."

Drake said nothing.

"'I can do all things through Him who strengthens me,'" Captain Swain said. "Just me and God talking, Drake." He walked over to the young man and put his arm around his shoulder. "Think of this as a rehearsal. Tell them about the next great Wright invention, the one that's destined to change life on the Outer Banks forever."

Drake looked at his feet for a few seconds. Then he took a deep breath and began what sounded like a well-rehearsed speech. "This is a vehicle called the Wright D-94 Wave Smasher. It's a new recreational water vehicle that I've been working on for the past several years. The D-94 is unlike any other recreational water vehicle because it can ride on the water or sail up to thirty feet above it with the flick of a switch. It's built tough enough to withstand a ten-foot wave, and the driver is completely protected in the cockpit, so he won't get hurt or wet."

"Or *she*," Bailey corrected him. "Girls can use it too, right?"

When Bailey saw Drake's shy smile she was positive that he fell into the "cute" category.

"Yes, girls can use it too," Drake answered. "But it's not a toy. It's for professional sportsmen—I mean sports people," he corrected himself.

"So why did you invent it?" Sydney asked.

"Well," Drake went on, "you can travel up and down the Outer Banks and see all sorts of fun things to do on the water. You can kite sail, hang glide, water ski, kayak, sail a boat. . .there are all kinds of activities. But there's nothing like the D-94. In the daytime, it's a superfast racing boat. You can zoom across the water, leap over waves, and even hover or sail up to thirty feet above the water. In fact, it even works on the beach. You just press a button, and it becomes a hover craft that rides on a cushion of air, or it can walk on its feet." He pushed a button, and four tennis-racket shaped platforms came out of the bottom of the craft.

"So *you* made those strange footprints and passed us on the beach," said Sydney. "You scared us half to death."

"Sorry about that." Drake smiled. "But I didn't think anyone would be out that early in the morning. I've had to be real careful so no one stole my idea until Cap here got me the patent."

"So you only tested it at night?" Bailey asked.

"Yeah," Drake answered. "But there's a reason for that. That D-94 is not only a daytime recreational water vehicle, it's actually a very expensive game piece."

"Huh?" asked Sydney.

"Well, you see," Drake said, "I've also invented a new water sport." He walked over to one wall of the equipment shed and pointed to a big drawing on a sheet of paper stuck to the wall. "Come over here," he said.

When the girls got closer, they saw the drawing looked like a football field off the shore of the ocean. There were pictures of D-94s positioned on the field and a goal post on either end.

"I don't have a catchy name for it yet," said Drake, "but it's all done with lights. Players compete on teams, and the goal is to get all your D-94s safely into your end zone. You play in the dark on an imaginary field on the ocean. A floating string of lights outlines both end zones. The only other lights are on the D-94s. The lights can be stationary or flashing, and they're used as a way to signal plays to other members of your team."

"Baseball players use hand signals, and in this game, the players use light signals instead," said Sydney.

"Yeah, that's right," Drake said, looking like his confidence was growing.

"Wow, this is so cool!" said Sydney. Just then, her cell phone started to vibrate. She excused herself and read a text from Kate. I THINK IT LOOKS TOO HEAVY TO BE A REMOTE-CONTROL DEVICE. I GOOGLED NATE WRIGHT. HE HAS A REPUTATION FOR CREATIVE FORMS OF TRANSPORTATION, SO I WOULD GUESS THAT IT'S AN EXPERIMENT THAT HAS SOMETHING TO DO WITH THAT. INVENTORS ARE OFTEN HUSH-HUSH UNTIL THEY HAVE THE KINKS OF THEIR EXPERIMENTS WORKED OUT AND UNTIL THEY GET A PATENT. B CAREFUL! K8

Sydney texted back: YOU'RE RIGHT. IT'S A WRIGHT D-94 WAVE SMASHER. MORE LATER.

"Can you imagine how awesome a game would look from the beach?" Bailey asked. "With all those lights scooting around and flying over the water?"

"I can," Sydney answered. "It was pretty exciting when we thought your D-94 was a UFO. People are going to love watching these things at night."

Mr. Wright was standing near his son, grinning. "And Drake here has taken extra-special care to make sure that it runs quietly so it doesn't disturb the residents. They already think we're crazy, you know. They don't get it that some of the craziest-looking ideas might change the world someday."

"Like the Wright brothers' flying machine," said Bailey.

"That's *right!*" said Captain Swain. Everyone laughed. "Girls," he said with a serious tone. "Always remember: 'Do not judge according to appearance, but judge with righteous judgement.' That's just me and God talking to you," he said.

"You like to quote God, don't you?" said Sydney.

"I do," the captain replied. "His Bible gives me the words, and I just speak them aloud."

"Just like our friend Bettyboo," Bailey answered. "She likes to quote scripture verses too." She walked over and stood next to Drake. He was about a foot taller than she was, and he had deep brown eyes. She was happy that he finally looked at her instead of down at his feet. "What are your plans for the D-94?" she asked.

Drake clammed up again, and his face turned red. Sydney noticed that he looked very uncomfortable. "Drake, I'm sorry for not getting to know you sooner, and even sorrier that I was suspicious of you and your dad."

"Me too," Bailey agreed. "I guess I let my imagination get the best of me."

Nate Wright took off his cap and scratched his head. "Imagination isn't a bad thing," he said. "Don't be sorry for letting it go when it wants to run, but remember that you have to reign it in once in a while. Otherwise, it *will* get the best of you."

"I'll remember, Mr. Wright," Bailey said. "So, how about it, Drake, what are you going to do with the D-94?"

Drake sat on some tires stacked in a corner of the shed. "Well," he said. "Dad and the captain think I need to promote it. You know, get it out there in the ocean in the daytime and show it off. They both think people are living in Corolla Light who have the money to back my invention and get it into the hands of the right people."

"Like companies that build recreational water vehicles and race boats and stuff?" Sydney asked. An idea was beginning to form in her head.

"Yeah, exactly," Drake replied. "Know anybody?"

It was a rhetorical question. He didn't really expect an answer, but Sydney had one for him.

"Mr. Kessler," she said.

"Who?" Mr. Wright asked.

"The Kessler twins' dad," said Sydney. "They have a house near my grandparents' place. Mr. Kessler runs a company that builds race boats and other water vehicles. I'm sure he'd be interested in seeing the Wright D-94 Wave Smasher."

"'God works for the good of those who love Him,'" said Captain Swain, smiling. "Where can we find Mr. Kessler?"

"They're in the Village at the crab fest," said Bailey. "The whole family is there. I think we should all go over there and find them, before the crab boil and all the stuff that goes with it is eaten up."

"And if you want an audience at the beach when you show off your invention, you only have to tell the Kessler twins about it. They're terrible at keeping secrets," said Sydney.

The Wrights washed up in an old sink in the equipment shed while the girls and the captain waited.

"I have a couple more questions, if you don't mind," said Bailey.

"Go ahead," Mr. Wright told her.

"Well, are the words on your bus a secret code?"

"Bailey!" Sydney scolded.

"Why would you even think that?" asked Drake.

Bailey felt a little embarrassed, but she wanted answers. "If you read the first letters of the words backward they spell *Roswell*, like that place in New Mexico where the spaceship crashed back in 1947. I thought maybe your invention was a UFO."

Drake laughed out loud.

"Okay, call me silly," said Bailey. "But what is that weird coffee mug that lights up inside. We heard you say that it belongs to you. I thought it was an alien weapon."

Drake looked at her wide-eyed. "A what! It's no weapon. It's my idea for a pinhole flashlight that's magnetically powered," he said. "It's another invention I'm working on. I'm hoping someday it'll be a fun thing for kids to use when they go ghost-crab hunting."

"Okay," Bailey said, slapping him on the shoulder. "You've passed the Camp Club Girls' interrogation. You and your dad are definitely *not* from outer space. Now, let's go find the Kesslers."

CHAPTER 12

The Wright D-94 Wave Smasher

Hi, Camp Club Girls.

Well, last night, at the Wrights' equipment shed, we solved the mysteries of the UFO and Captain Swain. The Wrights aren't space aliens, and Captain Swain isn't a ghost.

Drake has invented an awesome water vehicle called the Wright D-94 Wave Smasher (pictures attached). That's what we've seen over the water at night. He's been testing it. It's also what made the footprints on the beach and whooshed by us that day. Captain Swain helped Drake get a patent on it. The D-94 can race like a speedboat, jump waves, and hover or fly about 30 feet over the water. And Drake invented a new water sport to go with it. He doesn't have a name for it yet, but it's played in the dark, and the lights on the vehicle have a lot to do with the strategy of how its played.

Drake is really shy (Bailey says to tell you he's really cute too). He was nervous about showing his invention to anyone. We convinced him he has to or else he'll never sell it and become famous like his distant cousins the Wright brothers. So tonight he'll demonstrate the wave smasher at the beach. One of our neighbors runs a company that makes racing boats. I introduced him to Drake last night, and he can't wait to see the D-94 in action. Bailey and I are going to the beach now to watch.

That's all we know. Mystery solved. The only question that's still hanging out there is: What really happened to the sailors on the Carroll A. Deering? *Nobody knows for sure.*

Maybe you guys can all come here next summer, and we can crack that case together.

All for now,
Sydney

P.S. from Bailey: I'm really sorry that I called Drake "Digger." The captain said, "Do not judge according to appearances, but judge with righteous judgement." I think Drake Wright and his dad are awesome! Oh, and we forgot to tell you, Captain Swain is the nephew of the old Captain Swain, the lighthouse keeper. He dresses like the old captain when he volunteers at the lighthouse. Syd says to tell you the lighthouse lady is on vacation. Aliens did not abduct her.

Sydney put her binoculars and cell phone into her backpack, zipped it shut, and slung it over her shoulder. "Let's go," she said to Bailey.

Bailey went into the bathroom to check herself out in the mirror. She smoothed her straight, black hair and applied strawberry lip gloss to her thin, pale lips. "Can I use some of your banana-coconut body spray?" she asked Sydney.

"Sure," Sydney agreed.

Bailey spritzed some onto her arms and her neck. "So, do you think he's going to buy it?" she asked.

"Who?" Sydney wondered.

"Do you think that the twins' dad is going to buy Drake's idea?"

"I really think he might," Sydney answered. "He sure liked the Wave Smasher when he saw it in the Wrights' equipment shed, and since we gave the twins the job of spreading the word around Corolla, I think people will come out to see it."

Bailey took one last look in the mirror. Then she picked up her backpack and slipped her arms through its straps. "Okay, let's go," she said.

At twilight, the girls walked down the beach to Tuna Street. A crowd was starting to gather. Families spread blankets in the sand and sipped bottles of water. Several big floodlights were there to illuminate the beach, and a small set of bleachers was set up for special guests who might want to buy Drake's invention. The Wrights' bus was parked at the end of the access road. Drake, his dad, and the captain were rolling the D-94 out of a trailer that was hitched onto the back bumper. When Captain Swain saw the girls, he tipped the brim of his cap. "Good evening, young ladies," he said.

"Hi, Captain. Hi, Drake!" Bailey said, brightly.

"Hi," Drake responded without looking up.

"A lot of people are here," Sydney said as she noticed more curious onlookers arriving in cars, on bikes, and on foot. Several men in business suits, looking quite out of place, stood at the end of Tuna Street talking with Mr. Kessler. "I guess Carolyn and Marilyn got busy getting the word out."

"I guess *so*," Drake replied.

Bailey saw that he seemed nervous. "Hey, just imagine you're one of the Wright brothers," she said. "I'm sure they drew a big crowd with their flying machine. It's your turn now, Drake. Trust me. They'll love you."

The corners of Drake's lips curled into a tiny smile. "I don't want them to love me," he said. "I just want them to love my D-94."

"That too!" said Bailey.

"My boy," the captain said. "This is your shining moment. I don't think we should just launch the craft without a fanfare. Why, when they launch a ship there are speeches, and sometimes they even smash a bottle on the bow—"

"I don't want anything smashed on my invention!" Drake exclaimed.

"No, no, I didn't mean that." The captain chuckled. "I just think that we should make this an occasion. Do you still have that megaphone in the bus?"

Drake's face turned beet red.

"It's under the driver's seat," Mr. Wright said. "I agree with you, Cap. We should make this special."

Drake gulped. "Do I have to do all the talking? I mean do I have to tell everybody about my invention?"

"No," said the captain. "I'll introduce you as the inventor and give a brief account of what you are about to show them. I think, for now, we should keep the water sport part to ourselves. That's something that you can discuss privately with Mr. Kessler and his friends. You can meet with them after the demonstration and answer their questions."

The captain went to the bus to get the megaphone.

By now, the crowd was trying to push toward the Wrights to get a better look at the shiny machine. "Get back, please!" Nate Wright shouted. Everyone took a giant step backward. Before long, the beach security team showed up and stretched a line of yellow tape between two posts that they pounded into the sand. They patrolled the line, telling onlookers to stay behind the line. The Kessler twins showed up, and the officers let them through.

"We told security that they'd better get down here," said Carolyn.

"We told them to hurry, because we needed crowd control," Marilyn added. "Tons of people are here already!"

The only time Sydney had seen the beach more packed was on the Fourth of July. "How many people did you tell?" she asked.

"Hundreds!" said Carolyn.

"At least!" added Marilyn. "When we got home from the crab fest last night, we printed up flyers on our computer. We told everyone to come down here at eight o'clock tonight because a UFO was going to be on the beach."

"We used up two big packs of paper—" said Carolyn.

"And a whole black ink cartridge," said Marilyn. "Then we got up early this morning and started putting them in all the mailboxes."

"And after that, we went to the shopping centers," said Carolyn. "And we stuck flyers under the windshield wipers of all the cars in the parking lots."

"But then a guy came out and told us not to do it anymore, so we left," said Marilyn.

Captain Swain stepped out of the bus with the megaphone in his hand. He turned it on and pointed it toward the crowd. "Testing one, two, three, four. Testing." His deep voice boomed across the beach. He turned the megaphone off.

"I thought you didn't like crowds, Captain," Sydney said.

"I don't," the captain replied. "But this is an historical day. Why, once people see the Wrights as serious twenty-first-century inventors, we can only imagine how their inventions will someday change the world."

As twilight faded to darkness, Mr. Kessler and his friends ducked under the yellow tape. The twins' dad wore khaki shorts, a white tee shirt, and flip-flops. His friends were obviously not as prepared for the beach. They had taken off their suit coats, rolled their pants legs above their knees, and were barefoot. "Let's get this show on the road," Mr. Kessler said. "Are you ready, Drake?"

"Yes, sir," Drake replied.

Mr. Kessler and his friends joined several others who were seated on the bleachers.

Bailey was at Drake's side now. She stood on her tiptoes and whispered to him. "You can do it. Just keep repeating to yourself, 'I can do all things through Him who strengthens me.' That's what I did when I climbed the lighthouse."

Drake's face turned redder than ever.

The captain flipped a switch inside the bus, and floodlights wired from the bus turned the beach from darkness to daylight. He then walked to the front of the crowd and stood with the megaphone in his hands. "Ladies and gentlemen, boys and girls, may I please have your undivided attention?"

A hush fell over the crowd.

"I have the great privilege of introducing one of our own, Mr. Drake Wright!" He swept his left hand toward Drake.

Bailey, Sydney, and the twins moved out of the way, leaving Drake by himself next to the Wright D-94 Wave Smasher. They began to clap loudly.

"Let's hear it for Drake!" Bailey shouted. Then everyone on the beach clapped and cheered.

The captain continued, "Drake and his dad, Nate Wright, are well known around Corolla as inventors, and tonight Drake will show you an invention he has worked on tirelessly for the past several years. It is a recreational watercraft unlike anything you have ever seen. As soon as you have watched it in action, you will want a Wright D-94 Wave Smasher of your very own. I won't take up your valuable time explaining the fine points of his amazing invention. I will, instead, let it speak for itself. Drake, my boy, take it away!"

Drake climbed into the cockpit and pulled down the bubble-like cover. He started the engine and the soft whirring sound began. He pushed a button making the four snowshoe-like feet pop out of the bottom of the vehicle. Then another button raised the D-94 up on its legs. It started walking toward the water, and people in the crowd gasped.

"You haven't seen anything yet, ladies and gentlemen," the captain said. "Prepare to be amazed."

When Drake got within several feet of the water, he let the D-94 lift and hover a few yards above the beach. Then it started rotating.

"It walks. It hovers. It even spins!" the captain announced. "Around and around she goes!"

Drake let his invention spin faster and faster until it looked like a top spinning out of control. The crowd oohed and aahed. Then, slowly, Drake let the craft rotate counterclockwise to a complete stop. He set it down in the ocean, just offshore. The legs and feet folded up into the bottom of the vehicle and it floated.

"How about a game of leapfrog?" the captain asked the crowd.

With the spotlights fixed on his craft, Drake pushed the control stick forward, and the D-94 sailed out to sea, leaping over waves that got in its way. The crowd went wild. Captain Swain flicked a switch, and all the spotlights went dark. "Keep your eyes fixed on the horizon," the captain said. "The best is yet to come."

"Now what?" Carolyn asked in the darkness.

"Yeah, now what?" Marilyn repeated.

"Just watch," Sydney answered. "He'll make it look like a UFO."

"He's so awesome," Bailey remarked. "He can make the D-94 do just about anything."

Offshore, Drake turned on the signal light. It flashed bright white in a series of dots and dashes. "He says, 'Watch this, Dad,' " Sydney heard Mr. Wright say as he stood nearby. "I'm so proud of you, son," Mr. Wright said, although Drake couldn't hear him.

The Wright D-94 Wave Smasher lit up like a Christmas tree, first with red lights chasing around its middle, then with multicolored lights flashing on and off. As the crowd watched, Drake made the craft shoot like a bullet across the water. Its lights provided the only clue as to where it was. To make things even more interesting, Drake sometimes turned off all the lights and then changed places before turning them back on.

"He's over there!" someone in the crowd shouted.

"No, he's over there!"

"Look at how fast that thing can move."

"You can't tell if it's on or above the water!"

Drake put on an amazing show before bringing the craft back to shore. As he approached the beach, Captain Swain flipped the spotlights back on. The D-94 sailed to the water's edge and lifted off the sand with a puff of air. It scooted across the beach to where the bus was parked, and then Drake set it down to rest in the sand. He killed the engine and pulled back the cover on the cockpit.

"That was more wonderful than anything I could ever have imagined," said Bailey.

"Wow, that's saying a lot," Sydney replied. "You have the wildest imagination of anyone I've ever known."

"Ladies and gentlemen," the captain shouted. "Let's give a big round of applause to our resident inventor, *Mr. Drake Wright!*"

Everyone on the beach applauded, and many tried to get past the yellow tape. "Stay back!" Mr. Wright shouted.

"That's all for tonight," the captain announced. "There will be plenty more opportunities for you to see the Wright D-94 Wave Smasher in action. And before long, you might even have one of your very own." He shut off the megaphone and climbed down the ladder.

"Drake," Captain Swain said, approaching the D-94, "you were incredible!"

"Yes, you were!" Bailey agreed.

"We think so too," said Carolyn and Marilyn.

Drake climbed out of the cockpit, and Sydney shook his hand.

"You did that just like a pro," she said. "I was praying for you the whole time."

"Thanks, Sydney," Drake said with a lot more confidence in his voice. "I felt your prayers. I couldn't have done it without you guys—"

"And the Greatest Helper of them all," said the captain, pointing up at the sky.

"He means God," Sydney whispered to the twins.

Mr. Kessler had climbed down from the bleachers and was walking toward them.

"Here comes our dad," said Marilyn.

"Drake." Mr. Kessler said in a serious voice. "My associates and I would like to have a word with you and your dad. Over there, please." He motioned to the bleachers where his friends were waiting. The Wrights followed Mr. Kessler through the sand.

"What do you think will happen?" Sydney asked.

"They're going to set him up," Carolyn said.

"Huh?" said Bailey.

"We overheard our dad talking on the phone this morning," said Marilyn. "He said that if Drake's demonstration went well tonight, his company will start manufacturing the Wright D-94 Wave Smasher."

"And there's more," said Carolyn. "He's going to set up a dealership, right here in Corolla, and Drake's dad will run it, and everybody on the Outer Banks will come here to buy their D-94s."

"Before long, there will be dealerships up and down both coasts," Marilyn added. "And Drake and his dad will own them all."

Captain Swain beamed. "Praise our God! His deeds are wonderful, too marvelous to describe."

"You really need to meet our friend Beth," Sydney told him. "You two could have a contest to see who knows the most scripture verses."

"Why, Sydney Lincoln," said Captain Swain, "I'd be honored to meet your friend. Maybe she can come with you the next time you visit your grandparents."

A few yards away from them, they heard Drake Wright let out a joyful whoop! Mr. Wright threw his arms around his son and hugged him.

"Watch that boy," said the captain. "This is only the beginning."

Camp Club Girls:
Sydney and the Wisconsin
Whispering Woods

Things that Go Bump in the Night

"Look out!" Sydney Lincoln screamed.

Screeeeeeech!

The wailing of tires sliding on concrete echoed in her ears. A chill raced down Sydney's spine as Aunt Dee pulled the SUV onto the shoulder of the road.

"You almost hit that thing," Sydney gasped. "What was it?"

Alexis Howell sat in the backseat. Her hands gripped Sydney's headrest.

"It ran so fast I didn't get a good look at it. I saw something big and brown. A bear, maybe?" she said.

"A deer," said Aunt Dee. "It was a huge buck. Is everyone all right?"

Alexis checked on Biscuit, also known as Biscuit the Wonder Dog. He stood in his kennel cage in the back of the SUV. "Biscuit looks a little scared, but he's fine," she said.

Aunt Dee took a deep breath and pulled back onto the narrow woodland road.

Sydney had never seen a darker summer night. The moon and the stars were trapped above clouds behind hundreds of towering pine trees. As the three—and Biscuit—traveled along, they saw animal eyes peering out at them from the forest, reflected in the beams of the headlights.

"I think we're lost," Aunt Dee announced.

"Wonderful!" Sydney sighed. "It's almost midnight, and we're lost in the middle of a national forest."

"We're not in the *middle* of the forest," said Aunt Dee. "We're barely on the edge of it. And we're not *lost* lost. I know the resort is on this road, but in the dark I'm not sure exactly where it is."

Sydney put her window down. "You can turn off the air condition-ing. It's nice outside."

Aunt Dee flipped a switch on the dashboard, and the cool air stopped rushing from the vents. Just then, an awful smell filled the car.

"Skunk!" Sydney cried, quickly putting up the window.

"Eeeewwwww!" Alexis complained. "That's nasty. Did you see it?"

Sydney held her nose and flipped on the AC.

"I saw it lying dead on the road back there," said Aunt Dee.

"The poor little thing," Alexis said. "It died just trying to cross the street."

Sydney's aunt eased her foot off the accelerator, and the SUV slowed to a crawl. "Look for a long driveway to the right with a sign that says MILLER'S RESORT. It leads to the cabins and the lake."

"I think we passed it," Sydney said in a muffled voice. She still had her hands cupped over her face to block the skunk smell.

"What?" Aunt Dee said.

"About a half an hour ago," Sydney answered. "I saw a sign that said MILLER'S RESORT with an arrow pointing to the right. I would have said something, but I didn't know we were going there."

Aunt Dee pulled the SUV to the side of the road. "How in the world did I miss it?" She made a U-turn and headed in the opposite direction. "I guess we're all tired."

The long trip was almost over. The day before, Aunt Dee and Sydney had driven eleven hours from Washington DC to Chicago, Illinois. They had dinner there with Bailey Chang and her family, who came from Peoria to see them.

Then they spent the night in a motel and, this morning, they went to the Chicago Airport to pick up Alexis. Her plane, due to arrive at one, was three hours late. They didn't leave Chicago until almost five, and for the last six hours, they had been on the road driving from Chicago to northern Wisconsin.

"I can't wait to climb into bed and go to sleep," said Sydney. "Yester-day morning, I thought a road trip was a cool idea. Now I can't think of anything I'd like better than to get out of this SUV."

Ruff!

"Biscuit agrees," said Alexis. "He's *such* a good boy. Aren't you, Biscuit?"

The little dog perked up his ears and stuck one front paw through the bars of his kennel. Alexis reached back and held it. "It's probably not safe to walk in the forest at night. I mean, with bears and stuff around here."

After they backtracked several miles, Aunt Dee slowed down to make sure they wouldn't miss the sign again. "It should be on the left," she said.

"*Oh my goodness!*" Aunt Dee slammed on the brakes sending the girls flying against their seatbelts.

Sydney gasped. "A wolf!"

"No. That's a coyote," Aunt Dee said.

A large dog-like animal stood in the road in front of the SUV. It had big pointed ears, long legs, and a silver-brown coat. Frozen like a statue, it stared at them.

Ruff! Ruff! Ar-roof! Ruff! Ruff! Ar-roof! Biscuit barked wildly.

When the coyote heard Biscuit bark, the corners of its mouth turned up in a sneer. It showed its fangs, daring the SUV to come any closer.

"Biscuit, be quiet!" both girls exclaimed.

"Are all the windows shut?" Aunt Dee asked.

"They are," said Alexis, double-checking. She reached back and made sure Biscuit's kennel was latched.

"Look!" said Sydney, pointing to the side of the road.

Three coyote pups came out of the woods. Their mother yipped at them, and they quickly ran to her side. With a firm nudge of her nose, she sent them running. Then she trotted after them across the road.

"I've seen more wild animals in the last half hour than I have in my whole entire life," said Alexis.

"Isn't it cool?" Sydney asked.

"Way cool," her friend answered. "But, as much as I like animals, I'm afraid of bears. That's about the only thing we haven't seen so far, and I hope we don't run into any."

A soft, little *Ruff!* came from inside the kennel cage.

They drove another quarter of a mile before they saw the sign:

MILLER'S RESORT
LAKESIDE CABINS
OPEN ALL YEAR

"We're here," said Aunt Dee. She turned the SUV onto the long, winding driveway. "I can't wait to get some sleep. I have to be at the ranger's station at nine tomorrow morning."

Sydney's aunt was a forest ranger with the National Park Service in Washington DC. For as long as Sydney could remember, Aunt Dee had worked at the many landmarks and memorials in Washington. But now she wanted to try something new. She planned to interview for a ranger job at the Chequamegon-Nicolet National Forest in Wisconsin, and she had invited Sydney and her friend, Alexis, to come along and spend a week with her in the Northwoods.

Though Sydney was from Washington DC and Alexis was from California, the two girls had met at camp. The six girls in their cabin had solved a mystery together. Dubbing themselves the Camp Club Girls, though all of the six lived in different parts of the country and were different ages, they were all great friends. And they all worked together to solve mysteries.

"We need to check in at the resort office," said Aunt Dee. "Mrs. Miller promised to stay there until we arrive." She parked the SUV in front of a two-story, white cottage and shut off the engine. A red fluorescent sign above the door flickered OFFICE, and several bright outdoor lights lit the grounds. When they opened the car doors, they felt a blast of cool, woodland air.

"I'll let Biscuit out," said Sydney.

"Wait," Aunt Dee told her. "It's not safe for him to run around here in the dark."

Biscuit lay down in his cage and sighed.

"It'll only take a minute," said Aunt Dee as they walked up the steps and onto the wide front porch. A ragged, old note was taped above the doorbell. RING AFTER 9 PM. Aunt Dee pressed the button and waited.

After a few seconds, the door swung open. A short, round lady greeted them with a smile. She wore faded blue jeans, a white tee shirt, and a yellow baseball cap that said GREEN BAY PACKERS. "Miss Powers?" she asked.

"Yes," Aunt Dee agreed, stepping inside. "We're so glad to finally be here."

"You had a long drive," said Mrs. Miller. She walked toward the registration desk. "Come inside, girls, and shut the door behind you."

Sydney and Alexis entered the office and closed the door. A small television on a shelf behind the desk was tuned to a home shopping station.

"This is my niece, Sydney Lincoln," said Aunt Dee, wrapping her arm around Sydney's shoulder. "And her friend Alexis Howell from Sacramento, California."

Alexis smiled shyly.

"Goodness, all the way from Sacramento, are you?" Mrs. Miller said. "So, what do you think of the Northwoods?"

"From what I could see in the dark, it's very nice," Alexis said politely.

"So, there will be three of you then, staying in Cabin One?" asked Mrs. Miller getting out the guest register.

"Right. Three of us," Aunt Dee said.

"We have a little dog too," Sydney added. "Is that okay? We're taking care of him while our friend Kate is on vacation."

"We thought he'd enjoy spending time near the lake and the woods," Alexis added. "We found him when we were at Discovery Lake Summer Camp, and Kate adopted him."

Mrs. Miller opened the big registration book and asked Aunt Dee to sign her name. "Your aunt told me about the dog when she made the reservations. It's okay, as long as you don't let him run around and bother the other visitors."

"We'll keep an eye on him," Sydney promised.

"And be sure to put him on a leash after dark, and stay with him when you let him out to do his business at night," Mrs. Miller warned. "Some of the wild animals around here would hurt a friendly little dog."

"Are there bears?" Alexis asked.

"Oh yeah," said Mrs. Miller. "We have black bears here. Sometimes, they wander over by the cabins at night. But, if you don't bother them, they won't bother you. And make sure you don't leave any food outside. That's how most problems between people and bears start."

Alexis shivered.

Mrs. Miller took a set of keys from a wall behind the desk. "Here are your keys," she said. "Go to the end of the driveway. It's the first log cabin on your left, the one with the big front porch. You can park behind it to unload. Then move your car back here to the parking lot. Try to be quiet. Cabin Two is occupied, and the folks are asleep."

"We will," said Aunt Dee. "And thanks for staying up for us."

"No problem," said Mrs. Miller. "Enjoy your stay. My husband and I are here if you need anything. Good night, girls. Sleep tight."

"Good night," Sydney and Alexis answered.

"Oh," said Mrs. Miller, remembering something. "And do you have a flashlight?"

"I do," Aunt Dee replied.

"You'll need it then, to find your way. I put a couple more in the cabin on the table."

"Thanks," said Aunt Dee. She closed the door, and they got back in the SUV and headed down the driveway.

"We're almost there, Biscuit," said Alexis, reaching into the kennel. Out of the coal-black night, the headlights shone on a log cabin with a screened porch all along its front. A sign near the door said CABIN ONE.

"Oh, Biscuit will love the porch," Sydney said. "He can hang out there all day long and not have to worry about wild animals."

"Like skunks," said Alexis.

Aunt Dee parked the SUV behind the cabin and shut off the engine. While the girls unloaded the suitcases, Sydney's aunt used her flashlight to find the lock on the door. She unlocked it, pushed the door open, and fumbled for a light switch.

When she flipped it, thankfully, the light came on. The door opened into a quaint, little kitchen that had ruffled curtains on the windows and a flowered plastic tablecloth on the small, round table. Two flashlights lay on the table with a brochure that said MILLER'S RESORT—REST AND RECREATION. Gratefully, Sydney and Alexis plopped their bags onto the floor.

"I'll let Biscuit out," said Sydney.

"Remember the leash," Alexis reminded her.

Sydney found Biscuit's leash near his kennel. Carefully, she opened the kennel door and snapped the leash onto his collar. The happy little dog came bounding out of his cage and ran circles around Sydney. Then he stopped. He put his head up and sniffed the air. He sniffed it again and let out a little *Ruff!*

"What's the matter, boy? Do you see something?" Sydney asked. She looked toward the lake, but in the darkness, she couldn't see a thing.

Biscuit pulled hard on the leash and started to pant. He reared up on his hind legs. *Ruff! Ruff! Ar-roof! Ruff! Ruff! Ar-roof!*

"Quiet!" Sydney whispered. She thought she heard a bump. *Something's out there in the darkness*, she thought. *I'm almost sure of it.*

Just the idea that something or someone might be watching made Sydney nervous. "Come on, boy," she said, leading Biscuit back toward the cabin. "Do your business, so we can go inside."

Biscuit stood for a few seconds, anxiously staring into the darkness.

Then, obediently, he did what Sydney asked and followed her to the cabin's back door.

"Why was Biscuit barking?" Aunt Dee asked when Sydney brought him inside.

Sydney shut the back door and flipped the deadbolt lock. "I think he saw something by the lake," she said. "I couldn't see anything. Do you know how dark it is out there? At Discovery Lake, the paths are lit at night, and we sort of know what animals are around. But this is way different—and spooky."

Alexis hauled her suitcase into the girls' bedroom. "By tomorrow night, we'll be getting used to the darkness and all the weird noises."

"You're probably right," said Sydney, picking up her suitcase and following Alexis into their room.

Alexis found a lamp on the nightstand next to the bunk beds. She turned the switch, and the room lit up. On one wall hung a brightly colored Indian trading blanket. Above the closet door, a mounted deer's head stared down at them.

"Oh, gross! I hate it when hunters display the heads of animals they've killed," said Alexis. She put her suitcase on the lower bunk and opened it.

"Get used to it," Sydney grinned. "There's a moose head in the bathroom."

"No there isn't!" Alexis exclaimed.

"There is," Sydney insisted. "Hey, which bunk do you want?"

"I'll take the top one," said Alexis. She took her pajamas and toothbrush out of her suitcase and headed for the bathroom.

"You just don't want to sleep next to the window," Sydney said, "in case a big bear comes along and peeks in at you."

"You're right," Alexis agreed. "I don't like bears."

Aunt Dee had parked the SUV in the lot and settled in to her room on the other side of the cabin. Before long, the girls snuggled into their beds too.

"Lights out?" Sydney asked.

"Prayers first," said Alexis, pulling the cool sheet up under her chin.

"Okay. Say amen when you're done," Sydney told her.

The girls prayed silently for a few minutes.

"Amen."

"And amen," Sydney echoed. Then she reached over and turned off the lamp.

The girls were almost asleep when the bedroom door swung open. A rush of air swept through the room as Biscuit scurried in and leaped onto the lower bunk, landing on Sydney's chest.

"Get down!" said Sydney.

Biscuit didn't move.

"Biscuit, don't stand on me. Lie down."

He pretended not to hear.

"Oh, I know what's wrong," Alexis said from the top bunk. "He wants his doll. He has that rag doll that he sleeps with. It's in the car."

Sydney sighed. "I forgot," she said. "I guess I'll have to go get it." She climbed out from under the covers and put on her shoes.

"Don't forget the flashlight," Alexis reminded her. "And watch out for bears."

"Okay," Sydney said as she left the bedroom. She took one of the flashlights and the car keys from the kitchen table. Then she unlocked the back door and bravely walked up the driveway to the parking lot. She got Biscuit's doll from his kennel and headed back to the cabin.

When Sydney was almost there, she shined the flashlight toward the lake. The beam landed on a picnic table. She saw the gentle waves lapping on the shore, and then—a shadow. A mysterious hulking figure dashed from the beach and disappeared into the forest. Sydney heard whatever it was running through the edge of the woods.

Every ounce of courage drained from her body.

Something was watching her!

Mountain Man

"Alex, are you awake?" Sydney asked, hurrying into their bedroom. "I think something is out there."

"Huh?" Alexis answered sleepily.

Biscuit grabbed his doll from Sydney's hand and wrestled it on the floor.

"I just saw someone, or something, hurry into the woods. I could only make out its shadow, but it looked tall and kind of hunched over. I could feel it watching me."

Alexis rubbed her eyes and sat with her feet dangling over the edge of her bed. "Now I'm afraid to go to sleep," she said. "Bears don't walk upright and hunched over, right?"

Sydney lay on her bed on her stomach and looked out the window. "Circus bears walk on their hind legs," she said. "And I've seen people throw marshmallows to bears at the National Zoo—when the bears stand up to catch them, they look sort of hunched over."

"Are marshmallows good for bears?" Alexis asked.

"I don't know," Sydney said. "But they like them."

Biscuit hopped onto the bed and wiggled next to Sydney. He stuck his nose against the window screen and sniffed. "He smells something," Sydney whispered. "What is it, boy?"

Alexis and Sydney both sniffed the air.

"I don't smell anything, do you?" Alexis asked.

"Just fresh air," Sydney said. She reached over to pet Biscuit, and she noticed that his muscles were stiff. He stood at attention, focusing everything on his sense of smell. Then, he let out a low, soft growl. "Something *is* out there," said Sydney. "I'm sure of it."

Alexis climbed down from the upper bunk and lay on the bed with

Sydney. With Biscuit between them, they peered out the window. The clouds had begun to break up now, and a narrow ray of moonlight cast the faintest bit of light on the grounds outside the cabin.

"I think I see something," Alexis said. "You're right. It looks big and hunchbacked, but I can't tell what it is. It's moving around by the beach. At least I think a beach is out there. Who knows in this darkness? Now it's stopping."

Sydney saw the shadow too. "I wish I knew exactly where we are. The cabin is pretty close to the lake. When I came back with Biscuit's doll, the flashlight lit up the water and a picnic table. Hey, I think it's standing by the table."

Biscuit growled again, a low, menacing growl.

"What do you think it's doing?" asked Alexis.

"I have an idea," Sydney said, "I think it's a bear. Someone left food on the table, and it's after that. How brave are you?"

Alexis looked at her in the darkness. "Why?"

"Because I'm going to shine the flashlight out the window and see, once and for all, what's lurking around out there."

Biscuit shivered.

"Oh Syd, are you sure that's a good idea?" asked Alexis.

"We're the Camp Club Girls," Sydney answered. "Solving mysteries is what we do." She reached over to the nightstand and got the flashlight. "Are you ready?" she asked.

"I guess so," Alexis replied.

Sydney pointed the flashlight at the window and flipped the switch. "Oh!" she gasped.

Alexis caught her breath as Sydney turned off the flashlight and both girls ducked under the windowsill.

A man lurked outside, a big, burly man with a bushy brown beard and a ruddy complexion. He wore a floppy tan hat, khaki-colored clothing, and brown hiking boots. In one hand, he carried a long, thick walking stick. It looked bumpy—perhaps carved out of a tree branch. A huge, bulky backpack hung over his shoulders, and attached to it was a frying pan and a bedroll. The flashlight startled him. He grabbed something from the picnic table and ran off toward the woods.

Biscuit was barking wildly when Aunt Dee rushed into their room.

"What's going on?" she asked.

"Someone is out there," Sydney said. "A guy."

"What do you mean, a guy?" Aunt Dee said, sounding concerned.

"I went to the car to get Biscuit's doll, and when I was almost back to the cabin, I saw something big hurry into the woods," said Sydney. "It looked like a bear. So Alex and I looked out the window. We shined the flashlight outside to see if we could see anything, and we saw a guy. He looked like a mountain man. He's gone now. He ran into the woods."

Aunt Dee climbed onto the bed and looked out the window. "Was he looking in at you?"

"No," said Alexis. "I think we scared him. He was doing something at the picnic table when we turned on the flashlight, but we didn't see what. He took off running that way." She pointed.

Aunt Dee locked the window and drew the curtains closed. "Keep the window closed tonight," she said. "And Sydney, you shouldn't have gone out there alone to get Biscuit's toy."

Biscuit jumped to the floor, picked up his doll, and scampered out of the room.

"The ceiling fan should keep you cool enough," said Aunt Dee. "In the morning, we'll have a better idea of who and what you saw."

"It *is* morning!" said Sydney.

"I know." Aunt Dee sighed. "And we should all be asleep." She flipped on the ceiling fan and left the room, closing the girls' door but leaving just enough room for Biscuit to go in and out.

Alexis climbed the ladder to the upper bunk. "What do you think he was up to?" she asked.

"Beats me," said Sydney. "I think maybe he's camping in the woods or something. His clothes looked dirty and worn, and did you notice the bedroll?"

"I did," Alexis answered. "And the frying pan too. Obviously, he's a camper. I'm just glad we saw a person out there instead of a big grizzly bear. A camper guy I can handle, but not a bear that wants to make a snack out of my arms or legs."

Sydney laughed. "Oh Alex, what's gotten into you? You're usually so positive."

"Not when it comes to bears," Alex said. "Unless, of course, they're in a zoo. Then I think they're cute and cuddly."

Sydney rolled onto her side and adjusted the pillow under her head. "Well, I feel safe here with the window shut and the doors to the cabin locked. Tomorrow we can look for evidence and maybe find out what our mountain man was up to. Goodnight, Alex."

"Goodnight, Syd," Alexis said. "And by the way, Wisconsin doesn't have any mountains."

"I know," Sydney said, sleepily. "But still, he looked like a mountain man."

———•———

In the morning, the girls awoke to the sound of sausages sizzling in a frying pan. Aunt Dee was in the kitchen making a big country-style breakfast. She was already dressed in her park ranger uniform, and when the girls came to the kitchen table still in their pj's, she scooped scrambled eggs onto their plates. "Help yourselves to some pancakes," she said. "The sausages are almost ready. I was just about to come in and wake you guys up."

Sydney yawned and put several pancakes on her plate. "Thanks for making breakfast, Aunt Dee," she said. "I'm hungry enough to eat a bear." She looked at Alexis and grinned.

"I'm not *that* hungry," Alexis said. "But I am hungry enough to eat pancakes. Thanks, Miss Powers. This is great."

Aunt Dee carried the frying pan to the table and put two sausages on each of their plates. "You're welcome," she said. "You can make supper tonight."

She set the frying pan in the sink and sat down at the table. Before they ate, they thanked God for their food.

"So, did you sleep well?" Aunt Dee asked.

"Sort of," Alexis answered.

"Me too, sort of," Sydney added. "I dreamed about that guy we saw. Why are the drapes all shut?"

"I haven't had time to open them yet," Aunt Dee told her. "As soon as I woke up, I dressed and started breakfast. I have to leave in a few minutes for my interview."

Sydney got up and walked into the small living room. She pulled the cord that opened the drapes on the big picture window. Bright sunlight flooded the room.

Beyond the screened porch, Sydney saw a grassy front yard. It led down a gentle slope to the lake, which was only a short distance from the cabin's front door. A very narrow strip of sandy beach stretched along the water's edge, and an aluminum rowboat lay there upside down. The water glistened in the sunlight, and a pair of ducks floated on the surface near a long, wooden dock.

"This is cool!" Sydney said. "We're closer to the water than I thought."

She went back to the table and continued eating her breakfast.

"I'm sure you'll find plenty to do," Aunt Dee said. "The resort brochure tells about swimming, fishing, and rowing. A small grocery store is within walking distance—and also an ice cream and coffee shop with video games and internet access."

"Great!" said Alexis. "Then we can email our friends."

Sydney knew that Alexis referred to the other Camp Club Girls—Bailey Chang, Kate Oliver, Elizabeth Anderson, and McKenzie Phillips. Kate, the technological one, had set up a web page with a chat room. When they weren't at camp and since they lived in different parts of the country, it was like their own private cabin in cyberspace.

"We'll email them later," Sydney said. "We can tell them about the mountain man."

"And almost hitting a deer, and the skunk, and the coyote," said Alexis, before taking the last bite of her scrambled eggs.

"Maybe we should leave out the wild animals part," Sydney suggested between sips of orange juice from a red, plastic cup. "Kate might worry about Biscuit."

"You're right," said Alexis. "We'll leave that part out." She reached down to pat Biscuit on his head. He sat patiently at her feet, apparently hoping she would give him a bite of sausage.

Aunt Dee gathered her purse and briefcase. She nestled her tan ranger's hat on her head and picked up her car keys. "If you need me, you know my cell phone number. And you girls stay out of trouble today," she said. "Okay?"

"Who, us? Get into trouble?" Sydney smiled.

"Listen, girlfriend," said Aunt Dee. "I haven't forgotten that you and Elizabeth got mixed up in an assassination plot to kill the president. I still have gray hairs from that little adventure."

She meant the time when Sydney and Elizabeth followed some thugs who planned to set off a bomb at Fort McHenry. Sydney saved the president's life when she grabbed the bomb and dumped it into Baltimore Harbor. An event they'd dubbed Sydney's DC Discovery.

"We'll be fine," Sydney promised.

Aunt Dee waved and went out the door.

The girls cleaned the table, washed the dishes, and made sure Biscuit had food and water.

"So, what do you want to do now?" Alexis asked after they got dressed.

"I don't know," said Sydney. "Let's go outside."

They put Biscuit on the big, screened porch. Then Sydney locked the door and stuck the key in the pocket of her gray sweatpants. "Let's see if the mountain man left us any clues."

The other visitors weren't up yet, and the lake was quiet. Chipmunks scampered about looking for scraps of food, seeds, and other treats. Birds scurried from the ground to the trees, feeding their babies in well-hidden nests. The girls walked to the picnic table where they'd seen the man the night before. The rickety old table held nothing more than a small pile of peanuts, obviously left by some well-meaning guest who wanted to feed the animals.

"Maybe that's what he was doing," Sydney said. "Leaving food for the critters."

She tossed a peanut on the ground. Instantly a chipmunk skittered over and popped the whole thing into its cheek. Alexis tossed another one. The girls took turns tossing peanuts until the whole pile was gone.

"I don't like the idea of someone putting food out at night," said Alexis. "It might attract bears." She sat down on the picnic bench. "Ouch!" She jumped up, rubbing her behind.

"What's wrong?" asked Sydney.

"I sat on something sharp." Alexis checked out the spot where she'd sat. "Hey, look. What are these things?"

Three tiny bunches of brightly colored feathers lay on the ground. Each bunch was gathered tightly at the bottom with a small, sharp hook tucked inside.

"Fishing flies," said Sydney.

"Fishing what?"

"They're fishing flies," Sydney said. She picked one up and held it in her hand. "When you go fishing, you put one of these on the end of your line. When the little fishies see the colorful feathers swimming under the water, they bite. That's how you catch a fish."

"How do you know this stuff?" Alexis asked.

"My aunt's a park ranger," Sydney said. "I've been fishing lots of times."

"Hey! What are you doing with my fly?" A short, skinny, redheaded boy marched over to the picnic table. "Give it to me." He held out his hand.

Gently, Sydney placed the fly in the palm of his hand. She pointed to the others on the ground. "There's more," she said.

The boy bent and picked them up.

Sydney decided he was about the same age as she and Alexis. "Are you staying here?" Sydney asked. "We just got in last night, and we're in Cabin One. I'm Sydney, and this is Alex."

The boy scowled. "We're in Cabin Two. I need these for the fishing contest. Alex? What kind of name is that for a girl?"

"It's short for Alexis," Alex told him. She already sensed trouble. Nothing about this boy was friendly.

"And what's your name?" Sydney asked.

"Duncan," he answered sharply.

"So what about this fishing contest, Duncan?" Sydney wondered.

"What about it?" Duncan checked the flies to make sure they weren't broken.

"You said something about a fishing contest," Sydney said. "I always like a good contest, and maybe I want to sign up."

"You can't. Girls don't fish," Duncan said matter-of-factly.

Sydney got that expression on her face, the one Alexis recognized as determination. No one, absolutely no one, ever told Sydney Lincoln that she couldn't compete. She lived for competition.

"Oh yes, girls *do* fish!" Sydney told him. "Where do I sign up?"

Duncan looked at her. The corner of his mouth turned up in a sly smile. Then he shook his head back and forth, uttered a wicked little laugh, and walked away.

"Ooooo!" Sydney said under her breath. "I don't like him. *Girls can't fish!* Who does he think he is? I'm going to find out where to sign up for that contest, and you just watch. I'm going to win that contest if it's the last thing I do!" She sighed with exasperation.

"'A gentle answer turns away wrath, but a harsh word stirs up anger,'" said Alexis. "It's in the Bible. Proverbs 15:1."

"You sound like Elizabeth," said Sydney. Elizabeth knew an amazing amount of scriptures. "But I'm not angry," Sydney continued. "I'm just frustrated because he thinks girls can't fish, or shouldn't fish, or whatever. Let's go to the office and find out where to sign up." She headed toward the cabins.

"Hey," said Alexis. "What's this?" She picked up a paperback book from the grass: *Field Guide to Mushrooms*.

"Keep it," Sydney said. "It might belong to the mountain man."

"And look," Alexis said. "The bottom of the rowboat is covered in wet seaweed, and the squishy mud has big footprints in it. And what are these things?" She pointed to pieces of brown, slimy fungus at the edge of the beach.

"I dunno. We'll check it out later," said Sydney. "Right now, my mind's on that contest."

Northern Lights

Mrs. Miller sat behind the registration desk drinking a cup of coffee. "Good morning, girls," she said when Sydney and Alexis entered the office. "You're up bright and early."

"Hi," said Sydney. "I have a question. Where do I sign up for the fishing contest?"

"Which one?" Mrs. Miller asked. She opened a bakery box filled with donuts and offered them to the girls.

"No thanks," Sydney said as Alexis grabbed a crème-filled, chocolate-covered long boy. "There's more than one contest?"

Alexis kept busy studying a map of the lake hanging on the wall.

"There's always fishing contests on North Twin Lake," said Mrs. Miller. "Here's a list of our current ones." She handed Sydney a flyer.

FISHING CONTESTS
AUGUST 2 THROUGH 9
OFF SHORE: BIGGEST FISH—PRIZE $200 AND 50% OFF TAXIDERMIST
SERVICES AT SCALE AND HIDE TAXIDERMY IN EAGLE RIVER
DOCKSIDE: BIGGEST FISH—PRIZE: $100 AND
FREE ALL-YOU-CAN-EAT FISH FRY AT
CLIFF'S BOATHOUSE CAFÉ IN CONOVER

"The kid in Cabin Two, Duncan," said Sydney. "Which contest did he sign up for?"

"He probably signed up for the dockside contest," Mrs. Miller answered. "Children under 13 can only compete in offshore if they're with an adult."

Alexis walked to the desk and helped herself to another

chocolate-covered donut.

"Okay, I want to sign up for dockside," said Sydney. "And Alexis does too."

"I do?" said Alex, licking chocolate frosting from her fingers.

Mrs. Miller smiled. "Not a fisherman, are you?" she asked.

"I've fished a little," said Alexis, "but I've never fished in a contest."

"Well, you girls go up there to the end of the drive. Then you turn left and walk down the road a bit. You'll see Tompkins' Ice Cream Shop. Go inside there, and that's where you sign up. You sure you don't want a donut?" Mrs. Miller slid the box toward Sydney.

"No thank you," Sydney said again. "Come on, Alex. Let's go sign up."

The girls got Biscuit from the cabin, and Alexis made sure his leash was firmly fastened to his collar. Then the three of them headed up the drive toward the road.

Soon they came to a gas station and a row of quaint little shops. Tompkins' Ice Cream was the first two-story building on the left. A red-striped awning hung over the wide front window, and a sign in the window said:

COFFEE, REGULAR AND SPECIALTY
MUFFINS, SCONES, AND OTHER SWEETS
ICE CREAM AND FREE INTERNET ACCESS
OPEN EVERY DAY 8 TO 8

The girls opened the door and went inside.

Four small tables sat in the middle of the shop, and three huge, wooden booths lined one wall. The opposite wall had an old-fashioned soda fountain with a lunch counter and tall stools with round, red seats. The tables and booths were empty. Several men sat at the counter drinking hot coffee out of thick, black mugs.

"No dogs allowed," said a man wearing a white apron. He stood behind the counter writing the daily specials on a blackboard. "You can tie it to the hitch outside the front door."

Biscuit cocked his head and raised one paw to beg. Then he raced toward the man, pulling the leash out of Sydney's hand. He stood up with his paws against the man's knees and wagged his tail.

"There, there now," the man said, patting Biscuit's head. "I have to kick you out, buddy—the health inspector says so."

Sydney picked up the end of Biscuit's leash and apologized. "Are you the manager?" she said as Alexis took Biscuit outside.

"I own the place," the man said.

"Where do we sign up for the fishing contest—the one on the docks?"

"Right here." The man looked past Sydney. "Are you signing up for your dad, or your brother, or someone else?"

"I'm signing up for me!" Sydney said as Alexis came back into the shop.

A man at the counter chuckled. "Girls don't fish," he said.

Sydney felt the blood rush to her face. "We do too," she told him. "Where's the sign-up sheet?"

The owner walked to the end of the counter and came back with some papers attached to a clipboard. "Here 'tis," he said. "Do you know what you're fishing for?"

Sydney signed her name and *Miller's Resort, Cabin One*. "I'm fishing for the biggest fish dockside."

The man at the counter chuckled again. "What *kinds* of fish?" he asked.

Sydney had no idea what kinds of fish were in North Twin Lake, and she didn't like that the man tried to make her look stupid. "All kinds!" she replied firmly.

She handed the clipboard to Alexis. Alex hadn't planned to compete, but when she heard the man laugh at Sydney's answer, she signed her name too.

"May we use the computer?" she asked.

"Over there," the owner said, pointing to the corner of the room.

Sydney gave him back the clipboard. "Internet access is free, right?"

"Correct," the man said. He took a coffeepot from a heated plate behind the counter and filled the men's cups.

"Did you see that Duncan kid's name on the list?" Alexis asked as they walked to the computer.

"Yes, right at the top. He's Duncan Lumley. Age twelve."

They sat down at the computer, and Sydney typed in her name and password. Then she logged on to the Camp Club Girls' website. Bailey was online.

Sydney: *Hi, Bailey. Greetings from Tompkins' Ice Cream Shop in the Northwoods! Alex says hi too. We're on the shop's computer.*

Bailey: *Hi, guys! Alex, sorry I didn't get to see you when you arrived in Chicago.*

Alexis: *No problem. Maybe we can meet this weekend before I catch my plane.*

Sydney: *You'll never guess what we just did.*

Bailey: *What?*

Sydney: *Alex and I signed up for a fishing contest.*

Bailey: *Get out of town! How come?*

Sydney: *An obnoxious kid named Duncan is staying at our resort. He told me this morning that girls can't fish. So we're going to show him that girls not only fish, but girls WIN fishing contests.*

Bailey: *You show him, Sydneykins. A resort? That sounds fancy.*

Alexis: *Think again. It has an office, which is an old two-story cottage, and a row of small cabins not much bigger than our cabins at camp.*

Bailey: *Cool.*

Sydney: *So, do you know much about catching fish? That kid, Duncan, is using feather flies. I don't know what he uses for bait, though. What do you think? Worms?*

Bailey: *Hang on a minute.*

"Do you want an ice-cream cone?" Alexis asked Sydney.

"Alex! You just had a big breakfast and two donuts," Sydney exclaimed. "What's up with you? You usually eat healthy."

"I know," her friend answered, "but all this fresh air makes me hungry. I'll wait. Maybe I can get an ice cream when we leave."

Bailey: *Sorry guys. I went and asked my dad what he uses for bait. He fishes all the time. He said big fish like dough balls. Take a little glob of fresh dough, mix in some tuna, and roll it in corn meal. That's the secret, he said. Put them in the fridge overnight to firm up. Make sure to stick them onto the hooks good. Otherwise, they'll fall off.*

Sydney: *Tuna? That sounds like cannibalism!*

Bailey: *Fish are cannibals, Sydzie.*

Sydney: *Gross. But tell your dad thanks. Will you set up a chat with the girls for tonight at 6:30 CDT? We saw a strange guy near the cabin last night, and we want to know whether you think he's suspicious.*

Bailey: *Will do. Why do you think he's strange?*

Sydney: *He looked like a mountain man, and he ran off into the woods. We couldn't see much in the darkness.*

Bailey: *There aren't any mountains in Wisconsin, are there?*

Sydney: *I know. But that's the best way I can describe him. He looked like someone who lives alone in the mountains. Think of Heidi's grandfather, or better yet John the Baptist, the guy in the Bible who was a loner and wore clothes made of camel's hair. He stayed alive by eating locusts and wild honey.*

Bailey: *John lived in the desert, Sydz, and he was Jesus' cousin.*

Sydney: *Whatever. Just think of a big, bearded, lonesome guy, with a backpack and tattered clothes.*

Bailey: *OK. I'll tell the girls. We'll meet you here at 6:30. In the meantime, good luck with the old man of the woods.*

Sydney: *Thanks, Bailey. See you later.*

Alexis chewed a hangnail on her thumb, a bad habit she wished she didn't have.

"So, do you still want ice cream?" Sydney asked.

"No. I've changed my mind," said Alexis. "Maybe when we come back tonight. I have an idea, though."

"What's that?" said Sydney.

"There's a grocery store across the street. Let's get some frozen pizza dough and other stuff to make pizza. The dough will be thawed out by suppertime. We can make pizza tonight and keep some of the dough for bait. What do you think?"

"Great idea," said Sydney, shutting down the computer. "Let's go shopping."

"Happy fishing," the man at the lunch counter said sarcastically as the girls left the shop. Sydney and Alexis ignored him.

Biscuit sat patiently just outside the door, his leash tied to a big, iron hook screwed into the building's outer wall.

"Just a few more minutes, boy," said Alexis, petting his fluffy fur. "We're going across the street to buy groceries. Then we'll come back to get you."

Biscuit whined softly and raised his right paw as if to say, *Please don't leave me here.*

"I'm texting Aunt Dee," Sydney said as Alexis reassured Biscuit. She took out her cell phone and typed NEED LIST OF KINDS/SIZES OF FISH IN N. TWIN LAKE AND BEST WAY 2 CATCH THEM. WILL XPLAIN L8R. SYD.

"Okay, that's done. Now let's get the stuff for the dough balls."

The girls left Biscuit and crossed the street.

Sydney and Alexis loaded a large package of frozen pizza dough into their shopping cart. Then they added pepperoni, some olive oil, cornmeal, a big bag of shredded pizza cheese, and a can of tomato sauce.

"How about some mushrooms?" asked Alexis. "Do you like them on your pizza?"

"Sure," said Sydney. "And onions too."

Alexis put a carton of mushrooms and an onion into the shopping cart. Then they headed to the checkout counter. Just as they were about to pay for their groceries, Sydney remembered something. "Where can I find canned tuna?" she asked the cashier.

"At the end of aisle ten."

Sydney hurried off and returned with three cans of tuna.

"Three!" Alexis exclaimed.

"I want to catch lots of fish," said Sydney.

They left the store carrying paper bags filled with groceries, and headed back across the street.

"Hey!" Alexis said. "Biscuit's gone!"

Biscuit's leash and collar hung from the hook, but Biscuit was nowhere in sight. The owner of Tompkins' Ice Cream Shop stood outside. "That way," he said, pointing in the direction of the resort. "He slipped out of his collar and scampered off."

Sydney shoved her grocery bags at Alexis and sprinted as fast as she could down Twin Lakes Road.

"Wow, can that girl run!" the man said.

"She did track and field in the Junior Olympics," said Alexis, taking Biscuit's leash off the hook in the wall. She dropped it and his collar into one of the grocery bags. Then she hurried after Sydney. When she got to the resort, she found her friend alone on the cabin's front porch.

"I don't know what to do," Sydney cried. "He's lost!"

A sinking feeling swept through Alexis's stomach as she put up the groceries and hung up Biscuit's collar. "We have to find him, Sydney. But where do we start to look? He could be anywhere."

Ruff-ruff! Ruff-ruff! Biscuit's bark came from far away—deep in the woods surrounding the lake. "Biscuit!" they shouted. "Biscuit! Biscuit! Here, boy!"

When Biscuit didn't come, they dashed into the forest, hurrying toward the sound of his bark.

Alexis grabbed Sydney's arm, stopping her dead in her tracks.

"What?" Sydney protested.

"We need to mark our trail," said Alexis. "Remember? We learned it in camp. If we aren't familiar with our surroundings, we should mark a trail so we can find our way back."

She found some pinecones on the path and stacked them into a neat little pyramid. Then she laid a stick next to them, pointing in the direction they'd come from. "Whenever we make a turn, we have to mark the place," she said.

The girls continued in the direction of Biscuit's barking, stopping to mark the trail every time they turned. After a while, they didn't hear his barking anymore. They only heard birds chirping loudly in the trees.

"Why do you think he stopped barking?" Sydney asked. "Or. . .do you think that someone stopped him from barking?"

"I don't know," Alexis said. "But I just said a silent prayer and asked God to keep him safe."

"I'm praying too," said Sydney.

Tall trees blocked out most of the sunlight, and soft pine needles covered the cool forest floor. The girls looked for Biscuit's pawprints there, but found nothing.

"I hope he didn't run into a bear," said Alexis.

"I doubt it," said Sydney. "Besides, Biscuit could outrun a bear or any other wild animal. He's fast."

"I guess so," said Alexis, marking their trail with a little pile of stones.

Sydney walked on ahead of her and disappeared among the trees.

"Yeeeeeeah! No! No! Stop it!"

Alex ran toward her friend's screams. She found Sydney lying face down on the ground with her hands over her head. Biscuit licked her face with his long, pink tongue.

"Oh Biscuit!" Alexis gushed. She picked up the little dog.

"Eewwwww, Biscuit. You stink!"

"I know," said Sydney, getting up and brushing herself off. "He smells awful. Biscuit, where have you been? What's all that smelly stuff in your fur?"

Biscuit let out a sad whimper. Alexis put him down, and he sat in front of her. He raised a paw.

"He came out of nowhere and ran between my legs," Sydney said. "I tripped over him and fell. Stay with him. I'm going to walk over there and see if I can find out what he got into."

Sydney wove her way through the brush and the pine trees sniffing the air for anything that smelled like Biscuit now smelled.

"Alexis, come here," she called. "I see something."

Reluctantly, Alexis picked Biscuit up and went to where Sydney was.

"Look at that," Sydney said, pointing slightly to the right.

In the distance, deep in the forest, she saw an eerie purple glow. It was the color of lilac nail polish, not a deep purple, but soft and wispy. It lit up the trees, making the forest look enchanted.

"Whoa," said Alexis. "What do you think that is?"

"Should we go and check it out?" Sydney asked.

Alexis looked at Biscuit. "I don't trust him not to run again," she said. "Otherwise, I'd love to check it out. We'd better take him home."

"I guess so," said Sydney. "Unless—"

She saw a Virginia Creeper vine growing around a nearby tree trunk. She reached for it.

"Stop!" Alexis said, grabbing Sydney's hand. "It's poison ivy!"

"No, it's not. It has five leaves, not three." Sydney broke off a piece, and tied it around Biscuit's neck. "These vines are strong, and they'll make a good collar."

She broke off a longer piece and tied it to the collar like a rope. "There, now he has a leash. Oh Biscuit, you smell just terrible!"

Biscuit looked at her and sighed.

Cautiously, the girls walked through the forest toward the light.

"Maybe we're seeing the Northern Lights," Alexis suggested.

"Nice try," Sydney said. "But you can only see the Northern Lights at night."

They kept moving toward the purple glow. If they walked just a few more yards, they might discover what caused it.

WHOOOOOOSH!

Suddenly, the forest came alive. A noise surrounded them, like air rushing through a tunnel.

"Go back! Go back! Go back!"

At the sound of the loud whisper, Alexis screamed.

Sydney scooped Biscuit into her arms.

The girls ran for their lives!

Lost

"Run!" Alexis cried. "Hurry!"

The girls ran as fast as their legs could carry them. Then Sydney stopped.

"Wait," she said. She grabbed Alexis's arm. "I don't think it's following us."

Alexis quit running. She stood huffing and puffing, trying to catch her breath. Gigantic pine trees surrounded them, and she wrapped her arms around one of the trunks to brace herself.

"I can't hear it anymore," said Sydney. She set Biscuit down in a soft pile of leaves. "What do you think it was?"

"A bear, maybe?" Alexis answered.

"Bears don't glow purple and talk," Sydney said. *"Shhhhh."*

They listened. The whooshing had become a buzz, barely noticeable, locked deep inside the forest.

"Did you hear what it said?" asked Alexis. " *'Get out! Get out! Get out!'* "

"That's not what I heard," Sydney told her. "I heard *'Go back! Go back! Go back!'* But whatever it said, something doesn't want us here."

Biscuit rolled happily in the pine needles. He didn't seem bothered by the spooky sound in the woods.

"We need to get out of here," Sydney said. She picked up the end of Biscuit's viney leash and started walking.

"Syd?" Alexis asked, "Are you sure the resort is that way?"

Sydney stopped. She looked left and right and all around. "I think we came from over there," she said, pointing to her left.

"I think it's that way," said Alexis, pointing to her right. "I didn't pay attention to where we were going when we ran away. And unless we find our trail markers, I think we're"—she hesitated—"lost."

Sydney sighed. "Okay. We've been lost in the woods before. Let's just stay calm and practice what we learned at Discovery Lake Camp."

"Well, the first thing you're supposed to do is blow a whistle," said Alexis, "which we don't have. Or shout to get someone's attention. And the last thing we want to do right now is draw attention to ourselves. Whatever is out there probably wonders where we are. So making noise is not an option."

"I'm thinking," Sydney said. "We learned at camp to look for water, like a river or stream, and follow it. That way we might run into someone canoeing, or fishing, or whatever."

Alexis started chewing her hangnail again. "That would be great except that the only water around here is the lake, and we don't know where that is right now. Besides, we don't want to run into whatever it is that's trying to get us."

"We don't know for sure that it's trying to get us," said Sydney. "What's up with you, Alex? You're always the one with the positive, realistic attitude."

"Well, I think 'go back' or 'get out' or whatever it said is enough for us to know that it doesn't want us around," Alexis argued. "Anyhow, I'm sure we can find our way home. We just need to stay calm." She looked at her watch.

"What time is it?" Sydney asked.

"Almost noon."

Sydney handed Biscuit's leash to Alexis. Then she started walking in circles around the pine trees.

"What are you doing?" Alex wondered.

"Looking for moss. It grows on the north side of tree trunks. The woods are south of the resort, so if we can find north, then we'll know which direction to go."

Biscuit decided that Sydney was playing a game. He pulled hard on his viney leash until it snapped in two. Then, joyfully, he pranced around the tree trunks with her.

Alexis busied herself with marking the spot where they were. She piled up some pine branches and laid two sticks in a criss-cross on top of them. "There," she said. "This is our starting point. If we see this again, we'll know that we're walking in circles. Why don't you just call your Aunt Dee and tell her we're lost? You have your cell phone."

"Oh, right," Sydney complained as she inspected another trunk. "I'll call her in the middle of her interview and say, 'Aunt Dee, we're lost in the Chequamegon-Nicolet National Forest, and something wicked is in here with us. Do you think you might be able to get away for a few minutes and come find us?'"

"It was just an idea," said Alexis.

Biscuit stopped and sniffed the air. His ears perked up. He let out a little *Ar-roof*, and then off he ran into the forest.

"Oh no," said Sydney, "Not again! Let's go."

"Wait," said Alexis. "Remember what that thing said. Are you sure you want to go back in there?"

"Think about it, Alex—it's Biscuit. We *have* to go. If we lost him, Kate would never forgive us."

"She would too," said Alexis, stalling for time. "She has to. The Bible says to."

Sydney took off after Biscuit. Reluctantly, Alexis followed. "We have to be quiet," she said. "If we start calling for him, whatever it is might hear us."

"You're right," Sydney agreed.

The buzzing noise grew louder as they approached the spot where they'd heard the *whoosh*—where the voice whispered, *"Go back! Go back! Go back!"*

The forest seemed darker now, and they heard that noise, the persistent buzz, a low sound, almost a growl. Then, as Sydney and Alexis walked deeper into the forest, they saw the eerie purple glow.

"What's that?" Sydney whispered.

"It's the purple light. We saw it before," said Alexis.

"No," said Sydney. "Something is out there walking in the woods."

The words had no sooner left her lips than they saw the mountain man. He stood in a small clearing in the distance.

"Drop!" Sydney gasped. The girls fell to the ground and hid behind a huge log.

Alexis peeked around one side of it.

"Oh my goodness!" she whispered. "He's got Biscuit!"

The mountain man walked toward them with Biscuit held firmly in the crook of his left arm. In his right hand, he carried the walking stick. The backpack was gone, but he still wore the floppy cap and ragged clothes. As he came nearer, the girls heard his deep, gruff voice.

"I need to get you back," he said. "If they come looking for you, they might find out what I'm doing. It'll be in all the newspapers and even on television. And I'm not ready for that yet."

As he got closer, Alexis and Sydney prayed that Biscuit wouldn't bark or wiggle out of the man's arms and run to them. Even a whisper could be heard, so they just huddled together behind the log and looked at one another with desperation.

Baw-waw-waw!

Suddenly, a hollow, loud barking sound came out of the eerie purple glow. It echoed through the forest and made Sydney shiver. She felt Alexis grip her forearm.

"I never tied Fang up before," said the man's rough voice. "He's not at all happy about it. Now, once I get you back home, don't you come after us again, you hear? This is no place for a friendly little dog like you. You tell that gal to keep you on your leash."

The girls heard the mountain man's boots crunch pinecones against the forest floor. He was almost to the log now, and they plastered their bodies tightly against the ground.

Please, dear God, don't let him see us, Sydney prayed silently.

Biscuit began to whine, sensing that they were nearby.

"Whoa, slow down there, boy," said the mountain man, tightening his grip. "Nothing's going to get you."

Sydney could imagine Biscuit squirming to get out of the man's arms.

"Whew!" she heard the man exclaim. "Your owner's going to be mad when she gets a whiff of you. You shouldn't have rolled in my manure pile."

Certain that the man was far enough away, Sydney let out a sigh of relief.

"He saw you!" Alexis whispered.

"No, he didn't," Sydney replied. "He walked right on by."

"I don't mean now," said Alexis. "I mean when you were out with Biscuit last night. He said, 'Tell that gal to keep you on your leash.'"

"You're right," whispered Sydney. "So now what do we do?"

"We follow them," said Alexis.

The thing called Fang started barking again. Soon its deep *Baw-waw-waw*s mixed with long, mournful *AR-ROOoooooo*s.

"I think he has a wolf tied up out there," said Sydney.

"Oh, do you think so?" Alexis shuddered.

"Whatever it is sounds big," Sydney replied.

They got up from the ground and followed the mountain man,

making sure that they stayed well behind him and hidden in the trees.

"Do you know what?" Sydney whispered as she ducked under a low branch. "I just thought of something."

"What?" said Alexis, avoiding the same branch.

"We need to get ahead of them."

"Why?" Alexis wondered nearly tripping over a rock half buried in the soil.

"Because Biscuit is smart," Sydney said. "If we're behind them, he'll run right to us when the mountain man puts him down. Then we'll be caught for sure. And who knows what he'd do to us. Probably take us back to that purple glow where he has the wolf tied up." She squeezed around a Cockspur Hawthorne tree and caught her arm on one of its long, sharp thorns. "Ouch!" she squealed.

"Ssshhhh!" Alexis scolded.

It was too late. Biscuit heard Sydney's cry.

Ruff-ruff-aroof! Ruff-ruff-aroof!

"Oh no," said Alexis. "Dear God, please, please, let the mountain man hang on to Biscuit."

"Lord, hear our prayer," Sydney agreed, quickly wiping a dribble of blood from her arm.

They waited, expecting Biscuit to bound through the woods right to them. But nothing happened.

"Oh thank you, Lord," Sydney said.

"You're right," said Alexis as they slipped in and out among the trees. "We should get to the resort before Biscuit does. I sure wish we knew a shortcut."

"Ooof!" She tripped over something and fell flat on her face.

"Are you okay?" asked Sydney.

"I'm fine," said Alexis, pushing herself up onto her knees. "I just tripped over this. . .shovel."

A garden shovel with a long wooden handle lay in the dirt under Alexis. "This is a strange place for a shovel," she said, standing up. "Someone must have been digging here. Maybe looking for something."

"Or, maybe burying something," Sydney suggested.

The girls looked at one another. Without saying a word, each knew what the other was thinking. The shovel belonged to the mountain man.

"Hey," said Alexis, brushing dirt and pine needles off of her knees. "Look!" She pointed to the base of a nearby tree trunk. "Isn't that moss?"

Sydney checked it out. "It sure is," she confirmed. "That way is north."

She pointed in the direction that the mountain man went. "Let's hurry."

The girls squirmed around gangly bushes and past the branches of evergreen trees, and before long they saw bright sunlight not far ahead of them. The green grass surrounding the resort office came into view, and Sydney and Alexis hurried into the clearing.

"We got here before he did," said Sydney.

"I think it would be best if we were in the cabin," Alexis suggested. "That way, if he's watching, he won't know we were in the woods."

"Good idea," Sydney agreed.

They took off running, darting behind the resort office, staying away from the woods. They ran down a little hill to the back of their cabin. Sydney pulled the key out of her pocket and unlocked the door.

"Quick! Let's go to the front porch," said Alexis, rushing through the little kitchen and living room. She pushed open the front door and stepped onto the porch just in time to see Biscuit race out of the woods.

Ruff-ruff! Ruff-ruff! Ruff-ruff-aroof!

Alex opened the porch door and stepped outside to meet her furry friend.

"Biscuit, where have you been?" she said in a voice much louder than normal. "We've been worried sick about you!"

Sydney was close behind. "Why are you yelling?" she asked.

"I want that guy to hear me," said Alexis softly. "I want him to think that we were here all along."

Biscuit licked her hands.

Sydney looked toward the woods. The mountain man was nowhere in sight. "I think he's gone," she said.

Alexis held Biscuit at arm's length. "Oh, you smell *so* bad. We have to give you a bath. Why did you roll in that man's manure pile?"

"Manure pile!" Sydney shrieked.

"Didn't you hear him?" said Alexis. "He told Biscuit that he smelled bad, and then he said that Biscuit shouldn't have rolled in the manure pile."

"I must have missed that part," said Sydney, keeping her distance from Biscuit. "Manure is made up of animal droppings, like from cows and horses and sheep. Why in the world would he have a manure pile in the middle of a forest?"

Alexis picked Biscuit up and carried him onto the porch.

"Oh Alex, don't bring him in here," said Sydney. "He stinks."

"I know," her friend replied, "but if we don't keep him in the cabin, he might run away again. I'm not going back there. I'll get his leash and collar, and then we'll take him into the lake for a bath."

"I'll get them," said Sydney, walking toward the kitchen.

A few minutes later, Alexis buckled Biscuit's collar around his neck and hooked the leash onto the collar.

"Maybe the mountain man is keeping farm animals out there in the woods. Go get my shampoo from the bathroom, please," she told Sydney. "I'll meet you over by the dock."

Alexis opened the screen door and led Biscuit outside. He turned and pulled toward the woods. "No way, Biscuit!" she said. "You are *not* going back by that man. I wish you could talk, because I'd love to know what he's up to."

Sydney arrived with the shampoo. "Why would he have farm animals in the woods?" she asked. "It doesn't make any sense."

"Neither does the purple glow or the whispering woods," Alexis responded, kicking off her tennis shoes and wading into the water. "Come on, Biscuit." She held tight to his leash as the dog bounded into the lake splashing water all over her shorts.

"Okay, let's think about what we know," Sydney said as she opened the cap on the shampoo bottle. "We have a mountain man living in the forest. There's a spooky, purple glow in the woods, and something goes *whoosh* and talks. And a wolf, or whatever, belongs to the guy, and he has it tied up."

"Toss me the shampoo," said Alex. "And he has a manure pile. So that shovel probably belongs to him." She squeezed a generous amount of shampoo onto Biscuit's back. Then she tossed the bottle back to Sydney.

"And did you hear what he said about people finding out about him?" said Sydney. "He said if anyone found out what he was doing, it would be in the newspapers and on television. He's up to no good, Alex. I just know it."

"But he's kind to animals," her friend said. She was busy scrubbing Biscuit and had him so covered with lather that he looked like a little lamb. "Don't look now, but here comes that Duncan kid."

Duncan Lumley was heading for the dock carrying a fishing rod and tackle box. When he saw the girls washing the dog, he scowled. "What are you doing that for?" he said, walking right up to Sydney, almost getting in her face.

She took a step backward. "We're giving our dog a bath."

"Well, get him out of there," said Duncan. "You'll scare the fish away."

"Oh, for goodness' sake," Sydney said. "You act like you own the place."

"I do," he said. "We come here every year."

Alexis rinsed Biscuit off and led him out of the water. He shivered, sending a shower of water all over Duncan.

"Hey!" Duncan cried, jumping backward. "Knock it off!"

"So what do you know about the guy who lives in the woods?" Sydney asked indifferently.

Alexis shot her a look. She couldn't believe that Sydney had asked Duncan such a thing.

The boy grinned. "I know all about him," he said. "He's the ghost of Jacques Chouteau."

CHAPTER 5

Jacques Chouteau

"Who's Jock Show Toe?" Sydney asked.

Duncan smirked and shook his head. "Don't you know anything? It's a French name." Then, with a phony French accent, he said, *"Jacques Chouteau."*

Duncan's attitude irritated Sydney, but she tried to hold her temper. "Yeah, well, who is he?"

The redheaded boy walked onto the dock and opened his tackle box.

"I'm not telling," he said. He took a stubby, white Styrofoam container out of the box and opened the lid. He reached inside and pulled out a night crawler. "Catch." He flung it toward Sydney.

Sydney didn't flinch. The worm fell at her feet and quickly dug into the muddy soil.

"That's one less worm that you'll have for bait," Sydney announced. "Come on, Alexis, let's go."

"Yeah, you should go," Duncan told them. "I need to do some serious fishing."

Alexis walked ahead of Sydney, tightly holding Biscuit's leash. He trotted a few steps forward and then stopped to shake the water off his soggy fur coat. When they were almost to the front porch, Biscuit decided to lie down and roll in the dirt.

"No, Biscuit!" Alexis said. She swept him into her arms and hurried through the door. "There," she said, setting him on a chair. "You behave yourself. You've gotten into enough trouble today."

Sydney stepped inside and closed the door. "We need to talk to Mrs. Miller in the office."

"What about?" Alexis asked.

"We need fishing poles. That brochure on the kitchen table says that the resort has some we can use. I also want to find out where to get bait."

"But we have dough balls," said Alexis, pointing toward the pizza dough thawing on the kitchen counter.

"I know," said Sydney. "But I think we each should fish with a different kind of bait. It'll give us a better chance at catching fish."

The girls shut Biscuit on the porch and headed up the driveway toward the office.

"Do you think Duncan told the truth about a ghost in the woods?" Alexis asked.

"I don't believe anything he says," said Sydney. "He was just trying to scare us. You didn't believe him, did you?"

Alexis kicked a stone to the side of the driveway. "I don't believe in ghosts," she said. "That guy in the woods is probably a very nice man— but I wish I knew that for sure."

Sydney opened the front door to the office, and the girls went inside. Mrs. Miller wasn't at the desk. From somewhere inside the house came the sound of a soap opera on the television. Sydney rang the little metal bell next to a sign that read RING FOR SERVICE.

"Hey, look at this," said Alexis. She pointed to a painting on the wall. It showed a man dressed in a heavy fur coat with a big fur collar and a warm fur cap. In his left hand, he proudly held an animal skin. A caption at the bottom of the picture said *Jacques Chouteau, Fur Trapper.*

"Wow," said Sydney. "He really did exist."

Mrs. Miller pulled aside a curtain that hung in the doorway dividing the office from the living quarters. "Did you ring the bell?" she asked. She turned on the television behind the desk to her soap opera.

"I'm just wondering if we could get some fishing poles," said Sydney. "Alexis and I entered the contest."

A commercial interrupted the program, and Mrs. Miller turned her attention toward the girls. "Good for you!" she said. "Mr. Miller can certainly fix you up with some poles. Do you each have a fishing license?"

"No, ma'am," Sydney answered. "I didn't know that we needed one."

"You might," said Mrs. Miller. "My husband owns the bait shop. Go up to the road and turn right. In a little while you'll come to a restaurant called The Wave. The bait shop is next door. Charlie, that's my husband, will get you all fixed up." The commercial ended, and she turned back to the TV.

Sydney wanted to ask about the picture of Jacques Chouteau, but she could tell Mrs. Miller was too preoccupied with her program. "Thanks," she said as she and Alexis walked out the door. "See you later."

Charlie's Bait and Tackle was in a small, rundown building. It looked like an old garage set behind the parking lot of the restaurant, not far from the lakeshore. When the girls opened the front door, a strong, fishy smell filled their nostrils. They stood near a tank where hundreds of tiny gray fish darted to and fro. Fish trophies hung on the paneled walls. Around the trophies, the walls were lined with fishing poles and hundreds of fishing lures, spoons, and flies. An old paddle was propped in the corner behind the service counter. The words FISH TALES TOLD HERE were carved into it. A revolving rack on the counter held different kinds of fishing lines, and the front of the counter was a glass display case filled with various sizes of hooks.

"May I help you?" said a bald-headed man sitting behind the counter.

"The lady at the resort sent us," said Sydney.

"That would be my wife, Betty," the man said. "I'm Charlie."

Sydney walked over to the counter. "Mr. Miller, we need a fishing license and some poles," she said. "And we'd like some bait too, please."

The man smiled. "How old are you girls?"

"Thirteen," said Sydney.

"Kids under sixteen don't need a license," he said. "What kind of poles do you need?"

Alexis joined Sydney by the counter. "We're not sure. The brochure at the resort said that you have some poles that we can use," she said. "We're competing in the fishing contest."

"You are, are you?" said Mr. Miller. "Well, good for you. Usually, girls don't fish."

His comment irritated Sydney. *Why does everyone around here think that girls don't fish?* she thought.

"We're entering the dockside contest," she told him. "We're planning to catch the biggest fish."

"Well good. I hope you do," Mr. Miller said as he disappeared into a room next to the counter. He quickly returned with two fishing rods. "These are rods with reels," he said. "They're for the big fish."

Alexis took the pole and inspected it. "I've fished with cane poles," she said. "But I've never used one of these."

"I have," said Sydney. "But I'm not very good at it."

"Then come on outside, and I'll give you a lesson," Mr. Miller said.

It took a few tries for the girls to get comfortable using the rod and reel. Soon, they cast the line into the water like pros. The reel allowed them to hang onto the pole and throw the line a good distance into the water, way out where the big fish swim.

Mr. Miller was friendly and helpful. He seemed genuinely pleased that the girls had entered the contest. He told them that they could use the poles for free, and he gave them some bait—a small pail filled with water and two dozen tiny gray fish called minnows. He also gave them a Styrofoam container like the one Duncan had, filled with squirming night crawlers.

Neither of the girls liked the idea of using live bait, but Mr. Miller convinced them that they had to. "You can't fish without live bait," he said. "If you want to be serious contenders in the contest, then you have to get over being squeamish."

Sydney had one more question before she and Alexis left the bait shop. "What do you know about Jacques Chouteau?" she asked.

"Oh, he's quite the legend around here," Mr. Miller said. "Jacques Chouteau was a French fur trapper. He hung out in northern Wisconsin way back in the 1800s. Mostly, he trapped beavers around here. Then he skinned them and sold their pelts to the Indians across the lake."

Mr. Miller took two ice-cream bars out of a nearby freezer case and handed one to each of the girls. He opened a can of soda for himself and sat down on a stool behind the counter.

"They say Jacques made camp somewhere in the forest around here, though I don't know exactly where. There're caves deep in the woods, a bunch of 'em hidden under mounds of earth and among the trees, so you don't even know that they're there. Folks say old Jacques hid his furs inside those caves—and his money too." Mr. Miller took a long drink of soda before he continued. "One day, he told folks he was gonna take his canoe over to the other side of the lake to do some trading at an Indian camp. That's the last anyone saw or heard from him. He set out across the lake on a nice, clear day, and he never came back."

Sydney licked the last bit of her vanilla ice cream off the wooden stick. "A kid at the resort says the ghost of Jacques Chouteau haunts the woods. Is that true?"

Mr. Miller put his elbows on the counter and leaned forward.

"Well, it just might be," he said mysteriously. "The legend says that Jacques Chouteau died in the woods, and his soul cries out sometimes. It moans, begging for someone to come and save him—"

Suddenly, the door swung open, and the girls jumped. The man from the lunch counter at the ice-cream shop came inside. He had two buddies with him, and when he saw the girls with their fishing poles, he laughed.

"You girls are really serious about fishing in the contest, aren't you?" he said. "You haven't got a chance."

Sydney was about to give him a piece of her mind when Mr. Miller came to her defense. "Now, Fred," he said. "Leave 'em alone. I think they'll do just fine."

The man named Fred walked past the girls like they were invisible. He took a spool of fishing line from the rack on the counter and paid for it. "My boy, Duncan, is gonna win the dock contest," he said. "He doesn't need these girls getting in his way."

Sydney felt her face turn hot. She was tempted to speak when Alexis tugged on her arm. "Let's go," she said. She thanked Mr. Miller for his help, and then they walked out the door.

"So that's Duncan's dad," Sydney said as they walked back to the resort. "It figures. They're both rude."

"We don't know them that well yet," said Alexis. "I'm sure there's something good about them. I don't think they're bad people. I remember on one TV show I watched, everyone hated this dad and son because they seemed obnoxious. But they turned out to be really nice."

Sydney said nothing.

It was almost suppertime, and when they got back to the cabin, Aunt Dee was on the porch reading a book. "Hey, girls," she said cheerfully. "How was your day?"

Biscuit slept near her feet looking like an angel.

"It was okay," Sydney told her. "We entered a fishing contest, and we just got back from the bait shop. Did you bring that list of fish that I texted you about?"

"It's on the kitchen table," Aunt Dee said. "And what's that thawing on the counter?"

"Pizza dough," said Alexis. "We thought we'd make pizza for supper."

The girls got busy in the kitchen. They saved a glob of the dough for bait and put it in the refrigerator. Then Alexis rolled out the rest for the crust. Sydney sprinkled it with olive oil, spread on some tomato sauce, and put on the toppings. They made a salad, and before long the girls and Aunt Dee sat at the kitchen table eating delicious slices of gooey homemade pizza.

"This is so good, girls," said Aunt Dee. "I'm glad you thought of it. Since you made dinner, I'll take care of the dishes tonight."

Sydney popped the last bite of pizza into her mouth and drank some milk. "Thanks, Aunt Dee," she said. "We went to the ice-cream shop this morning where they have a computer and free internet. We set up a group chat with the Camp Club Girls for 6:30. We'd better get going."

"Be back before dark," Aunt Dee said.

"We'll leave Biscuit here," Alexis said. "He's not allowed inside the ice-cream shop."

When they got to Tompkins' Ice Cream Shop, they found the tables and booths filled with customers enjoying after-dinner cones, malts, and sundaes. Sydney and Alexis walked to the back of the room and sat at the computer. They logged on to the Camp Club Girls' private chat room where the other girls were waiting.

Sydney: *Looks like we're all here.*

Kate: *How's Biscuit?*

Sydney: *He's fine. How's Arizona?*

Kate: *Really hot, but fun.*

Bailey: *I told everyone about the mountain man.*

Sydney: *Well, here's an update. Biscuit ran into the woods today, and the mountain man got him.*

Kate: *NO WAY! Why did you let him off his leash? Is he all right?*

Alexis: *It's okay, Kate. He pulled out of his collar and ran into the woods, but he's fine. We went after him.*

Sydney: *We followed Biscuit into the forest. Then we saw this weird, purple glow, and heard a whooshing noise. It sounded like someone whispered, "Go back. Go back." So we ran and hid.*

McKenzie: *Wow, who do you think it was?*

Alexis: *We don't know. It didn't sound human. It sounded like trees were whispering.*

Bailey: *Trees don't whisper, Alex.*

Elizabeth: *Be careful. A forest can be dangerous.*

Alexis: *I know, but we had to get Biscuit. We hid and saw the mountain man carry Biscuit back to the cabin.*

Sydney: *We think he's up to no good. He told Biscuit if people found out about him, he'd be in the newspapers and on TV.*

Elizabeth: *That man sounds creepy. Do you think he's a terrorist?*

Sydney: *He doesn't look like a terrorist, but neither did those guys we caught in Washington who planned to kill the President. We heard the ghost of an old fur trapper named Jacques Chouteau haunts the forest. Of course, we don't believe that. But we can't explain the purple light or the whispering. We need to investigate some more.*

Kate: *Be careful. The hotel we're at has overnight mail service. I'll send you some gadgets that might help you spy on him. Arizona is two hours behind Wisconsin, so I can send them today. You'll have them in the morning.*

Sydney: *Cool. We entered a fishing contest. Do you have any tips for catching big fish?*

McKenzie: *My brother always says be quiet, or you'll scare them. And you have to think like a fish and try to outsmart them.*

Bailey: *Dough balls for bait.*

Sydney: *We're making them tonight.*

Kate: *I'll send you my mini-microcamera and some other stuff. Maybe you can use some of it when you fish.*

Alexis: *Awesome!*

Elizabeth: *And I'll pray that God sends you tons of fish, just like He did when He fed the five thousand people in the Bible!*

Sydney: *I don't think we need five thousand fish, Beth. Just pray for us to catch the biggest one. We met this disgusting kid, Duncan, who acts like he's already won the contest. We're going to show him.*

Elizabeth: *Remember James 4:6 says that "God opposes the proud, but gives grace to the humble." Trust God to do what's best.*

Sydney: *Will do. Have to sign off now. Someone's waiting for the computer.*

A man and a little boy stood patiently near the workstation at the back of the shop. The boy was eating a chocolate ice-cream cone, and it melted and dribbled down his arm.

Kate: *Please take very good care of Biscuit.*

Alexis: *I promise.*

Bailey: *Text me if anything happens, and I'll tell the girls.*

Sydney: *OK. Good night, everyone.*

As the girls walked away from the computer, Sydney's cell phone rang.

"Sydney?" Aunt Dee said. "I'd like you girls to come home. Mr. Miller just found a dead coyote on the beach. The man in Cabin Two saw something big run into the forest. He thinks it was a bear. I'd feel better if you were here."

Ghost Dog

When the girls got to the resort, Mr. Miller was walking toward the office. He carried a shovel, and his T-shirt was spattered with blood.

"Are you okay?" Sydney asked.

He wiped the sweat from his forehead. "I just buried a dead coyote. Something got him good. Nearly tore him apart."

Sydney's stomach churned. She loved animals. "What do you think did it?" she asked.

Mr. Miller set the shovel on the ground and wiped his hands on his overalls.

"I'm guessing a bear," he said. "I can't think of anything else that would tear an animal apart like that. Usually, a coyote can hold its own."

Alexis shuddered. "Do bears often kill things around here?"

"Not that much," said Mr. Miller. "When they do, it's mostly late at night, and they drag their prey into the woods to eat it. A bear coming at dusk and leaving what it killed isn't a good sign. It means it might be sick." He picked up the shovel. "You girls stay inside tonight, and keep your dog inside too."

"Charlie, telephone!" Mrs. Miller stood on the front porch. She held a cordless phone.

Mr. Miller said, "If you need anything, call the office. Don't be out in the dark."

Alexis linked her arm in Sydney's as they walked to the cabin. "I just had a scary thought," she said.

"What about?" asked Sydney.

"Well, last week, I was playing a new Nancy Drew video game. It happens at a cabin on a lake. In it, a pack of howling ghost dogs attack her friend's house at night." Alexis took a deep breath. "Syd, you don't think—"

"Oh Alex, you don't believe the howling we heard in the woods was a ghost dog, do you?"

"I don't believe in ghosts," Alexis said. "But if I did, I'd think that the mountain man is the ghost of Jacques Chouteau, and Fang, his wolf or whatever that thing is, is a ghost too. Of course, I don't believe that."

"So, we have to go back in the woods and find out what's really going on," said Sydney.

They were almost to the back door of the cabin. The sun had set behind the trees, and the sky was becoming dark. Whatever was in the woods was lurking in the darkness.

"We're not going into the woods tonight, Syd," said Alexis. "It's too dangerous with that bear, or whatever it is, hanging around." She opened the door to the cabin.

"I didn't mean tonight," said Sydney. "But tomorrow, maybe, in the bright daylight."

Biscuit ran to the back door to meet them. Alexis bent and patted him on the head. "What about the bear?" she asked.

"We'll need something to protect us," Sydney said.

"Protect you from what?" Aunt Dee's voice came from the living room.

"Careful," Sydney whispered. "Excellent hearing."

She closed the back door and flipped the lock.

The girls went into the living room where Aunt Dee sat on the floor playing the card game solitaire.

"We were just talking about what would happen if we ran into the bear in the daylight tomorrow," said Sydney. "We were wondering how to protect ourselves."

"I've already thought of that," said Aunt Dee. "I'm going to give you some pepper spray to carry. It's a good idea for you to have protection in case you run into something, but only use it in a dire emergency. Understood? Only if your life depends on it."

"Understood," Sydney agreed.

"In the meantime, I called a ranger from the forest office. He's coming to look at the dead coyote. He should be able to tell what killed it." Aunt Dee uncovered the ace of spades and put it above the other cards on the floor.

"Good luck," said Sydney. "Mr. Miller already buried it."

"You're kidding!" Aunt Dee exclaimed. She put the two of spades on top of the ace.

"Nope," Sydney said. "We met him on the driveway, and he told us all about it. He had a shovel in his hands, and his shirt was bloody."

Aunt Dee uncovered the king of hearts and laid it face up. "Well, maybe Ranger Geissman can find some evidence where the body was."

"Do we know for sure that a bear killed it?" Sydney asked.

"Mr. Miller said the man in Cabin Two saw something, but he couldn't say for sure what it was," said Aunt Dee. "He said that it was big, and it moved very fast."

Sydney took the leftover dough out of the refrigerator. "Cabin Two is the Lumleys.'"

"How do you know that?" asked her aunt.

"We've seen the kid, Duncan, a couple of times. He's rude. So is his dad. He thinks it's really dumb that Alex and I entered the fishing contest."

Sydney opened a can of tuna, and Biscuit came running into the kitchen to investigate the smell. "He told Mr. Miller that he doesn't want a couple of girls getting in the way of Duncan winning the contest."

Sydney mixed the tuna with the dough and rolled it into little balls. Then she rolled them in cornmeal.

Soon, the beams from a car's headlights flashed through the cabin windows. Sydney looked outside and saw a park service car pull up to their back door. "I think the ranger's here," she said.

The girls and Aunt Dee went out to meet him.

"So, where's the dead coyote?" Ranger Geissman asked.

"The resort owner buried it," said Aunt Dee. "But maybe we can find enough evidence to get some idea about what killed it."

She got her flashlight from the kitchen table, and they all walked to the shore. "It was right over here," said Aunt Dee.

Ranger Geissman shined his flashlight on the sandy strip at the edge of the lake. The only pieces of evidence left were a few spots of blood and gobs of matted, gray fur. "Well," he said, "looks like there was a struggle here. Looks like the coyote tried to fight off whatever got it. Usually, a coyote won't get much of a chance to fight with a bear. A bear attacks, and that's it."

He walked around the area looking for clues. "This is interesting," he said. "Looks like two sets of canine footprints here. Charlie Miller found just one body, right?"

Aunt Dee shined her flashlight on the ground to get a better look at the prints. "That's right. Just one dead coyote, and the man in Cabin Two saw something run away."

"Did he say what it was?" asked Ranger Geissman.

"He thought it was a bear, but he wasn't sure. He just said it was big and fast."

AR-AR-AR-ROooooooooooooooooooooo.   .AR-AR-AR-ROooooooooo-oooooooooooooo... A mournful cry came from deep in the forest. Sydney whispered in Alexis's ear. "It's Fang!"

"Well, there's your answer," said the ranger. "I think a big wolf killed your coyote. If you look at this other set of prints, you can see they're huge. They're not coyote, but definitely canine and probably a wolf."

He walked up and down the narrow beach looking for more evidence. "I don't see any sign of a bear," he said. "And no blood trail leading into the woods, so the other dog must not have been badly injured. Looks like a dog fight to me. Most likely your coyote tangled with a good-sized wolf."

Aunt Dee sighed with relief.

"Well, that's good to hear," she said. "The last thing we need is a sick bear wandering around. Will you stop at the office and tell the Millers what you found?"

"Will do," said Ranger Geissman, walking to his car. "And I hope you get the job at the ranger station," he added. "You'd be good on our team."

"Thanks," said Aunt Dee. "I hope so too."

The ranger drove to the office, and Aunt Dee and the girls went back inside.

Boom! Boom! Boom!

Someone pounded hard on the front door.

Boom! Boom! Boom!

"Now who would that be?" Aunt Dee wondered. She walked to the door and peeked through the curtains on the window. "It's Mr. Lumley from Cabin Two." Aunt Dee opened the door. Fred Lumley stood there with Duncan at his side.

"We want to know what's going on over here," Mr. Lumley said.

Aunt Dee invited them in. "Why, nothing's going on," she said. "What do you mean?"

Mr. Lumley looked around the cabin as if he expected someone to be there. Meanwhile, Duncan stood next to him with a snide grin on his face.

"Dunk here said you were all wandering by the lake with flashlights.

Then he saw a police car drive away. If there's trouble, I want to know."

Aunt Dee got her backpack from the bedroom and unzipped it. She took out her ranger identification badge and handed it to Duncan's dad. "I'm Dee Powers," she said. "I'm a US Park Ranger. Another ranger and I were trying to find out what killed the coyote on the beach."

Duncan's face lit up. "You're a park ranger!" he said. "No way."

"Way!" said Aunt Dee, smiling.

"But ladies can't be park rangers—can they, Dad?"

Duncan's father looked at the ID and smirked. "Looks like they can, Dunk," he said, handing the ID back to Aunt Dee. "So what did the other ranger think happened to the coyote? I told the Millers that I saw something big hurry into the woods. I'm sure it was a bear."

"You're sure it was a bear, or you *think* it was a bear?" said Aunt Dee.

Mr. Lumley ignored her question. "So what did the guy ranger say?"

Duncan stood with his hands on his hips. Once in a while, he glanced toward the kitchen at the cookie sheet filled with dough balls.

The smile disappeared from Aunt Dee's face. Sydney could tell she was as irritated with Fred Lumley as Sydney was with Duncan.

"Nothing proved it was a bear attack," said Aunt Dee. "We saw another set of tracks on the beach, probably a wolf's. Ranger Geissman and I agreed that the coyote's death was the result of a dog fight. So Mr. Lumley, you and Duncan have nothing to worry about. There's no bear, and everything is under control."

"Come on, Dunk," said Mr. Lumley, putting his hand on his son's shoulder. "Let's go." They turned and walked out the door. As they did Fred Lumley mumbled, "I know what I saw."

"Have a nice evening," Aunt Dee replied cheerfully.

Neither Mr. Lumley nor Duncan answered.

"Well, those are a couple of happy fellows, aren't they?" said Sydney's aunt, shutting the door.

"You haven't seen the worst of them," Sydney told her. "Duncan is a real pain, but I'm going to show him. Tomorrow, when Alex and I start fishing, he'll wish that he'd never come to North Twin Lake."

She went to the kitchen and loaded the dough balls into a plastic bag. "I've got a secret weapon. While Alex fishes with live bait, I'll be fishing with these—some nice, tasty tuna treats for the big guys."

"Well then, you'd better turn in early," Aunt Dee said. "The fish bite best at dawn."

Sydney and Alexis went to their room to study the fish booklet that Aunt Dee had brought from the ranger station. They needed to research which fish were the biggest and how to catch them.

"Muskies," said Sydney.

"Huh?" Alexis wondered.

"We need to fish for muskies. *Esox masquinongy* is the scientific name. Also known as muskellunge, lunge, maskinonge, and great pike. The Ojibwa Indians called them *maashkinoozhe*, which means ugly fish. It says here that you catch them by casting, and they like spoon lures or live bait."

"What's a spoon lure?" asked Alexis. She took some hand lotion from her bag, put a glob in the palm of her hand, and offered some to Sydney.

"I'm not sure exactly," Sydney said, squeezing lotion onto her hands. "The bait shop probably has them, but I think we should just stick to our live bait and the dough balls. It says that the world record for the biggest muskie is almost 70 pounds."

"Oh Syd! How will we handle a 70-pound fish? We don't weigh much more than that." Alexis sat down on Sydney's bed.

Sydney continued reading. "The average size for a big muskie in North Twin Lake is 35 to 40 inches. It doesn't say how much a fish that size weighs. The rules for the fishing contest say that the fish are measured by length, not weight. Here's a picture." She handed the booklet to Alexis.

"Oh, it's ugly!" Alexis exclaimed. "But it can't help the way it looks. Poor fish."

The picture showed a long, silver-brown fish. It had brown stripes on its body and spots on its tail. The eyes were glaring and the nose was short. Its lower jaw stuck out in a long underbite.

"It has teeth!" said Alexis.

"Yeah, I know," Sydney said. "Look at the caption under the picture. It says the teeth are as sharp as surgical scalpels, and you should never stick your hand into its mouth."

"As if I would want to stick my hand in there," said Alexis. "I'm sure we'll be fine. But Sydney, do you really want to do this?"

"I do!" said Sydney. "We're going to show Duncan Lumley how to fish. Tomorrow we'll catch the biggest muskie in North Twin Lake."

"Well then," Alexis said, standing. "We'd better get ready for bed and get a good night's sleep. We have to be up before dawn."

She headed for the bathroom holding her toothbrush and pajamas. "And if we catch one of those things, you're going to take it off the hook."

Before long, the girls turned off the light in their room, said their prayers, and settled into their beds. Sydney rolled over and faced the window. She opened it a few inches to let in some fresh air.

"Hey," she said. "I can see that purple glow."

Alexis climbed down from her bunk and looked. "Oh yeah," she said. "The tops of the trees are glowing lavender. Is that spooky or what?"

Sydney sat up in her bed and made room for Alexis. The two of them gazed out the window at the purple light.

"What do you think causes it?" Alexis asked. "It's pretty in a strange way."

Sydney put the window up a little more. "I can't think of anything in a forest that lights up," she said. "When Bailey came to visit me at my grandparents' house at the ocean, we saw the waves glowing at night. It was something called *bioluminescence*. Billions of living organisms in the water glowing from a chemical reaction. It was really pretty. Everything glowed sort of green and blue."

Alexis put her face nearer the window screen. "So do you think maybe some sort of giant organism is out there in the forest that's causing it to glow purple?" she asked.

"You mean like a giant glowworm, or a monster mutant firefly?" Sydney grinned.

"Very funny," said Alexis. "But what if billions of tiny organisms live deep in the forest, and they glow purple? That's a possibility, isn't it?"

"I suppose," said Sydney.

Suddenly, Alexis gasped. "Did you see that?"

Sydney did see. Something big was out there again lurking near the picnic table. It was in the shadows, just like the night before. And this time, the girls were certain that it was the mountain man. The moon was bright enough for them to see his form. He walked about slowly with a long stick, picking at the earth.

"What's he doing?" Sydney whispered.

"I'm not sure," said Alexis. "I think he's digging in the dirt." She moved over so Sydney could get a better look.

"He has some sort of bag," Sydney said. "It looks like he's collecting things. He is! I just saw him pick something up and put it in the bag. What do you think?"

"I think you're right," said Alexis. "*Shhhh!* Listen."

From just beneath the window, came a soft, rhythmic panting sound. Someone, or something, was breathing hard like it had just run a race, and then—

"Oh!" Sydney cried, slamming down the window. Looking in at them was the head of a huge, black dog. Its eyes glowed, and its open mouth was filled with sharp menacing teeth.

CHAPTER 7

Girls Can Fish

The sun was just peeking over the horizon when Sydney and Alexis went out to fish. Neither girl had slept much the night before. The dog's head had scared them both. It disappeared so quickly when Sydney shut the window that she wondered if they had only imagined its wild eyes and spiky teeth.

No. She was sure of it. The mountain man and his dog were real.

Sydney carried her fishing rod and the bag of dough balls onto the dock. Alexis followed with her pole and a small pail filled with minnows.

"You dropped a dough ball," Alexis said. She bent over to pick it up. "Hey, this isn't a dough ball. It's a big mushroom!"

Sydney set her fishing pole on the end of the dock. She looked at the brown mushroom, about as big as a ping-pong ball, in the palm of Alexis's hand. "That's weird," she said.

"Look, I see more floating in the water," said Alexis.

A dozen mushroom caps floated in the water beside the dock.

"Someone must have made a salad or something and tossed them away," Sydney said. She took the mushroom from Alexis's hand and threw it as far as she could into the lake. The mushroom barely landed on the water's surface when a big fish leaped up into the air. It made a narrow arch and plunged back into the lake with a splash, taking the mushroom with it.

"Wow, did you see that?" Sydney asked.

"I think it was a muskie," said Alexis.

The girls sat on the dock and got their fishing lines ready.

"I hate this," Alexis said, sticking the hook into one of the minnows. "I feel like a murderer. I don't know why I let you talk me into using the live bait."

Sydney was busy loading a dough ball onto the end of her line. At first, the dough didn't stay on the hook, but after a while she figured out how to squish it just right so it stuck.

"Don't look now, but here comes trouble," said Alexis.

Duncan Lumley and his dad walked toward the dock. Sydney and Alexis cast their lines into the lake and pretended not to see.

"Get out of my spot," Duncan said.

"I didn't see your name on it," Sydney replied.

"I always fish here," said Duncan.

Mr. Lumley stood by his son. A toothpick dangled from his mouth. He wore a life jacket and carried a fishing rod and tackle box. "This is where Dunk fishes," he said.

Sydney refused to look at him. "Each cabin has a dock, and this one is ours. Duncan can fish on his own dock."

From the corner of her eye, she saw Duncan step forward. His dad grabbed him by the arm and stopped him.

"They're girls, Dunk," he said. "They don't know any better. Come on. You can fish with me in the boat."

"If I fish from the boat, I can't enter what I catch in the contest," Duncan complained. "And I wanna win!"

"Well then," his dad said, "I suppose you'll have to fish from *our* dock." He gave the girls a dirty look, and then he walked away.

Sydney turned and smiled at Duncan. His green eyes flashed, and he stormed off stomping his feet.

"Don't you bother my boy while he's fishing," Mr. Lumley called to them over his shoulder. "Cast away from his line, and don't get in his space."

"Will do," Sydney said.

Mr. Lumley stepped onto the dock by Cabin Two. As the girls watched, he untied the aluminum boat from the dock. He pulled the cord on the outboard motor and revved it. Then he steered the boat into the lake, speeding past Dock One, nearly clipping the lines from Sydney's and Alexis's poles.

"Ooooo, he's just as irritating as Duncan!" said Sydney. She reeled in her line and cast it again, trying another spot farther out. At the same time Duncan stood at the end of his dock and cast his line into the water.

"Hang in there, Syd," said Alexis. "Remember what the Bible says: 'Losing self-control leaves you as helpless as a city without a wall.' That's Proverbs 25:28."

"You've gotten almost as good as Beth at quoting scripture," said Sydney.

Alexis reeled in her line a little bit. "I'm trying to learn a verse a day.

"Hey, I think I've got something!" The tip of her pole bent down toward the water.

"Reel it in, Alex! Reel it in!" Sydney cried.

Alexis leaned back and pulled against the tension on her line. She turned the crank on the reel hard and fast.

"Go, Alex! Go!" Sydney shouted. "Don't look now, but Duncan has something too."

Duncan stood on Dock Two reeling in his fish just as hard and as fast as Alexis. Then, all of a sudden, he yelled. "Stop! Hey! Stop reeling in your line!"

Alexis glanced over at him. "I think he's yelling at me," she said.

Duncan was jumping up and down. "Stop reeling!" he shouted. "You're tangled in my line!"

But it was too late. The fishing pole flew out of Duncan's hands and splashed into the water. As Alexis turned the crank on her reel, she watched his pole moving nearer to her dock.

"Oh, oh," said Sydney. "Here he comes."

Duncan rushed onto the dock where the girls were fishing. He took the pole out of Alexis's hands and reeled in her line. When he reached down to pick his pole out of the water, Sydney felt like pushing him in.

"This is why girls shouldn't fish," Duncan said, untangling his line from Alexis's.

"*Listen*," Sydney said, raising her voice a little. "We were here fishing first. You knew where we'd cast our lines, and you *deliberately* threw yours near ours. So don't blame *us* for the trouble."

She stood and faced Duncan. He stepped back. She realized she was at least a head taller than he was, and she had muscles—Sydney kept in shape. Duncan, on the other hand, didn't look at all strong.

"Let's just try to get along," she said, lowering her voice. "Okay?"

Duncan backed off. "Okay," he said, nearly whispering. He freed the last bit of his line and reeled it onto his pole.

"Hey, what's this stuff?" He pointed to the bag of dough balls.

"Bait," said Sydney. She picked up the bag and held it protectively.

"What kind of bait?" asked Duncan.

"Secret bait," Sydney said.

"Yeah, well, it's not as good as mine," Duncan told her. "Hey, did you hear that howling last night?"

Alexis put another minnow on her hook. She asked Sydney and Duncan to stand back, and with all her might, she cast her line into the lake. "We heard it," she said. "What do you think it was?"

"The ghost of Jacques Chouteau," Duncan said matter-of-factly.

"What makes you think so?" Sydney asked. She picked up her pole from the dock and continued fishing.

"Everyone knows the story," said Duncan. "Old Jacques got trapped in a cave in the forest. An avalanche or something trapped him inside, and he died in there. Now, his ghost howls to get out. *Ow-wooooooo....* And sometimes he says, 'I'm gonna get you. I'm gonna get you. I'm gonna get you!'" Duncan put his arms in the air and walked like a monster toward the girls.

"Just ignore him," Sydney said.

"I am," Alexis agreed.

"Aw, come on." Duncan sighed, putting his hands on his hips. "Don't you have a sense of humor?"

"You're not funny," said Sydney.

Then something pulled hard on her line. She held tight to the pole with both hands and yanked. All at once, the crank on her reel spun around and around making the line shoot forward.

"Hang on! You got something," Duncan cried. "Here, let me do it." He reached for Sydney's pole.

"Get away!" Sydney said, shoving him with one shoulder.

"Aw, come on," said Duncan. "You got something big on there. Let me reel it in. You don't know what you're doing."

"No!" said Sydney.

Alexis thrust her pole into Duncan's hands. "Here," she said. "Hold this." Then she grabbed the handle of Sydney's pole with both hands and helped her to hang on. "Reel it in, Syd," she said.

"Nice and slow," Duncan added.

Sydney let the fish take a little more line. Then she reeled it in. She did it again and again. Suddenly, she felt a strong jerk on the line. Then the fish shot up and out of the water! It was about twenty yards offshore, and when it splashed back into the lake, it fought hard against the hook.

"Oh man, you got a muskie on there," said Duncan.

Sydney couldn't tell if he was excited or complaining. She fought the fish until it was too tired to fight. Then she reeled it in. "Here it comes," she said. "Here it comes."

The fish's long snout appeared near the dock. The muskie opened and closed its mouth and thrashed in the water.

"It's huge!" Alexis squealed.

The fish was way too heavy for Sydney to lift by herself, besides she was afraid of its teeth. "Now what?" she asked.

"I dunno," said Alexis. She looked at Duncan.

"You gotta get it in your net," he said. Then he looked around the dock. "Don't tell me you don't have a net."

Sydney hadn't even considered that they might need one. She should have known that they would need help lifting a big fish up onto the dock.

Alexis sensed Sydney's embarrassment.

"We can do it," she said. "Come on, Syd. We can both grab it and lift it up." Alexis got down on all fours and leaned over the edge of the dock.

"No," said Duncan. "Wait." He turned and sprinted toward Dock Two. Soon he was back with his net. "Here, I'll help you."

"Thanks, but no thanks," said Sydney. Secretly, she wished she hadn't said it. She needed that net, but she didn't trust Duncan to help her.

"Aw, come on," Duncan said. "I'm not going to do anything. Besides, I can tell already that it's not a winning fish."

He pushed between the girls and scooped the fish into his net.

Sydney saw that he struggled to lift it up. She reached over and grabbed onto the handle, and together they pulled the net onto the dock. "Remember," she said. "Helping me to net it doesn't give you any rights to the fish."

"I don't want your dumb old fish," said Duncan. Carefully, he removed the hook from the fish's mouth. Then he took a small tape measure from his pocket and measured it as it lay gasping on the dock.

"Thirty-two and a half inches," he said. "Not big enough."

"How do you know?" Alexis asked.

Duncan took his cell phone out of his back pocket. He punched in some numbers. "Didn't you read the rules?" he said. "When you catch a fish, you call Tompkins' and text FISH. They'll send you a message saying what the biggest catch is so far. If it's less than that, you've gotta let the fish go."

"I don't believe you," said Sydney.

Duncan's cell phone rang. "Look," he said, handing her the phone. "The message on the screen says 34 INCHES. See? Not big enough."

Sydney looked at the muskie flopping on the dock.

"He's right, Syd," said Alexis. "I read the rules again this morning. If it's not the biggest fish, you're supposed to release it."

She reached down and grasped the fish around its middle, steering clear of the razor-sharp teeth in its huge, gaping mouth. The fish's body was motionless; it seemed to melt in her hands. With all her might, Alexis pushed it off the dock and into the water.

"Swim away," she said. "Go on. Swim."

The big fish treaded water just below the surface. Then, sensing that it was free, it shot away from the dock.

"Wow," said Duncan. "You touched it and everything."

"Yeah," said Alexis. "So what?"

"So, girls don't touch fish," Duncan said. But this time his voice sounded confused.

Sydney sighed deeply.

"Listen," she said. "I've had it with all this *girls don't* stuff. Girls do a lot of things that boys do. If your mom wanted to, *she* could fish. So could your sister. And if they wanted to, they could touch the fish and *everything*!"

"I don't have a mom, and I don't have a sister," said Duncan. "It's just me and my dad."

Suddenly, Duncan seemed different and not so much of a bully.

"Well, anyhow," Sydney said softly, "thanks for your help."

Duncan picked up his net. "Not a problem. And don't forget, I'm going to win the contest."

He started walking toward the end of the dock. "And don't get your line anywhere near mine." He looked over his shoulder at Alexis. "Next time, I won't be so understanding."

He went back to Dock Two, baited his hook, and cast his line into the water.

"I can't figure that kid out," said Sydney. "For a minute there, I thought maybe he wanted to be our friend."

Alexis threw her line back into the lake. "He is a bit strange. And what did you make of what he said about Jacques Chouteau's ghost? Do you think he was really trapped in a cave and died there?"

Sydney put another dough ball on her hook and cast her line. "It all adds up with what Mr. Miller said. Remember? He said Jacques hid his money and furs in a cave and that he died in the woods."

"But he didn't say anything about him dying in a cave," said Alexis.

"No," Sydney said. "The legend says that he died in the woods, and he haunts them."

Alexis was quiet for a while. "Well, I don't believe it, do you?"

"Do I believe that he's a ghost? No," said Sydney. "But we know that Jacques Chouteau was a real person, so it's possible he might have died in a cave in the woods. Something is out there. And it lurks in a spooky, purple light, and it hangs around with some sort of big dog that howls and maybe kills coyotes."

"Oh Syd," said Alexis, easing her grip on the pole. "Do you think that thing we saw last night killed the coyote? It sure didn't look like a wolf."

Sydney turned the crank on her reel and added some slack to her line. "I'm sure it wasn't a wolf," she said. "It was much bigger than a wolf, and black, and not at all shaggy. And Alexis, when that thing stood up, it must have been six feet tall!"

"I know," said Alexis. "I don't even want to think about it. I couldn't believe my eyes."

"Neither could I," said Sydney. "In fact, when I woke up this morning, I wondered if it had all been a dream—just something in my imagination."

Alexis reeled in her line a bit. "It wasn't your imagination, Sydney. I saw it too. I think it was his dog—*Fang*."

They fished silently for a while. The sun was up over the trees now, and its reflection on the water hurt their eyes. Alexis watched Sydney's pole while Sydney went back to the cabin and got their sunglasses.

"You know," Sydney said when she returned. "I just saw that mushroom book on your nightstand, the one you found on the ground yesterday morning."

"Yeah, what about it?" Alexis said lazily.

"Well," Sydney continued, "it's a field guide to mushrooms. And we just found a mushroom on the dock and more floating in the water. Do you think they're somehow connected?"

"They could be," said Alexis. "What are you thinking?"

"I don't know yet what I'm thinking," said Sydney. "But maybe they have something to do with the mountain man."

"Could be," said Alexis. "Maybe he's a farmer or something."

"No," said Sydney. "My instinct tells me that he's not a farmer. I don't know yet what he is, but we're going to find out. And when we do, we'll know what that purple light is too, and the howling."

"*Whoo-hooo!*"

A shout came from Dock Two. Duncan stood, pole in hand, fighting with something on the end of his line. As the girls watched, he reeled it in. He dunked his net into the water and, after almost falling in, he scooped a big fish onto the dock.

Duncan took out his tape measure.

"Thirty-five and a half inches!" he shouted.

Into the Woods

Kate's package arrived as promised.

"Great," said Sydney. "Let's see what's in here." She put the box on the kitchen table and got a sharp knife from the drawer. Carefully, she cut the tape that held the box shut.

"Hurry," said Alexis. "I want to see what Inspector Gadget sent us."

The lid popped open. The first thing Sydney saw was a watch.

"Cool!" she said. "Kate sent us the Wonder Watch."

Kate loved inventing things, and the Wonder Watch was one of her best creations. It could connect to a computer, surf the net, and read email. Kate set it up so that with the push of a button, the girls would be connected to the Camp Club Girls' chat room.

Also in the box was a plastic bag, carefully wrapped and surrounded by Styrofoam peanuts. Sydney removed the wrapping and pulled out a pair of mirrored sunglasses.

"Check this out," she said. "Kate gave us a note. 'If you wear these, you can see what's behind you.' "

She handed the glasses to Alexis.

"Whoa," Alex said after she put them on. "This is weird. Depending on where I look through the lenses, I can see straight ahead or behind me. These are awesome, but they'll take getting used to. Here. You try them."

Sydney put the glasses on and looked in front of her. "Oh!" She gasped.

"What?"

"I saw someone looking in the window behind me." Just then, there came a soft knock on the back door. The girls saw Mr. Miller standing on the little concrete porch. "Hi, Mr. Miller," Sydney said, opening the door.

"Howdy," he said. "Nice sunglasses. Say, I hear that you might need one of these." He held up a fishing net. "And one of these too." He handed Sydney a metal tape measure. "So, you caught a big one this morning, huh?"

"You must have been talking to Duncan," said Alexis.

Mr. Miller took off his baseball cap and scratched his head. "Well, let's just say that a little bird told me."

He gave Sydney the net, and she put it on the table next to Kate's box.

"Well, that little bird has been giving us plenty of trouble since we got here," Sydney said. "And his dad hasn't been very nice either."

Mr. Miller plopped his cap back on his head. "Well, that's kinda what I wanted to talk to you about. You see, Duncan's not a bad kid. His family's been comin' here since he was a baby. Then a couple of years ago, his mom and sister were killed in a car accident. Duncan and his dad haven't been the same since. His dad's still mad that it happened, and poor Duncan gets the worst of it sometimes. I don't think he has many friends."

A guilty feeling sank into the pit of Sydney's stomach. "I'm glad you told us," she said.

"Me too," Alexis added. "We'll pray for them."

Mr. Miller smiled. "You seem like nice girls. I figured you'd give Duncan a break and try to be friends with him."

"We'll try," said Sydney. "And thanks for the net and the tape measure."

"You're welcome," he said. "Good luck with your fishing, and may the best man. . .er. . .I mean. . .um. . .may the best man or woman win!"

He tipped the brim of his cap and walked back toward the office.

Sydney closed the door. "Well, that might explain why Duncan is so mean," she said. "I can't imagine how I'd feel if my mom and brother died."

"Me neither," said Alexis. "We'll add Duncan and his dad to our prayers every night. And Syd, let's be nice to Duncan—as hard as that might be."

There were three more things in Kate's box. One was a GPS locator.

"Great!" Sydney said. "Now we won't have to worry about making trails in the woods and getting lost."

The second item was a tiny camera, about the size of a matchbox. Kate had included another note:

This is a mini-microcamera with a hand-held monitor. It takes pictures and videos. You can set it up like a security camera and watch the monitor to see what's going on. You can also use it under water. I programmed it so every picture you take will automatically show up on our website.

Sydney unpacked the monitor, which was about the size of a cell phone.

"This is so cool," she said. "So do you want to do some exploring?"

"You mean sleuthing?" Alexis asked.

"That's exactly what I mean," said Sydney. "Let's go into the woods and find out what that mountain man is up to."

Sydney loaded the gadgets inside her waist pack and strapped it around her middle. In the meantime, Alexis slipped the Wonder Watch over her wrist. She took her cell phone out of her pocket and started a text.

"I'm texting Kate to let her know that we got the package. Then I'll text the other girls and tell them that we're going into the woods. Maybe some of them will be online if we need them."

"Good idea," said Sydney.

"And Syd, don't forget the pepper spray in case we run into a bear," Alexis reminded her.

"I got it," said Sydney.

The girls entered the forest following the same route they'd taken the day before. After they'd walked about ten minutes, they noticed the shovel on the ground.

"Hey look," said Sydney. "Someone's been digging again."

The earth near the shovel was freshly turned over, and the tip of the shovel was caked with mud.

"Do you think that's where Mr. Miller buried the coyote?" Alexis asked.

"I don't think so," said Sydney. "We're too far from the resort. And look at how the ground is dug up. Whoever dug here didn't dig one big hole. The person dug a bunch of little ones."

Alexis gave the earth a closer look. "It looks like clumps are missing out of the soil."

Sydney picked up the shovel.

"What are you doing?" Alexis asked.

"I'm going to dig and see what's here," Sydney said. "Maybe I'll find the lost treasure of Jacques Chouteau." She grinned.

"Don't," said Alexis. "At least not now. Whoever dug here will probably come back. We'd better not mess things up. Otherwise, whoever it is will know for sure that we're watching them."

"You're right," said Sydney. She put the shovel back on the ground, careful to place it exactly as she'd found it.

"What are those things over there?" Alexis asked. She pointed to a brownish-white mass on the forest floor a few yards away.

"Mushrooms!" said Sydney. "Gigandimundo mushrooms."

She took a closer look and snapped a picture with the mini-microcam. "I don't know what kind they are, but there's a ton of them all over the place. I didn't notice them when we were here before."

"Neither did I," said Alexis.

Dozens of mushrooms popped out of the rotted leaves and pine needles on the forest floor. Their umbrella-shaped caps were rough and bumpy like the wool on a sheep, and their edges were ragged. The black-and-white caps sat atop thick little trunks that were scaly and peeling.

"Do you think they're edible?" Alexis wondered.

"I don't know," said Sydney. "Some mushrooms you can eat, but others are poisonous. I think we should leave them alone. Definitely, though, we need to check out this spot and find out who's digging here."

"Maybe it's one of the visitors at the resort," said Alex. "These things are probably edible, and someone is digging them up for cooking."

The girls walked farther into the woods searching for clues as they went. After a while, they found a narrow path going east and decided to follow it.

"I think we're walking toward the lake," said Alexis. "I hear a motorboat."

"Me too," said Sydney. "A bunch of boats were on the lake when we left. *Shhhh!* Listen."

Alexis heard it too. Someone whistled a quick and lively tune. It came from the south—in the woods—and with each happy note it got closer.

"Hide!" said Alexis. "Over there in those bushes."

The girls scrambled behind a thick cluster of honeysuckle. They stood silently, watching the path through the dense leaves. Sydney took the mirrored sunglasses out of her waist pack and put them on.

"I don't want anyone sneaking up on us," she whispered.

The whistling stopped. The girls heard a rustling. Something was trying to force its way through the brush on the other side of the path.

Twigs snapped, and the tops of small saplings swayed.

"Doggone it!" a man grumbled. More twigs snapped. The brush on the other side of the path trembled. "Come on. . . . *Ugh! Ooof! Umph!*"

Suddenly, a bright-orange object thrust through the bushes and fell onto the path. It was nine feet long, and it looked like a giant kazoo. The middle part was hollowed out to form a little place with a seat. A long pole was strapped to the side of the thing with a rounded paddle on either end.

"It's a kayak." Sydney whispered so softly that Alexis could barely hear.

A heavy brown boot emerged from the thicket, then a leg wearing worn khaki pants, a thick brown belt, a red plaid shirt, an arm, a hand. Finally, the mountain man pushed through the brush and onto the path. His cap had come off, and he held it in one hand. Burrs and brambles covered his shaggy beard and hair.

"Dad burn it!" he complained. "There has to be a better way through the woods to this path."

He picked up his cap and plopped it onto his head. "Ow!"

He took it off again and picked the brambles out of his hair. While the girls watched, he tilted the kayak onto its edge with the bottom facing him. He gripped the center rim, hoisted the boat onto his upper leg, and then wrestled it onto his shoulder. "There," he puffed. Then off he went down the path, whistling his happy song.

"Let's follow him," whispered Alexis. "Are you going to take off those glasses?"

"I think I'll leave them on," said Sydney. "In case Fang is nearby."

They followed a safe distance behind as the mountain man slogged along toward the shore.

"Wait!" said Alexis.

"What's the matter?" Sydney asked.

"The Wonder Watch is doing something. I feel it jiggling on my wrist." Alexis looked at the face of the watch. Words flashed across the screen. MESSAGE WAITING: BAILEY. "What do I do?" she asked.

"Push the button on the side," Sydney said.

Alexis pushed the button, and Bailey's message scrolled across the watch's big, round face. WHAT'S WITH THE UGLY 'SHROOM? HAVE YOU GUYS SEEN THE OLD MAN IN THE WOODS YET?

"Can I text back on this thing?" Alex asked.

"No, but you can talk back," said Sydney. "Just say what you want, and a microchip inside will translate it into printed words. They'll show up in the chat room."

"I forgot all the extra stuff that Kate built into this thing," said Alex. "I've never used it."

She put her lips up to the face of the watch and spoke softly. "They're growing all over the place in the forest. We don't know what kind they are. We're following the mountain man now. More later."

"Come on. Let's go," said Sydney. "He's probably to the lake already."

By the time they got to the lakeshore, the mountain man had already launched his kayak. They could see him paddling swiftly across the lake, heading directly to the other side.

Sydney searched the muddy earth for clues. "Hey, I think these are his boot prints," she said. "A word is on the bottom of the soles."

She took out the mini-microcam and took a picture. "I can't read it very well, but maybe the Camp Club Girls can enlarge it and tell us what it says. Send a message on the Wonder Watch. Ask them to blow up the picture."

While Sydney and Alexis waited for the girls to reply, the mountain man steered his kayak to the other side of the lake. He pulled it up onto the shore and disappeared into the forest.

"The watch is jiggling again," said Alexis. "It's a message from Elizabeth." She held out her wrist and pushed the button so Sydney could see.

I ENLARGED THE PHOTO. THE WORD ON THE SOLE IS *ÉSPRIT*. I TOOK FRENCH LAST SEMESTER. IT MEANS SPIRIT.

Sydney felt a chill. "This is spooky, Alex," she said. "I mean, think about the legend of Jacques Chouteau. He paddled off across North Twin Lake and was never heard from again. He was French. Now, we find this French word on the bottom of this boot print, and it means 'spirit.' It's too weird."

"You know what's weird?" Alex said. "Seeing my reflection in those mirrored sunglasses!"

"Sorry," said Sydney. She took off the glasses and put them in her pack.

"Syd, you don't really believe that he's the ghost of Jacques Chouteau, do you?"

Sydney hesitated. "No," she said. "But you have to admit it's strange." She started walking up the narrow path and into the woods.

Alexis followed her. "Where are we going now?"

"We're going to find the purple glow," said Sydney, "and see what's really going on here in the forest. I'm sure it's over this way—the direction the mountain man came from. We should be safe now that he's on the other side of the lake."

The girls pushed their way through the brush and the brambles. Before long, they heard the buzzing noise. They followed it.

"Unless something terrible happens, let's agree not to run away," said Sydney.

"Agreed," said Alex.

The noise grew louder. Then finally they saw the familiar purple glow. It was straight ahead of them lighting up the tops of the trees.

"Careful," said Sydney. "Let's go slow." She opened her waist pack and took out the mirrored sunglasses. "I'll put these on in case he comes back."

They walked a little farther until they came to a clearing. They peeked out from the bushes and saw a campsite bathed in the eerie, purple light. There was a campfire ring made of stones, a folding table, and a collection of pots and pans. A bedroll was neatly placed on the table by a small canvas sack. Sydney noticed a seat made from a split-timber log next to the fire ring. "This is where he lives," she said.

"What's that awful smell?" Alexis asked.

"The manure pile," said Sydney. She pointed to a stinking pile of debris at the edge of the clearing. "Now we know where Biscuit was."

Bravely, the girls walked into the campsite.

"The light is coming from over there," said Alexis. "Near the base of that gnarly, old pine tree."

"Let's go check it out," said Sydney.

"Oh Syd, do you really think we should? I feel like we're trespassing or something."

"The forest doesn't belong to him," said Sydney. "It belongs to everybody."

She walked toward the glowing purple light. The buzz grew stronger. The light flashed off Sydney's sunglasses and bounced like prism light across the tree trunks.

"Oh my goodness," said Sydney. "Look at that!"

They were at the entrance to a cave. Its gaping doorway was almost hidden by the low, sweeping branches of an evergreen tree. The purple light came from inside. The buzzing sound echoed from deep within. It ricocheted off the cold, stone walls and sounded like a swarm of angry bees.

Sydney stopped just outside the entrance. She squatted down and tried to look inside. "What do you think is making the purple light?" she asked. "And what's that noise?"

"I don't know," said Alex. "But maybe we shouldn't be here."

"I think we should do some spelunking," said Sydney.

"Some what?" asked Alexis.

"Cave exploring." Sydney explained. She stood and took a few steps into the cave. Then bravely, she took a few steps more. When she did, the buzzing noise stopped.

Suddenly, a great *whoosh* of icy-cold air rushed through the cave. It hit Sydney in the face, sending a chill down to her toes. The buzz turned into a sound that was like a whirling helicopter blade—*whop-whop-whop.*

Out of the noise came a raspy voice whispering, *"Go back! Go back! Go back!"*

The girls turned and ran as fast as they could.

"Alex! Run for your life!" Sydney screamed.

Through the lens of the special sunglasses, she saw something behind them. It was the monstrous dog—the same one that had looked into the bedroom window. It raced after them now, lunging at their heels.

Nice Doggie

Sydney felt the dog's huge front paws wrap around her ankles. She fell to the ground facedown. Then came a thud as the animal leaped onto her back. The wind rushed out of her lungs, and she thought for sure that she would die. But then a long, wet tongue licked the side of her face.

"Sydney!" Alexis screamed when she saw her friend lying there helplessly.

The big, black dog lifted its head and looked Alexis straight in the eyes. *Wuf!* Its jowls shook like jelly when it barked.

"Nice doggie," Alexis said, standing still.

Sydney stayed on the ground, not knowing what to expect from the big animal stretched across her back.

"Sydney," Alexis said softly. "I think he's friendly."

She took a few steps toward the dog with her hand extended, palm up. The dog sniffed the air, perhaps wondering if she held a treat.

"Get it off me," Sydney demanded.

"I'm trying," said Alexis quietly. "Nice doggie. Follow Alex now." She kept her hand extended and took a few steps backward.

The dog stood. Its belly was at least three feet above Sydney's back, and she felt as if she were under a table. As it walked away from her and toward Alex, Sydney noticed its long, gangly legs.

"What *is* this thing?" she asked.

"It's a very nice doggie," Alexis said sweetly as she coaxed the animal to come near to her.

"And it has a head the size of a big pumpkin," she continued, "and spooky brown eyes and sharp teeth, and the closer it gets to me, the more scared I am. But I'm going to save you, Sydney, no matter what. Now, while I'm talking real nice to the doggie and have its attention, why don't you get up very quietly and get out of here? Nice doggie, come here. . . . Nice doggie."

"I'm not leaving you alone with it," said Sydney, getting up on all fours. "We're in this together."

"It's all right," Alexis replied. "I'll be fine." She shivered as the dog's black nose, at least the size of a baseball, thrust into her hand and sniffed. "I wish I had a dog biscuit or something."

Sydney stood up. "I stuck one in my waist pack. Oh my, he's huge!"

Now that she was standing, she could see just how big the dog was. The top of its back was higher than her waist. It had a thick, muscular body, a long tail that curled upward, and short, floppy ears.

"Sydney. . .I think the doggie wants a biscuit *now*," said Alexis. The dog was eagerly licking her hand.

Sydney unzipped her waist pack and found one of Biscuit's dog treats on the bottom.

"Here, dog," she said. "Hungry?"

As soon as the dog saw Sydney pull the biscuit out of her pack, it stopped licking Alexis's hand and rushed toward her. Before Sydney could get out of the way, it stood on its hind legs and plopped its paws squarely onto her shoulders, knocking her backward into a tree trunk. She stood there, pinned between the tree and the dog, its big head looking down at her.

WUF!

"Oh Alex." Sydney gasped. "He's way taller than I am!"

"Maybe you should give him the biscuit," Alexis suggested.

A voice in Sydney's head whispered, *Stay calm. You're in charge. Tell him to get down.*

"Get down!" Sydney said, firmly.

WUF!

"I said, *get down!*" Sydney repeated.

The dog dropped his paws from her shoulders and stood in front of her, looking her straight in the eyes.

"Now, *sit*," she said.

Surprisingly, the dog sat. Sydney tossed the biscuit to him, and he scarfed it down in one big gulp. Then he sat there waiting for another.

"Now what?" Alexis asked.

Sydney took the mini-microcam out of her pack and snapped a quick picture of the animal as it sat there. "I don't know what to do next," she said. "I think this is what we heard howling and barking in the woods. I'm pretty sure its Fang—*his* dog. Let's see how well he follows commands. Fang, *stay!*" she said. The dog didn't move. "Great. Come on, Alex. Let's go."

The girls started to walk. They only went a few yards before Fang got up and began following them.

"Go back!" Sydney commanded.

Fang sat down and whined like a puppy.

The girls started off again, and once more Fang trotted along behind them.

"Sydney, I think we're going to have to take him back to the camp-site," said Alexis. "Otherwise, he's going to follow us all the way to the cabin. We can't risk the mountain man discovering that we've been snooping around."

Sydney sighed. "I guess you're right. Come on, Fang. Let's take you home."

The girls turned and walked in the opposite direction, with Fang playfully romping at their side. As they approached the campsite, they were keenly aware that the whooshing noise had disappeared. Once again, the forest was quiet except for the buzzing sound deep within the cave.

"Wait," said Sydney. She stopped in the bushes at the edge of the clearing. "You stay here with Fang. I'm going to circle around and make sure the mountain man hasn't come back yet."

Fang was happy to have Alexis pet him while Sydney explored the campsite. She made a wide circle around the grounds, careful to stay hidden among the trees. Everything was silent—the mountain man hadn't come back.

Then Sydney made a strange discovery. In the forest floor was a large rectangular-shaped hole covered with a metal grate. When she got closer, she heard the buzzing sound deep inside the earth. A hazy, purple light shined up through the grate and lit the tops of the pine trees nearby. A tall cyclone fence with a gate surrounded the hole, and a big padlock secured the gate. Sydney was curious. She wished that she could get closer and look down through the hole into the earth. Some-thing mysterious was going on down there. She was sure of it.

Sydney was so quiet when she came up behind Alexis and Fang that they didn't hear her. "All clear. He's not there," she said.

Alexis jumped. Fang whirled around, and his lips curled up in a growl.

"Nice doggie!" Alexis exclaimed. Then she said to Sydney, "Don't scare him like that, or me either."

"I'm sorry," Alexis said. "I wasn't thinking. Come on. I found where the light comes from." She led Alexis to the hole in the ground.

"Well, what do you make of that?" Alexis asked.

"I don't know," said Sydney. She took a picture with the mini-microcam. "But I'd love to get a closer look." She handed the camera to Alexis. Sydney put one hand into the wire mesh of the fence, then the other. Carefully, she lifted one foot and stuck the toe of her shoe into the mesh. Then Sydney began to climb.

"No!" said Alexis. "Syd, don't you dare! You don't know who or what's down there. It might be dangerous!"

She grabbed on to Sydney's leg and kept her from climbing any farther.

"Alexis!" said Sydney. "Let go."

"No," Alexis said firmly. "We'll find another way."

Reluctantly, Sydney got down.

Alexis sniffed the air. "Something smells different here," she said. "Did you notice? It smells earthy, like after a spring rainstorm."

"You're right," Sydney agreed. "It smells like wet dirt. Maybe an underground stream flows through the cave."

"But it wouldn't have dirt around it," Alexis countered. "Caves are made of rock."

"You're right again," said Sydney.

The Wonder Watch on Alexis's wrist began to jiggle.

MESSAGE WAITING: MCKENZIE. A message scrolled across the watch's face. I'M THE ONLY ONE IN THE CHAT ROOM LOOKING AT THESE PICTURES. *WHERE ARE YOU GUYS?* AND WHERE'D YOU GET THE BERNADANE?

Alexis spoke softly into the tiny microphone. "We're sleuthing in the mountain man's campsite in the forest. We saw him row his kayak to the other side of the lake, so he's not here. We found a cave. Near it, there's a hole in the forest floor with a fence around it. What's a bernadane?"

McKenzie's reply flashed on the screen. A BERNADANE IS A CROSS BETWEEN A SAINT BERNARD AND A GREAT DANE. I SAW ONE AT OUR STATE FAIR LAST SUMMER. THEY'RE HUMONGOUS!

"Tell me about it," said Alexis. "The bernadane is standing next to us. His name is Fang, and he's the mountain man's dog. He's friendly. We can't talk now. The mountain man will be back soon, and we have exploring to do. More later."

His name is Fang? Be careful. Take lots of pictures. And shout if you need us.

The screen went black.

"So, he's a bernadane," said Sydney. "That's comforting. At least he's not part wolf." She reached over and patted Fang on the back of his thick neck.

"Sydney," said Alexis. "You don't think Fang killed that coyote on the beach last night, do you?"

"I've been wondering about that, Alex. But if he did kill it, then why? He doesn't seem like a mean dog. Maybe he was just defending himself."

Fang ran circles around the girls, wanting to play.

"Mr. Lumley saw something big run off into the woods," Alexis said. "They thought it was a bear. But think about it, Syd. If you saw Fang running in the dark, you might think he was a bear. He's black and big like a bear. Maybe Fang has a dark side."

Sydney didn't even want to think about that. "Well, right now, we have the problem of getting Fang to stay here so we can go back to the resort. Any ideas?"

"No," said Alexis. "Unless we tie him up."

"If we do that, the mountain man will know that someone was snooping around here," said Sydney.

"That's right," Alexis answered. "But he won't know who it was. I don't know what else we can do, Syd. Otherwise, he'll follow us."

"Let's go inside the cave," Sydney suggested. "Maybe Fang has his own room or something, and we can leave him there."

"But what about that horrible sound we heard and the whispering?"

"I have a feeling it won't hurt us," Sydney told her. "I think the mountain man made it as a trick to scare people away. And since the mountain man is nowhere around, I'm not going to be afraid to go inside."

Sydney and Alexis hurried toward the cave's entrance with Fang romping ahead of them. He trotted inside, and the girls followed. Alexis linked her arm through Sydney's. The only light in the cave came from daylight seeping through the entrance—and it was rapidly fading away. Ahead of them lay nothing but a faint purple glow.

"Do you remember in *The Wizard of Oz*, how the scary wizard turned out to be Professor Marvel, an ordinary man?" Alexis said. "He was hiding behind a curtain making things work to create a vision of the wizard. It was all done with tricks."

"I remember," said Sydney.

"Well, maybe the mountain man is like that. Maybe he's not scary at all, but a very nice man like Professor Marvel."

They were about a dozen yards inside the cave now.

"Maybe," said Sydney. She stopped and took a flashlight from her waist pack.

"Hey, what's that?" Alexis asked. An old canvas knapsack was propped against one of the cave's stony walls.

Sydney went to check it out. "Shoot! The flashlight batteries are almost dead. I see something written on the knapsack, but I can't read it."

"Hang on a minute," Alexis said. She pulled out her cell phone.

"You'll never get a signal in here," Sydney warned.

"I'm not going to call anybody," Alexis answered. "My phone has a built-in flashlight." She pushed a button on the phone, and the light lit up. She pointed it at the canvas sack.

"J.C." said Sydney. "It's the initials J.C. Are you thinking what I'm thinking?"

"Jesus Christ," Alexis said in almost a whisper.

"No! Although I'm sure Jesus is here protecting us. J.C., as in Jacques Chouteau. This thing is old enough to be his," said Sydney. "This must be the cave where he hid his stuff."

"Maybe the mountain man is a thief," Alexis suggested. "Maybe he found Jacques's money and furs in here, and he's selling them for his own profit."

"You might be right," Sydney agreed. She shined the light around the rough, rocky wall. "Check this out," she said, focusing the beam on a series of lines.

"There must be a hundred or more lines carved into this wall," Alexis said. "It looks like someone is keeping score."

"Or keeping track," Sydney said. "Maybe Jacques Chouteau was trapped in here and kept track of the days. Remember? Duncan said that he got trapped in a cave and died there."

"But that's a legend," Alexis told her.

"But maybe the legend isn't a legend," Sydney said. "Maybe the story is true. Jacques Chouteau died here, and the mountain man found his body. Maybe the mountain man has been excavating this site, digging away at the debris from the avalanche and searching for buried treasure. Maybe that place in the woods where we found the shovel is where he buried Jacques!"

"Ewwww, do you think so?" Alexis asked.

Sydney snapped pictures of the knapsack and the etchings on the wall.

Meanwhile, Alexis counted the marks. "One hundred twenty-six," she said. "Do you think Jacques could have stayed alive in here for one hundred twenty-six days?"

"Only if there was a source of air and water," Sydney answered. "If that was the case, then he probably starved to death."

GRRRRRAH, pant, pant. Fang trotted toward them holding something in his teeth.

"What do you have, boy?" Alexis asked. She took a closer look. "He has a bone, Sydney." She gasped. "Maybe it's human!"

Fang dropped the stubby, white bone at their feet.

Sydney inspected it. "It could be from an animal. At least, I hope so. On the other hand, I still wonder what's buried in the forest near those mushrooms we saw?"

"Oh Sydney!" Alexis exclaimed.

Wuf! Wuf!... Wuf! Wuf...

"I think he wants us to follow him."

Reluctantly, the girls accompanied Fang deeper into the cave toward the purple light. After a few minutes, they entered a small room filled with stalactites and stalagmites. The formations glistened in the neon purple glow.

"Oh, it's beautiful, like an ice castle!" said Alexis.

Fang led them around, sniffing as he went.

"Ack!" Alexis squealed.

A cold drop of water had dripped from a stalactite on the cave's roof onto Alexis's face.

In the corner of the room, they found a door made of thick, wooden planks. Its heavy iron latch was padlocked shut. Cut into the bottom of the door, there was an opening about a foot square. Fang lay down and sniffed it. Then he whined and started digging at it with his paws.

Sydney got on her hands and knees and looked inside. "All I can see is a bright purple light. And it smells really musty in there. I wish I were small enough to climb through this opening, because I think we've found the treasure room."

Alexis got down on the floor too and stretched out on her stomach trying to get a better look.

"I can't see anything either," she said. "I think we should go to

Tompkins' and chat with the girls. We need to make a plan."

"I agree," said Sydney, standing up. "We need to come back here and find out what's behind this door."

Suddenly, Fang perked up his ears. He cocked his head. Then he raced toward the cave's entrance.

"Oh no," Sydney said. "Trouble. I think the mountain man is back."

"We're trapped!" Alexis gasped, standing up. "Oh Syd! What are we going to do?"

Think positive, Alexis, she said to herself. *Remember Isaiah 43:5, "Fear not, for I am with you." Everything is fine. It's all good. Besides, on all the TV shows and movies, the heroines always get out of the situations just fine.*

"The only way out is through the front door," said Sydney. "Let's go. No, wait!" She took several quick pictures of the door and its mysterious opening. "Now let's go."

They ran toward the cave's entrance. Sydney was prepared to fight the mountain man if she had to. But as they came nearer to the door, they heard Fang barking in the distance. *Baw-wha-wha! Baw-wha-wha!*

"It sounds like he's found something," said Alexis.

"Or some*one*," Sydney suggested.

The girls hurried out of the cave and into the fresh, woodland air. They were relieved that no one was in the campground. But then they heard it—the whistling. The mountain man was back, and he was walking through the forest heading into camp.

Sydney reached into her waist pack and took out the GPS locator. "That way to the resort," she said, pointing north. "Run! We have to get out of here before Fang gives us away."

The girls ran through the forest, back to the resort as fast as their legs could carry them.

The Plan

More visitors had arrived for the weekend, and all of the cabins at Miller's Resort were occupied. Little children splashed in the water near the narrow beach. Moms sat in lawn chairs reading novels, while dads fished in motorboats. Each cabin's dock had at least one young boy fishing. When the girls came running out of the woods, they noticed Duncan fishing on theirs.

"Don't yell at me, okay?" he said when he saw them. "You guys were off somewhere playing, and I didn't think you'd mind if I used your dock."

Sydney debated whether to tell Duncan about the mountain man. She thought he might know something and maybe provide some clues.

"We weren't playing," she said. "We were spying on a guy in the forest."

Duncan looked at her suspiciously.

"There's a guy living in a cave in the forest," said Sydney. "He looks like a raggedy, old mountain man, and he has a gigantic dog. Standing up on its hind legs, it's more than six feet tall. A purple glow comes from the cave, and we discovered a secret room inside, and there are noises—buzzing and whooshing and someone whispering in the trees."

"Ah-ha!" Duncan laughed out loud. "You guys can't fake me out. There's nothing in that forest but a bunch of wild animals."

"No, she's telling you the truth," said Alexis.

"Yeah, right," Duncan replied. "You're not going to scare me off this dock with a ghost story. You just want me to believe you so I'll go look. Then, while I'm gone, you'll fish in my spot. No way!"

Sydney looked at Alexis and shrugged. "Well, we tried," she said. "And by the way, Duncan, this isn't *your* spot. Who's winning the dock-side contest, so far?"

"I am," he said. "Thirty-five and a half inches. My fish is on ice at Tompkins.'"

"Well, enjoy the lead while you can," Sydney told him. "We have an errand to run, and then we'll be back here to catch the biggest muskie in North Twin Lake."

Duncan laughed. "Whatever," he said. As the girls walked away, they heard him mutter, "Purple glow. It's nothing but the Northern Lights. Dumb girls."

Sydney and Alexis went to Tompkins' Ice Cream Shop. Just inside the front door, they saw Duncan's fish on display in a freezer case.

"You've got to admit his fish is really big," said Alexis. "Do you think we can catch an even bigger one?"

"We're going to try," said Sydney. "Take a look at that monster fish that someone caught from a boat."

A forty-two inch muskie lay next to Duncan's. The tag on it read FRED LUMLEY.

"Well, it looks like both of the Lumleys are in the lead," said Alexis.

"Great," Sydney said sarcastically. "And if they win, Duncan will think for sure that girls can't fish."

"I thought we were going to be nice to Duncan," said Alexis.

"We can be nice and still win the contest. I was reading my Bible last night, and I memorized a verse. Do you want to hear it?"

"Sure," Alexis answered.

" 'You know that many runners enter a race, and only one of them wins the prize. So run to win!' That's what it says in 1 Corinthians 9:24."

"But I don't think the Bible means a fishing contest," said Alexis.

"Well, I think the verse means that God wants us to always try to do our best," said Sydney. "So that's what I'm going to do. I'm going to be nice to Duncan *and* fish to win."

They went to the back of the shop, booted up the computer, and logged on to the Camp Club Girls' website. Once they got to the chat room, they found the other girls trying to make sense of the pictures Sydney had snapped with the mini-microcam.

Sydney: *We're back at the ice-cream shop.*
Elizabeth: *Thank goodness! We've been praying for your safety.*
Alexis: *We're fine. Got out of the camp just as the mountain man was returning.*
Kate: *I researched Jacques Chouteau. He did exist and*

disappeared one day. I found tons of legends about him. He's almost as famous in the Northwoods as Paul Bunyan.

Sydney: *We think the mountain man found the cave where Jacques Chouteau died. That old knapsack inside has Jacques' initials on it. We think Jacques was trapped in the cave, and marked off the days by scratching lines on the wall.*

Bailey: *So that's what those marks are.*

Alexis: *That's what we think. Fang brought us a bone when we were in the cave.*

Elizabeth: *Fang?*

Sydney: *That's what the mountain man calls his dog. Mac says the dog is a bernadane, part Great Dane and Saint Bernard.*

Elizabeth: *I can't believe that picture. He looks huge.*

Sydney: *He is, but he's friendly. When he chased us, he just wanted to play. We wondered if the bone was one of Jacques'.*

Bailey: *Eewwwwww.*

Sydney: *Someone was digging in the forest. We wondered if the mountain man was burying Jacques' bones there.*

Bailey: *Eewwwwww!*

McKenzie: *Why'd you take pictures of mushrooms?*

Alexis: *We found a bunch in the forest. This morning we found a mushroom on the dock and more of them floating in the water. We also found a* Field Guide to Mushrooms *book near the picnic table.*

McKenzie: *What's up with that?*

Alexis: *We don't know, but it seems like more than a coincidence.*

Sydney: *Maybe something evil is happening in that cave. We found a hole in the ground with a locked fence around it. Purple light shines up through the hole. We heard a sound like a helicopter. A cold wind blows, and the trees whisper "go back." And there's a secret room in the cave. We think that's where Jacques kept his treasure.*

Elizabeth: *Syd, trees don't whisper. There has to be a logical explanation. Remember how the land of Canaan was a mystery to Moses and his people? It could have been anything. So Moses sent his guys to check it out, and they discovered something good. I believe behind that secret door, you'll find a logical explanation, and hopefully, a good one.*

Sydney: *I hope you're right, Beth. But how do we get into the room? The door is locked. It has a trapdoor at the bottom that's way too small for Alex or me to get through.*

Bailey: *Can you stick the camera through the trapdoor and take pictures?*

Sydney: *I didn't think of that.*

Kate: *I have a better idea, but first you have to promise me that if you use my idea, the mountain man and his big dog won't be anywhere around.*

Sydney: *We promise.*

Kate: *Okay. Send Biscuit into the secret room with the mini-microcamera strapped to his collar. He's small enough to fit through the trapdoor. You can watch the monitor and see what's inside. But take very good care of him!*

Sydney: *You know we will. That's a great idea, Kate!*

Bailey: *What kind of mushrooms are they?*

Sydney: *I don't know. Why?*

Bailey: *I'm just curious. You usually know stuff like that.*

Alexis: *I'll see if I can find them in the field guide. We'll go back in the woods tomorrow and wait for the mountain man to leave. If he does, I'll babysit Fang while Sydney takes Biscuit into the cave.*

McKenzie: *Sounds like a plan.*

Kate gave instructions for programming the mini-microcamera to send live video to the Camp Club Girls' website, and Sydney wrote the instructions down. The girls promised to keep in touch.

"Tune in tomorrow," said Alexis. "We'll be broadcasting live from the Chequamegon-Nicolet National Forest."

When they went back to the cabin, Sydney got their poles ready for fishing. In the meantime, Alexis looked through the *Field Guide to Mushrooms*.

"There are tons of pictures in this thing," she said. "I don't know where to look. Wait. I found a list in the back of the book that tells which mushrooms grow in which states. That should be helpful. Let's see. . . Washington, West Virginia. . .Wisconsin! Here it is."

Alexis thumbed through the pages while Sydney got dough balls out of the refrigerator.

"I think I found it," she said. "You're going to love this, Syd. It has the scientific name and everything. The mushrooms that we saw are called *Strobilomyces floccopus*. It means, 'a wooly mushroom that looks like a pinecone.' The common name is the Old Man of the Woods. *Strobilomyces floccopus* only grow in the eastern half of North America, and it says here that you can eat them, but they taste bad."

Sydney checked the minnows swimming in the pail near the kitchen door. "If they taste bad, then why would anyone be digging them up in the forest?"

"That's what I was just wondering," Alexis said. "But I still think that someone was digging up clumps of them where we saw the shovel."

The girls got their fishing gear and headed for the dock. Duncan was still there fishing. He pretended not to see them.

"Duncan, it's time for you to move to your own dock," said Sydney.

Duncan didn't answer.

"Duncan?" Sydney stood there waiting.

"Aw, come on," he said. "Can't we all fish from here?"

Alexis and Sydney sat down on the dock and got their poles ready.

"Why do you have to fish from *this* dock?" Alexis asked. "What's wrong with Dock Two?"

Duncan turned around with a serious look on his face. "Because right out there," he said, pointing, "is the best fishing hole on North Twin Lake. Some of the biggest fish have been caught right there—straight out from this dock. I'm doing some serious fishing here, not just playing around like you girls are. So this is where I should fish." He turned back and sat facing the lake with his legs hanging off the end of the dock. Again, Sydney felt like shoving him in.

Forgive me, God, she prayed silently. *Help me to be nice to him.*

"Duncan," she said. Her voice sounded overly sweet. "You've been fishing here all day. Now it's our turn. That's only fair, don't you think?"

Duncan sighed deeply. "I guess so," he said. "I'll move." He took his time reeling in his line and packing up his gear. Then he walked to the dock by Cabin Two.

"Maybe we should try spoon lures on our lines," said Alexis. "The fish book says muskies like them. Maybe we can find out where the big ones are swimming."

Sydney caught her breath. "Alex, you just gave me an idea."

"Huh?"

"When you said, 'Maybe we can find out where the big ones are swimming,' it gave me an idea. Why don't we use the mini-microcam?

It's waterproof, and if we attach it to the end of one of our lines, we can see where the big fish are. What do you think?"

"I think your idea is *brilliant*," said Alexis, casting her line into the water. "Will you go back to the cabin and get it? And let Biscuit come sit with us. He's been cooped up on the porch all day."

"Will do," said Sydney.

In a little while, she returned with Biscuit trotting at her heels. "Okay, here's what we'll do," she said. "We'll put the camera on the end of your line without any bait or anything. Then you'll cast and slowly reel it in. In the meantime, I'll watch the hand-held monitor here. If we see a big fish, you stop reeling. I'll cast my line as close to yours as I can get it. Then we'll wait for the big one to bite."

"Sounds like a plan," said Alexis. She reeled in her line. "I'm ready." Carefully, Sydney tied the mini-microcam to Alex's line using a Palomar knot.

"I'm glad I took that knot-tying class at camp," she said. "Your fishing line will loop right through this little thingy on the side of the camera and the knot will hold it tight. It's a super strong knot."

With the knot tied and the camera attached, Alexis stood up and cast her line as far into the lake as she could. "Don't look now," she said. "But you-know-who is looking at us." Duncan was on Dock Two watching every move the girls made. He reeled in his line and then cast it near Alexis's.

"Stay clear of my line!" Alexis shouted. "I don't want to get tangled up with you again."

Duncan pretended not to hear.

Sydney loaded a dough ball onto her line. She made sure that it was firmly attached to the hook and double-checked it. The last thing she wanted was for it to fall off if a big fish came along. She turned on the monitor for the mini-microcam. It showed nothing under the water but some green algae.

"Start reeling in your line," she told Alexis. "But go really slow."

Alexis turned the crank on the reel while Sydney watched the monitor. Some small fish swam by—blue gills, sunfish, and perch.

"Nothing but little guys," Sydney said.

Alexis reeled her line closer to the dock. "Do you want me to cast it out again?" she asked.

"Yeah," Sydney answered. "See how far you can throw it."

Alexis stood and took a couple of steps backward.

"Move, Biscuit," she said. "I don't want you in the way."

Biscuit sniffed the wet mini-microcam hanging on the end of the fishing line. Then he sat down and watched Alexis cast the line with all of her might. It arched toward the sky and landed far into the lake.

"All right! Way to go, Alex!" Sydney exclaimed. "That was a great cast!"

She looked at the screen on the monitor in her hand. "Oh my goodness. Look."

She held it in front of Alexis. The camera had landed in the fishing hole—the one where the big ones swam. Several muskies were circling it, probably wondering if it held some food.

"Okay," said Sydney. "Now, I have to cast my line close to yours before they eat the minicam."

She stood and checked the dough ball one last time. It was stuck hard to the hook.

"Wish me luck, 'cause here I go." She stood back, trying to avoid Biscuit. Then with all her strength, she cast her line. It flew through the air and landed with a *splash* just a few yards from Alexis's line.

"All right!" she yelled. "Bull's-eye!"

Duncan watched more avidly than ever.

"Now I guess we just have to wait," said Alexis.

She had barely said the words when the end of Sydney's pole bent sharply toward the water. Then the reel started spinning uncontrollably, unraveling yards of line. Sydney grabbed the pole and held the reel crank to stop it from spinning.

"I've got a big one," she gasped.

Biscuit barked wildly, *Ruff! Ruff! Ar-roof! Ruff! Ruff! Ar-roof!*

That got Duncan's attention. "Need any help over there?" he yelled.

"We're fine!" Sydney shouted.

By now, the other boys on the other docks were watching too.

For fifteen minutes Sydney fought with the fish. She let it take some line, and then she reeled it in. She kept doing that until the fish was tired out. Then finally, she reeled it up to the dock.

"It's huge!" Alexis cried. She leaned over the edge of the dock and scooped the muskie into the net. It took every ounce of her strength to help Sydney haul it onto the dock.

Biscuit ran to the fish and sniffed it as it lay there flopping.

"Careful, boy. It has sharp teeth," Alexis warned.

The little dog backed away and whined.

Sydney took out the tape measure and measured her catch.

"Thirty-nine inches!" She yelled over to Duncan. "We're heading over to Tompkins' to put it on ice."

CHAPTER 11

A Fungus Among Us

The next morning, the girls quietly prepared for another adventure in the forest. They both knew returning to the mountain man's cave was risky.

"I think we should leave Biscuit here," said Sydney.

"We can't," Alexis argued. "He's the only one who will fit through the trap door."

"I know," Sydney said, as she stuffed their sleuthing equipment into her waist pack. "But if Biscuit barks, he'll give us away. We should go to the campsite alone. Then, when the mountain man leaves, one of us can come back here and get him."

Alexis slipped the Wonder Watch over her wrist. "And what do we do about Fang? If he senses we're nearby, he might run to us or bark or something."

"That's a chance we'll have to take," Sydney said. "We need to be super quiet when we're at the campsite."

Alexis tucked the pepper spray into her pocket just in case they ran into a bear. "Scooby-Doo, where are you?" She sighed as they left the cabin.

"What?" Sydney asked.

"I was just thinking about Scooby-Doo," Alexis explained. "He's always nervous when he goes sleuthing, and I wondered how he would sneak into the campsite."

"Are you nervous?"

"A little," Alexis answered. "Let's check out the mushrooms first and see if anyone has been digging."

When they arrived at the spot where the mushrooms grew, they found them—*gone!*

"Were there hundreds of mushrooms here yesterday or was it all my imagination?" Alexis asked in disbelief.

"They were here," Sydney confirmed. "And now they're not." Someone had dug up the mushrooms, raked the soil, and covered it with dead leaves and pine needles. The shovel was gone too.

Sydney probed the soil with her foot, looking for clues. "Check this out," she said, pointing to a spot on the ground.

"Ésprit!" said Alexis. "It's the mountain man's boot print! But why would he want so many mushrooms?"

Sydney was busy thinking. "Do you know what, Alex?" she said after a while. "I'm sure he's the one who left the *Field Guide to Mushrooms* on the ground at the resort. And I'm sure too that he's responsible for the mushroom we found on the dock and the others floating in the water. And remember, the first night we were here we saw him, and then in the morning the bottom of the boat at our dock was wet, and you noticed a brown, slimy fungus at the edge of the beach."

"That's right," said Alexis. "And mushrooms are a fungus. And that night, after the coyote was killed, we saw the mountain man near our cabin. He was picking at the earth with a stick and putting stuff into a bag."

"Mushrooms!" Sydney added. "Alex, he was searching for mushrooms there in the dark, but why?"

"That's what we have to find out," Alexis said.

They approached the campsite cautiously, stopping briefly when the buzzing noise from the cave turned to the familiar *whop-whop-whop* followed by "Go back! Go back! Go back!"

"I'm not afraid of that anymore," said Sydney. "It's obviously triggered by something we step on or walk by. I think the mountain man is using spooky sounds to keep people away."

"Like the professor in *The Wizard of Oz*," said Alexis.

"Yeah, just like him," Sydney agreed.

They peeked through the bushes at the campsite. The kayak was gone, and so it seemed, were the mountain man and Fang.

"I'm going to check it out," said Sydney. "You stay here." She walked around the campsite, staying well hidden in the brush. She passed the stinking manure pile at the edge of the clearing. Then she went toward the hole in the ground. The purple glow shot up from the hole as it had the day before, and the buzzing noise whirred down below. The fence was still padlocked shut.

"They're not here," Sydney said when she circled back around to where Alexis stood. "Stay put, and I'll get Biscuit."

Sydney sprinted back to the cabin. Biscuit was waiting for her on the screened porch. Before they'd left that morning, Sydney had attached the mini-microcamera to his collar so he'd be ready to go.

"Come on, boy," she said, snapping his leash onto his collar. Biscuit sensed that he was on an important mission. Instead of barking and running playfully into the woods, he sniffed the ground following the trail that the girls had taken. Before long, he led Sydney right to the campsite where Alexis was.

"I have the monitor turned on and ready," Alex said, "and I alerted the other Camp Club Girls that we're about to go in. Kate sent a message that she's worried. I told her we'd make sure Biscuit stays safe."

"Good," said Sydney. "I think only one of us should go into the cave with him."

Alexis said nothing.

"I'll go," Sydney offered.

"I'll stand guard," Alexis said. "And Sydney, be very, *very* careful."

"We will," Sydney promised. Then she and Biscuit walked into the purple glow of the clearing and headed toward the entrance to the cave. Biscuit pulled and strained hard on his leash. He made a gagging, gasping sound as the collar choked him, and he dragged Sydney inside.

"Slow down, boy!" she said. But Biscuit hurried on ahead.

They went through the wide stone-cold corridor toward the secret room, and Sydney noticed that the knapsack was missing—the one with the initials J.C. They rushed past the marks etched on the wall and into the little room with the stalactites and stalagmites. Biscuit seemed to know exactly where he was going. He led Sydney directly to the corner of the room and the locked door. Then he sat and looked at her.

"Are you ready to do some exploring?" Sydney asked him. Biscuit stood on his hind legs and put his paws on Sydney's knees. She reached for the mini-microcam on his collar and switched it on. Video of the outside appeared on the small monitor that Alexis held in her hand. First, the blue denim of Sydney's jeans, then her white sneaker with the lace half tied, then the stone floor of the cave, and finally the wooden planks of the heavy, padlocked door.

"Here we go," Alexis whispered into the face of the Wonder Watch. She took a deep breath and prayed. "Dear God, watch over Biscuit."

"Okay, Biscuit," said Sydney. "You go through this little door and check things out, and be quick about it too." She unhooked the leash from Biscuit's collar and let him go. He lay down on his fluffy belly and then slithered and squeezed his body through the little trapdoor.

Sydney ran back to where Alexis was so they could watch the monitor together. "He's in," she said, peeking over Alexis's shoulder.

"So far, all I can see is purple," said Alexis.

"He must be sitting or standing just inside the door," said Sydney. "He's not moving. Why?"

"I don't know," said Alexis. "He's just sitting there."

Suddenly, the monitor went black.

"What's wrong with this thing?" Sydney complained. "We just lost our picture. Wait. . .no. . .I think the camera is taking a picture of something black. Look. Whatever it is, it's moving."

The blackness on the screen bounced up and down and back and forth and then—

"Oh my goodness!" Sydney gasped. A huge, black nose appeared on the screen, sniffing. Then a sparkling, brown eye looked into the camera lens, and a long, pink tongue licked it. "Fang!"

The Wonder Watch jiggled on Alex's wrist. MESSAGE WAITING: KATE. A message scrolled across the screen. THAT'S NOT BISCUIT'S NOSE! WHAT'S IN THERE WITH MY DOG?

Alexis held the watch toward Sydney. "You tell her," she said.

Reluctantly, Sydney pushed the button on the watch and spoke into its face. "Fang is with Biscuit. I had no idea he was in there. But he's friendly, Kate. I'm sure of it."

GET HIM OUT OF THERE THIS MINUTE!

Alexis answered this time. "Kate, we can't. It'll be just fine. I promise. Watch the pictures, and if anything goes wrong, we'll go right in to get him."

PROMISE?

"I promise," said Alexis.

Sydney looked on helplessly. "The only problem with that," she said to Alexis, "is that we *can't* go in and get him. The door is locked."

"I forgot," said Alexis. "So now what?"

"Pray," said Sydney.

"I am," Alexis said. "*I am!*"

The picture on the screen changed to a thick, black tail wagging like a windshield wiper on a car. Then the girls saw all of Fang's behind as he trotted ahead of Biscuit.

"What's that?" Sydney asked.

A long table showed up on the screen. On it were jars of various sizes. Each jar was filled with a clear liquid, and each held a single large mushroom. The mushrooms seemed to glow in the eerie purple light.

"I see labels on the jars, but I can't read them," said Alexis. "It looks like he's handwritten a name and date on each one."

Biscuit must have sensed that the jars were important. He put his paws up on the table and gave them a closer look.

MILLER'S RESORT: 8-1

FOREST: 7-31

WATER'S EDGE: 8-2

"Each one has a label telling where the mushroom came from and when he found it," said Sydney. "Look, Biscuit's going into another room."

The purple glow grew softer as Biscuit left the room and entered another. The girls could see Fang running ahead of him.

"It's some sort of laboratory!" said Alexis.

Biscuit sniffed around the room, and the girls saw beakers, bottles, flasks, and test tubes. Some of them had green and pink liquids inside.

There were microscopes and Bunsen burners and magnifying glasses and culture jars.

"Maybe he's a mad scientist," said Sydney.

"Oh," said Alexis. "He's not mad. He can't be! Like Beth said, there's a perfectly logical explanation for all of this."

"Yeah, well. . .then what is it?" Sydney asked, pointing to the monitor screen and ugly, gray spores growing in a culture dish.

"I don't know," said Alexis. "He's obviously doing some experiments."

"Obviously," Sydney agreed.

Biscuit wandered past thermometers, trays, tubes, tweezers, scales and stirrers, and blenders and buckets.

"Check that out," said Alexis.

A large beaker sat atop a hot plate. A shimmering, green liquid bubbled and boiled inside, and radiant chartreuse steam rose from the top and hung in the air. The beaker came closer and closer as Biscuit moved in to investigate it. He stuck his nose near the steam and jumped back.

"I think maybe he burned his nose," said Sydney.

"Or else it smelled bad," said Alexis. "What do you think the mountain man is cooking?"

"I don't know," said Sydney. "But Biscuit doesn't like it. And have you noticed that Fang is nowhere in sight?"

"I didn't," said Alexis, "but now that you mention it. . ."

WUF!

Alex and Sydney whirled around. There stood Fang. He ran toward the girls and put his big paws on Alex's shoulders, knocking her to the ground. He started licking her face.

"Get him off!" she cried. "Get him off me!"

Sydney reached down and wrapped her arms around Fang's middle. She pulled, trying to lift him off of her friend, but Fang rolled over, pulling Sydney down too. Soon the girls were on the ground wrestling with the big, black dog.

"He thinks we're playing with him," Alexis complained. "Fang, no! Fang, stop it! *Sit down!*"

Fang sat. He looked at the girls with sad, brown eyes and cocked his head.

"I think he gets it," said Sydney. She stood and wiped dirt from the seat of her jeans. "Where did he come from? The door to the secret room is locked with a padlock."

A sick look came over Alexis's face. "What if there are two of them?"

"Two of what?" asked Sydney.

"Two Fangs," Alexis answered, standing up. "Maybe that's another dog inside the cave with Biscuit."

Sydney picked up the monitor that Alexis had dropped when Fang pushed her down. "I don't see another dog," she said, "but where is Biscuit going? Everything is really purple now, and it looks like he's in *another* room." She handed the monitor to Alexis.

Fang sat quietly at the girls' feet.

"I see something," said Alexis.

Biscuit was wandering around a room filled with racks of shallow, dirt-filled trays. As he got nearer to them, the girls saw mushrooms popping out of the soil.

"Alex, there must be thousands of mushrooms in those trays," Sydney said. "Big ones, little ones, all sizes! The room is filled with mushrooms. And do you see that book next to one of the trays? The title says *Cancer Fighting Foods*. I think I know who the mountain man is and what he's doing."

The Wonder Watch jiggled. MESSAGE WAITING: KATE. IT'S A MUSHROOM FARM. WE HAVE THEM IN PENNSYLVANIA. I KNOW ABOUT

A BIG ONE IN KENNETT SQUARE. THE MOUNTAIN MAN IS GROWING MUSHROOMS IN THAT CAVE BECAUSE THE CONDITIONS ARE PERFECT: COOL, DARK, AND DAMP.

"You're right," said Sydney. "The cave is a perfect place for a *scientist* to work. I think the mountain man is a scientist, and he's doing some sort of research with mushrooms."

"See," Alexis whispered. "I told you he's not a *mad* scientist. He's a *good* scientist."

YOU MIGHT BE RIGHT, SYD. WE LEARNED IN CLASS THAT SCIENTISTS ARE EXPERIMENTING WITH MUSHROOMS TO HELP SICK PEOPLE. THAT COULD BE WHAT HE'S DOING. WHERE IS FANG? I HAVEN'T SEEN HIM ON THE MONITOR.

Alexis spoke into the watch. "Fang is with us."

HOW DID HE GET WITH YOU IF THE DOOR IS LOCKED?

"We don't know," Alexis told her, leaving out her theory that there might be two dogs.

SOMETHING FISHY IS GOING ON THERE, AND I DON'T LIKE IT. WHAT IF WE'RE WRONG, AND HE REALLY IS UP TO NO GOOD?

Just then, Fang leapt up and took off running through the forest.

"Oh. Oh," said Sydney. "I don't like this either." Fang's bark echoed through the trees as he ran away from the campsite. "I'm going inside to get Biscuit, and he'd better come when I call him."

Sydney ran to the cave leaving Alexis alone.

"Sydney is going back inside to get Biscuit," Alexis said into the watch. "I think we've seen enough for one day."

Grrrrrrrrrr. . . . A deep, soft growl came from an alder thicket behind her.

"Fang, is that you?" she asked.

Grrrrrrrrrr. . . . The growl was a little louder now.

"Fang, stop it. You're scaring me," said Alexis. She took a few steps toward the thicket and peeked through its branches.

There, just a few yards away, stood a huge gray wolf. The sides of its mouth curled back, revealing its razor-sharp teeth. *Grrrrrrrrr. . .*

Alexis didn't dare move. She remembered the pepper spray in her pocket, but she was afraid to reach for it. Even the slightest move might make the wolf attack.

Dear God, please help me, she prayed silently.

BAW-WAW-WAW. . . . AR-ROOooooooo. . . . BAW-WAW-WAW!

Fang barreled through the brush and lunged at the wolf, scaring it. The frightened animal ran off through the forest with Fang in hot pursuit.

BAW-WAW-WAW! Baw-waw-waw. . .baw-waw-waw. . . The barking faded into the distance.

Alexis sighed with relief.

Then, just as her pounding heart was slowing down, she heard—

"Young lady, what are you doing here?"

It was the mountain man! He stood behind her, strong and tall. He held his walking stick and a plastic bag filled with mushrooms. The knapsack, the one with the initials J.C., was flung over one shoulder. Alexis noticed that his bushy, brown beard twitched, and his brow was creased with a frown. His blue eyes flashed. "I asked what you're doing here."

Alexis was trapped. A still, small voice inside told her to be polite. "Hello, sir," she said brightly. "I'm Alexis Howell. Pleased to meet you."

She extended her trembling right hand toward the man.

He reached out and gave it a little shake. "Professor Joshua Cantrell." He introduced himself. "Now, Alexis, what are you doing here?"

Alexis didn't know what to say. She heard herself babbling. "Oh, so you're a professor! We thought you might be a scientist or something. We didn't know for sure, but we figured that you were a perfectly normal person, a very nice man just out here in the woods camping—"

"Little girl, are you lost?" the man asked.

Little girl! Alexis thought. *I'm not a little girl.*

"No, sir," she said. "The truth is our dog is in your cave, and my friend went in to get him."

CHAPTER 12

The Secret Revealed

Sydney arrived with Biscuit on his leash.

"Oh. Oh," she said when she saw Alexis with the mountain man.

"So, this must be your friend," Professor Cantrell said. "And I've seen your dog here before. In fact, I took him back to the resort just the other day."

"We know," said Alexis. "We saw you. Sydney, this is Professor Joshua Cantrell."

"You *saw* me?" said the professor. "What are you girls doing this deep in the forest? You shouldn't be wandering out here alone."

Sydney picked up Biscuit and handed him to Alexis.

"A better question, Professor Cantrell, is what are *you* doing here in the woods? We know all about you and your mushrooms."

"You do?" said the professor. "Just what do you know?" He reached over and scratched Biscuit's ears.

"We know that you sneak around in the dark picking mushrooms. We know that you dug up a ton of them in the forest and that you're growing more of them in your cave and experimenting with them. We hope that you're doing something good."

"And that you're not a mad scientist!" Alexis added, wishing that the words wouldn't have slipped from her mouth.

Professor Cantrell laughed. "You're right, I'm a scientist," he said. "And yes, sometimes I get a bit grumpy, but no, I'm not mad."

Wuf! Wuf! Wuf!

Fang shoved his body through the thicket and ran to his master. The professor checked him over.

"Are you okay, boy?" he asked. "That was a good boy for chasing the wolf."

"Wolf?" said Sydney.

"I was almost attacked by a wolf. Fang saved me." Biscuit squirmed in Alexis's arms. "And how did Fang get out of the cave?" she asked the professor. "The door to the secret room is locked."

"Secret room!" said Professor Cantrell. "Have you girls been inside my laboratory? You didn't touch anything, did you?" He was getting irritated now. "How did you get in, and how do you know my dog's name?"

"We've been watching you," said Sydney. "And you can't do anything to us, because right now you're being filmed—live."

"What!" the professor exclaimed, looking around for a camera. "Young ladies, we need to talk." He invited the girls to sit down on the log near the campfire ring. "Tell me what you know," he said.

Sydney and Alexis explained about being in the forest and seeing the purple glow and hearing strange sounds coming from the cave. They told him about seeing the hole in the ground with the padlocked fence and the old knapsack inside the cave and the marks on the wall. And finally, about their theory that he, somehow, had found Jacques Chouteau's treasure.

"We know you're a scientist who's sneaking around in the woods," said Sydney. "And that must mean that you're doing something wrong."

"Girls, girls, girls," the professor said, scratching Fang's ears. "I'm not doing anything wrong."

They heard a rustling in the brush nearby. Then Aunt Dee and Mr. Miller stepped into the clearing.

"Are you girls all right?" Aunt Dee wailed. "Bailey called me and said a man in the forest kidnapped you! I've been frantic!"

"Hello, Charlie," said Professor Cantrell.

"Hi, Josh," said Mr. Miller.

"You two know each other?" Sydney said.

"We do," Professor Cantrell answered. He hesitated. Then he looked at the girls. "Charlie, can they be trusted?"

"I think so," Charlie Miller answered. "I *know* so!" he added, winking.

The professor took a deep breath and let it out slowly. "Girls, if I tell you a secret, do you promise not to tell anyone, *ever*?"

Alexis switched off the mini-microcamera on Biscuit's collar.

"Wait a minute, Alex," said Sydney. "Can all of *you* be trusted not to tell if *we* share a secret?"

The professor, Aunt Dee, and Mr. Miller all gave their word not to tell.

Sydney explained about the camera and the Wonder Watch and promised that the other Camp Club Girls wouldn't tell if they too could hear the professor's story.

"That's quite a gadget," Professor Cantrell said, inspecting the watch. "As long as the other girls promise, I'll tell all of you what's going on."

"You'll have their word," said Sydney. She pushed the button on the watch.

"Girls," she said. "Everything is fine here. This is Professor Cantrell. Listen to what he has to say. All of this is top secret—not to be shared outside of our group, *ever*. Do you absolutely, positively promise never to tell another living soul?"

ELIZABETH: I PROMISE.
KATE: ME TOO.
MACKENZIE: PROMISE.
BAILEY: DITTO!

Sydney handed the watch to the professor and reminded him to push the button so it would pick up his voice.

He held the watch near his lips. "It's true that I've been out at night picking mushrooms at the resort," said the professor. "Very rare mushrooms grow under the trees near the cabins. They only sprout up from the ground in the dark, and I've been harvesting them secretly. You see, these mushrooms might someday be a cure for certain kinds of cancer."

"Kate was right!" Sydney interrupted.

"I've been growing and synthesizing them, and other mushrooms from the forest, in my laboratory. But for now, I need to keep it all a secret. If the press discovers what I'm doing, they'll be all over the place out here."

"So that's why you've been so sneaky," said Sydney. "It all makes sense now. *Strobilomyces floccopus.* Wow, a cure for cancer right here in the Northwoods!"

Suddenly, the buzzing from the cave turned to a *whoosh*, followed by *whop-whop-whop* and "Go back! Go back! Go back!"

"What about those noises?" Sydney asked. "We keep hearing them coming from the cave."

"I've put two huge fans in the cave," said the professor. "They exchange the air every forty-five minutes to keep the climate controlled.

Come on, let me show you." He led the group to the fence and unlocked the padlock.

"This is the exchanger," he said, pointing to the hole in the ground. "One fan blows the air up and out of the cave, and the other sucks fresh air in. I keep it locked up so animals don't get curious and fall down into the fans. If you looked carefully, you'd see six other smaller vents covered with metal grates out here in the forest floor."

Alexis set Biscuit down so he could play with Fang. The two dogs ran off together into the cave.

"The purple light is part of my experimenting," the professor explained. He took off his knapsack and laid it on the ground. "I've found that the cultures I grow from the mushrooms need a special kind of light. With a combination of the purple light and certain chemicals, I'm close to finding a substance that might be the cure."

"That's amazing," said Aunt Dee. "I can understand why you'd want to keep it quiet for now. So, the Millers have known about you living and working here in the woods?"

"Betty and I have known Josh for years," said Charlie Miller. "He spends summers working in the cave and harvesting mushrooms from our property."

Just then, Biscuit came running from behind a stand of pine trees.

"Hey," said Sydney. "Where did he come from? I saw him go into the cave a few minutes ago with Fang."

"I dug out a back door in the mushroom-growing room," said the professor. "Putting a door close to the manure pile made it easier for me to get the trays ready for planting."

Fang trotted out of the cave's entrance. He sniffed the professor's knapsack where it lay on the ground.

"Do you want a treat, boy?" he asked, picking up the knapsack. He opened it and took out two dog biscuits. "Here's one for you and one for your friend."

"So that's your knapsack then, and not Jacques Chouteau's," said Sydney.

"Jacques Chouteau's! Why would you think it belonged to Jacques Chouteau?" the professor asked.

"Because of the initials J.C.," Alexis responded.

"Oh, goodness, no." The professor laughed. "But I'll tell you another secret, and this is a good one. A cave-in happened way back in the mine, and I think, behind all those rocks might lay the body of poor old

Jacques. There are tick marks on the walls just inside the cave. I think Jacques made those, counting off the days that he was trapped inside. When I first discovered the cave, the front entrance was blocked. So I had to dig my way in."

"We thought the same thing about the marks," said Sydney. "Our friend Elizabeth said that there was probably a logical explanation for everything, and there is. And Alexis always assumed that you were a nice man."

"Why, thank you, Alexis," said the professor.

Aunt Dee looked puzzled. "Who's Jacques Chouteau?" she asked.

Sydney grinned. "Oh, just some old ghost that haunts the Chequamegon-Nicolet National Forest. I'll tell you about it when we drive home tomorrow."

"Well, you'd better," said Aunt Dee. "I need to know everything about this forest because I just found out that I got the job."

"Oh Aunt Dee, that's great!" said Sydney, hugging her. "I'll miss you living with us in Washington, but how cool is it that I can visit you here all the time. And can Alexis come too?"

"Alexis and all the other Camp Club Girls," Aunt Dee said. "And tonight we're going to have a long talk about how dangerous it was for you girls to be sleuthing in the woods!"

"Over and out," Sydney said into the Wonder Watch. "We'll head for Tompkins' in a little while and chat online."

BETH: OVER AND OUT.
KATE: OVER AND OUT.
MACKENZIE: OVER AND OUT.
BAILEY: DITTO!

They left Mr. Miller and the professor talking about the wolf that killed the coyote on the beach.

"Well, that's another mystery solved," Sydney said as they walked through the woods.

"You girls and your detective work," Aunt Dee complained. "One of these days, you're going to get yourselves into trouble, and then what?"

"Then the Camp Club Girls will come and rescue us," Sydney replied. "But for now, Alex and I have some fishing to do."

When they got back to the resort, Duncan was fishing on Dock Two.

"Catch anything?" Sydney yelled to him.

He ignored her.

Alexis took out her cell phone and punched in the number for Tompkins' Ice Cream Shop. Then she texted the word FISH. In a few seconds, her phone rang. "Thirty-nine inches," she said. "We're still in the lead."

"Awesome!" Sydney exclaimed. "And I plan to keep it that way. Let's get our poles."

Biscuit pulled and strained against his leash. Sydney bent down to set him free.

"No," said Aunt Dee. "You need to keep him on the leash. Otherwise, he'll run right back to the campsite to play with the professor's dog."

"You're right," Sydney agreed. "Sorry, Biscuit."

In a few minutes, Sydney and Alexis were on their dock fishing. This time, they knew where to cast their lines.

"I sort of feel bad that we're beating Duncan," Alexis said as she sat on the end of the dock with her bare feet dangling in the water.

"You do?" said Sydney. "Why?"

"I don't know," Alexis answered. "Something about him is just so sad."

"Sad!" Sydney exclaimed. "He's a bully." She reeled in her line and cast it out again.

"That's not a very Christian attitude, Sydney. Remember what McKenzie always says, 'Mad is usually a cover up for sad.' She might be right. Mr. Miller said that Duncan doesn't have many friends."

"Yeah, and I can tell you why," Sydney answered.

"We promised to be nice to him," Alexis continued. "I mean, look over there. Boys are fishing on every dock, and none of them seem to know Duncan. You'd think that since he and his dad come here every summer he'd know some of the kids and hang out with them." She reeled in her line just a little.

"Maybe they're first-time visitors, like we are," said Sydney.

"Maybe," Alexis said. "And maybe not." She fished silently for a while. "I'd be really sad if my mom and sister died in an accident," she continued. "He's gotta be sad, Sydney. You don't just forget about something like that."

"You're right," Sydney answered. "But Alex, I really want us to win this contest. If we don't, he's going to think that girls can't fish. If nothing else, I want him to learn that he's wrong about that."

The tip of Alexis's pole bent down. She grabbed tight to the reel and started turning the crank. "I don't think it's very big," she said. "It doesn't feel like the other fish we caught."

Duncan watched them from his dock.

Alexis reeled in her line and found a small sunfish dangling from the hook. Carefully, she removed the hook and set the fish free.

"Ah-ha-ha!" Duncan laughed loud enough for the girls to hear. "Nice one, Alex," he called to them. "That'll win the prize for sure."

"See what I mean?" said Sydney.

Just then, Duncan's pole jerked in his hands. He stood up and pulled back, setting the hook in the fish's mouth. Then he tried to reel it in. The fish was strong, and it put up a gigantic fight. While the girls watched from their dock, Duncan pulled hard. He let the fish run with the line. Reeled it in. Let it run. Reeled it in, again and again. The fish kept fighting. Duncan pulled and yanked and reeled, but he made little progress.

"Do you think we should go help him?" Alexis asked.

"Goodness no," said Sydney. "He'd never accept our help anyway."

Then it happened—something the girls could never have imagined. They heard Duncan scream, *"Ah-ah-yeeeeeeahhhh!"* The scream was followed by a humongous *splash!* The strength of the fish pulled Duncan right off the end of the dock and into the water.

The girls' first instinct was to laugh. There he was, soaking wet, thrashing around near the dock. Sydney saw his pole in the water, flying toward them. She reached down and grabbed it. Alexis set her pole on the dock and grabbed Sydney's ankles just in time, or she would have been thrown into the water too.

Sydney managed to get herself upright. Then, just like Duncan, she fought the fish with all of her might.

"Help me! Help me!" Duncan screamed. "I—I c–can't sw–swim!"

The other boys didn't notice, or they didn't care.

"Oh my!" Sydney gasped. She handed her pole to Alexis, and then she sprinted to Duncan's dock.

She jumped into the water, wearing all of her clothes, and grabbed hold of Duncan's shirt just before his head disappeared under the water. He sputtered and spit and flogged around.

"Duncan, calm down!" Sydney demanded. "You're fine."

She pulled him to the side of the dock into shallow water.

"Put your feet down. You can reach the bottom now."

Duncan did as he was told, and the two of them walked up onto the shore.

By now, everyone on the docks was watching. "Everything all right?"

a boy shouted from Dock Three.

Duncan stuck his hand in the air and waved him off.

"How come you embarrassed me like that?" he said to Sydney. "All the guys are lookin' at me now."

"Embarrassed you!" Sydney said, standing there dripping wet. "If I hadn't *embarrassed* you, you'd be dead!"

Duncan hung his head.

"I'm sorry," he whispered. "I guess you saved my life."

"Hey! Hey! Come here!" Alexis shouted from Dock One. She'd managed to reel the big fish in. "I need someone to net this monster."

Sydney and Duncan hurried over to help her. It took all three of them to pull the muskie up onto the dock. The fish's gaping, tooth-filled mouth swung open and shut as it still fought against the hook. Sydney took out her tape measure and measured it.

"Forty inches," she announced.

Duncan stood there red faced. "Well," he said. "I guess you guys won. The contest ends in an hour, and I'm done fishing."

Alexis wiped her wet hands on her jeans. "What do you mean, Duncan? You won," she said. "You did all the work. I just helped you to pull it in."

Duncan's face brightened.

"Do you mean it?" he said. "I won?"

"It's your fish," said Sydney. "Congratulations." She put her hand out, and Duncan shook it. "There's just one thing," she said.

"What's that?" Duncan asked suspiciously.

"I want you to say that *girls can fish* and mean it."

Duncan looked down at the dock. "Girls can fish, I guess."

"You guess?" said Alexis.

"Naw," he replied. "Girls *can* fish."

When Duncan's dad heard about Sydney rescuing Duncan from the water, he insisted on treating them and Aunt Dee to supper at The Wave Restaurant. As it turned out, Duncan and his father were good company. Mr. Lumley knew a lot about the lake, and he seemed eager to find out more about Aunt Dee's job as a forest ranger.

"I had fun tonight," said Alexis, as she and Sydney got ready for bed. "Duncan and Mr. Lumley turned out to be all right."

Sydney sat on her bed reading her Bible. "They did," she agreed. "Alex, isn't it strange how sometimes you can read the Bible and it seems to speak to you about what's going on right now? Do you want to hear the verse I just read?"

"Sure," Alexis answered.

"I found it in Leviticus 19:18," said Sydney. "It goes like this. 'Do not seek revenge or bear a grudge against one of your people, but love your neighbor as yourself.' Duncan's not the only one who learned a lesson this week. I learned that revenge isn't good. During supper tonight, I realized that Duncan might have been a friend. We could have had fun hanging out with him all week."

"Well," said Alexis. "Maybe next summer. With your aunt working here, you can come back anytime."

"That's true," said Sydney.

Darkness had fallen on the Wisconsin woods. Sydney reached across her bed to shut the curtains on the window. A dark, shadowy figure moved about near the beach. "Professor Cantrell is out there searching for mushrooms," she said.

Alexis climbed into Sydney's bunk and looked.

"No, Syd," she said. "It's not the professor. Look again. It's a bear! Isn't that cool?"

"Cool?" Sydney asked. "I thought you were afraid of bears."

"I was," said Alexis. "But after what we've been through this week, a big, old bear doesn't scare me at all."

Camp Club Girls:
Sydney and the
Curious Cherokee Cabin

CHAPTER 1

Galilahi

" 'Run, Syd, run!' I kept telling myself. 'You have a ticking time bomb in your hands. If you don't throw it into the harbor in like, two seconds, you'll be dead!' "

"At least you would have been with the Lord," said Elizabeth Anderson, as she poured maple syrup onto her buckwheat pancakes. "Although I tried not to think about it at the time."

Sydney Lincoln, her Aunt Dee, and Elizabeth were eating breakfast at Peter's Pancakes and Waffles in Cherokee, North Carolina. The girls were reminiscing about the week Elizabeth had visited Sydney at her home in Washington, DC. The week had ended up full of adventure as Sydney and Elizabeth had landed full-steam in what they and their friends, the Camp Club Girls, had dubbed, Sydney's DC Discovery.

"Yeah, well, *I* thought about it," Sydney answered. "I've never run so fast in my entire life." She reached across the table for the pepper shaker and added pepper onto her already spicy, cheesy, jalapeno omelet. "I just wanted to toss the bomb in the water and climb into the boat where I knew I'd be safe with you and your uncle."

"When you were running toward the dock, I shut my eyes tight and prayed harder than I ever have," said Elizabeth. "I held my breath until I heard the big splash, and Uncle Dan hauled you into the boat."

She stabbed a piece of pancake with her fork and swirled it around in the syrup on her plate. "Moose and Rusty were the dumbest thugs in the world. And to think that they almost succeeded in killing the president."

"If it hadn't been for us," Sydney reminded her.

A hummingbird flittered around a birdfeeder hanging outside the window next to their table. The noisy breakfast crowd had thinned out now, and it was easier to hear a conversation.

Aunt Dee looked out the window at the Oconaluftee River and shook her head. "I can't believe the things you girls have gotten yourselves into. If I'd known you were chasing criminals who planned to assassinate the president of the United States, neither of you would have left the house while Elizabeth was visiting. You would have stayed in Sydney's room texting with your friends, or whatever you do."

Sydney grinned. "Not to worry, Aunt Dee. I don't plan to get to heaven until I'm at least a hundred years old, and besides, the Camp Club Girls have solved enough mysteries to be real detectives. In fact, that's what I'm going to be someday. I'm going to college to study criminal justice. When I get out, I'm going to start my own detective agency—"

"Will you hire me?" Elizabeth interrupted.

"Of course!" Sydney responded. "You and all of the Camp Club Girls."

"Lord, help me," Aunt Dee prayed, as she poured herself a cup of coffee from a white carafe on the table.

It was two weeks before the start of a new school year. Aunt Dee was temporarily working as a park ranger at Great Smoky Mountains National Park, and she'd invited Sydney and her friend Elizabeth to stay with her for a week.

"I'm sorry I can't get off work more while you're here," said Aunt Dee. "I expect you to keep out of trouble. There's plenty for you to do in Cherokee. You can shop, hike the nature trails, go horseback riding—"

"Or how about a helicopter ride?" said a voice from the next table. The girls turned around to see another girl who looked about the same age as Sydney and Elizabeth. She had long, shiny, crow-black hair and eyes the color of almonds.

"I hope you don't mind that I heard your conversation," she said, "but I was thinking: Maybe, since you're so good at solving mysteries, you can help me solve the mystery surrounding my grandmother."

The girl got up and walked around to their table. "I'm Galilahi Lowrey," she introduced herself. A man and woman got up from the table and followed her. Sydney noticed that their skin, like the girl's, was the color of sandstone.

"These are my parents, Jack and Melvina Lowrey," she added.

"I'm Sydney Lincoln." Sydney responded. "And this is Elizabeth Anderson."

Aunt Dee introduced herself to Galilahi's mom and dad.

"So what's this about a helicopter ride?" asked Sydney.

"We moved here from Oklahoma in June," said Mr. Lowrey. "I worked at an oil refinery there, but it shut down. We have friends here on the Cherokee reservation. One of them owns a helicopter-tour attraction, and he offered me a job."

Mr. Lowrey reached into his pocket and pulled out a small folder filled with business cards. He gave some to Aunt Dee and the girls. The cards had a photograph of a black-and-yellow helicopter and the words: *"Helicopter Tours, See the Smokies from the Sky."*

"I'm a pilot with the company. You're welcome to come and take a ride any time. My treat."

"Cool!" said Sydney. "Can we, Aunt Dee?"

"That sounds like fun," her aunt answered. "And thank you, Mr. Lowrey," she added.

Elizabeth slid the business card into a pocket in her tote bag. "I didn't know Cherokee has an Indian reservation," she said.

"Oh, yes," Mrs. Lowrey answered. "The Eastern band of Cherokee. The reservation is next to Great Smoky Mountains National Park."

"That's where Aunt Dee works," Sydney exclaimed.

"I'm a park ranger there right now," Aunt Dee told them. "I'm filling in for a ranger who was injured in an accident. I'm familiar with the reservation. In fact, girls, I was just going to suggest that you check out some of the attractions near there. There's plenty to see and learn about."

Sydney took the last bite of her omelet. She squished up the paper napkin that had been on her lap and laid it on her empty plate.

"Do you live on the reservation?" she asked the Lowreys.

"No," Mrs. Lowrey said. "I'm embarrassed to say we don't know much about the Cherokee culture. When my grandmother was a girl, she lived on the reservation in Oklahoma, but when she grew up and got married, she and my grandfather moved to Blackgum. They owned a little diner and bait shop there near Lake Tenkiller."

"Great-Grandma Rogers is the one who named me," said Galilahi. "She gave me an old family name."

"*Galilahi* means 'attractive'," her mother added. "A beautiful name for our beautiful daughter."

Galilahi blushed.

A waitress came to the table and asked if Aunt Dee wanted more coffee. Aunt Dee said she didn't, and the waitress handed her the bill.

"So is that the grandma whose house you're looking for?" Sydney wondered.

"No," Galilahi answered. "I'm looking for the house of my fifth great-grandmother. She's the one Great-Grandma Rogers named me after."

Aunt Dee opened her wallet and counted out money to pay the bill. She laid a tip for the waitress on the table.

"You have *five* great-grandmas?" said Sydney.

"No," Galilahi responded. "I probably should have said it's my great-great-great-great-*great* grandmother, but that's a mouthful."

"It sure is," Elizabeth laughed. "Let's just call her Grandma Number Five."

"Or Grandma Hisgi," said Galilahi. "*Hisgi* means 'five' in Cherokee."

"*Heeshk*," Sydney repeated. "Am I saying it right?"

"You are," Galilahi confirmed.

"Galilahi knows more Cherokee words than we do," Mrs. Lowrey told Aunt Dee. "My husband and I never learned the language. Lea is very close to my grandmother, and she's learned a lot about the Cherokees from her."

"Great-Grandmother is very old now," said Galilahi. "She's almost ninety."

"Do people call you Lea?" Elizabeth asked.

"Only my parents," said Galilahi. "I like my real name."

"Then that's what I'll call you," said Sydney. "*Oo-lee-LOW-hee.* I like the way your real name sounds."

The waitress came to their table again, and Aunt Dee handed her the money.

"Why don't we walk down to the river?" Mr. Lowrey suggested. "It's a pretty day to be outside, and we can get better acquainted—unless you have other plans."

"No, that would be nice," said Aunt Dee. "I'm happy the girls have found each other."

They left the restaurant and walked to a wooded area on the bank of the Oconaluftee River. It was peaceful compared to the clattering of plates and silverware in the restaurant. Birds sang from their perches in the trees, and the narrow river flowed in a gentle ripple. Occasionally, a big fish would leap into the air, making a big splash as it swam downstream.

"Trout," said Mr. Lowrey. "Keep your eyes open. Some birds like to hang out around here and fish for trout and the fingerlings."

"Fingerlings?" said Elizabeth.

"Baby trout," Mr. Lowrey explained. "It's a little early in the season, but you just might see some osprey swoop down and grab the fish right out of the water. Lunch to go!"

"Dad!" Galilahi protested.

"Well, honey," her father said, "it's all a part of the food chain."

"I know," said Galilahi, "but I'd rather not hear about it."

The Lowreys and Aunt Dee sat down at a picnic table on the river-bank. Meanwhile, the girls walked a little farther downstream. They sat on the edge of the river, took off their sandals, and stuck their feet into the water.

"So, tell us about Grandma Hisgi," said Sydney, "and why do you want to find her house?"

"Well, it's a long story," Galilahi began. "Great-Grandmother Rogers told it to me, and it goes back hundreds of years."

"Cool!" said Elizabeth. "I love old stories."

"Grandma Hisgi was Great-Grandmother's great-great-grand-mother," said Galilahi.

"She's the one who had your name," said Elizabeth.

"Right," Galilahi answered. "I was named Galilahi after her."

A large bird circled over them, its wings stretched out gracefully.

"Grandma Hisgi was born in 1828, probably in Cherokee," Galilahi continued. "Of course, this area was all wilderness then. The Cherokee people lived here for hundreds of years before the European explorers arrived."

"That's a long time ago," Sydney said. "I can't even imagine it!"

"When the settlers started arriving in this area, they didn't under-stand the Cherokee people's lifestyle. A lot of them thought the Chero-kee should be just like them: live in the same sort of houses, wear the same kinds of clothes, and speak their language."

"That's not right!" Sydney protested.

"I know it isn't," Galilahi said. "But that's how it was. The settlers didn't like it that the Cherokee weren't like them. So over time they started taking land away from the Cherokee people and making it their own."

"Didn't the Cherokees fight back?" asked Sydney.

Galilahi dipped her fingers into the cool water and splashed some onto her short, thin legs.

"They tried, but there were so many settlers by then, that the Chero-kees couldn't do much. The Cherokee people even tried to be more like the settlers so they would blend in. None of it mattered, because the settlers wanted them to get off the land and go someplace else."

"That's not fair," said Elizabeth. "The Cherokee people were there first."

"You're right, Elizabeth," said Galilahi. "But things were different back then. Even President Thomas Jefferson and, later, President Andrew Jackson, felt the Cherokee should give up their land. By that time, Grandma Hisgi was ten years old. And that's when things got really bad."

An osprey swooped to the water not far from where the girls sat. With lightning speed, it plunged its talons into the water, and carried a trout as it smoothly arced back into the sky.

"So, then what happened?" Elizabeth asked.

"The government forced the Cherokees off their land. It was a terrible thing to happen to the Cherokees," Galilahi said. "They went, but it broke their hearts to leave. They were forced to immediately get on the road.

"The route they took was called the Trail of Tears," Galilahi explained. *"Nunna daul Tsuny.* It means 'the trail where they cried.' "

"Nuh nah dah ooh la chuh yee." Sydney said each syllable slowly. Galilahi took her feet out of the water and slipped them into her sandals.

"No wonder they cried," said Elizabeth. "Where did they go?"

"To Oklahoma," Galilahi explained. "Where I used to live. Only they didn't go on their own. Soldiers went along to make sure that they went where they were supposed to go, to a reservation that the government set up there. Not very many settlers lived in Oklahoma at that time—the white men hadn't taken it over yet.

"The Cherokee people, almost fourteen thousand of them, had to walk more than a thousand miles from North Carolina to Oklahoma. The sick and old ones sometimes rode in wagons with the little children, but the rest of the Cherokee walked. It was cold and rainy a lot of the time.

"Great-Grandmother said that they walked for a whole year, and all sorts of terrible things happened along the way. By the time they got to Oklahoma, four thousand of the Cherokees had died."

The girls sat quietly watching the fish jump.

"So Grandma Hisgi was part of the Trail of Tears?" Elizabeth asked.

"No, she wasn't actually with them," Galilahi said.

"What do you mean?" Sydney plucked a piece of grass and twisted it around her finger. She wished she'd brought along her notebook to write this down.

"Well, Great-Grandmother Rogers told me that Grandma Hisgi's mother—she was my great-great-great-great-great-*great*-grandmother—"

"In other words, Grandma Number Six," Elizabeth interjected.

"Yes. She left Grandma Hisgi behind," Galilahi said.

"She just took off without her kid?" Sydney exclaimed.

"No," Galilahi replied. "Not exactly. A few hundred Cherokee people got to stay here in North Carolina. It had something to do with them being official United States citizens. Anyway, Grandma Hisgi's mom left Grandma Hisgi with one of those families."

"Why? Seems like they would have wanted their daughter with them," Elizabeth said.

"I don't know why," Galilahi explained. "Great-Grandmother Rogers never explained, and I never thought to ask."

"Maybe she was sick and couldn't make the journey. Or maybe for some reason they were afraid for her safety on the road," Elizabeth speculated.

"Maybe," said Galilahi.

"Did Grandma Hisgi ever see her parents again?" Sydney asked.

Galilahi tossed a stone into the river and watched the tiny circle-shaped ripples it made in the water. "I don't know. Since her great-granddaughter, my Great-Grandmother Rogers, was in Oklahoma, we know that Grandma Hisgi had at least one child. And we know that one of her children or grandchildren went to Oklahoma at some point. Great-Grandmother Rogers's parents died when she was very young, so no one seems to know how Grandma Hisgi's great-great grandchildren ended up in Oklahoma."

"So no one knows how your family got to Oklahoma—you don't know if Grandma Hisgi ended up there or stayed here in Cherokee," Sydney said.

"Yes. There's only one other thing my great-grandmother knew," Galilahi said.

"What's that?" asked Sydney. She took her feet out of the water and slipped on her sandals.

"The name of the cabin that Grandma Hisgi grew up in here in Cherokee," said Galilahi. "It was called the Cabin of the Rising Sun. I guess in those days they named their houses. They were probably named for where they were, like the House on the Hill, or the House on the Oconaluftee River."

There was a *splash* as another trout jumped in the water.

"Or, the House Where the Trout Jumps," said Sydney.

The girls laughed.

"And you don't have any idea where the cabin was," Elizabeth stated.

Galilahi stood up and brushed off the seat of her shorts. "That's what I hope you guys can help me find out. I promised Great-Grandmother Rogers that when I moved here, I'd try to find the Cabin of the Rising Sun.

"I want to do it for her, but I also really want to find the cabin myself," Galilahi said. "I don't know if I can explain why."

"I think I understand," Elizabeth said. "I like knowing about our family history. It gives me a sense of where I've come from. It makes me feel like I belong."

"Yes, I think that's part of it for me too," Galilahi said. "I love reading about history. So the history of my people, the Cherokees, interests me. And I want to know about this woman I was named after.

"I need to find out what happened to Grandma Hisgi. I know that the house was here somewhere. No one from my family has ever looked for it before, but I *know* that I can find it or find a trace of it."

"Finding the house will help Grandma Hisgi come alive to you, won't it?" Sydney asked.

"Yes, it will help make her more real to me. If I'm named after someone, I want her to become real in my life. I can feel it in my heart that I need to look for the cabin, like my ancient ancestors are speaking to me."

"Or maybe it's God speaking to your heart," Elizabeth suggested.

"Maybe," Galilahi replied. "So, what do you think? Do you want to help me?"

"Of course we do!" said Sydney. "Don't we, Beth?"

Elizabeth shook the water off her bare feet. "Of course," she agreed.

"Aaaaaaaaaaaaaahhhhhhhh!"

Suddenly a scream split the air.

Sunrise in the Smokies

"Aaaaaaahhhhhhhgggg!"

The scream destroyed the calmness again, as this time it gurgled away in a little sob.

Galilahi jumped backward away from the riverbank. Her scream quieted as her parents and Aunt Dee rushed over.

"Yeeeeeech!" Galilahi said. A bit sheepishly she pointed at the water. "It's a spider. I don't like them. It almost bit me."

A brown water spider skimmed along the surface. "There's an old Cherokee legend that says a water spider brought fire to the Cherokee people," she said.

"The way the sun brings fire to the sky when it rises in the east," Sydney announced. "The Cabin of the Rising Sun. Girls, I think we have a mystery to solve."

●━━━●━━━●

The next morning, before daybreak, Mr. Lowrey and Galilahi arrived at Aunt Dee's apartment to pick up the girls. They found Elizabeth prodding a very sleepy Sydney out the front door.

"Come on," Mr. Lowrey called from the driver's seat of the old, blue SUV. "The Smoky Mountains are beautiful at sunrise."

Sydney rubbed the sleep from her eyes. "Even at Discovery Lake Camp, we didn't get up this early," she mumbled, sliding into the backseat.

"Oh, but it's the best time of day," said Mr. Lowrey as Elizabeth climbed in beside her. "You can see the world wake up, little by little."

"On our way!" he said, giving the gas pedal a push. The car backfired and chugged and then kicked into gear. "The heliport is about a half hour's drive from here. The helicopter tours moved out of Cherokee awhile back, because of the noise. People complained."

"I can understand why," said Elizabeth. "There were helicopters in the Amarillo Air Show last summer. They were really noisy, especially when they flew over our heads."

Mr. Lowrey laughed. "Well, you can expect our ride today to be noisy too. There's not much that I can do about it. If the noise stops, then you have to worry."

"Not funny, Dad," said Galilahi. "So, Elizabeth, are you from Texas?"

"I am," Elizabeth answered. "My family's lived in Amarillo forever. We love everything about it—especially our church."

"Beth is the queen of scripture verses," Sydney announced. "She studies the Bible, and she has a verse for just about everything. Do you go to church?"

"Sometimes," said Galilahi. "Great-Grandmother goes to church, so when we lived in Oklahoma I went with her. A few times, I've gone to a church here in Cherokee."

Sydney thought about asking Mr. Lowrey if he went to the church too, but something in her heart told her to wait. She'd learned to trust those feelings.

In a few minutes, they arrived at the heliport site—a big, grassy field surrounded by groves of trees. As they pulled into the gravel parking lot, a wild cloud of swirling dust shrouded the car.

WHAP-WHAP-WHAP! WHAP-WHAP-WHAP!

Elizabeth ducked and put her hands over her head as a helicopter took off right over the car.

"Oh, that's scary," she exclaimed. "Especially in the dark."

"You get used to it," said Mr. Lowrey. "A helicopter rotor kicks up a lot of dust. That was Jay. He's doing a charter run to Nashville this morning."

Galilahi's dad took the girls inside the ticket office, a white brick building with two orange wind cones flying from its roof.

"Hey, Billy John!" he said. "Kind of early for a soda, isn't it?"

A teenaged boy stood behind the ticket counter with a Coke in his hand. "Breakfast!" he said with a smile. "I didn't expect you till later, Mr. L."

Galilahi's dad picked up a clipboard from the counter. "I'm taking my daughter and her friends up for a ride," he said. "Galilahi, Elizabeth, Sydney, this is Billy John Kingfisher. He works here during the summer."

Billy John said hello and shook each of the girl's hands. Sydney thought that he was handsome. He was tall with auburn skin, like the

Lowreys', and his face was interesting. His features were prominent and perfect, almost as if chiseled in stone.

"I've seen you at church," Galilahi said.

"Resurrection Church?" Billy John asked.

"Yes. You played the drums in the contemporary worship service," she said.

"Yup, that was me," Billy John admitted with a smile.

Galilahi's dad was busy writing on the clipboard. "Billy John, I want you to come up with us and shoot some video for the new web page. Grab the camera, and let's go so the girls can see the sunrise."

The boy gulped down the rest of his soda and disappeared into a back room. He returned with a video camera and three pair of headphones.

"All set," he announced.

"Lock up," Mr. Lowry reminded him as they headed out the door.

The heliport was in the field, a short walk down a steep hill from the ticket office. Two helicopters waited there, lit by tall, bright floodlights. Mr. Lowrey led the group to the bigger of the two.

"It's a lot like riding in a car," he said, swinging the door open. "You girls, sit in the back. Billy John will ride up front with me."

Sydney climbed in first. She sat next to the window and noticed that there wasn't much room for her long legs. She strapped on her seatbelt. Elizabeth got in next and then Galilahi.

Billy John handed each a set of headphones with microphones attached. "Put these on," he said. "They cut down on the noise. We can hear each other through them and talk."

"Cool," said Sydney. She slipped the headphones over her cornrows and adjusted the microphone so it was nearer to her mouth.

"Testing, one, two, three," she said. "Ready for lift-off."

"I can hear you," Elizabeth responded.

"Me too," said Galilahi. "This is neat."

Billy John joined Mr. Lowrey in the cockpit.

"Girls," Mr. Lowrey's voice came through the headphones, "when we take off, it's going to feel a little like a roller coaster. Your stomachs might jump, like when you're in an elevator. Okay?"

"Okay," the girls answered in unison.

Galilahi's dad started the engine. "It takes a little while to warm up," he said.

WHAP-WHAP-WHAP!

Sydney heard the rotors begin to turn. As they spun faster, the engine sounded like a vacuum cleaner. Turning faster still, it whirred like a blender. The helicopter shivered.

"Here we go!" said Mr. Lowrey.

Sydney looked out the window as the ground fell away. Her stomach flip-flopped.

"It's a little bumpy now," Mr. Lowrey explained. "In a few seconds, the ride will get smoother."

Sydney enjoyed the roller-coaster feeling that she got from the lift-off, but when it disappeared and they flew into the darkness, she was disappointed. "It's too dark out there to see anything," she complained.

"But just for a little while," said Mr. Lowrey. "Right now, I'm taking us southwest over the mountains. Then, we'll swing east. By that time, the sun should be coming up."

They flew without talking, looking out the windows at only a few lights below. Sydney was glad when she felt the copter swing east.

Suddenly, the helicopter dipped and shook. Elizabeth grabbed onto Sydney's arm. "Oh no!" she gasped.

"Dad?" Galilahi blurted. "What's wrong?"

Sydney squeezed Elizabeth's hand for what seemed like forever until Mr. Lowrey's voice came through the headphones.

"It's nothing," he said. "Just a little turbulence. That happens some-times over the mountains."

"I hope it goes away soon," Elizabeth groaned. Her stomach was doing somersaults, and she worried about losing her breakfast.

"There are airsick bags in the pockets on the seatbacks," Billy John said. "In case you need them."

Elizabeth hoped she wouldn't.

"Look. Over there!" Galilahi pointed out her window. "Is that a for-est fire?" A gleaming, orange glow stretched along the horizon. With each minute, it crept higher, painting the sky with shades of peach, salmon, and gold. Mountains appeared out of the darkness, shrouded in a smoky-blue mist.

"*Shaconage*," said Galilahi. "It's a Cherokee word that means 'land of the blue smoke.' "

"Oh, it's beautiful!" Sydney gasped. "*Sha-kon-o-hey*."

"That's not a forest fire," Mr. Lowry explained. "You're watching sunrise in the Great Smoky Mountains. Watch the horizon now. Any second, the sun will come up."

He turned the copter south and told the girls to look to their left.

A sliver of a brilliant white ball came into sight as the sun met the sky.

Sydney noticed something strange. "Hey," she said. "What's that little green thing?"

A glowing, green disc rested atop the sun. It was there for just a second or two, and then it disappeared. "Did you see it?" she asked.

"I did," said Elizabeth.

"Me too," Galilahi agreed.

"That was weird," Billy John's voice came through the headphones. "I've never seen anything like it."

Mr. Lowrey agreed. "Maybe it was a UFO."

"There's no such thing," Sydney insisted, not sure if Mr. Lowrey was serious or kidding them. "My friend Bailey and I spent a whole week thinking that we saw a UFO over the ocean near my grandparents' house. But it turned out to be a kid experimenting with a new kind of watercraft. UFOs don't exist."

Before long, the morning sun shone brightly on the mountains. Mr. Lowrey flew the copter over the tops of trees and rocky cliffs. Then Sydney spotted some cabins down below.

"Could one of those be Grandma Hisgi's?" she wondered out loud.

"I doubt it," said Mr. Lowrey. "Most of those are rental cabins. The mountains are filled with them. Any really old cabins that belonged to the Cherokee people are probably long gone."

"Or not," Billy John said softly.

"What did you say?" Sydney asked.

The boy hesitated.

"Nothing," he said. "Look down there. It's Big Cove and Mingo Falls. We're flying above Cherokee and Great Smoky Mountains National Park."

"Maybe we can spot your aunt's apartment building," said Elizabeth. "Or the ranger station where she works."

Sydney wished she had brought along her binoculars.

"I don't think Grandma Hisgi's cabin will be out in the open," said Galilahi. "I mean, it has to be ancient. I imagine it's hidden deep in the woods or something."

Mr. Lowrey made the copter swoop down over the waterfall. The water spilled over the top of the jutting land and cascaded more than a hundred feet down in dozens of long, twisted braids.

"The early Cherokee people lived near rivers," said Billy John. "Their houses were made from river cane plastered with weeds, grass, and clay. Later they lived in log cabins. That's probably what you're looking for, an old log cabin." He'd been listening to the girls talk about Grandma Hisgi.

"How do you know about the earlier Cherokees?" Sydney asked.

"Mostly from going to Indian Village near the reservation," he said. "You can go there and see reproductions of their houses and stuff."

"Put that on our list," said Elizabeth. "We can check it out tomorrow."

As they flew over the mountains, Sydney tried to imagine what it would be like to live there in the wilderness.

"The Cabin of the Rising Sun," she said, thinking out loud. "Did it face east, in the direction of the sunrise? Does it have something to do with the morning? Did Grandma Hisgi grow sunflowers?"

"Sunflowers?" said Galilahi.

"Sunflowers always face the morning sun," said Sydney. "The flowers face east."

"They *do*?" Elizabeth said.

"Trust me," Sydney answered. "I know this stuff. Mr. Lowrey, please fly low so we can see what's down there."

Billy John's voice came through the headphones again. "You won't see anything," he said. "It's so well hidden that a trained bloodhound couldn't find it."

"Find what?" asked Sydney.

"Nothing," said Billy John. "I mean *anything*! Everything down there's very well hidden."

Sydney felt that Billy John was getting annoyed with her, but she didn't know why.

For almost an hour, they flew over treetops, creeks, rocks, and ridges. Billy John shot video for the company's web page. The girls tried to spot anything that looked like a really old cabin.

"Can you think of other clues?" Sydney asked Galilahi. "Anything else that your Great-Grandma Rogers said?"

Galilahi thought for a minute. "Not really. Except Great-Grandmother often says that she looks forward to meeting Grandma Hisgi in heaven, because then she'll know the rest of the story."

"So, if your Grandma Hisgi is in heaven, then she must have been a Christian, right?" said Elizabeth.

"I guess so," said Galilahi. "Great-Grandmother Rogers is a Christian. She knows a lot more about God and heaven than I do."

The helicopter shook again. It reminded Sydney of riding a bicycle on a gravel road.

"Turbulence?" asked Elizabeth. Her hands held tight to the seat.

"Turbulence," Billy John confirmed. "Don't worry."

"Galilahi, how did your great-grandma know the name of the cabin?" Sydney asked. "If the story ends with Grandma Hisgi being left behind, then how does your great-grandma know the name of the cabin she lived in? There must be more details that she didn't tell you."

"I don't know," said Galilahi.

"Maybe she just forgot," said Elizabeth. "Sometimes, old people forget things."

"Maybe," said Galilahi.

"Or maybe it's all just a story," Billy John interrupted.

"Why would you think that?" she asked him.

"I don't know. . .um. . .I don't know why I said it. . .uh. . . Hey, look down there. It's a bear!"

The girls looked down through the trees.

"I don't see anything," said Elizabeth.

"Neither do I," said Galilahi.

Sydney didn't see the bear either.

"You just missed it," Billy John told them. "It ran off into the woods. That way." He pointed out his window.

Sydney remembered the summer when she and Alexis were in the Northwoods of Wisconsin. They thought they'd seen a bear, but it ended up being something very different, something that had helped them solve another mystery.

"Or maybe not," Sydney said.

"Huh?" Billy John's voice came through the headphones.

"Oh, nothing," said Sydney. "I was just thinking out loud."

Two can play this game, she thought to herself.

For a few minutes they flew, saying nothing. Sydney watched the ground below, wondering if Billy John had really seen a bear.

"We must be flying in circles," she said. "I remember seeing that ridge a couple of times before."

"Good eyes," said Mr. Lowrey. "We *are* flying in circles. With each one, I'm taking us a little lower until we get back to the heliport."

"Did you know that the circle is an important symbol to Native Americans?" said Galilahi. "Black Elk—he was a leader in the Sioux tribe—said: 'The sun comes forth and goes down again in a circle. The moon does the same, and both are round. Even the seasons form a great circle in their changing and always come back again to where they were.' "

"Sort of like *you* coming back to your roots, to where your family came from," said Sydney.

"That's right!" Elizabeth agreed. "If you find the Cabin of the Rising Sun, it'll be like you're completing a circle. You'll be connecting with your ancestor, the grandma who had your name."

"I hadn't thought about it that way," said Galilahi, "but it *would* be like coming full circle, wouldn't it? You know, I can't help but think that I might learn more about myself if I find Grandma Hisgi. Right now, it's like a part of me is missing."

The helicopter swooped toward the heliport. It hovered above the ground, and then inched downward.

Suddenly the helicopter began to shake and swerve.

"What's going on? More turbulence?" Sydney asked.

She'd been so wrapped up in talking to Galilahi that she hadn't been paying attention to the flight.

"Hold on!" Billy John shouted.

"Oh dear God, please help us!" Elizabeth cried out.

Sydney looked up and gasped.

A flock of birds zoomed straight toward the helicopter windows!

CHAPTER 3

A Curious Letter

Sydney felt the helicopter abruptly swoop. She clutched her seat and closed her eyes tightly. She didn't know much about helicopters, but she did know that helicopters and birds didn't mix! A bird strike could tear off a rotor blade.

That could make a helicopter crash. And people died in helicopter crashes!

The helicopter abruptly swung sideways. Sydney felt her stomach flip. Then the helicopter righted itself. It bumped a few more times.

Thump!

The helicopter skids gently landed on the helipad.

"It's okay, Sydney, you can open your eyes now," Galilahi said, gently touching her new friend's hand.

"The Lord protected us," Elizabeth added.

Sydney breathed a prayer of thanks.

Everyone sat silently for a few moments, as if in shock. Then Billy John broke the silence.

"Where did those birds come from?" he exclaimed.

Mr. Lowrey slowly let out a big breath as he took off his headphones.

"Well, I've never had that happen before!" he said. "Looked like a bunch of pigeons. We must have disturbed a whole gathering of them."

"Maybe they were having a party," Sydney said with a snicker, ready to laugh now that the scary moment was over.

"Might have been a worship service," Elizabeth said. "Especially if there's a bird sanctuary nearby." She giggled.

"Yeah, or maybe a pigeon family reunion," Galilahi added with a laugh.

The girls laughed helplessly for a few minutes. Billy John just shook his head, and Mr. Lowrey grinned as he got ready to climb out of the helicopter.

As the girls jumped out of the plane, Sydney's head still spun for a moment. Part of her felt like kissing the ground. Then she looked at the concrete that was already heating up for the day.

Nah, I'm thankful, but I don't think I'll do that! she thought.

The girls stretched. Then they dashed up the hill toward the office.

Mr. Lowrey treated the girls to Cokes.

"Back to the mystery—do you have any ideas about where to begin?" asked Elizabeth as she snapped open the top of her can.

"Just one," said Galilahi. "I have an old family Bible. Great-Grandmother gave it to me just before we left. She said the names of some of my ancestors are written inside. I haven't taken it out of its box yet. It's so old and fragile that I'm afraid it might fall apart."

"Then let's start there," said Sydney. "That old Bible might hold some clues."

"There's just one problem," Galilahi said. "The Bible is written in Cherokee, and I don't read Cherokee. So I don't think I'll be much help."

"Don't worry about it," Sydney answered. "We Camp Club Girls can do just about anything."

Billy John laughed.

"What's so funny?" Sydney asked him.

"Nothing," Billy John replied.

Something about the boy made Sydney uneasy. He talked in circles, and he avoided answering questions. All at once, Sydney felt that finding the Cabin of the Rising Sun was very important. She didn't know why, but she'd learned to trust her instincts.

"Galilahi," she said. "Let's go to your house and look at that Bible."

Mrs. Lowrey picked up the girls from the heliport and swung them by Aunt Dee's place to get Sydney's laptop.

When the girls arrived at the Lowrey home, Elizabeth and Sydney sat at the kitchen table with the computer while Galilahi went to get the Bible.

In moments, Galilahi came from her bedroom holding a flat, white box. She put it on the kitchen table near the computer.

"I can't wait for you to meet the girls," Sydney said. "Last night we sent them an email about you and Grandma Hisgi."

Elizabeth attached the AC adaptor to the side of the computer and plugged the cord into a nearby outlet.

"We have our own web page with a chat room where we can talk privately," she revealed.

"Among other things," Sydney added. "You'll be amazed at all the ways we have to communicate with each other. Kate is mostly responsible. She's invented gadgets that even Inspector Gadget doesn't know about."

Galilahi laughed. "Well, after we've looked at the Bible, maybe we can go to your chat room and tell them about it."

"Better yet," said Sydney, "you'll get to meet them in person—well, sort of. We sometimes use webcams to talk with each other. Mine is built right into my laptop."

"But we only use them to talk with each other," Elizabeth told her. "You can't be too careful on the internet, especially with webcams."

Sydney turned the computer on. The screen went from black to blue, and it started cycling through the start up. "I texted the girls and told them to stand by," she announced. "We might need their help."

Galilahi lifted the lid from the box. She folded back several layers of crisp, white tissue paper to reveal a rectangular package wrapped loosely in an old linen cloth. Carefully, she removed the wrapping to uncover an old family Bible that was tattered and worn. Its cover was barely attached to the book, and the yellowed pages were ragged with their edges sticking out every which way.

Elizabeth placed her hand gently on the chocolate-brown cover. "Oh," she said. "This is ancient."

"I'm not sure how old it is," Galilahi replied. "But Great-Grandmother Rogers's mother gave it to her."

"Your great-great-grandma," said Sydney.

"Right," Galilahi confirmed. "She died when Great-Grandma Rogers was a baby."

"So, Great-Grandma Rogers never got to ask her mother about the Bible," Elizabeth observed.

"No. All that Great-Grandmother knows is that this Bible belonged to her mother, and that someone wrote family names inside."

"Check out this neat design." Sydney pointed to a series of symbols on the cover.

"That's not a design," said Galilahi. "Those are words written in Cherokee."

"They probably say 'Holy Bible,'" Elizabeth suggested.

"But the words aren't made of letters," Sydney declared. "They're symbols."

"That's the problem," said Galilahi. "Words in Cherokee don't look at all like words in English. The language has its own special alphabet. Like I said, I don't know how to read it, so I won't be much help." She sighed.

"Don't worry about it," Elizabeth assured her. "We'll figure it out." She pulled her chair closer to Sydney's.

"Can I open it up?" Sydney asked. "I'll be really careful."

"Sure," said Galilahi. "I trust you. This is the first time that I've had it out of the box. Actually I'd never even seen it until I watched Great-Grandmother pack it up before we left. She treated it like gold."

"So you've never looked inside?" Elizabeth wondered.

"Not until now," said Galilahi.

Sydney opened the Bible's front cover. An old smell drifted from the pages and reminded her of lavender and mothballs. The Cherokee words were repeated on the first page. Beneath them was written: *"February 28, 1863—The Lord is my Shepherd."*

"Look," Sydney said. "Someone wrote in here in English. Maybe it was your great-grandma?"

Galilahi looked at the writing. "No. That's not Great-Grandmother's handwriting. She writes much smaller and straighter up and down. But maybe *her* mother, my great-*great*-grandmother, wrote it."

"Which makes sense," said Elizabeth. "Because the Bible belonged to her."

Sydney looked at the inside front cover. "Here are the names. It looks like they were written in different handwritings, though. Some are neat and others are sloppy. They're even different shades of ink."

Elizabeth and Galilahi listened as Sydney read them aloud.

"Galilahi Adair Coody."

"That's my great-great-great-great-*great*-grandmother!" Galilahi said. "That's Grandma Hisgi."

"Hers is the first name on the list," said Sydney.

Sydney read the second name. "Salli Coody Lightfoot."

"I don't know who that is," said Galilahi.

"Lucy Lightfoot Kingfisher?"

"I don't know her either," said Galilahi.

"How about Nanny Kingfisher Fields?"

"No."

"The next name is Mary Fields Rogers," Sydney said.

Galilahi gasped. "That's Great-Grandmother!"

Carefully, Sydney moved the Bible toward Galilahi so she could see. "Is that her handwriting?" she questioned.

Galilahi studied the small, straight up-and-down writing.

"Yes," she confirmed. "That's how Great-Grandmother writes. And look. My grandmother's name is under hers, 'Nancy Rogers West.' And my mother's name is the last one on the list, 'Melvina West Lowrey.' "

"It looks like your grandma's name was written by your great-grandma," said Sydney. "The handwriting is the same."

Elizabeth had been jotting down the names on a piece of paper. "I think I know what this is," she said. "It's a list of mothers and daughters. The middle name is each woman's maiden name, in other words, their last name before they were married. So, Salli was Galilahi's daughter, Lucy was Salli's daughter, Nanny was Lucy's daughter, and your great-grandma was Nanny's daughter—"

"What about your grandma?" Sydney asked Galilahi. "Your mother's mother. Why haven't you mentioned her?"

"Because she ran off, and nobody knows where she is," Galilahi said. "It happened a long time ago, when my mom was a baby. I don't know much about it, but my mother was raised by Great-Grandmother. Nobody talks about it."

Galilahi went to the refrigerator and took out a plastic pitcher filled with lemonade. She poured some for each of her friends.

Sydney pulled the Bible closer. She began turning the pages, being ever so careful.

"This book is *so* old that some of the pages are falling apart," she said. "Whoever owned it underlined some of the words and, once in a while, wrote in the margins. It's in English, but the ink is so faded that I can't figure out the words."

"Let me see," said Elizabeth. She leaned closer to Sydney. "I can't make it out either. And do you know what's strange? This Bible isn't very thick. It's about half the size of a regular Bible."

"Maybe the Cherokee symbols don't take as much space as English letters and words," Sydney suggested. She sipped her lemonade and then swirled the rest around in her cup.

"Maybe," Elizabeth agreed.

"Or maybe it's not a Bible at all," Galilahi offered.

"Oh, it's a Bible all right," Elizabeth affirmed. "I can tell by how the chapters and verses are set up and numbered."

Sydney continued turning the pages. "Oh, I'm sorry," she said. "A few of the pages at the very back were stuck together. And when I turned them, they pulled right out of the binding. Good thing they were blank pages at the back. Hey, what's this?"

A thin paper envelope was tucked between the pages. Like the book, it was old and yellowed. The handwriting on the envelope was barely readable, but Sydney could make out the words. They were written in English: *"To my family Adair."*

The envelope was sealed with a thin blob of wax.

"Adair," said Galilahi. "If Elizabeth is right, that was probably Grandma Hisgi's last name before she was married."

"Right," said Sydney. She took another drink of her lemonade. "Did you notice that the handwriting on this envelope is the same as the handwriting used for Grandma Hisgi's name?"

Galilahi pulled her chair nearer to get a better look. "Sydney," she said. "Do you think this is Grandma Hisgi's handwriting?"

"I do," Sydney agreed. "And do you know what else I think?"

Galilahi gasped. "This is Grandma Hisgi's Bible!"

Elizabeth smiled. "Good thinking! We'll have to make you an honorary Camp Club Girl."

Galilahi took the envelope from Sydney and held it gently in her hands. "And Grandma Hisgi wrote this letter."

"I think so," said Sydney. "Do you want to open it?"

"We have to," Galilahi exclaimed. "It might hold a clue."

Galilahi turned the envelope over. She gently broke the wax seal with her fingernail. Then she looked into the envelope and pulled out a single sheet of paper. It was thin, like tissue paper, and on it were written many rows of Cherokee symbols. At the bottom was a simple line drawing of the sun rising over the mountains. Underneath it were a few more Cherokee words.

"I wish I could read this," Galilahi said. "But it's all written in Cherokee."

Sydney swirled the remaining lemonade in her cup. "That's where the other girls come in," she said. "Let's text them and tell them to turn on their webcams."

Sydney logged in and switched on the webcam on her laptop.

"Kate has this set up so we can all see each other at once," she told Galilahi.

Elizabeth had been on the phone texting the Camp Club Girls.

"We're fortunate," she said. "Everyone seems to be at home right now. They're going to get on their computers."

Soon, the image on the screen divided into fourths and four faces appeared. A girl with black, chin-length hair and bangs waved to the camera.

"That's Bailey Chang," Sydney said.

"Hi, everybody!" Bailey said, cheerfully.

"Hi, Bailey," Sydney replied. "Girls, this is Galilahi Lowrey."

Galilahi smiled and waved toward the screen. "Hi," she said. "Nice to meet you."

"And this is Alexis Howell," said Sydney, pointing at another girl on the screen. Alexis, with dark brown hair and lovely, blue eyes waved and said hello.

"And McKenzie Phillips," Sydney continued. A cute girl with a smattering of freckles across her face smiled and waved.

"And Kate Oliver."

"I love your name," Kate said.

Just then, a shaggy little dog scampered into the picture behind Kate and slid across the floor. *Ruff-ruff A-roof. Ruff-ruff A-roof!*

"And this is Biscuit the Wonder Dog," said Kate.

"Oh, he's so cute," Galilahi said.

"So, what's going on?" Kate asked. "Have you looked at the Bible yet?"

"We have," Sydney answered, "And we have a ton of stuff to tell you."

Sydney, Elizabeth, and Galilahi explained all about the Bible and their theory that it had belonged to Galilahi's great-great-great-great-*great*-grandmother.

"Can you scan the letter?" Kate wondered. "So all of us can see it."

Sydney looked at Galilahi. "Do you have a scanner?"

"My dad does, in the den. I'll go scan it. Where should I send it?"

Elizabeth wrote down the girls' email addresses for Galilahi. "Be careful when you're scanning," she cautioned. "That letter is so fragile."

"Oh, I will," said Galilahi. She disappeared into the next room.

Kate scowled, which meant she was thinking. "While you guys were talking I went online and did some research," she said. "Not all of the books of the Bible have been translated into the Cherokee language. So what you have there is probably just the New Testament."

"That would explain why the book is thinner than most Bibles," said Elizabeth.

"And while you were doing that, I was sleuthing on my own," McKenzie announced. "I looked up the Trail of Tears. The Cherokee people were forced off their land in 1838. Galilahi said that Grandma Hisgi was ten years old then, so she was born around 1828. She probably didn't get the Bible until she was a young woman, so that was probably around 1850. That would make the Bible more than a hundred and sixty years old."

"Wow," said Sydney.

The scanner in the next room whirred. "I'm sending the letter right now," Galilahi called. "Let me know when they get it."

"Did you hear that?" Elizabeth asked the girls.

"I heard," said Alexis. "I just got mine."

"Here comes mine," said Bailey.

Kate and McKenzie opened their copies too.

"If you give me a couple of hours, I think I can translate this," Kate said. "I found a website that tells all about the Cherokee alphabet. I'll send you the web address."

"Okay" said Sydney. "Let's meet back here at 2:30. I can't wait to hear what that letter says."

After logging out of the webcam, Sydney, Elizabeth, and Galilahi went to the website Kate had suggested.

"It says here that the Cherokee symbols were invented in the early 1800s by a man named Sequoyah," said Elizabeth. "His mother was Native American and his father was an English fur trader. Sequoyah's English name was George Gist. It says that until Sequoyah invented the syllabary, the Cherokee people didn't have a written language."

"What does *syllabary* mean?" asked Sydney.

"Let's check an online dictionary," Elizabeth said. She opened another window on the screen and searched for the definition. "*Syllabary* is a language that has characters that represent syllables." She went back to the language page. "It says that this syllabary has eighty-four different symbols that represent eighty-four syllables the Cherokee people use when they speak. Today, the words are often written phonetically in English."

Galilahi pulled her chair nearer the laptop. "What does that mean?"

Sydney picked up a pen and wrote something on a scrap of paper. "This is how your name would look if it were spelled phonetically," she said. "If it were written the way it sounds: 'ooh-lee-low-he.' "

Galilahi looked at her name on the page. "It sure would be easier if the letter were written like this," she said. "I hope Kate can figure it out."

"Oh, I'm sure she can," Elizabeth told her. "Kate can do anything." She read some more on the language page. "This is cool. There's a pronunciation key here. It tells how each of the vowels would sound if you wrote a word phonetically. In other words, if you read the words aloud phonetically and use this pronunciation key, you'll be speaking Cherokee."

Galilahi sighed. "This is a bit confusing. I think I'd rather learn the language by listening to Great-Grandmother."

Time passed quickly until it was time for the girls to go back online, at 2:30 sharp.

"So, Kate, did you figure it out?" Galilahi asked.

"I did," Kate answered, "But I'm not sure what it means."

"Tell us," said Bailey.

"Yeah, I can't wait to know," said Alexis.

"I've been on pins and needles," McKenzie agreed.

"Okay," Kate said. "Here goes." She read from a sheet of paper: " 'The sun rises and the sun sets, and hurries back to where it rises. The wind blows to the south and turns to the north; round and round it goes, ever returning on its course. All streams flow into the sea, yet the sea is never full. To the place the streams come from, there they return again.' "

Kate set the paper down.

"That sounds like the circle thing you quoted this morning in the helicopter," Sydney said to Galilahi. "The quotation from that Indian leader, Black Elk. Say it again for the girls."

Galilahi repeated the quote. " 'The sun comes forth and goes down again in a circle. The moon does the same, and both are round. Even the seasons form a great circle in their changing and always come back again to where they were.' "

Bailey sneezed. "Excuse me," she said. "Hay fever. Anyway, the similarity is interesting."

"Do you think the letter is just someone writing a version of the Black Elk quote?" asked Alexis.

Elizabeth picked up her tote from the floor. She unzipped it and took out her Bible. "I think I know what it is," she said.

The girls sat quietly, anxiously waiting for Elizabeth to say something. She flipped through her Bible and stopped. "I found it!" she announced. She began to read, " 'The sun rises and the sun sets, and hurries back to where it rises. The wind blows to the south and turns to the north; round and round it goes, ever returning on its course. All streams flow into the sea, yet the sea is never full. To the place the streams come from, there they return again.' That's in Ecclesiastes 1:5 through 7."

"So, it's a scripture passage!" said McKenzie.

"And there's one more thing," Kate remarked. "That line of symbols under the drawing of the sun? It says—'I am here.' "

"Now," said Sydney. "We have to figure out what this all means."

Biscuit barked in agreement.

The Secret Message

"So, Grandma Hisgi wrote down a Bible verse for her family," said Galilahi. "But why? I mean, if she wrote them a letter, wouldn't she want to tell them something more?"

"Maybe she did," Alexis speculated. "Maybe she sent them another letter telling them to look at this one in the Bible. Only, maybe it didn't arrive or maybe she didn't send it."

"But why wouldn't she just give all the information in one place? Especially in those days when sending letters was rare," McKenzie reasoned. "Maybe this letter is her full message."

"Maybe, maybe, maybe! I'm so confused." Galilahi cried.

"Think about it," Alexis suggested. "Nancy Drew, Encyclopedia Brown, Scooby Doo. . .all of them, at one time or another, discovered a code that they needed to break in order to solve a mystery. I think that's what we have here, Ecclesiastes 1:5 through 7 is a code."

Sydney played with her cornrows, something she often did while thinking. "Or, maybe, Ecclesiastes 1:5 through 7 was just Grandma Hisgi's favorite Bible passage—"

"Except that she might not have known *that* Bible passage, because it's in the Old Testament," Kate interrupted. "Her Bible only has the New Testament."

Elizabeth sighed. "But do we know that for sure?" she said. "This Bible is written totally in Cherokee. We don't know for sure if it's just the New Testament. And why would she have to write to her family in code? How would she know this Ecclesiastes scripture if she only had the New Testament?"

Biscuit pressed his nose against Kate's webcam. Kate peeked around his furry head. "Maybe because she was hiding, or because the soldiers would punish her family if they knew that her family had hidden

Grandma Hisgi before they left on the Trail of Tears.

"Who knows? There's no address on the envelope, just the words 'To my family Adair.' I don't think she ever meant to send this letter. I think she meant it to be found," Kate said.

Sydney opened a new window on her computer screen. She went to the web page where she'd seen the Cherokee syllabary. "Can you print this for us?" she asked Galilahi. "Make a copy for yourself and one each for Elizabeth and me, please. We're going to have to translate each heading to see which books of the Bible we have here."

"That will take forever!" Galilahi exclaimed.

"Not if we work together," Sydney promised. "Good sleuthing takes time, but it's always worth the work in the end."

Galilahi took the laptop computer into her father's den and printed the copies. She returned and handed the girls the set of symbols. Each symbol was matched with the sound it made.

D a		R e	T i	Ꮼ o	O u	i v
Ꮟ ga	Ꭴ ka	Ꮝ ge	Ꮽ gi	A go	J gu	E gv
Ꮧ ha	Ꮂ he	Ꮙ hi	Ꮵ ho	Ꮒ hu	Ꮤ hv
W la	Ꮷ le	Ꮲ li	Ꮐ lo	M lu	Ꮴ lv
Ꮞ ma	Ꮉ me	H mi	Ꮲ mo	Ꮏ mu	
Ꮎ na	Ꮆ hna	Ꮑ ne	Ꮒ ni	Z no	Ꮕ nu	O nv
Ꮖ qua	Ꮖ que	Ꮙ qui	Ꮹ quo	Ꮼ quu	Ꮟ quv
Ꮖ sa	Ꮜ s	Ꮢ se	Ꮒ si	Ꮩ so	Ꮋ su	R sv
Ꮭ da	W ta	Ꮥ de	Ꮶ te	Ꮧ di	Ꮨ ti	V do	Ꮪ du	Ꮲ dv
Ꮣ dla	Ꮮ tla	L tle	C tli	Ꮰ tlo	Ꮳ tlu	P tlv
G tsa	V tse	Ꮵ tsi	K tso	Ꮶ tsu	C tsv
Ꮤ wa	Ꮺ we	Ꮼ wi	Ꮼ wo	Ꮽ wu	Ꮾ wv
Ꮿ ya	Ᏸ ye	Ᏹ yi	Ꮵ yo	G yu	B yv

"Let's get to work," Sydney instructed.

"In the meantime, we'll put our heads together and see if we can crack the Ecclesiastes code," Bailey chimed in. "Let's meet back here in an hour, okay?"

The girls agreed, and as they shut off their webcams, their screens went blank.

Painstakingly, Sydney, Elizabeth, and Galilahi began translating the headings: MATTHEW, MARK, LUKE, JOHN.

"Now I'm sure it's the New Testament," said Elizabeth.

"Let's keep going," Sydney suggested. "We need to know exactly what's in here."

"But Matthew, Mark, Luke, and John are the first four books of the New Testament," Elizabeth protested. "Why do we have to go on?"

"Yeah, this is hard," Galilahi agreed. "Why do we have to translate the rest of the headings?"

Sydney was hard at work. "Because that's what good detectives do. They leave no stone unturned." She carefully flipped to the next page in the Bible. "Look here on the first page of the Book of Acts. It's that same drawing of the sun, and some of the words in the text are underlined."

She translated them from the Cherokee symbols. "Grandma Hisgi underlined this part of Acts 8, verse 36: 'As they traveled along the road, they came to some water.' "

"A clue!" exclaimed Galilahi.

"Maybe," said Sydney, "or maybe not. Let's keep going. Look for that sun drawing, and see if anything else is underlined."

The girls worked together, turning each page carefully.

"There it is again!" said Elizabeth. "There's a sun drawn in the margin in the Book of Jude. Grandma Hisgi underlined some of the words in Jude 1, verse 12." Elizabeth translated them: " 'trees, without fruit and uprooted—twice dead.' "

They were getting close to the end of the Bible. "There's one!" Galilahi said, after Sydney turned a page. "Right there, in the Book of Revolution—"

"*Revelation*," Elizabeth corrected her. "It's the last book of the New Testament."

"The sun is next to the number six," Galilahi said. "I think that means chapter six. And Grandma Hisgi underlined words in verse number fifteen. Let's see what they mean." She got busy deciphering the symbols. "The words translate: 'Every slave and every free man hid in caves and among the rocks of the mountains.' "

"That seems to fit as a clue," Sydney said. "We're here in the Smoky Mountains, and during our helicopter ride this morning, we saw plenty of rocks. There have to be caves there, somewhere."

"And think about it," said Elizabeth. "When the soldiers came to take the Cherokee people off their land, some of them might have hidden in those caves."

"Maybe some of the free people too," Galilahi said. "Remember? Great-Grandmother Rogers told me that some of the Cherokee people were free to stay because they were United States citizens."

"I'd forgotten about that," said Sydney.

The girls continued to the end of the Bible. On the very last page, they found one more sun and a few words.

"It looks like Joshua 10:6," Galilahi translated.

"Let me look it up," Elizabeth said, grabbing her own pocket Bible once more. "The men of Gibeon quickly sent messengers to Joshua at his camp in Gilgal. 'Don't abandon your servants now!' they pleaded. 'Come at once! Save us! Help us! For all the Amorite kings who live in the hill country have joined forces to attack us.' "

"I wonder what that means," Galilahi commented.

"It almost sounds like a cry for help," Sydney said thoughtfully.

Then they went back, carefully checking each page to see if they'd missed any more suns. But there were only four in all.

"There are things written in English in the margins in the four Gospels," Elizabeth observed, "But from the writing I can make out, they don't seem to be clues. It looks like the only clues are the ones that have the sun picture."

Sydney put her elbows on the table and rested her chin on her hands. Elizabeth twisted a strand of her long, blond hair. "I'm trying to put these Bible verses together in my head to see if I can make sense of them."

"What do you think they mean?" Galilahi wondered.

"I don't have a clue," said Elizabeth. "We have plenty of puzzle pieces to figure out."

"And I have another one," Galilahi offered. "Why didn't anyone else open the envelope or discover these clues? After all, the Bible was handed down from mother to daughter, right?"

Sydney had written the clues on a sheet of paper, and she was busy studying them.

"Except your grandmother probably never got the Bible," Sydney said. "I think that's true because your great-grandma wrote her name inside."

"I've been thinking," said Sydney. "Maybe the women wrote their names when they got married. That's why both their birth names and their married names are listed."

"The Bible was handed down through the Coodys," Elizabeth recalled. "And the letter and clues were specifically for the Adairs. So, unless the other owners of the Bible were into genealogy, they probably weren't looking for clues."

"It could be," Sydney added, "that no one ever looked through the Bible and found the envelope. After all, if you inherit an old book you can't read, even if it is a Bible, you may not thumb through it."

Galilahi put her hands on her head and grunted. "I'm *so* lost. Please explain what you just said—and what's *genealogy*?"

Elizabeth slipped her arm around Galilahi's shoulder and gave her a little hug.

"I'm trying to be patient," Galilahi insisted. "But there's just too much information for my brain to take it all in."

"That's why we're here," Sydney grinned. "We're not only going to help you make sense of it all, but the Camp Club Girls will help you find the Cabin of the Rising Sun."

"I'm glad you're so sure," Galilahi sighed.

"Genealogy is when you explore your family history—what some people call a family tree—and try to find out who your ancestors were," Elizabeth explained. "Imagine that there are two main branches coming out from a tree trunk. One is for your father's side of the family; the other is for your mother's side. Your ancestors are all the little branches coming off of those main branches. The ancestors on your father's branch aren't the same people as the ancestors on your mother's branch, right?"

"Right," Galilahi agreed.

"So," Elizabeth continued. "We're trying to find information about your mother's branch on the tree. We know that Grandma Hisgi was born into the Adair family. But, when they were forced from their land during the Trail of Tears, Grandma Hisgi's mother left her with another family, and we don't know who they were."

"Those people weren't her relatives," Sydney chimed in. "They were nice people who took her in. So Grandma Hisgi's connection with the Adairs stopped when her mother gave her away."

"And," Elizabeth said, "When Grandma Hisgi grew up, she married a man with the last name of Coody. That's why, in the Bible, she wrote her name as Galilahi Adair Coody. Eventually, the Bible got handed down to her daughter, whose last name was Coody. As the years went by, the

Adairs were all but forgotten."

"Except by us!" Galilahi observed. "And Great-Grandma Rogers. At least the part of the story of Grandma Hisgi's life, the part where she was left behind, was handed down from generation to generation. I think I get it now."

Sydney was doodling on her paper now, another habit she had when she was deep in thought.

"You know what?" she said. "I think she did it deliberately. I think Grandma Hisgi stuck those pages together so her letter would be hard to find. She wanted this letter to get to the right people. Maybe she was afraid that it might be lost or thrown away. There's definitely some sort of important message hidden here for the Adairs."

"And you're an Adair descendant," Elizabeth said to Galilahi. "So, you have every right to this letter."

The girls had much to talk about when they went back online. Sydney, Elizabeth, and Galilahi were eager to share their clues.

The other Camp Club Girls had each been studying Ecclesiastes 1:5–7 and were also excited to share ideas.

"We think the scripture verse is like a treasure map!" Bailey blurted out. "Everything is written in code. If you follow the directions, you'll find the Cabin of the Rising Sun—"

"The sun rises and sets, and hurries back to where it rises," Bailey continued. "Maybe that's a clue for the direction *east*. We think it means that you should look to the east for the cabin. That fits with the name, *Cabin of the Rising Sun*. The sun rises in the east."

Sydney wrote that down.

"And then, there's this part about the wind," said Kate. " 'The wind blows to the south and turns to the north; round and round it goes, ever returning to its course.' We think that means after you've gone east for a while, you need to go south."

Sydney wrote that down too.

"After that, you have to find a stream," Alexis added. "The scripture verse says, 'All streams flow into the sea, yet the sea is never full.' Since there are no seas near Cherokee, North Carolina, forget about that part. Just look for a stream."

"Once you've found the stream," McKenzie continued, "you have to find out where the stream comes from. The verse says, 'to the place the streams come from, there they return again.' "

Sydney wrote *"stream"* on her sheet of paper. "That might fit with our clue 'as they traveled along the road, they came to some water.' "

Elizabeth twisted a strand of her hair again. "It's beginning to make sense," she said. "And that picture of the sun? It's a symbol for the cabin. When Grandma Hisgi wrote 'I am here' underneath it, I bet she meant that anyone searching would find her at the Cabin of the Rising Sun."

"The reference to Joshua 10:6 at the back of the Bible makes it seem like she was in trouble and wanted help," Kate mused, "but what kind of trouble?"

Sydney looked at what she'd written. "Well, we sure have a lot of clues here, but we're missing the most important one."

"What's that?" Galilahi asked.

"Where do we begin?" Sydney said. "Do you have any ideas?"

"Not even one," her friend answered. "So now what?"

"We think about what we know," Elizabeth told her. "We have some clues about directions and landmarks. You've lived here a few months, Galilahi. Think hard. See if you can remember a road that leads to water, or dead fruit trees that are uprooted and laying on the ground, or a cave hidden in some rocks."

Galilahi sighed again. "I don't know! I haven't explored very much since I've lived here."

"It's all right," McKenzie said, sensing Galilahi's frustration. "We'll get to the bottom of this. You'll see."

"Where are you guys going next?" Kate asked.

"We're going home soon," Sydney answered. "It's almost time for Aunt Dee to get off work, and I promised that I'd make supper. We're having spaghetti."

"Oh, that sound good!" said Kate. "With meatballs?"

"With meatballs," said Sydney. "And lots of Parmesan cheese, and a nice, leafy, green salad and garlic bread, and—"

"Can I come?" Kate said and laughed.

"I'll keep it warm for you," said Sydney.

"Oh, and seriously, that green thing you saw from the helicopter, the disc on top the sun, that was probably a green flash."

"What's a green flash?" Sydney asked.

"It's a phenomena where a tiny part of the sun suddenly changes to green," Kate said. "It lasts for only a few seconds."

"Hey, Sydzie!" Bailey piped up. "Do you remember when we saw the bioluminescence at your grandparents' house on the beach? The ocean waves glowed green at night? Your green flash reminds me of that."

"Usually, a green flash happens at sunset," said Kate. "It's pretty rare to see it at sunrise, so you guys were lucky."

Elizabeth said, "Maybe we should follow the sunrise. In other words, to go east."

Galilahi smiled as she had a revelation. "And green means go! I think you're right, Elizabeth. We need to head east to look for the cabin."

Sydney folded her sheet of paper and tucked it into her jeans pocket. "Right now, we need to head home," she said to the Camp Club Girls. "Tomorrow, we're going to the Indian village. This kid we met at the heliport this morning, Billy John, said it has replicas of old Cherokee houses. Maybe that will help us know what the Cabin of the Rising Sun looks like."

"Great idea!" said Alexis. "I have to sign off now too. Let me know what you find out."

"Me too," said McKenzie, slipping a sock onto one of her bare feet.

"I'll keep pondering the clues," Kate promised.

"Buh-bye, fellow sleuthies!" said Bailey. "The Bailster is signing off. Over and out for now."

The monitor screen went blank.

Sydney logged off the internet, shut down her laptop, and snapped the lid closed. She detached the AC cable from the side of the computer and pulled the cord out of the wall outlet. Then she rolled it up and stuck it, along with the laptop, into her tote.

"So, tomorrow we'll go to the Indian village," she said. "Do you know where it is, Galilahi?"

"I do," she replied. "It's easy to get to from your aunt's apartment, and it's on the way to her work. Tell your aunt to leave you at the stoplight on River Road. Walk east along the road until you come to the water. I'll meet you there at nine."

Back in Time

As Sydney entered Indian Village, she felt as if she were being transported back to 1750. The village was created to show how the Cherokee people had lived in those days. The girls could see people all around the village dressed in clothing like the Cherokee people had worn in the eighteenth century and working on crafts from that time.

Sydney noticed the smell of wood fires drifting through the air, and she could hear the distant, haunting melody of a river-cane flute floating through the trees.

"This is like a living museum," said Sydney as she and Galilahi stepped aside for a big group of tourists.

Elizabeth looked at the trees. "It's so peaceful here. It's like our century is gone: no sounds of car engines, televisions, loud music—"

"Chee-lew-gee!" A handsome man dressed in native Cherokee clothing approached the girls. "My name is Wa-ya a-di-si, but you can call me Running Wolf."

"O-si-yo, Running Wolf!" said Galilahi.

Sydney rolled her eyes and laughed. "Okay, you guys. Speak English. What do *chee-lew-gee* and *o-si-yo* mean?"

"*Chew-lew-gee,* means 'welcome', " Running Wolf said.

"And *o-si-yo* means 'hello', " Galilahi answered.

"O-si-yo," said Sydney. "O-si-yo, Wa-ya a-di-si!"

Running Wolf nodded and smiled.

The man began to walk, "Come," he said. "Let me show you the village and how people lived more than two hundred and fifty years ago." He strode down a dirt pathway with the girls following closely.

First, they stopped to watch several women sewing beads together to make belts, headbands, and necklaces. The women explained how they did this. Sydney wished she could try.

"I make jewelry from paper," she told them. "Maybe I could learn to do this too."

Then the girls and their guide walked past several more women weaving wool to make shawls and blankets. They watched people forming pots from clay and placing them around an open fire to make them hard; then they'd be watertight and ready to use.

They saw ladies weaving baskets who explained the traditional plant dyes used to color the basket material. On they walked, past men making arrowheads and a man demonstrating a blowgun used to hunt small game.

The girls looked at countless traps: bear traps, fish traps, figure-four traps. It was all very interesting, but they still hadn't seen the Cherokee houses.

"Running Wolf, we're interested in the kinds of houses the Cherokee people lived in," Sydney said. "We heard that you have some of those here." Running Wolf didn't say a word. Instead, he signaled the girls to follow him. Quietly, they walked into the woods on a narrow path lined with rhododendron thickets. As they traveled along the path, they came to a streambed and passed a tiny waterfall that trickled over stones. Then they came to a clearing and several old houses made of woven saplings plastered with mud.

"Wow!" Sydney gasped. "Who would have known that these were back here in the woods?"

"I can almost imagine my Cherokee grandmother living in one of them," Galilahi said.

"You have a Cherokee grandmother?" Running Wolf asked.

"My whole family is Cherokee," Galilahi told him. "My great-great-great-great-*great*-grandmother was left behind during the Trail of Tears."

"Really?" Running Wolf said.

"Grandma Hisgi's mother asked another family to take her little girl and keep her," Sydney explained.

Galilahi walked up to one of the houses and ran her hand along the rough wall. "Grandmother's real name was Galilahi Adair Coody. She lived somewhere around here in a cabin called the Cabin of the Rising Sun."

"Have you heard of it?" Sydney asked him.

"Never," Running Wolf replied. "But if you want to see homes like those from the 1800s, these aren't the ones. By then, the Cherokee people lived in log cabins. I'll show you."

They walked on until they came to a man tending a fire burning in the center of a huge log. The log was lying on its side.

"What's he doing?" Elizabeth asked as they stopped to watch.

"The Cherokee people often used logs from fallen and dead trees," said Running Wolf. "This one is being made into a canoe. In the old days, the people used fire to hollow out the center of the log to make the inside of the canoe. The man is watching the fire closely and adding clay to control how much it burns." Running Wolf nodded at the man, and then he walked on, leading the girls further into the woods.

A little jog in the path took the girls around a grove of trees and to another clearing. There, a short distance away, the girls saw a small log cabin. Smoke wafted from its stone chimney. It had no windows, and on the front wall hung several dried animal skins. Next to the front door sat an old, wooden bucket and a ladle made from a tree branch.

"This is a house like the one your ancestor might have lived in," Running Wolf said. "Go. Look inside."

The door stood wide open. Inside was a single, dark room. A woman sat cooking something in an iron pot hung over a fire in the fireplace. A bitter smell came from the pot while whatever was inside bubbled and boiled.

"O-si-yo," the woman said.

"O-si-yo," the girls answered in unison.

"I am making a fish stew," the woman explained. "If I were not cooking or sleeping, I would be outside. In the old days, homes were used just for cooking and sleeping. That is why you see little furniture here. Only a bed to sleep on and a place to sit."

The woman invited the girls to sit down on a narrow bench near the fireplace.

Galilahi told her about Grandma Hisgi and their search for the cabin.

"Your grandmother may have lived in a log cabin nicer than this one," the woman said. "By the mid-1800s, many of our people lived much the same as the white settlers did."

"Have you ever heard of the Cabin of the Rising Sun, or Galilahi Adair Coody?" Galilahi asked.

"No," the woman answered. "But Adair is a common name among the Cherokee people." The woman poked at the burning logs with a long, metal tool, and the fire grew stronger. "I don't think, dear, that you'll find what you're looking for. As far as I know, none of the old cabins exist anymore. A few of them were moved here years ago. But the rest are gone."

The girls sat on the bench watching as the woman stirred the pot.

"I know I'm going to find *something*," Galilahi blurted. "I have this feeling that Grandma Hisgi's cabin still exists, and I'm not going to give up."

"And you shouldn't give up," the woman replied. "When you search for your ancestors, you find yourself."

Running Wolf entered the cabin with more tourists. The girls thanked him for showing them around and then left to explore on their own.

"You know," said Sydney as they walked up the path, deeper into the woods. "I can't get that canoe out of my head. There was something about that old tree trunk lying there on its side."

" 'Trees without fruit and uprooted—twice dead'!" Elizabeth said. "I know, Syd, I was just thinking the same thing."

Galilahi dodged a branch that was blocking the path. "But that old tree trunk wasn't lying there when Grandma Hisgi was alive. This museum village is only about fifty years old. So that can't be the tree that she meant in her letter."

"Yes," said Elizabeth, "but there's just something about this place. I don't know what it is. . ."

Sydney had a feeling about the place too. She wondered if it was just the feeling of being transported back in time and living among the Cherokee people.

"But you know," she said, "we did walk east along the path until we came to some water—that little stream, remember?"

"And that was another clue in the Bible," Elizabeth said. "Acts 8:36: 'As they traveled along the road, they came to some water.' Syd, do you think this is the place?"

"I don't know," Sydney sighed. "There must be tons of roads that lead to water in and around Cherokee."

"And plenty of uprooted trees," Galilahi said.

"O-si-yo!"

A voice that came from the side of the path startled the girls. An old woman sat on a tree stump picking leaves from some plants and putting them into a basket.

"I'm harvesting herbs to use for medicines and cooking," she said. "Are you girls enjoying your visit to our village? I heard you talking about the canoe as you came along the path, and about the water and the trees. Is there something special that you're looking for?"

Again, Galilahi told the story of her Grandma Hisgi. This time, she included their theory about the clues in the letter.

"Maybe the trees you're searching for never had fruit," the woman said. "Listen. I'll tell you a Cherokee legend about the sparrow and the trees. Perhaps it holds a clue."

She set aside her basket of herbs and began telling the tale.

"Long ago trees and birds talked to each other. After all, they lived very close together, so they could not help but be friends. In spring, summer, and fall, the birds lived among the tree branches. But in winter, when the cold winds came, the birds flew away. They went south to where it was warm.

"One year when the cold winds came, Sparrow broke his wing. He could not journey south with the others. He knew he would die unless he found shelter among the trees.

" 'Oak, Oak!' he cried to the oak tree. 'Will you give me shelter from the winter storms?'

"Oak was a disagreeable old tree, and he did not relish the idea of having a winter guest.

" 'Go somewhere else to spend the winter,' he told Sparrow. 'I do not want you spending it with me.' So Sparrow left with hurt feelings.

"Next, he went to the maple tree. 'Maple, Maple!' he cried. 'Will you give me shelter from the winter storms?'

"Maple was a selfish and vain tree, and she did not want to entertain Sparrow all winter long. 'Go somewhere else to spend the winter,' she said. 'I do not want you spending it with me.'

"So Sparrow left with his feelings hurt even more.

"One by one, Sparrow went to all the trees in the forest and asked for shelter in their leaves. And all of the trees said, 'No.' Every one turned Sparrow away, and he was very sad. He lost all hope of living through the cold, harsh winter and sat on the ground waiting to die.

"There was one more tree in the forest who was often ignored. His name was Pine, and the birds didn't roost among his branches. His leaves were sharp, like needles, and his branches were few and not filled with beautiful leaves, like the others.

"While Sparrow had begged the trees for help, Pine watched. He was sorry for Sparrow and thought: *I am the least of the trees in the forest, but still, maybe I can help.* So he called out to Sparrow, 'Sparrow! My leaves are but needles and my branches are few. But you are welcome to share what I have.'

"Sparrow joyfully spent the winter with Pine, nestled safely among his needles, and protected from the winter storms—"

"That's a very nice story," Sydney interrupted. "But what's the clue?"

"Oh, I'm not finished yet," the old woman said. "There's more.

"Now, the Great Creator was watching. He saw how the trees had turned Sparrow away, and he also saw Pine's kindness. So, when spring arrived, he spoke to the trees. 'You, to whom I've given so much, would not share the least of what you had with Sparrow. Because of this, when the cold winds come again, your leaves will wither and die and blow away.'

"Then, he spoke to the pine tree. 'Pine, you are the least of the trees, but you have given so much. Of all the trees in the forest, you shall keep your leaves throughout the seasons. You have given me a great gift by providing shelter for Sparrow.'

"And that, girls, is why, when the cold winds come to the land, all the leaves wither and die except for those on the pine trees. Look all around you. The least of the trees has become the greatest in the forest."

Sydney looked up and around, and for the first time she noticed that almost all of the trees were pine trees.

"So we should be looking for pine trees?" Sydney asked.

The old woman resumed picking her herbs. "Only the Great Creator knows for sure what you should be looking for. But the woods are filled with pines. And I know where many are uprooted and lying on their sides."

Galilahi had been listening closely to everything the old woman said. "You do!" she exclaimed. "Where?"

"It's a place called Blowing Rock, but it's not nearby. It's almost four hours from here. It's an amazing tourist attraction that you girls should visit while you're here in North Carolina. You can pick up a brochure in the gift shop on your way out."

Suddenly, Sydney had a sinking feeling. She thanked the woman and set off on the path in the direction that they'd come from.

"Why are you dashing off?" Galilahi asked as she hurried to catch up with her.

"Yeah," Elizabeth agreed. "I liked talking with her." She brushed past a thicket that grew out over the path.

"Because," said Sydney. "She's at the end of the tour, right? It's probably her job to tell visitors a legend and then try to sell them tickets to another attraction. I mean, think about it. We can 'pick up a brochure in the gift shop.' I think she just wanted us to buy stuff."

Galilahi squeezed past the thicket. "Well, what if you're wrong?" There was a hint of indignation in her voice. "What if the fallen pine trees at Blowing Rock are the clue that we're looking for?"

The girls reached the clearing now, where the old cabin was. They continued past the man burning out the inside of the canoe, and to the next clearing where the older houses stood.

"We have to give it more thought," Sydney said, gently. "We need more information. If we don't plan wisely, we could be on a wild goose chase, running all over the place."

"I'll text the girls and get them going on it," said Elizabeth, pulling out her phone.

By now, the girls had reached the place where the women were sewing beads, almost to the exit and the gift shop.

"Hey, isn't that Billy John Kingfisher?" Elizabeth asked.

"Where?" Galilahi looked around.

"Over there, by the exit gate," Elizabeth said.

It was Billy John. He spotted the girls and waved.

What's he doing here? Sydney wondered.

Billy John leaned on the gatepost and grinned as the girls approached him. "Hey girls," he said. "What's going on?"

"What's going on with you?" Sydney asked.

"Not much," he said, swinging the gate open for them to exit. "Just hanging here, waiting for some friends."

"We found the houses that you told us about," Galilahi said.

"Are you still searching for that silly old cabin?" Billy John laughed. "Give it up. You're not going to find it."

Something in his voice struck Sydney as odd.

"What makes you so sure?" she asked him.

"Nothing," the boy replied, looking away.

At that moment, Sydney Lincoln vowed to herself to find out what Billy John Kingfisher was hiding!

Teamwork and Technology

When the girls got back to Galilahi's house, an email was waiting from Bailey:

> *We researched Blowing Rock. It's a cliff that juts out over a gorge 4000 feet above sea level. The wind there blows up and down. If you throw something off the rock, it will blow back up to you. There's an old story that a Cherokee brave jumped off the cliff, but the wind picked him up and blew him back. His girlfriend was standing there and saw the whole thing. (Of course, it's just a legend. It didn't really happen. But I think it's a neat story.) Anyhow, check with Kate when you get home from Indian Village. She's working on other stuff.*
>
> *Huggers,*
> *Bailey*

"Maybe Blowing Rock fits with the clue in Ecclesiastes 1:5 through 7," said Sydney.

Elizabeth quoted the scripture verse. " 'The wind blows to the south and turns to the north; round and round it goes, ever returning on its course.' You're right, Syd. There does seem to be a similarity with that and what Bailey wrote."

Sydney doodled on a scrap of paper. She drew a circle, labeled it *Earth*, and scribbled the words *north, south, east,* and *west* to show the relative compass points.

"Hey," she said, thinking. "Hey! North and south are up and down when you look at directions on a map. The wind blows up and down at the Blowing Rock. That fits with 'the wind blows to the south and turns to the north!' "

"See!" said Galilahi. "The lady was telling us the truth. We should go there." She picked up her cell phone. "I'm calling my dad at the heliport to see if he'll fly us to the Blowing Rock. After all, it fits with the wind clue and it fits with the tree clue. That *has* to be where the cabin is."

Sydney was about to tell Galilahi to keep Billy John Kingfisher out of their business. But it was too late. Billy John answered the phone at the heliport office. Galilahi was already divulging the contents of Bailey's email and their desire to visit the windy cliff.

"Good detectives keep clues to themselves," said Sydney when Galilahi ended the call. "It's best if Billy John doesn't know what we're up to."

"Why?" Galilahi said. She sounded slightly annoyed. "He works with my dad."

"Whenever we've mentioned the cabin around Billy John, he's laughed or said we'll never find it, or he's changed the subject," she said. "I'm beginning to think he knows something and is keeping it from us."

Elizabeth typed a note to Bailey, telling her that they were hoping to take a trip to the rock.

"Are you sure about Billy John?" she asked Sydney. "I didn't get that impression, but I wasn't paying much attention."

"There's just something about him that I don't like." Sydney turned to Galilahi. "How did he react when you told him about Bailey's message?"

"He was fine," Galilahi replied. "But—" she hesitated. "You're not going to like this."

"Like *what*?" Sydney asked suspiciously.

"Billy John is going with us to the Blowing Rock."

"What!" Sydney exclaimed. "Why?"

"Because he said it's no place for us to be wandering by ourselves. Plus, he said that it's a really neat place to explore, and we'll all have fun together."

"Oh, for goodness' sake!" said Sydney. "I don't want him hanging around with us. If we need a chaperone, let's ask your dad instead."

"It might be okay if Billy John comes," Elizabeth suggested. She disliked conflict.

"Dad *can't* go with us," Galilahi countered. "He has to work. As a matter of fact, he's in the helicopter right now giving a tour. That's why Billy John answered the phone."

"So we're stuck with Billy John Kingfisher." Sydney sighed. "Wonderful."

The girls were quiet for a few moments. Finally, Elizabeth said something. "I think it's strange that he's eager to join us. I'm remembering the stuff that he said in the helicopter. You're right, Syd. If he knows where the Cabin of the Rising Sun is, he doesn't want us to find it. But wouldn't he discourage us from going to the Blowing Rock, if that's where the cabin is?"

"You would think so," said Sydney, still drawing doodles. Her laptop chimed. "Incoming email," she said, looking at the screen. "It's from Kate."

Bailey just emailed that you're at Galilahi's house. Let's talk on the webcams. I'm standing by. K8

Sydney logged in and switched on her webcam. Kate's face appeared on the screen. Her glasses were perched at the tip of her nose.

"How was Indian Village?" she asked.

"Interesting," Elizabeth answered. "We saw what the cabin might have looked like."

"Only it would be better than the one we saw," Galilahi added. "A tour guide said in Grandma Hisgi's time, the Cherokee people lived in cabins like the ones the settlers lived in."

A strange snuffling noise came from the laptop's speakers. Biscuit had his nose pressed up to Kate's webcam and was sniffing it. Kate pushed him aside. "I know," she said. "I looked up Oconaluftee Indian Village online and found pictures of the cabins. Then I found an article that told about the Cherokee people living in log cabins in the mid-1800s. After that I looked for pictures that showed what those cabins might have looked like. I found some, and I have a pretty good idea of the cabin's approximate dimensions."

Sydney was doodling pictures of log cabins. "There are miles to explore in and around Cherokee, North Carolina," she said. "With nothing more to go on, how in the world are we supposed to find one ancient cabin in the wilderness?" She drew a dead-end sign on her paper. "And now we're planning to travel four hours away from Cherokee, in case that's where Grandma Hisgi lived. It just doesn't make any sense to me."

"I have a few more interesting things to tell you," Kate said. "There are caves in the area of the Blowing Rock. One of them is an attraction that people can visit called the Linville Caverns. I'm sure that there are more caves hidden there among the rocks."

Elizabeth gasped. "That fits with Revelation 6:15: 'Every slave and every free man hid in caves and among the rocks of the mountains.' "

"It makes even more sense," Kate told her, "because the Blowing Rock website names specific mountains that you can see from the rock: Hawksbill Mountain, Grandfather Mountain, and Mount Mitchell. It also mentions Table Rock. So we have rocks and mountains and caves—"

"And that all fits with the clues," Sydney conceded.

"See?" said Galilahi. "And the village lady said that there are dead trees there."

"But what about the water part?" Elizabeth asked. "Acts 8:36."

"It's there too," said Kate. "The Blowing Rock overhangs Johns River Gorge, so there has to be water down there somewhere, and my guess is that you have to travel along a road to get to it."

"Oh my goodness!" said Elizabeth. "Maybe we're really on to something."

"But," Sydney added, "it'll be like finding a needle in a haystack."

Kate flashed her never-fear-Kate-is-here smile. "That's where I can assist," she said. "Do you remember when you guys were chasing the would-be assassins in Washington DC, and I rigged up a cell phone as a tracking device?"

"How could we forget?" Elizabeth answered. "It helped save our lives."

"Well, I've created something similar. It involves tapping into satellites and the technologies used by explorers who searched for Noah's Ark. I've created software that can help you find certain objects from the air."

"You mean like Superman's x-ray vision?" said Galilahi as she looked at the doodles on Sydney's paper.

"Not exactly," Kate answered. "You can't see through things, but this technology can detect shapes of objects down below and create a rough computer model of what it sees. The best thing is that you can load the program onto a cell phone and use the phone as the locator."

"Cool!" said Sydney. "How exactly does it work?"

"Well," Kate explained, "let's say that I'm looking for a cabin. I can program some rough dimensions into my cell phone. That gives the device a clue about what I want it to search for. Then I punch in a numerical code that connects the cell phone to a satellite feed. The data

I programmed into the cell phone bounces up to the satellite and back down to Earth. I can point my cell phone at the ground while I'm in an airplane, and if it detects something down below that fits the data, it creates a computer model that I can view on my cell phone screen. It will also lock in and store the latitude and longitude. So, when I'm back on the ground, I know exactly where to go to find what the locater found."

"Wow, Kate, that's awesome!" Sydney said. "But it won't help us if it's on *your* phone in Philadelphia."

"You can load the software onto any cell phone," Kate answered. "Either of yours will work fine. I've just uploaded the program to our Camp Club Girls' web page. Why don't you go there right now and download it to your laptop? Then I'll tell you how to load it onto your phones. We'll fix it so one of you can look for cabins and the other can look for caves. How's that?"

"Perfect," said Elizabeth.

"Ditto," Sydney echoed.

While Sydney and Elizabeth downloaded the software and programmed their cell phones, Galilahi looked again at Grandma Hisgi's Bible. She thought that maybe it held other clues that they might have missed. She opened the cover and read to herself the list of names: Galilahi Adair Coody, Salli Coody Lightfoot, Lucy Lightfoot Kingfisher— She hesitated. Nanny Kingfisher Fields—Mary Fields Rogers!

Oh my, she thought. *It couldn't possibly be.* She jotted the names down on a sheet of paper and slipped the paper into her jeans pocket.

"Sometimes it's best to keep a secret," she said out loud.

"What?" Sydney asked.

"Oh, nothing," Galilahi responded.

"Oh. Right," said Sydney. She was preoccupied with figuring out how to use the software.

Galilahi hadn't been paying much attention. She was thinking about Billy John Kingfisher and wondering what he knew. In the past few minutes, as she'd read the names, Galilahi decided that Sydney was right. Billy John might be hiding something from them.

"Okay, Kate." Sydney said. "I think we have both phones programmed. Explain to us how to use them."

Kate pushed her glasses up on her nose. "Syd, yours is programmed to look for a cabin. The dimensions we entered are similar to an average-sized log cabin where settlers might have lived during the mid-1800s.

Tomorrow, as you're flying over the Blowing Rock in the helicopter, just point your cell phone toward the ground like you're taking a picture. If it detects anything down there that fits the dimensions, it'll let you know by vibrating. Then look at the screen. The software will create a simple line drawing of what it found. If you save the drawing, you will also save its latitude and longitude coordinates. Understand?"

"I get it," said Sydney.

Elizabeth was writing down Kate's instructions in case the girls needed to refer to them later.

"Does my cell phone work the same way?" she asked.

"Almost," Kate answered. "Beth, you point your cell phone at the ground, and it will look for caves. When it finds one, your phone will vibrate to let you know. You won't get a drawing, though. Instead, you'll receive data about how big the cave is and its longitude and latitude. That's the best I can do for caves. My advice is to look for a place where a bunch of caves are close together."

Elizabeth wrote down: *"Look for a bunch of caves."*

Sydney's forehead wrinkled with frustration. "You realize, Kate, that we'll be flying over miles and miles of wilderness and mountains. We're bound to find more than one cabin down there."

"But think about it," Galilahi said. "We're looking for an old cabin hidden in the wilderness, and it has to be close to caves and rocks. If we see anything that doesn't fit, we should ignore it."

"And any cabin we find has to fit with the wind and water clues too," Elizabeth contributed. "So that should further eliminate some of them—"

Kate interrupted. "And, then again, you may not find *anything* that fits the criteria. But you can trust my software. It works. And one more thing, I've set it up so all of the Camp Club Girls can see the data from your phones. We'll be analyzing what you've found, and we can text you with our thoughts."

Galilahi's phone rang. She looked at the caller ID. "It's my dad," she said, taking the call. She went into the living room so she wouldn't disturb the girls' conversation.

"Alexis and McKenzie are working on the genealogy angle," Kate said. "They're trying to find out more about Galilahi Adair Coody."

"Grandma Hisgi," Elizabeth said.

"Right," Kate confirmed. "But instead of searching for information about the Adair family, they're looking at the Coody family and their ancestors. There might be a connection that mentions Grandma Hisgi."

"That's a great idea," said Sydney. "If we find out about Grandma Hisgi's husband, that might help us learn more about her."

"Send us a text message if you uncover anything important," Elizabeth told her.

"I will," Kate promised. "And Bailey is working on the name, Cabin of the Rising Sun. Her mom knows a docent at a historical museum near their home. The docent has Cherokee relatives, so maybe she can help us."

"What's a *docent*?" Sydney asked.

"Someone who takes you on a tour and explains things," Elizabeth said. "I know because they have docents at the Amarillo Museum of Art."

Galilahi walked into the kitchen. "We're all set, if it's okay with your aunt, Sydney. Dad will fly us to Blowing Rock tomorrow morning. That's not only the name of the cliff, but also of the town where it is. He almost didn't let us go, but I convinced him. He trusts Billy John, and as long as he comes with us, we have Dad's permission."

"I'm sure Aunt Dee will give us permission to go as long as you got your dad's permission," Sydney said. "Tomorrow the *four* of us will go to Blowing Rock. But, Galilahi, Billy John is *not* to know about Kate's software. Our spy stuff is top secret. Do you promise?"

"I promise," Galilahi said.

Trailing Through the Woods

The next day, Sydney asked Mr. Lowrey to fly low over the Blowing Rock and the rugged terrain around it.

"The Blowing Rock is North Carolina's oldest attraction," said Galilahi's dad. He swung the helicopter toward the rock and flew in wide circles above it. "It's been open to the public since 1933. Blowing Rock is actually a cliff that overhangs a gorge several thousand feet below. It got its name because the walls of the gorge make a chute, a sort of chimney, and the northwest wind shoots up it. Sometimes, the wind is so strong that objects thrown over the cliff will fly right back up."

Galilahi laughed. "Dad, you sound like a tour guide."

"I *am*, honey," he said. "I know all about this part of North Carolina. In the few months since I've been on the job, I've seen just about everything from the air."

"Except the Cabin of the Rising Sun," Galilahi said with a sigh. "You're still looking for it when you fly around, aren't you?"

Her dad didn't answer.

"There *is* no such thing." Billy John's voice came into the girls' headphones.

Sydney felt her face turn hot.

"Billy John," she said as calmly as she could. "Do you know something about the Cabin of the Rising Sun that you're not telling us?"

His answer was terse. "I've never heard of it."

"Then how do you *know* that it doesn't exist?" Sydney blurted.

The boy turned in his seat and looked at her.

"Because," he said, "I *know* that most of the old cabins around here were destroyed as settlers came to North Carolina and built neighborhoods with modern houses. A few of the old Indian cabins were moved to the Indian Village museum where you were yesterday.

"If a mysterious old Cherokee cabin was hidden somewhere in the mountains, don't you think someone would have found it by now? It would be as famous as the Blowing Rock."

It wasn't the answer Sydney had hoped for. She sat quietly, silently counting to ten, trying to calm herself.

He's such a know-it-all, she said to herself. *One. . .two. . .three. . . four. . .*

Elizabeth pointed her phone toward the ground. "Mr. Lowrey, would you mind circling over the area so we can take pictures? We want to send them to our friends."

Sydney aimed her phone at the ground too. "Yes, we'd like to record the whole experience of flying in a helicopter over the North Carolina wilderness," she added. "It'll be like our friends are taking a virtual field trip."

Mr. Lowrey obliged. He flew low over the area, occasionally identifying points of interest. "Over there, to the southwest, you can see Hawksbill Mountain and Table Rock. If you look due west, you'll see Grandfather Mountain."

"That's the highest peak in the Blue Ridge Mountains," said Billy John.

"And Mount Mitchell," Galilahi's dad continued.

"The highest peak east of the Mississippi River," Billy John added haughtily.

Sydney felt the muscles in her face tighten. She tried to stop the scowl that swept across her forehead. "How do you know so much?" she asked.

"Because I explore," Billy John responded. "That's how you learn stuff. You explore and you ask plenty of questions."

"And I suppose you always get straight answers," said Sydney.

Suddenly, Elizabeth's cell phone vibrated. She looked at the screen and saw rows of numbers spilling onto it. She didn't understand any of them.

"Oh," she gasped, "I hope Kate is watching this and analyzing the data." Then, realizing that she'd said it out loud, she looked to Sydney.

"Who's Kate?" Billy John asked. "What data?"

Elizabeth saved the numbers to her cell phone's memory. "Um. . . Kate is our friend in Pennsylvania," she said. "She's been helping us with. . .uh. . .with a project that has to do with a new invention. . .

a technological invention. . . "

Sydney looked at Elizabeth and caught her eye. *Don't say too much,* she thought.

Elizabeth looked back at her with desperation.

"Did you know explorers are planning to search again for Noah's Ark?" Sydney didn't know why she said that, but the words just came out. She had to say something to move the conversation away from Kate and the data.

"What's that have to do with anything?" said Billy John.

"Mountains," Sydney replied, thinking quickly. "I thought about it because of the mountains. A lot of people believe that Noah's Ark is still on Mount Ararat in Turkey."

They flew without talking for several minutes. Elizabeth's phone continued to vibrate, and she saved the data, hoping Kate and the girls were making sense of it. "Mr. Lowrey," she said, "are there any caves around here?"

Billy John was the one who answered. "We're getting near the Linville Caverns."

Sydney kept her cell phone pointed at the ground and waited.

"The Linville Caverns are deep inside Humpback Mountain," Billy John said. "They were discovered more than two hundred years ago and were used as a hide-out for Civil War soldiers. A stream runs through the caverns. If you got lost, you could follow the flow of the stream to find your way out."

Sydney grew excited. She and Elizabeth exchanged a knowing look. Galilahi caught it, and her face brightened.

"Water, mountains, and rocks!" Galilahi exclaimed. "That has to be the place!"

Sydney poked her with her elbow. "That's very interesting, Billy John," Sydney said. "Mr. Lowrey, do you think you could fly low over where the caves are, so we can get a better look?"

The copter made a wide sweep to the southwest.

Sydney recited Ecclesiastes 1:5-7 to herself and thought about the clues. *"The sun rises and the sun sets, and hurries back to where it rises"*—East. *"The wind blows to the south and turns to the north; round and round it goes, ever returning on its course"*—Blowing Rock, where the wind blows up and down. *"All streams flow into the sea, yet the sea is never full. To the place the streams come from, there they return again"*—A stream cut a path through Humpback Mountain *and it still flows there today.*

She thought hard, remembering the other scripture clues. "*As they traveled along the road, they came to some water; trees, without fruit and uprooted—twice dead*"; "*every slave and every free man hid in caves and among the rocks of the mountains.*"

She didn't know yet how all the clues fit together, but she had a feeling the answer might lie near the caves.

Mr. Lowrey made a wide circle, and they approached the caverns from the east. Suddenly, Sydney's phone vibrated. A line drawing of a cabin appeared on the screen, and Sydney looked at the earth. She could barely make out a rough shingled roof among the towering pine trees.

"Look, down there!" she said. "I think I see a cabin."

Galilahi and Elizabeth looked to where Sydney was pointing. "I see it too!" Galilahi exclaimed. "It's hidden in the woods. Maybe it's the Cabin of the Rising Sun."

"Lea, we've talked about this before," her dad protested. "Your great-great-great-great-great-grandmother's cabin no longer exists. Your mother and I said you may look for it, just for fun, but this is getting out of hand."

Billy John turned and looked at the girls. "Mr. L. is right. There are hundreds of cabins down there, mostly owned by people who can afford a vacation house in the mountains."

Sydney wasn't going to give up. She had a feeling about the area around the Linville Caverns, and she wanted to check it out.

"But *this* cabin seems to be tucked in the woods away from the others," she said. "I think we should go there. We've seen the Blowing Rock from the air. I vote that we check out the caverns instead."

She looked at the other girls, silently pleading with them to agree.

"I vote for the caverns too," said Galilahi.

"Me too," Elizabeth said.

Mr. Lowrey looked at Billy John. "Well, what do you think?" he asked.

"Set her down near the caverns," Billy John answered. "I'd rather hang out there than at the Blowing Rock anyway. It's a hot day, and it'll be cool inside the mountain. You'll have to radio Jay at the office, though, and have him get permission for you to put down near the caves. There's an old parking lot about a hundred yards from the entrance. If they'll let you, you can set her down there."

Galilahi's dad radioed the heliport office and asked Jay to get permission for them to land near the caverns. While they waited for a reply, Sydney got a text message from Kate: YOU ARE 50 MI SOUTHWEST OF BLOWING ROCK. ASK TO GO TO LINVILLE CAVERNS. 411 SHOWS IMP LANDMRKS. CAVES & RIVERS BELOW. K8

Sydney replied: WE KNOW. THAT'S THE PLAN. SEE CABIN EAST OF CAVERNS. WE'LL CHECK IT OUT.

"They said you can land in the parking lot north of the entrance." Jay's voice crackled in their headphones. "Then head back here, Jack. We have a group of tourists waiting."

"Ten-four," said Mr. Lowrey. The helicopter swooped toward the northwest, and Galilahi's dad lowered it onto the empty lot. He shut down the engine.

"Enjoy yourselves," he said. "But don't wander off and get lost. When you're done at the cave, there are plenty of marked trails that you can hike and other public places to explore. Billy John knows his way around, so listen to what he says. I'll be back at three o'clock to get you." He looked at his daughter. "Do you understand?"

Galilahi slid open the helicopter's door.

"We'll be good, Dad," she promised. "And by the time you come to get us, we'll have found the Cabin of the Rising Sun."

Billy John shook his head and laughed.

As Sydney climbed out of the helicopter, her cell phone vibrated. It was another message from Kate: LOOK 4 TRAIL EAST OF CAVERN ENTRANCE. FOLLOW IT ABOUT 1 MILE TO THE CABIN. K8

She showed the message to Elizabeth and Galilahi. Luckily, Billy John didn't notice. He was getting last-minute instructions from Mr. Lowrey.

"I'll take good care of them, Mr. L.," Billy John was saying. "You don't have to worry."

Sydney winced. *Take good care of us! He's barely older than Elizabeth.*

While Billy John was preoccupied, Sydney shared her theory with the girls. "Listen, she whispered. "I think that the Blowing Rock, where the wind blows north and south, was Grandma Hisgi's clue that she wasn't in Cherokee, North Carolina, anymore. She'd moved away."

"And where we are, right now, is east of Cherokee," Galilahi said. "In the direction of the rising sun!"

"Good thinking," said Sydney. "The stream and the cave clues seem to work together. I think Grandma Hisgi knew that these caves were a hiding place during the Civil War, which fits with the date written inside her Bible—1863. And she must have known that a stream flowed through this particular cave. So she used that clue to bring her family here. Next, we have to walk east until we find that cabin that we saw from the air. It's all beginning to fit."

"What's beginning to fit?" Billy John said. They hadn't seen him coming.

The helicopter's rotors started to turn, and the girls and Billy John ducked and ran toward the cavern entrance away from the wind created by the blades. Billy John must have forgotten about his question.

"I'll get our tickets," he said. "You have to buy tickets to see the caverns." He turned and started walking.

Sydney grabbed his arm. "Wait!" she said. "Let's do some exploring first. We can see the caverns later, closer to when Galilahi's dad is supposed to pick us up. That way, we'll be sure to be here on time."

Billy John put the money Mr. Lowrey had given him for the tickets into his pocket. "Where do you want to start?" he asked.

"That way," Sydney said, pointing to the east.

Sydney was sure they'd find a trail nearby. Kate had sophisticated mapping software that could hone in on a certain area and identify roads and trails. She must have found something before she sent her text message.

"Where are we going?" Billy John asked.

"Just trust me, okay?" said Sydney. She marched forward with a purpose. "We're looking for a trail that heads east toward that cabin we saw from the air."

Billy John hurried to catch up with her. "Oh, for goodness' sake," he moaned. "Are you back on that cabin idea again? Okay, let's go. I'll do anything if it will prove to you that you're wrong."

After they'd walked several hundred yards, they came to a dirt road. It led east into a heavily wooded area, and Sydney took it.

"Hang on there," Billy John warned her. "You promised Mr. L. that you'd stay on the public trails. I can't let you go."

A shiver rushed up Sydney's spine. She stopped and spun around.

"What do you mean you can't *let* me go? Just try and stop me."

She knew she shouldn't have lashed out at Billy John, but she couldn't help herself. *I'm sorry, God*, she prayed as she continued walking. She stopped and faced the boy.

"I'm sorry I yelled at you," she told him. "But look."

She pointed to a small wooden post with a number carved on it about twenty feet up the road.

"That's a trail marker," she said. "And trail markers mark public trails."

Billy John looked at her sheepishly.

"I didn't see it," he admitted.

As they walked, the dirt road narrowed. It curved slightly to the right, and the air suddenly felt cooler and fresher. A rippling sound came from the distance. As they continued on the road, it grew louder. Before long, they saw a small waterfall that spilled into a narrow stream. The stream flowed on, deeper into the woods. Right there, the road ended.

" 'As they traveled along the road, they came to some water,' " Elizabeth declared.

"I was thinking the same thing," Galilahi exclaimed. "We're not far from the cabin."

Billy John picked up a stone and tossed it into the stream.

"*Who* traveled along the road and came to some water?" he asked. He picked up another stone and tossed it.

"Nobody in particular," said Elizabeth. "I was just thinking out loud."

"Whoa!" said Billy John. "Look at that big school of fish! I sure wish I had a fishing pole right about now."

A small trout jumped in the stream. Suddenly, Sydney had an idea of how she might get Billy John to leave them alone for a while. "You know you can catch fish without a pole," she said.

The boy looked at her suspiciously. "How?"

"We learned survival tricks at Discovery Lake Camp," Sydney told him. She hoped she could remember what she'd learned. There was a stand of strong, tall grass at the side of the stream. She picked some. "Take long pieces of really tough grass and tie a bunch together to make your fishing line."

She showed him, creating a line about twelve feet long.

"Beth, can I have one of your hair clips, please, one you don't want back?" Elizabeth took a clip out of her long, blond hair and handed it to Sydney. "Now, I'll bend this clip to make a hook and tie it onto the end of the line," Sydney said. She fashioned the hook and tied it. "There you go, Billy John. All you need now is a worm or something for bait, and you can fish all you want."

Billy John looked skeptical. "Does it really work?" he asked.

"Sure!" Sydney said. "Why don't you stay here and fish while we check out the cabin. The trail is marked. It's a public place. We'll be fine."

A trout splashed again. "Well. . .I guess it'll be all right," Billy John said. "Come back here as soon as you're done."

Sydney smiled and winked at her friends. They took off on the trail.

Trail Ends Here

"Are you sure this is the right way?" Galilahi asked. "Are you even sure this is a trail anymore?"

They had walked a few hundred yards into the woods, and the trail had turned into a narrow path covered with dead leaves and pine needles. The girls had to step over dead branches and small rocks that were in their way.

"Don't ask me," said Elizabeth. "I'm just following Sydney."

"It's a trail," Sydney said. "Just not well traveled. The trail markers look old, and some of the numbers are all but worn away, but I'm sure this has been a public trail."

"Listen," said Galilahi, stopping dead in her tracks. The girls heard a strong beat coming from high above them in the trees. "That sounds like some kind of code. Someone is beating a drum."

Sydney laughed. "No, it's just a woodpecker," she said. "Probably a pileated one."

"I don't think so," Galilahi argued. "The Cherokee people used drums to communicate, and that sounds like a drum to me. What's *pileated*?"

Sydney looked up and all around trying to find the noisy bird. "Pileated woodpeckers are giant woodpeckers that are about a foot and a half tall."

"You're kidding!" Galilahi exclaimed.

"And when they peck on trees, it sounds a lot like someone beating on a snare drum; not so much like the water drums we heard at the museum yesterday."

The noise got louder, and then Sydney saw it. The pileated woodpecker drilled its beak into the bark of an old, dead tree. The red crest on its head flashed up and down as the bird worked hard to catch insects that lived inside the trunk.

"Look, there it is now!" Sydney pointed toward the tree and up about twenty feet.

"You *were* telling the truth," said Galilahi. "That thing is huge!"

"I told you so," Sydney said. "And that woodpecker might be giving us a clue."

"What are you thinking?" Elizabeth wondered. Usually, she and Sydney were in sync with their thoughts, but this time Elizabeth couldn't imagine what clue Sydney had uncovered.

The big bird gave up its hunt for a quick meal and flew in the direction the girls were walking. It found a perch in another tree and screeched loudly.

Kuk-kuk-kuk, kuk-kuk-kuk.

"I'm thinking," said Sydney, "that pileated woodpeckers often make nests in the holes of dead trees. Listen, I hear another one."

The girls stood silently, listening for the sound. The loud *kuk-kuk-kuk* of the first woodpecker was answered by a distant *kuk-kuk-kuk, kuk-kuk-kuk.*

"That must be its mate. Let's follow the calls." Sydney dashed up the path.

"Why are we following birds?" Galilahi asked. "What do woodpeckers have to do with finding Grandma Hisgi's cabin?"

Elizabeth scurried to keep up with Sydney's long, quick stride.

"Dead trees," she said. "Trees without fruit and uprooted—twice dead."

"Oh, I get it!" Galilahi exclaimed. "I never would have thought of that when I saw that goofy-looking bird."

"Sydney's a nature nut," Elizabeth explained. "You should see her in the woods at Discovery Lake Camp. She can name almost every plant, bird, and animal."

Sydney was several yards ahead of them now. Suddenly, she stopped and looked into the woods. "Check it out," she said when her friends caught up.

There, lying on their sides, were two old pine trees. They were uprooted, probably ripped from the ground by a windstorm. Over time, all of their needles had fallen off, and their branches had died, rotted, and fallen to the earth. All that remained were huge, broken trunks and dirt balls that encased their ancient roots.

"Trees without fruit and uprooted—twice dead!" Sydney announced.

"See, I told you," Galilahi declared. "Just a little bit further, and we'll find Grandma Hisgi's cabin!"

Something rustled in the woods behind the girls. Then dead twigs snapped.

"Did you hear that?" Elizabeth whispered. She looked behind her. "What do you think it was?"

Sydney looked around too.

"I *did* hear it," she agreed. "But I don't see anything. Maybe it was an animal. That bothers me a little because of that episode Alexis and I had in the Wisconsin woods."

Galilahi's eyes widened. "*What* episode?"

Sydney hesitated slightly before she answered. "We thought a bear was hanging around our cabin, but it turned out to be something else—another mystery the Camp Club Girls solved. I'll tell you about it another time. Come on. We have to hurry. Let's go."

Sydney knew whatever was in the woods was big. Was it a bear?

The trail grew narrower and the markers became harder to see. Sometimes the girls had to move sideways to squeeze through the brush, but they pushed onward with Sydney leading.

Suddenly, Sydney stopped. Nailed to a tree trunk was a sign: TRAIL ENDS HERE. PRIVATE PROPERTY.

"Oh no!" Elizabeth complained. "We've reached a dead end."

Galilahi read the sign and kept walking.

"No we haven't," she declared. "I haven't come this far to turn back now. If Kate is so great at directions, the cabin we saw is straight ahead. I'm not leaving until I find it."

She disappeared through the rhododendrons.

"We can't let her go in there alone," Sydney said. She grabbed Elizabeth's arm, and they pressed through the rhododendron bushes, trying to catch up with Galilahi.

"Syd, did you hear that? Someone is following us." Elizabeth whispered as the girls heard leaves rustle.

Sydney walked faster. "You're right. Someone or *something* is following us," she responded. "I don't like this."

"Dead end. *Dead. . .end!!!*" Galilahi's voice echoed through the woods.

Sydney and Elizabeth suddenly spotted a clearing. In the middle was an old, run-down shack. A cement driveway led away from it, and in the distance the girls could see a newer house with a car in its driveway.

Galilahi stood next to the shack, looking distraught. "It's just an old storage shed," she wailed. "There's a lawn mower in there, some bikes, and a bunch of other junk. It's not the Cabin of the Rising Sun!" She looked ready to cry. "Kate was wrong. This is a dead end."

"No, she wasn't!" Sydney protested. "We spotted what we thought was a cabin when we were in the helicopter. The dimensions fit what we're looking for. Kate just told us how to get here so we could check it out."

Elizabeth interrupted. "We need to get out of here. We're on someone's property." She began walking back where they'd come from. She nervously looked around, trying to spot whatever had been in the woods behind them.

"I sure hope if that was a bear following us that it's gone now," she said. "Does anyone know what to do if a bear is following?"

"I read a brochure that they hand out at the park office," Sydney said. "It said bears don't usually bother people. You're supposed to watch the bear. Back away watching it, and it will probably be okay. If it acts aggressive, don't turn and run, but start hollering and try to make yourself look bigger than you are. Make a lot of noise and scare it."

"Maybe I'd better grab one of these big sticks," Elizabeth said. "Or some rocks."

"Might be a good idea," Sydney said. "Usually bears in this area only bother people if they want food. That's why you're never supposed to feed a bear—it makes them start bothering people for food. I think I'll grab a stick too, to be safe."

Galilahi didn't seem to be following this trail of conversation. She just watched the path with a sad look on her face.

As the girls pushed through the bushes and thickets, Galilahi continued. "Maybe we'll never find Grandma Hisgi's cabin. Maybe I should believe it when everyone says that it no longer exists."

They were almost to the path now. "Sydney, maybe you've been right all along. Maybe Billy John Kingfisher is *sure* it doesn't exist, and he's keeping that from us. Maybe he's watching our wild goose chase and laughing. But do you know what? He's not the only one who has a secret. I might know a secret about him!"

Suddenly there was a huge racket in the bushes near them!

Sydney and Elizabeth grabbed their weapons. Sydney felt as if her heart was going to beat out of her chest!

The bear or whatever it was started to push through the brush.

Gililahi's scream echoed against the trees.

CHAPTER 9

An Unexpected Ally

"What secret?"

Billy John stood on the path facing them.

"*Aah!* You scared us to death!" Elizabeth said. She dropped to a tree stump next to the path. Sydney and Galilahi sat down on large rocks nearby.

"Were you following us?" Sydney asked. She was angry to see Billy but grateful that he wasn't a bear. "I thought you were fishing."

Billy John smirked. "I promised Mr. L. I'd keep an eye on you. So, have you solved the case of the missing Cabin of the Rising Sun?"

The girls stood silent.

"I didn't think so," Billy John laughed. "And Lea, what secret do you know about me?"

"*Galilahi!* My name is Galilahi," she said.

Billy John walked back along the path. The girls stood and followed.

"Come on, spill it," he said smugly. "What's your secret?"

Sydney and Elizabeth were anxious to hear the secret too. They hoped Galilahi wouldn't tell Billy about Kate's gadgets, or any of the other Camp Club Girls' secrets she'd learned during the past few days.

The girls exchanged uneasy glances as they walked along the path. They were at the place where the path widened now, and Galilahi and Billy John were walking side by side, only a few steps ahead of them.

"How much do you know about your family tree?" Galilahi asked him.

"Some," he answered. "I know about my ancestors a couple of generations back. What's that have to do with anything?" He stepped over a branch in the path.

"Do you know the name of your great-great-grandmother on your dad's side?" Galilahi asked.

"I suppose if I thought hard enough I could come up with her name," Billy John replied. He walked a little faster.

"Well, *think*!" Galilahi said.

Elizabeth and Sydney looked at each other, wondering what Galilahi was getting at.

"Was your great-great-grandmother's name Nanny Kingfisher Fields?" Galilahi asked him. "And did she die when she was young?"

Billy stopped. He looked at her disbelievingly. "How do you know that?" he said.

Galilahi looked him straight in the eyes. "Because Nanny Kingfisher Fields was *my* great-great-grandmother too on my mother's side."

"You didn't tell us that part," Sydney interrupted. She still had no idea where all of this was leading. Neither did Elizabeth. But they couldn't wait to find out.

"It didn't seem important to tell you," Galilahi told Sydney. "But yesterday, I started thinking about the names in the family Bible, and I wondered if Billy John and I were related."

Billy John looked confused. "You and me? Related? How?"

They all stood together on the path, and everyone except Galilahi was trying to figure out how the pieces of this genealogical puzzle fit together.

"Our great-grandmothers were sisters," Galilahi explained. "Great-Grandmother Rogers told me that after her mother died—she was our great-great-grandmother, Nanny Kingfisher Fields—her father couldn't take care of all the children. They were sent to live with aunts and uncles. Some went to live with the Kingfishers. So, Billy John, that means we're distant cousins."

Billy John stood quietly, shaking his head. "I'm not good at figuring this stuff out," he said. "Are you sure?"

Galilahi stood straight and tall, feeling proud of herself. "I'm sure," she announced. "Now, if you know anything at all about our Grandma Hisgi and the Cabin of the Rising Sun, you'd better tell me!"

Billy John started walking again, much more slowly. "I've never heard the name Hisgi mentioned in my family," he said. "*Hisgi* means 'five' in Cherokee."

Sydney answered as they hiked along the path. "We've been calling her Grandma Hisgi because she's Galilahi's, and *your*, fifth great-grandmother. It's easier than saying all the greats. Her real name was

Galilahi Adair Coody. Does that name mean anything to you?"

They had arrived at the stream now. The makeshift fishing hook and line were in the middle of the path.

"I've never heard of her," Billy John answered. "Sorry, Galilahi, but I don't think my dad knows much beyond what happened to Nanny King-fisher, way back when. We talk about family history sometimes at family get-togethers. I don't remember much about it." He stopped, picked up a stone, and tossed it at a fish swimming in the water.

Sydney was disappointed. They had followed the clues, and all the landmarks seemed to fit their theory. She had been so sure that they would find the Cabin of the Rising Sun, but just like Galilahi said, they'd reached a dead end.

"Why are you so certain the cabin no longer exists?" she asked Billy John.

He picked up the crude fishing line from the path, then cast the hook into the water, forgetting he hadn't put any bait on it. He stood on the stream bank.

"Stop stalling," Sydney scolded him. "Tell us what you know."

Billy John sighed. "Well. . .I know a few of the old Cherokee cabins were saved. They were restored and moved to Indian Village."

"We know that!" said Elizabeth. "We were there yesterday. So, tell us something we don't know."

"Well. . . " He tugged a bit on the makeshift line. "There might be one more cabin that exists out there somewhere." He wound some of the line around his right hand.

Galilahi took a step forward and stood shoulder to shoulder with her distant cousin. "*Might* exist, or *does* exist?" she asked.

The boy unwound the line from his hand and let the whole thing slip away in the stream. "Okay!" he blurted. "One old cabin still exists, and I know where it is."

"Where?" Sydney and Galilahi both said at the same time.

Billy John looked down at his feet. "I can't tell you," he said quietly. "But I'm sure that it's not the cabin that you're looking for."

Sydney was determined to squeeze out every drop of information that Billy John Kingfisher had about the old cabin.

"Why won't you tell us where it is?" she insisted.

"Because," he said, looking at her and wiping his hands on his jeans, "I'd have to break a promise, and I don't break promises."

"What can you tell us without breaking your promise?" Sydney asked.

They all began walking west on the dirt road.

"There's this old woman," said Billy John. "She's ancient, about a hundred years old. She lives in a cabin—I can't tell you where, because that's what I promised. She practices the old Cherokee ways, and she's lived in the cabin her whole life. I found it one day when I was exploring. I made friends with her, and I visit her a lot and listen to her stories. I don't think anyone knows about her, or if they do they've forgotten or they just don't care anymore. I bring her food sometimes, and I help out around her place when she'll let me. She's a tough old lady. She likes to do everything on her own."

Sydney was beginning to feel differently about Billy John. Maybe he wasn't so bad if he was helping an old lady.

"Billy John," she said. "If she's that old, then she must know a lot of history about the Cherokee people who lived here after the Trail of Tears. Do you think you could get her to talk with us? I'm not asking you to break your promise."

Billy John thought for a minute.

"We're apparently family," he said to Galilahi. "And now I'm curious about Grandma Hisgi too. Let's meet at the entrance to Indian Village tomorrow at noon. I'll see what I can do."

●—●—●

That night as the girls got ready for bed, Sydney felt uneasy.

"I still don't know if I trust Billy John," she said. "Do you think he's just playing around with us, and when we get there tomorrow, it'll be another dead end?"

Elizabeth sat on her bed brushing her hair in the guest room at Aunt Dee's apartment.

"I don't know, Syd. But I think we have to follow through for Galilahi's sake. We promised that we'd help her." She pulled her hair back and fastened it with a ponytail holder.

Sydney sat on her own bed, browsing through a magazine.

"You're right. We did promise," she answered. "Let's see what the other girls think."

She closed the magazine and logged onto the Camp Club Girls' chat room where the girls had agreed to meet at nine o'clock. Kate, McKenzie, Alexis, and Bailey were already waiting, eager to hear about what had happened that day. Sydney was just as eager to share her thoughts about Billy John.

McKenzie: *I agree that you can't be sure about Billy John. Your first instinct was that he wasn't being totally honest with you guys. How do you know he's being truthful now?*

Sydney: *I can't, but we've reached the end of the line. We've followed every clue and have come up with nothing. It seems our next chance of finding the Cabin of the Rising Sun is to talk with the old Cherokee woman.*

McKenzie: *If she even exists.*

Elizabeth: *I think we have to give Billy John an opportunity to prove he's being honest. He regularly goes to church, so I'm guessing he must be a Christian.*

McKenzie: *Maybe, but hasn't he been lying to you?*

Elizabeth: *He's kept a secret and has made remarks about our looking for the cabin, but I don't think he's lied.*

Sydney: *He talks in circles and never gives a straight answer. He says, "Oh, never mind" or changes the subject.*

Bailey: *I think you have to give BJ a chance to prove himself. What's the worst that can happen?*

Alexis: *Bailey's right. We can't give up yet. I can't tell you the number of times I've almost given up trying to solve a Nancy Drew mystery. Then, I follow one last clue, and I get it!*

Kate: *Is there anything that I can do to help?*

Sydney: *Thanks, K8, but no. Your software worked great. It really helped that you gave us directions to the trail. It just turned out to be a dead end. We'll go to Indian Village with G. at noon tomorrow and see if Billy John is there.*

Kate: *Keep in touch. We're only a text message away.*

Sydney: *Will do. We're signing off now. Nighty-night.*

Bailey: *Nighters, fellow sleuthies.*

McKenzie: *Sleep tight.*

Alex: *Don't let the bedbugs bite.*

Kate: *Biscuit says good night too.*

As Sydney shut down the computer, she was lost in thought.

"Penny for your thoughts?" Elizabeth asked.

"Just keep thinking about Billy John," Sydney said. "Something in me just keeps telling me that maybe we just can't trust him."

The Curious Cherokee Cabin

"Well, where is he?" Sydney snapped, looking at her watch.

The girls had spent the morning shopping with Aunt Dee. At noon, they went to Indian Village where they found Galilahi waiting. A heavy rain the night before had left the woods smelling musty and damp, and now, thick, gray clouds hid any hint of sunshine. It was a chilly, summer day in North Carolina. Visitors to the village wore windbreakers and carried umbrellas.

"Where do you think Billy is?" Sydney said again.

"It's just a quarter past twelve," Elizabeth answered. "Let's give him some time."

Sydney leaned against a signpost and crossed her arms.

"I'm waiting until 12:30 and that's it," she said, after a few minutes.

"He'll be here," Galilahi responded. "I'm sure of it."

"I'm not so sure we can trust him," Sydney said.

The girls waited, barely talking. Sydney kept checking her watch.

"That's it," said Sydney when 12:30 arrived. "I'm done. Billy John Kingfisher had his chance, and he blew it." She started to walk away.

"No!" Galilahi insisted. "We have to wait for him. He'll show up. Just give him five more minutes!"

"Yeah! Give me five more minutes!"

Billy John trudged out of the woods just a few yards away. His face was ruddy, he was almost out of breath, and his shoes were caked with gooey dirt mixed with pine needles.

"It's muddy in there," he said, pointing into the woods. "It took longer than I expected to get back here. But I hurried."

Sydney almost felt sorry for him.

"Get back here from where?" she asked.

"From Mrs. Hummingbird's place," he said. "I had to ask permission for you guys to meet her. And, lucky for you, she agreed. But with one condition."

"What's the condition?" Sydney asked suspiciously.

"You have to promise—and I mean *promise*—that you won't tell a single soul about her or where she lives. She doesn't know you so she doesn't trust you. But she trusts *me*, and I've given her my word. And Lea, I mean *Galilahi*, it's only because we're cousins that she's agreed to talk with you." Billy John said nothing for a few seconds, still trying to catch his breath. "So, do you promise?"

"Yes, I promise," Galilahi said, enthusiastically.

"I do too," Elizabeth agreed.

"I guess so," said Sydney.

"I need better than 'I guess so,'" Billy John warned.

"Okay, okay, I promise!" Sydney blurted. "Take us to the hummingbird lady."

Billy John smirked. "Patience, Sydney. I'm worn out from my hike, and before I head back in there again, I'm getting some lunch. Care to join me?"

Reluctantly, the girls followed Billy John Kingfisher to Indian Village's snack bar.

Less than a half hour later, the friends began their trek into the woods. Billy John was their guide, and they had no choice but to trust him.

"There aren't any trails back here," Billy John said. "I know the way through the woods, so it's real important we don't get separated. Stay close behind me and be quiet. I don't want anyone following us."

"Like anyone would follow three kids," Sydney grumbled.

"Ouch!" Galilahi rubbed her forearm where a bramble bush had poked her. "There's stickers and stuff in here."

Billy John stopped so abruptly that Sydney almost ran into him. He swung around and faced the girls.

"I have to know right now if you girls are strong enough to make this hike. We have more than a mile to go, and some of it is really rough. If you don't think you can do it, we'll turn back now."

"Don't worry; we can do it!" Sydney said. She gave his arm a little shove. "Get going."

"Well, this is called the Gulch of Fallen Trees. And it isn't called that for nothing," he snapped.

"You mean they call it that because so many people fall down around here?" Elizabeth asked. "That's different than normal."

"No, they call it that because for some reason this land is not good for the trees," said Billy. "They tend to grow tall and fast, but then instead of lasting for years as most trees do, they fall. That's the way it's been for hundreds of years. In former days, braves came here to pull out the fallen trees, and make canoes of them in the clearings."

"Twice dead," Elizabeth murmured. "Falling once, and then made into canoes."

"What?" Billy John asked.

"It's nothing," Sydney said. "Why do the trees fall here so much?"

"I don't know," Billy John answered. "I don't know if it's some sort of pest that destroys the trees, or that they don't get enough sunlight or water or whatever. Your aunt might know since she works with trees.

"But it does mean it's always been a rough area, and if you can't make it through, we need to stop now. Do you want to go on?"

The girls nodded. Billy John looked at each of them for a moment, then abruptly turned and led.

They walked east for a while, pushing their way past low-hanging branches and through bushes and thickets. The mud quickly piled up on their shoes. Every so often they stopped at an old log or a rock and tried, as best they could, to scrape the mud from the soles of their shoes.

"What a mess!" Galilahi complained. "I don't like this at all."

Before long, the group came to a small open stretch of land lined with rocks that were almost as tall as the girls. This rocky wall seemed to separate one part of the woods from the other.

"What's this place?" Sydney wondered.

"I'm not sure," Billy John told them. "And she isn't either. Mrs. Hummingbird, I mean. But we think it's left from a war, maybe the Civil War, or a war before that between the Cherokee people and the Europeans. Who knows? I think it's what's left of an old fort. There's a cave over there, about a half mile." He pointed south. "Mrs. Hummingbird says soldiers and Indians used it as a hiding place, but not at the same time."

Sydney and Elizabeth gave each other knowing looks. They were in the Gulch of Fallen Trees, and now, as they hiked in the mountain woodlands, they'd come to some rocks, and there was a cave nearby. Neither had said anything. They knew this could be another dead end. Still, what they saw seemed to fit with the clues.

Sydney peeked over the rocks. On any other day, she might have been eager to explore and try to discover the meaning of this strange, stone wall. But today she was on a mission to find the Cabin of the Rising Sun.

"So now what?" she asked.

"We climb over it," Billy John answered, matter-of-factly.

That wasn't a problem for Sydney. She had once competed in the Junior Olympics and was tall. But the other girls weren't so sure.

"I'm too short!" Galilahi objected.

"Billy John and I will help lift you over," Sydney said.

"I can lift her by myself," Billy John argued. "Come on, Galilahi. I'll give you a boost. It's a piece of cake; you'll see."

Galilahi walked up to the wall. Billy John and Sydney stood on each side. *One. . .two. . .three. . .* They lifted her until she was able to grab onto the top of one of the rocks and pull herself over.

"Are you okay?" Sydney asked.

"Yeah, I'm fine," Galilahi said from the other side.

"Your turn, Beth," said Sydney.

Elizabeth approached the wall. "I think if I jump and you guys help just a little, I can make it over," she decided.

"Okay. Ready?" Sydney asked.

"Ready," said Elizabeth. She jumped, and Sydney and Billy John boosted her up and over the rocks.

Now, Billy John looked at Sydney and smiled. "You're next Sydney. May I help you?" he said with a bit of sarcasm.

Sydney smiled right back at him. "I don't need your help, Billy John. Thank you very much."

She walked a short distance back, away from the wall. Then she sprinted toward it, jumped, grabbed onto the top of the rocks with both hands, and pulled herself to the other side.

"There," she said. "I'm over. Come on, Billy John. We're waiting for you."

Not to be outdone, the boy did the same thing. He ran, jumped, and pulled himself over.

"Carry on," he said, leading them deeper into the woods.

They made a little jog south, and few minutes later they came to a rushing stream.

"Careful now," Billy John cautioned. "There are some deep ruts here in the ground. She says this used to be an old, dirt road that settlers used. These ruts are actually old wagon wheel tracks."

The sound of rushing water grew louder. Sydney and Elizabeth exchanged another knowing look. They pushed their bodies through a thick stand of bushes, and there, right in front of them, was a river, swollen by last night's rain. The white-capped water seemed to bubble and boil.

"The stream feeds into the river here. We have to walk along the bank to get to her place," Billy John told them. "Watch your step. It's narrow and slick. I don't need any of you girls falling in."

"Careful," Sydney warned her friends. "If we fall into that, we'll drown for sure. No one can swim in water that rough."

They inched along the riverbank, carefully following in Billy John's footsteps. As they went, he pointed out low branches they could hang onto to help them keep their footing.

"I can see why you were late meeting us today," Sydney told him. "This is a rough hike."

"Told you so," Billy John agreed. "But we're almost there. This is the worst part. Just a little ways ahead, and there's a path that leads from the water back through the woods to her cabin."

Sydney was anxious to get there. She and Elizabeth had plenty of experience trekking through the woods but Galilahi hadn't. They made sure she walked between them, and they watched her, ready to grab her if they had to keep her from falling into the river.

Billy John stopped again.

"Here's the path," he said softly. "We're almost there now. I want you girls to be very quiet. I told Mrs. Hummingbird I'd come and tell her before I brought you all up to the door. She's a very private person, and she's not used to company. This is a very big deal for her. Do you understand?"

"We get it," said Sydney.

Billy John led them up the path, just a bit further through the trees and bushes. Then they saw it—a small log cabin that looked somewhat like the one at Indian Village. The roof was constructed from hardwood shingles and, over time, moss had grown over them. As a result, the cabin blended with the woods. The walls were made solidly from logs and an earthy kind of plaster between them.

Like the cabin at Indian Village, this one had no windows. A stone chimney was built against one outer wall. A thin ribbon of curling smoke escaped from its top and disappeared into the gray clouds above. The smell of burning wood wafted through the trees. A shabby porch stretched across the cabin's front, and an old, wooden rocking chair was set next to the door. The door was slightly ajar.

A gentle rain had started to fall. The girls could hear it splattering against the leaves on the trees where they stood, but the leaves were so thick the raindrops were stopped from falling onto the woodland floor.

From inside the cabin came the sound of someone singing.

"I know that melody," Elizabeth whispered. "That's 'Amazing Grace.' My, she sings loudly for an old woman!"

"She sings it a lot," Billy John answered. "It's sometimes called the Cherokee National Anthem. The Cherokee people sang it on the Trail of Tears. Listen. She taught me the English words."

As Mahalia Hummingbird sang in the Cherokee language the boy translated the words of her song.

> U ne la nv I u we tsi
> "God's Son," Billy John whispered.
> I ga gu yv he i
> "paid for us."
> Hna quo tso sv wi yu lo se
> "Now to heaven He went"
> I net s yv ho nv
> "after paying for us."
> A se no I u net se i
> "Then He spoke"
> i yu no du le nv
> "when He rose."
> ta li ne dv tsi lu tsi li
> "I'll come the second time"
> u dv ne u ne tsv
> "He said when He spoke."
> e lo ni gv ni li s qua di
> "All the world will end"
> ga lu tsv ha i yu
> "when He returns"
> ni ga di da ye di go i
> "We will all see Him"
> a ni e lo ni gv
> "here the world over."
> u na da nv ti a ne hv

"The righteous who live"
do da ya nv hi li
"He will come after."
tso sv hna quo ni go hi lv
"In heaven now always"
do hi wa ne he s di
"in peace they will live."

"Mrs. Hummingbird must be a Christian," Elizabeth commented.

"Oh yes," Billy John answered. "She loves God more than anyone I know."

Mrs. Mahalia Hummingbird

Billy John stepped onto the cabin's porch. He waited outside the open door and called loudly, "Mrs. Hummingbird? Mrs. Hummingbird, it's me, Billy John."

The old woman stopped singing. She said something to him, and he went inside. Sydney, Elizabeth, and Galilahi waited in the woods, unable to hear what was going on.

Before long, Billy John came out onto the porch. He walked to where the girls were waiting.

"Okay," he said. "One more time, do you promise not to tell a living soul about Mrs. Hummingbird and where she lives?"

"Yes! We promise!" said Sydney impatiently.

Elizabeth and Galilahi agreed.

"Now, remember," Billy John told them, "she's very old and hard of hearing. And don't let her scare you. She's just that way."

"Just *what* way?" Sydney asked.

Billy John walked toward the cabin without answering. "Come on," he said. "Follow me. And be quiet and polite."

Sydney bristled. *Be polite! Who is he to tell us to be polite?*

They stepped onto the cabin's porch. The wood planks sagged and felt soft under Sydney's feet.

"Watch your step," she warned the girls. "This old floor could go at any time."

"Sshhh!" Billy John whispered. "I'll fix it someday, but don't say anything to her about it. She doesn't like it when I try to help."

He knocked on the open front door. "Mrs. Hummingbird, I'm bringing them in now," he said.

The warm, damp smell of the cabin reminded Sydney of the way the kitchen in her house smelled when her mom made stew on a cold, winter day.

Billy John went inside and invited the girls to follow him.

As Sydney stepped onto the clean-swept, hardwood floor of the one-room cabin, she could imagine what it was like to be a settler living in the Great Smoky Mountains in the late-1800s. Dried herbs, cast-iron pots and pans, and even a pair of snowshoes hung from the rafters. Cheerful, brightly-colored blankets were nailed to three of the walls. Sydney assumed that they helped keep out the cold on winter days.

The fourth wall held a stone fireplace and rows of crooked, wood shelves resting on brackets. The shelves were packed with covered crocks, jars, boxes, and old tin cans. One corner of the room was separated from the rest by a curtain. It was sewn from a bright, flower-patterned fabric.

When Sydney took a few steps to her right, she saw a mattress behind the curtain, covered with another native blanket. There was a small, black cooking stove in the opposite corner. A wood fire provided its fuel, and a coal black chimney pipe stretched from its firebox through the cabin's roof allowing smoke and soot to escape.

A pot of something steamed and boiled on the stovetop. A fire in the stone fireplace took some of the dampness from the cabin and provided a little light for the windowless room. In front of the fireplace was set a small, wooden bench and a rocking chair like the one on the porch.

Mrs. Mahalia Hummingbird sat there, rocking, with her back to the visitors.

Billy John brought the girls closer to her. "Mrs. Hummingbird," he said. "These are my friends, Sydney, Elizabeth, and Galilahi."

The woman turned toward them slowly. Her brown eyes stared at the company standing in her cabin. Her skin was bronze, like Billy John's, and wrinkled, like a wilted rose. Her face, like his, had chiseled features, a prominent chin and smooth, high cheekbones.

"Which is Galilahi?" she asked. Her voice sounded younger than her ninety-plus years.

Galilahi took a step closer. "I am."

The old woman lifted a gnarled finger and pointed to the bench next to her. "Sit here," she commanded. "Billy, bring more chairs."

Billy John got chairs from a ramshackle table in the center of the room and set them near the fire.

"And light the oil lamp on the table," Mrs. Hummingbird ordered.

"We need more light in here."

The boy lit the oil lamp and turned the wick high. The room brightened in a soft yellow glow that merged with the flickering light from the fire. It brought warmth to the misty gray daylight that shone through the open front door.

For what seemed like forever, they sat by the fireplace not saying a word. Usually, Sydney would have been asking questions by now. She might even have been writing in her sleuthing notebook, or setting up her tiny recording device to record Mrs. Hummingbird's words. But today, she kept both of these tucked into her pocket. She waited while the old woman rocked.

Mrs. Hummingbird's sharp voice cut through the silence like a knife. "I want Galilahi to speak now and tell me her story."

Billy John looked at Galilahi and nodded.

"Yes, ma'am." Galilahi spoke up. "My family is Cherokee. We just moved here from Oklahoma this summer. My dad is a pilot for the helicopter tours and my mom is looking for a job in Cherokee. She worked at a convenience store back home—"

"I thought you said that she needed my help to find out about her family," the old woman snapped, looking at Billy John.

Billy John leaned forward in his chair. "She does," he said gently. "It just takes her a little time to explain herself."

"My great-grandmother, my mom's grandmother, has taught me a lot about the Cherokees and our ancestors," Galilahi went on. "Great-Grandmother is, like, as old as you are—"

Mrs. Hummingbird shook her head. "You don't know how old I am."

Galilahi thought before she continued. "My great-grandmother—"

"Her name, please."

"Pardon?"

"Her name!" Mrs. Hummingbird repeated. "What is your great-grandmother's given name?"

"Oh," said Galilahi. "Her name is Mary Fields Rogers."

"I don't know her," said Mrs. Hummingbird. "But go on."

Sydney wondered if Galilahi would ever be able to tell her story without the old woman interrupting.

"I was named after one of my ancestors," Galilahi said. "Her name was Galilahi Adair Coody. She was my great-great-great-great-*great*-grandmother."

"We've been calling her Grandma Hisgi," Elizabeth said.

"Go on," Mrs. Hummingbird said. She seemed to have a new interest in Galilahi's story.

"Great-Grandmother told me a very interesting story about the Trail of Tears," Galilahi said.

A sad look swept across the old woman's face. "Nunna daul Tsuny," she said. "The trail where they cried."

"Yes, ma'am," Galilahi said. "My great-great-great-great-*great*-grandmother and her family were affected by Nunna daul Tsuny."

The room fell silent again. No one spoke as the old woman stared into the fire. Suddenly, she exclaimed, "We *all* were affected by Nunna daul Tsuny!"

Elizabeth shuddered.

"You, me, Billy John. All of the Cherokee people were victims."

Again, no one said a word.

"What are you waiting for?" the old woman asked. She stared at Galilahi with piercing, brown eyes. "Continue," Mrs. Hummingbird demanded, rocking more quickly.

Galilahi went on speaking. "Great-Grandmother says that Grandma Hisgi, I mean my great-great-great-great-*great*-grandmother, lived here in Cherokee when the Trail of Tears happened. When President Andrew Jackson got some of the Cherokee people to agree to move west."

Mrs. Hummingbird stopped rocking and looked at Galilahi. "A *small* group of our people agreed to move west," she said. "Most wanted to stay on their land. This was their home."

Sydney and Elizabeth sat silently, hoping that once Galilahi had told the whole story, Mrs. Hummingbird would provide some information about the Cabin of the Rising Sun. The rain fell harder now. It pounded on the cabin's roof, and thunder was rumbling in the distance.

"Ga-li-la-hi," Mrs. Hummingbird said, spitting out the syllables of her name. "You *still* haven't told me *one* thing about Galilahi Adair Coody. Why exactly have you come here?"

Billy John shifted in his chair. "Yeah, Lea, we really do have to move this story along."

"I'm sorry!" Galilahi moaned. "I'll get to the point right now."

The old woman sighed.

"Galilahi Adair Coody, my great-great-great-great-*great*-grandmother, was ten years old when the Trail of Tears happened. She and her parents were going to be taken away by the soldiers. But before the soldiers came, Galilahi's mother went to a family she knew. I guess a small group of Cherokee people didn't have to leave their land, because they made a deal with the government or something. That family was one of them. So Galilahi Adair Coody's mother asked them to take Galilahi as their little girl. The family agreed, and when the soldiers came, they took Galilahi's parents away, but Galilahi stayed behind. The soldiers thought she was the other family's child."

"Wow," Billy John interrupted. "That's really something. I didn't know that part. I'm related to Galilahi Adair Coody too, you know," he said to Mrs. Hummingbird.

"Yes, Billy," she said. "Is there any more of your story?" she asked Galilahi.

The fire in the fireplace sputtered again.

"She's getting to the most important part," Sydney announced. "Tell her, Galilahi. Explain why we came here."

Billy John slid his chair nearer the fire. "She's getting there, Sydney. Give the girl a chance."

Galilahi noticed that Mrs. Hummingbird was looking at her now with an almost eager expression on her face.

"We don't know much that happened after that," Galilahi said. "But Great-Grandmother heard that Grandma Hisgi, I mean my great-great-great-great-*great*-grandmother, lived around here in a place called the Cabin of the Rising Sun. I promised Great-Grandmother Rogers that when I moved here from Oklahoma, I'd try to find the old cabin. I want to know what became of Grandma Hisgi."

"And we were hoping that you could help us," Elizabeth added. "The only clues we have are in Grandma Hisgi's old Bible, which Galilahi has."

Galilahi reached into her jeans pocket and took out a folded sheet of paper. "There was a letter in the Bible," she said. "written in Cherokee. I made a copy."

She handed it to Mrs. Hummingbird.

As the old woman read the letter, Sydney's eyes wandered around the room. Something caught her attention. She wanted Elizabeth to see it too. She slid her right foot over and gave her friend's ankle a little kick.

When Elizabeth looked at her, Sydney rolled her eyes toward the back of the open front door. She nodded her head, slightly, in that direction.

At first, Elizabeth thought that Sydney had seen something outside. She looked hard, but she saw nothing out of the ordinary. Again, Sydney rolled her eyes toward the door.

Then Elizabeth saw it. Could it be? It was hard to tell from across the room, because it was so small, but it looked like a symbol of the sun had been etched or branded onto the back of the old, wooden door. It was the same sun symbol that had been at the bottom of Grandma Hisgi's letter and in the margins of her Bible.

Elizabeth's eyes widened as she looked at Sydney.

Mrs. Mahalia Hummingbird finished reading the letter. She laid it on her lap. Then she bowed her head for a few seconds. "Amen," she whispered. When she looked up at Galilahi, she smiled.

"Yes, Galilahi," she said. "Yes, I think I can help you."

CHAPTER

12

Secrets Revealed

"Do you realize what this is?" Mrs. Hummingbird held up the copy of Grandma Hisgi's letter.

"Yes," Galilahi said. The stern look on the woman's face almost made her afraid to continue. "It's a letter my great-great-great-great-*great*-grandmother wrote to her family."

Mrs. Hummingbird sighed again and slowly shook her head.

"What I'm asking," she said bluntly, "is do any of you know what these *words* are?

No one spoke. All were afraid of giving the wrong answer.

The fire in the fireplace had died now, and the old woman stood up. She shuffled to the stove and stirred whatever was simmering in the pot. "These words are a passage from the Bible," she announced. "Billy John, move the chairs to the table."

The boy got up and moved his chair first.

"Our friend Kate translated the Cherokee words," Sydney said as she got up.

Elizabeth stood up too. "They're from the Old Testament, Ecclesiastes, chapter 1, verses 5 through 7."

Mrs. Hummingbird pointed to the table. "Sit over there, where the light burns," she commanded.

Billy John and the girls pulled the chairs close to the table and sat down.

Mrs. Hummingbird stopped her stirring and joined them.

"The book of Ecclesiastes was written by Solomon, a king of Israel," she said. "He was searching for the meaning of life."

She read from Grandma Hisgi's letter: " 'The sun rises and the sun sets, and hurries back to where it rises. The wind blows to the south and turns to the north; round and round it goes, ever returning on its course. All streams flow into the sea, yet the sea is never full. To the place the streams come from, there they return again.'

"When Solomon wrote those words, he was unhappy. He was looking for a purpose in his life. He was saying life was just filled with all the same worthless things, every day, going 'round and 'round."

It was the most Mrs. Hummingbird had said since they got there. Sydney was surprised that she knew so much about the Bible, and she was also surprised by Mrs. Hummingbird's explanation of the words.

"By the end of the book of Ecclesiastes," the old woman continued, "Solomon had changed his mind. He decided that life is only the same old thing, day after day, if you don't have faith in God. But, if you *do* have faith, then every day is filled with hope. It's a brand-new day full of magnificent things. Do you understand?" she asked.

"Yes!" Elizabeth answered. "When you believe in Jesus, you become brand-new, and you see life the way He saw it. It's like you're a new person inside."

"Exactly!" Mrs. Hummingbird agreed.

Galilahi sat in her chair looking anxious. "But what does any of this have to do with the Cabin of the Rising Sun where my Grandma Hisgi was raised? Do you know where her cabin is?"

The old woman answered tersely. "No, I do not."

The look of eager anticipation faded from Galilahi's face.

"You don't?" she asked. "I thought you said that you did!"

Sydney felt Galilahi's disappointment. The look on Elizabeth's face showed that she did too. They had tried so hard to help their new friend, and they had reached yet another dead end.

"You did say you could help?" Sydney reminded her.

Mrs. Hummingbird folded her hands and rested them on the table.

"There are things that I can tell you," she said. "But I don't know anything about the cabin where Galilahi Adair Coody grew up. And I *did not* say that I did!"

"Then tell us what you do know, please," she begged the old woman.

A thin trail of sooty, black smoke rose from the oil lamp's glass chimney. Mrs. Hummingbird turned down the wick, and the light dimmed.

"When I was a very small child," she said, "I attended the burial of Galilahi Adair Coody."

Galilahi gasped. "You did! You knew my great-great-great-great-*great*-grandmother?"

Mrs. Hummingbird raised her hand slightly, a signal for Galilahi to stop talking. "I did not say that I *knew* her. I said I attended her burial. I did so with my mother and my sister. I was very young then, and your ancestor was very old when she passed. I remember little about the burial. But I do remember standing at her grave and one of the men playing 'Amazing Grace' on his flute. A large crowd of mourners was there dressed in tribal attire."

Tears filled Galilahi's eyes, not so much from thinking about Grandma Hisgi's funeral, but because they had reached another dead end. It seemed that Grandma Hisgi had taken the secret of the Cabin of the Rising Sun to her grave.

Sydney's mind was racing. "But Mrs. Hummingbird, if you didn't know her, why did you and your family go to her funeral? And you said that a whole crowd of people were there."

Whatever was on the stove was boiling. Mrs. Hummingbird got up and took the pot from the stovetop. She set it on the hearth to cool.

"Galilahi Adair Coody was a much-loved member of our community.

"After Nunna daul Tsuny, there was much anger and sadness among the people who remained here. Like King Solomon had written, life went around and around in a circle without any meaning."

She returned to the table and sat with her guests. "For many years, the people were sad and without hope."

She stared up at the ceiling rafters, looking at nothing. "I don't know where Mrs. Coody lived when she was young, but she was among our people, watching all the sadness. She grew up with sadness. First, losing her parents, and then having to give up the ways of her people to live the settler's ways."

Mrs. Hummingbird sighed. She lowered her head and looked at the flame in the oil lamp. Again, she adjusted the wick.

The room was silent. Sydney, Elizabeth, and Galilahi were eagerly waiting to hear what else the old woman would say.

"Is that it?" Billy John asked loudly. "Is that all you know, or is there more?"

Sydney was surprised when he spoke up. All the while, he had been sitting there, barely saying a word.

Mrs. Hummingbird looked at him, and then slowly she shook her head yes. "There is more."

"Then tell us!" Galilahi exclaimed. "I want to know all of it."

The light from the oil lamp played shadows on Mrs. Hummingbird's face. "I was a young woman when my mother told me about Galilahi Adair Coody. Mother said that after Nunna daul Tsuny, white missionaries came here and lived among the Cherokee people. The missionaries tried to get the Cherokee people to give up their beliefs in gods and spirits and to believe in the one true God instead.

"But the missionaries came and went, and when they left, there was no one to lead the people in worshipping God. Many of them fell back to their old ways."

Mrs. Hummingbird rocked hard and continued. "My mother said that, one day, a young missionary man arrived here. He was half Cherokee. His father had been taken from here by the soldiers and sent on Nunna daul Tsuny with the others. The father, who was a young brave then, had survived the long journey. When he grew up, he married an English girl. Through his wife's Christianity, the missionary's father came to know the God of the Bible, and they raised their children in the Christian faith."

Galilahi couldn't help herself. "But, how does all this fit with Grandma Hisgi?" she interrupted.

"I think I know," said Sydney. "The missionary's last name was Coody—Galilahi Adair married him."

"I think you're right," said Elizabeth. "Galilahi, the missionary was your great-great-great-great-*great*-grandfather. Are we right, Mrs. Hummingbird?"

"You are correct," the old woman said.

Galilahi's face brightened. "Please, Mrs. Hummingbird, tell us more," she begged.

The rain had stopped, and the sun was out. The light streaming through the open front door was much brighter. Billy John got up and opened the door all the way. The room flooded with late-afternoon sunshine.

"Galilahi," the old woman said sharply, "your ancestor grandparents remained here in Cherokee, and they lived among the people. They went into the homes and taught people God's Word. They prayed over the sick, and they baptized as many as were willing. In fact, the river that you walked along to get here is the river where the baptisms happened, all those many years ago."

"The river Grandma Hisgi mentioned!" Sydney exclaimed.

Mrs. Hummingbird didn't seem to notice Sydney's interruption.

"Do not think it was always easy for your grandparents, my child," she said. "At one stage, the Cherokees were very resistant to the message of the Bible, the white man's Christianity. My mother told me that for a time they had to live in caves, to hide from a Cherokee brave and his friends who swore to kill them for dishonoring the Cherokee religion."

"What happened?" Elizabeth asked breathlessly.

"They grew tired of hiding. They returned to their home. As it should be. They were willing to die to bring their people the Truth."

"I bet during that time is when they wrote the letter," Sydney whispered to Elizabeth.

"What about the brave who swore to kill them?" Galilahi asked.

"He met them on their porch," she said. "Instead of killing them, he dropped to his knees, begging to know the God whom they were willing to die for."

"Wow!" Galilahi whispered.

Scriiitcch! Bak-ka-kak!

The loud screech from the front porch startled the girls. A rooster strutted into the cabin and made himself at home.

"Oh, don't worry about him," said Mrs. Hummingbird. "The chickens are out now that the rain is gone."

"You have chickens!" Sydney exclaimed.

The stern look filled Mrs. Hummingbird's face again. "Of course, I have chickens, and an old goat too. Where do you think I get my milk and eggs?"

Sydney didn't answer. She tried to hide a grin. She'd noticed that Billy John had jumped higher than all of them when the bird had announced its presence.

Mrs. Hummingbird went on. "My mother said none of the people around here could read the Bible because it hadn't been scribed into the Cherokee language yet. So, your ancestor grandparents started having church services outside on Sunday mornings. They'd translate to Cherokee from their English Bible and explain what the scriptures meant. Before long, they had a crowd there on Sundays. They decided to build a church. It was the first church in these parts. It was near the Oconaluftee River off of what they now call the Bureau of Indian Affairs Highway—"

Sydney was sorry to interrupt, but she just had to. "That's near where we were when we met you!" she told Galilahi. "Right by the pancake restaurant. Is the old church still there, Mrs. Hummingbird?"

"No, it is not," she answered. "And that's what I was about to tell you."

She shooed the rooster away from the table and then sat for a minute or so, saying nothing.

"The Reverend Coody died in a smallpox epidemic," Mrs. Hummingbird finally said. "Mother said it swept through here like a windstorm, and many people died. Your ancestor grandmother and her daughter, by the will of God, didn't get sick, and they helped nurse and minister to the people during that terrible time. Many Cherokees turned to God through their sickness, and it made the church grow even stronger."

Mrs. Hummingbird got up, checked the pot, and then returned to the table. "Mrs. Coody kept that church going all on her own after her daughter got married and moved to Tennessee. Even in her old age, she kept right on preaching, every Sunday morning, just like her husband did when he was alive. But then something awful happened—"

"What?" Galilahi gasped.

"*Shhh!*" said Billy John. "Let her finish!"

"There was a fire."

"Oh no!" said Elizabeth. She put her hand up to her mouth.

"The old church was on fire, and your grandmother ran inside to save whatever she could. She made several trips in and out of the burning building, even though folks tried to stop her. The last time she went in, she didn't come out."

Galilahi's eyes filled with tears, and this time they were for her great-great-great-great-great-grandmother.

"My Grandma Hisgi died in the fire," she said softly.

Elizabeth wrapped her arm around Galilahi's shoulder.

"Galilahi," the old woman said. "I have something else to tell you, something that will dry your tears."

"What?" Galilahi asked, her voice cracking.

"Your grandmother's church had a name. It was called the Church of the—"

"Rising Sun!" Sydney blurted it out.

Mrs. Hummingbird straightened in her chair, folded her hands on the table, and nodded. "Son, spelled s-o-n."

"Like God's Son, Jesus Christ, rising from the dead," said Elizabeth.

Sydney sat there dumbfounded. She had never expected the story to end that way. "So, Galilahi's great-grandmother was wrong about the name," she suggested. "It was the Church of the Rising Son, and not the Cabin of the Rising Sun."

"Maybe she was wrong, and maybe she wasn't," the old woman

replied. "I don't know about that. But the word *sun*, in the name of the church, was spelled s-o-n to mean the resurrection of Christ, the risen Son of God."

Galilahi sat quietly, her mouth slightly open. She was trying to take in everything she had just learned about Grandma Hisgi.

"I feel so strange." The words seemed to stick in her throat. "I'm sad that Grandma Hisgi died in the fire, but I'm proud of her for all of the wonderful things that she did here. Wow, the very first church in Cherokee was built by my ancestors! I'm so happy that I didn't give up looking for her, and thanks to all of you for helping me. I do still wish we could find her house, though."

Mrs. Hummingbird reached with one hand toward Galilahi and patted her arm. It was a soft, caring gesture that Sydney had not expected from the crabby, old woman.

"Never stop looking for your ancestors," Mrs. Hummingbird said. "Look at the stars tonight and think of them as pinholes in the curtains of heaven. There are thousands of ancestors waiting for you just beyond the stars."

Elizabeth felt that the Lord had worked a miracle by bringing them to Billy John and, through him, to Mrs. Hummingbird.

"What do you think that the letter meant?" she asked. "Do you think that Grandma Hisgi ever connected with her family?"

"I don't know," Sydney answered. "We may never know, but I've been wondering, Mrs. Hummingbird, do you remember where Galilahi Adair Coody's grave is?"

The shadows were growing long on the cabin's floor. "I do," Mrs. Hummingbird answered. "It's in the Old Church Cemetery, and if my memory serves me, it's up near the top of the hill."

"I know where that cemetery is," said Billy John. "I'll take you girls there tomorrow. It's too late to go there now."

Mrs. Hummingbird got up and walked toward the door. "I have things to do," she said. The girls and Billy John got up and followed her. "You promise me, now, never to tell anyone about me or this place."

"Yes.

"Yes, ma'am."

"Except the other Camp Club Girls," Elizabeth confessed.

After hearing about the Camp Club Girls and making Sydney and Elizabeth promise that they wouldn't tell either, Mrs. Hummingbird agreed that Alexis, Bailey, Kate, and McKenzie could know the story too.

The corners of Mrs. Hummingbird's lips curled upward into the slightest of smiles.

"I choose to live here quietly and peacefully with the old ways." Instead of shaking their hands or saying goodbye to them, she raised her right hand. "The Lord bless you and keep you. The Lord make His face shine upon you and be gracious unto you. The Lord lift up His countenance upon you, and give you peace."

Sydney had one more question. She couldn't leave the cabin without asking it. "Mrs. Hummingbird," she said. "The symbol of the sun that's etched on the back of your door, what is that?"

Galilahi and Billy John looked at the back of the door, wondering what Sydney was talking about.

"Oh my goodness!" Galilahi exclaimed. "It's the same symbol that was on the letter and in the margins of Grandma Hisgi's Bible."

"Yes. I noticed it on the letter too," said Mrs. Hummingbird, "But I have no answer for you. That etching has been on this door for as long as I can remember. And I've lived here all of my life."

Completing the Circle

That night Sydney and Elizabeth couldn't wait to tell the Camp Club Girls all that had happened. After they had separated from Galilahi, they had formed a theory, and they wanted to share it with their friends. It was too much to type, so they used the webcams.

"Do you think Galilahi knows?" McKenzie asked after they'd explained their theory. "It took me awhile to figure it out, but then, as you were talking, I got it." She pulled back her hair and plopped her favorite baseball cap onto her head.

"I don't think she does," Sydney said. "And Beth and I have decided not to tell her. It's only a theory, after all. We could be wrong."

Elizabeth sat cross-legged on her bed in the guest room. "I don't think we're wrong, but if the story got out, it could get in the way of Mrs. Hummingbird's privacy, and we don't want any part of that."

Bailey's face popped onto the screen. "What did I miss while I was in the bathroom?" she asked.

"You missed the best part," said Alex. She sat near her computer, polishing her nails. "What do you think, girls, should we tell her?"

"Oh, I don't know," Kate teased. "It's a gigandamundo secret, after all."

Bailey frowned. "Come on, guys! What did I miss?"

Sydney wished that she didn't have to repeat the last part of their story, but she didn't want Bailey to be left out.

"Well," she said. "After we left Billy John and Galilahi at Indian Village, Beth and I got to thinking about all the Bible clues. The other day, when you guys read Ecclesiastes 1:5 through 7, the part that says, 'The sun rises and sets, and hurries back to where it rises,' you thought it was a clue that we needed to head east to find the cabin. Today, we walked east when we went into the woods with Billy John. Then, we made a little jog to the right, so that meant we were heading south."

Kate chimed in, "Remember, Bailey? That's what I thought when I read, 'The wind blows to the south and turns to the north; round and round it goes, ever returning to its course.' I told Syd and Beth, 'After you've gone east for a while, you have to turn south.' "

Bailey shrugged her shoulders. "I'll take your word for it."

"And then," Elizabeth continued, "Alex mentioned the part about the stream. 'All streams flow into the sea, yet the sea is never full, and to the place the streams come from, there they return again.' She thought that we needed to find a stream and discover where it comes from. That's what happened today. We came to a stream and discovered that it merged with a river."

Bailey's eyes widened. "Okay, I'm starting to get goose bumps—"

"Are you cold, dear? I can get you a sweater." Bailey's mom was in the kitchen behind her computer, getting something out of the refrigerator.

"I'm okay, Mom," Bailey said. "We're just chatting."

"Tell the girls hello," said Mrs. Chang as she left the room.

"So then what happened?" Bailey asked.

"So then," Sydney continued. "Billy John said that we were walking along what used to be an old wagon road. It ran right along the river, and the settlers went that way when they traveled to their homesteads."

"*And*," Kate added, "that fits with the clue: 'As they traveled along the road, they came to some water.' "

"Ooo, more goose bumps!" said Bailey. "This is getting good."

"You haven't heard the half of it yet," said McKenzie. "Just wait."

"While we were walking," said Sydney, "Beth and I saw some uprooted pine trees in the woods."

" 'Trees without fruit, uprooted, twice dead,' " said Kate. "But wait. It only takes, at most, around a hundred years for a tree to decompose."

"Decom-what?" asked Bailey.

"Decompose," said Kate. "A fallen tree will eventually be eaten up by insects and will become nothing but a pile of dust and chemicals returning to the ground. Any groups of trees that had fallen in Grandma Hisgi's time would be long gone."

"True," said Sydney, "they couldn't be the same trees. But get this—"

"That area is called the Gulch of Fallen Trees," Elizabeth exclaimed with a squeal.

"It's an area known for trees falling," Sydney explained. "Braves used to go get the trees and make canoes of them."

"Twice dead!" Kate said.

"Then we came to that wall of rocks," Sydney continued. "Billy John said that there was a cave nearby."

" 'Every slave and every free man hid in caves and among the rocks of the mountains!' " said Bailey. "Hey, you matched all the clues!" A blank look swept across her face. "Okay, so you matched all the clues, but you still didn't find the Cabin of the Rising Sun. So, it was another dead end, wasn't it?"

"We don't think so," said Alexis.

"Okay, I give up," Bailey conceded. "I haven't a clue what you're talking about."

"The next part is the secret," said Sydney. Then, with a very serious expression, she asked, "Do you, Bailey Chang, solemnly promise never to reveal to a living soul what I am about to tell you?"

"Of course I do!" Bailey complained. "I suppose that you didn't make the other girls promise."

McKenzie laughed. "Don't worry about it, Bailey, we were just teasing you."

"So what's the secret?" Bailey asked.

"Well," said Sydney. We think that Mrs. Hummingbird is living in the Cabin of the Rising Sun, and she doesn't know it."

"*What?*" Bailey squealed.

"Think about it," said McKenzie. "She's lived in that cabin all her life, and she's almost a hundred years old. She said that the sun symbol has been on the back of the door for as long as she can remember. The cabin is older than the settlers' cabins. We know that because it looks so much like the cabin in Indian Village. It was built with the same kind of stuff, and it has no windows."

"Our theory," said Sydney, "is that Grandma Hisgi lived in that cabin with her adopted family. Maybe she moved out when she married the missionary, or maybe at some point her adopted family moved out and she and her missionary man lived there."

"And she's the one who carved the sun symbol on the door?" Bailey asked.

"We don't know," Elizabeth answered. "It could have been put there by whoever built the cabin. That's a part of the puzzle that only God knows for sure. And a family or two might have lived there between Grandma Hisgi and the Hummingbirds."

"But it's only a theory," said Sydney. "We can't prove any of it. We also don't know why Grandma Hisgi wrote the letter, or if it really was in code, but in theory, it all seems to fit."

"Wait, I bet I know," said McKenzie. "You said Mrs. Hummingbird talked about a time when Grandma Hisgi was hiding in the cave. Maybe she sent her Bible to her family in Oklahoma at that time with the letter hidden inside."

"Then it might be natural for her to put it in code so that her family could find her, but her enemies couldn't," said Kate.

"Maybe the caves they were hiding in were those near the cabin," McKenzie said.

"They probably had some way to peek out and watch the cabin," Alex said. "Like in old Westerns. Then they would have seen if any of their family arrived to help them."

"Well, from what Mrs. Hummingbird said, it sounds like they didn't have anyone arrive to help them," Sydney said. "I guess no one ever found the letter hidden in the Bible. Or else Grandma Hisgi never sent it and just never took the letter out."

"It seems like Grandma Hisgi and Grandpa Coody figured out that the Lord would be their helper since they left hiding," Elizabeth said. "Just like the Bible tells us—He is a present help in time of need."

Bailey leaned back in her chair. "What did Galilahi and Billy John think when you told them that you thought Mrs. Hummingbird's house is the Cabin of the Rising Sun?"

"We decided not to tell them," said Elizabeth. "We would if we knew for sure, but we don't. If the word got out, Mrs. Hummingbird's privacy would be ruined. Can you imagine? Why, everyone in Cherokee would want to meet her."

"My lips are sealed," said Bailey. "So is the case closed?"

"Not entirely," Sydney answered. "Tomorrow morning, we're going with Billy John and Galilahi to find Grandma Hisgi's grave. It's in the Old Church Cemetery, here in Cherokee. We're hoping that the grave is marked."

"You can always ask the caretaker," Kate said, setting Biscuit on the floor. "Even if there's no headstone, the caretaker can probably tell you where it is. Most cemeteries have records."

"I didn't know that," Sydney said. "Thanks for the tip."

"You're welcome," Kate answered.

The girls said good night to each other and turned off their webcams.

"You know, I was just thinking," said Elizabeth. "We should take flowers to the cemetery tomorrow."

"That's a good idea," Sydney answered. "They sell flowers at the grocery store on the corner. We can get some in the morning before we meet Billy John and Galilahi at the cemetery."

Elizabeth settled into her bed. "I hope you wrote down the directions for getting there. I haven't a clue where we're supposed to go."

"Not to worry. I've got them," Sydney said as she turned off the light in their bedroom. She lay down and pulled up the covers. "I know exactly where we're going."

●—●—●

Billy John and Galilahi were waiting for them outside the big iron gates at the Old Church Cemetery. A stone wall surrounded the cemetery, and a narrow, gravel road led inside. Sydney carried a mixed bouquet of delphiniums, asters, and carnations. Galilahi had her own bouquet.

"I see you brought flowers too," Sydney said.

"Sunflowers," Galilahi answered. "I thought they'd be appropriate." She looked down at her feet. "I'm a little nervous. I feel like I'm meeting someone important for the first time. Sort of like last night."

They walked through the open gate and started along the winding road.

"Who'd you meet last night?" Sydney asked.

Billy John lagged behind.

"When I got home from Mrs. Hummingbird's, I felt like I should pray. So I went in my room and shut the door and knelt down by my bed. You guys might think that I'm weird for telling you this."

"Not at all," Elizabeth answered. "Go on."

"I started to pray, and I asked God to help us find Grandma Hisgi's grave today, but then the strangest thing happened."

She stopped. They'd come to a fork in the road, and they didn't know which way to go. Billy John caught up with them and pointed in the direction of a hill on the north end of the cemetery.

"That way, I think," he said and took off up the road.

"So, what happened?" Sydney asked.

Galilahi hurried along behind Billy John, not wanting him to get too far ahead. "Well, as I prayed, finding the grave didn't seem so important anymore. Don't get me wrong. I hope that we do find the grave, but if we don't, I'm okay with it. It seemed more important to thank God for Grandma Hisgi and all the good things that she and her husband did for the Cherokee people. The more I prayed, the more it became about thanking God than asking Him for stuff. Isn't that strange?"

A chipmunk skittered across the road in front of them. It stopped for a second or two, looked at the group walking toward it, and then dashed off among the headstones.

"I don't think it's strange at all," Elizabeth told her. "God loves it when we put Him first. That pleases Him more than anything."

The road grew steeper as they started up the hill.

"Whenever I've prayed before," Galilahi continued, "I've never really felt much, but this time I did. I felt that God was really there and listening to me, and that felt good. It was like I was meeting Him for the very first time."

"Maybe you were," Sydney suggested.

"The whole experience made me feel sort of nervous, or maybe I should say *different*," Galilahi confessed. "But in a good way."

Billy John stopped. "We're here," he said.

The headstones on the hillside were set in uneven rows. Sydney noticed that they were all very old. Some were toppled over. Others were so weatherworn that you couldn't read the words.

"I think we should split up," Billy John suggested. "It'll go faster that way. Galilahi, you take that row," he said, pointing. "Liz, take that one." He pointed again. "And Syd, you—"

"I'll take *this* one," Sydney interrupted, choosing her own row. "Remember," she added, "the name on the headstone is most likely Coody, not Adair. Look for a birth date around 1828. Mrs. Hummingbird is almost a hundred years old, so—"

"She's ninety-six," Billy John said. "She told me that, but you didn't hear it from me."

Sydney was busy doing the math in her head. "So, that means that Mrs. Hummingbird was born around 1915, and the death date on Grandma Hisgi's headstone has to be after that."

"But not too many years after that," Elizabeth cautioned. "Because Mrs. Hummingbird was a little girl when Grandma Hisgi died."

Billy John scratched his head. "Say all that again."

"Look for a headstone that says Coody," Sydney said, bluntly.

"And Adair too," said Galilahi. "Just in case she used that name. Okay? Let's go."

Galilahi, Billy John, Elizabeth, and Sydney each took a row of headstones. They walked slowly among them, carefully reading the words.

When they came to the ends of their rows, they'd found nothing that said Coody or Adair.

"Don't get discouraged," Elizabeth told Galilahi. "We'll keep looking."

Billy John assigned another set of rows, and they continued on. Back and forth they went among the stones. Again, they found nothing. They kept looking until they were almost at the top of the hill and on the verge of giving up.

"There's that big headstone on the very top of the hill," said Billy John. "Do you want to go check it out?"

"I doubt that Grandma Hisgi would have a big headstone, especially in an old and forgotten cemetery like this one," said Galilahi. "It's probably a marker for someone who was very important way back when. I think she'd have a little headstone."

"If she had one at all," Elizabeth offered.

"I'm checking it out anyway," Billy John told them. He trudged up the steep hill, dodging any headstones that were in his way.

"There's one more row to check here," said Sydney. "Let's do it." She, Elizabeth, and Galilahi set out together, carefully reading the inscriptions on the stones. There were no Coodys and no Adairs.

"I think we've reached another dead end," Galilahi declared. "But that's okay. Just knowing about Grandma Hisgi and learning about her faith in God makes me happy. I feel like I've found a piece of me that was missing."

"You've completed the circle," said Sydney. "You connected with the great-grandma who had your name."

"And just think," said Elizabeth. "If it hadn't been for her, your name would be something other than Galilahi."

All of a sudden, Billy John let out a loud whoop.

"*Whoo-hoo!*" his voice echoed through the deserted cemetery. "I found her!"

The girls looked at each other in disbelief, then sprinted up the hill to Billy John.

"Hers *is* the biggest headstone," he said as they got nearer. "Check it out."

The upright, white stone was as tall as Sydney. It was shaped somewhat like a steeple with a rounded top. A cross was etched near its top, and the words below the cross were weathered but still easy to read. Galilahi read them aloud:

IN LOVING REMEMBRANCE OF
GALILAHI COODY
BORN IN CHEROKEE CO., NC.: FEB. 28, 1828
DIED: APR. 11, 1919
SHE IS NOT DEAD BUT SLEEPETH
ALTHOUGH SHE SLEEPS HER MEMORY DOTH LIVE
AND CHEERING COMFORT TO HER MOURNERS GIVE,
SHE FOLLOWED VIRTUE AS HER TRUEST GUIDE,
LIVED AS A CHRISTIAN,
AS A CHRISTIAN DIED.
"WITH THANKS FROM THE PEOPLE OF CHEROKEE"

"Grandmother," Galilahi whispered.

Sydney noticed a tear trickle down her friend's cheek.

"I think the townspeople put up this headstone," she said, "as their way to say thank you to your Grandma Hisgi."

Elizabeth was standing just to the right of her friends. She looked down at the headstone next to her and gasped.

"Oh my! *He's* here too—the missionary." She read the inscription aloud:

IN MEMORY OF MY HUSBAND
REV. NATHANIEL COODY
DIED NOV. 6, 1882
"TO LIVE IN HEARTS WE LEAVE BEHIND
IS NOT TO DIE"
THY WILL BE DONE
FOREVER IN HEAVEN WITH GOD

"Wow, my great-great-great-great-*great*-grandfather," said Galilahi. She read the words on his headstone again. "Let's take another look around up here. Maybe we'll find some Adairs."

Galilahi, Billy John, Elizabeth, and Sydney looked closely at all the remaining headstones on the hill, but there were no Adairs among them.

"I think we've seen them all," said Billy John.

They returned to Grandma Hisgi's headstone, and Galilahi laid the sunflowers against it. "I still wonder if she was ever reunited with her family. Maybe if I keep at it and dig even deeper into my family's history, I'll find the answer some day."

Sydney laid her bouquet on Nathaniel Coody's grave. "You may never find the answer," she said. "Sometimes God keeps secrets."

"But there's one thing for sure," Elizabeth added. "Since you believe in Jesus, you'll go to heaven when you die, and when you get there, you'll have all the answers you need."

"The first thing that I'm going to do is write a very long letter to Great-Grandmother Rogers," said Galilahi. "Before long, Great-Grandmother will be with Grandma Hisgi in heaven, and then she'll know all the secrets about the Cabin of the Rising Sun."

"And one day," said Sydney. "We all will too."

Don't Miss the Rest of
the Camp Club Girls Series!

Camp Club Girls: Elizabeth
Whether the Camp Club Girls are uncovering a decades-old mystery at Camp Discovery Lake, investigating a bag of mysterious marbles in Amarillo, untangling a strange string of events in San Antonio, or solving the case of a missing guitar in Music City, you will encounter six delightful, relatable characters who combine their mystery-solving skills to crack the case.
Paperback / 978-1-68322-767-0 / $9.99 / Now available!

Camp Club Girls: Bailey
Whether the Camp Club Girls are investigating the whereabouts of eccentric millionaire Marshall Gonzalez, encountering out-of-control elk stampedes in Estes Park, uncovering the rightful ownership to a valuable mine, or solving the case of frightening events in Mermaid Park, you'll encounter six charming, relatable characters who combine their mystery-solving skills to save the day.

Paperback / 978-1-68322-828-8 / $9.99 / Now available!

Camp Club Girls: Kate
Whether the Camp Club Girls are saving the day for a Philadelphia Phillies baseball player, investigating the sabotage of a Vermont cheese factory, going on a quest to uncover phony fossils in Wyoming, or solving the case of twisted treats in Hershey, Pennsylvania, you'll encounter six charming, relatable characters who combine their mystery-solving skills to save the day.

Paperback / 978-1-68322-854-7 / $9.99 / Now available!

Check Out More Camp Club Girls!

Camp Club Girls: McKenzie
Whether the Camp Club Girls are in the middle of a Wild West whodunit, investigating a mysterious case of missing sea lion pups, uncovering the whereabouts of a teen girl's missing family member, or unearthing clues in an Iowa history mystery, you'll encounter six charming, relatable characters who combine their mystery-solving skills to save the day.

Paperback / 978-1-68322-879-0 / $9.99 / Now available!

Camp Club Girls: Alexis
Whether the Camp Club Girls are trying to save a Sacramento nature park, soaking up British history during the London Bridge festival in Lake Havasu, Arizona, witnessing odd incidents at a Lake Tahoe animal refuge, or filming a documentary for kids in Washington State, you'll encounter six charming, relatable characters who combine their mystery-solving skills to save the day.

Paperback / 978-1-68322-991-9 / $9.99 / June 2019